*also published
The Tears?*

*Shiraz
Durrani*

THE
BURNING
ORCHARD

Published 2009 by
Prakash Books India Pvt. Ltd.
1, Ansari Road, Daryaganj
New Delhi 110 002, India.
E-mail: sales@prakashbooks.com
Website: www.prakashbooks.com
Tel: 91-11-23247062-65

© 2009 Prakash Books India Pvt. Ltd.
© 2009 Text Anita Krishan

All rights reserved. No part of this publication may be reproduced, stored in a retrieval system or transmitted in any form or by any means, electronic, mechanical, photocopying, recording or otherwise, without the prior permission of the copyright holder.

This is a work of fiction. Names, characters & incidents are purely the product of the author's imagination. Any resemblance to any actual person, living or dead, and the events, is purely coincidental.

ISBN: 978 81 7234 298 2

Printed & bound in India: Raveindia. www.raveindiapress.com

THE BURNING ORCHARD

ANITA KRISHAN

PRAKASH BOOKS

Author's Note

I came upon the idea to write this book in the summer of 2004, during my first visit to Kashmir. Though I have lived my entire childhood and the early youth in the hills of Shimla, I found the beauty of Kashmir overwhelming. A drive to Gulmarg through the tranquil green mountains with the backdrop of snow clad peaks of the Pir-Panjal range of the Himalayas; or a peaceful walk at the banks of the river Liddar in Pahelgaon were a few exotic experiences worth the mention. But the stunning environs veiling the underlying uneasiness set my mind wondering as to how unrest could possibly exist in such peaceful surroundings. It was so unreal.

The beauty of the Kashmir valley had noticeably been stained by fear at every inch of the valley. There was an obvious air of dread, distrust and unease. I could see it in the eyes of the inhabitants; could feel it everywhere... in the busy market places...on the deserted roads...in homes... in the patrolling men in uniform.

Terrorism is a plague which is slowly fraying the fabric of the Kashmiri society.

The gravity of the situation became evident when we were being driven to Pahelgaon. On reaching the busy market place, the driver, an elderly Kashmiri Muslim, abruptly applied the brakes and rushed to remove the beacon light of the official vehicle. Getting back on the vehicle he remarked, "What a blunder it would have been if the beacon light had remained. We would have surely become the targets of the terrorists." The poor man appeared agitated and his tone revealed panic; that was more than enough to cause my husband and me to be highly alarmed. I immediately began scrutinizing the people around with suspicion. This mood of distrust undoubtedly stained the spirit of adventure.

The beauty of certain places that we visited was so captivating that we let go of our fears and walked around for hours. One such place was the Betab Valley. It is situated on Pahelgaon-Chandanbari route and named after a Bollywood movie shot at the location. We walked for almost a kilometre along the enticing, bubbling mountain stream and then right into a dense fir forest. Around a blind curve, we abruptly came face to face with a group of about a dozen local people; men and women. Accompanying them were their flock of sheep and mountain goats, and a train of ponies carrying their baggage. The first idea to crop up in our distrustful minds was that they could be carrying weapons…rifles could easily be hidden in their baggage. We didn't run; though we desperately wanted to; for we knew we couldn't have escaped even if we tried. Instead, we stood aside to let them go by. We soon realized that it was a harmless group of nomads on their way to the higher mountains for summer settlement. The pastoral group innocuously passed by, some even throwing sweet innocent smiles at us; very obviously they considered us the guests of their state and thus assumed that we deserved the honour of their attention.

We thus concluded that the situation was not as bad as projected. After all, we had been strolling around in forlorn spots and had remained unscathed.

It was only a day later that an engineer helping to lay the railway line in Srinagar-Baramulla section was abducted from an area not far from where we were located and mercilessly slaughtered. His younger brother, barely a teenager, too was not spared. This was only one of those uncountable killings that have soiled the divine beauty of the valley of Kashmir.

And to apprehend the culprits, how many innocents might have suffered at the hands of the keepers of the law!

The danger has been lurking now for years. There has been enough suffering. The inhabitants are sick of the continuous unrest. They want peace and prosperity to return. Though we are cognizant of the situation, are we making a difference?

This work is dedicated to
the Innocent Victims of the Senseless Violence

For Arvind, Aman, Peter and Amber
my pillars of support

Who Will Douse The Fire?

In this milieu of teeming billions,
Only a few concerned voice sane opinions;
Save the Earth; every plant, every creature,
Else disappearing species will endanger our future.
All God's gifts must be preserved,
Or pay the penalty, we will then deserve.

Man; who holds the power to save,
Has turned out to be the most knave.
Disappearing fauna and the declining woods,
Global warming and the polluted neighbourhood.
Added to such dismal legacy for our progeny,
Appended crimes against humanity are many.

Some think blood comes cheap,
Trivial excuse and it can be drained in heaps.
There is abundant to drench the land,
And without regret soak hands.
The victims were innocents, no one can contest,
Blasted into shreds are those who protest.

For many an opulent, own convenience is the only concern,
Others' plight; why should they want to discern?
When they own enough comforts and wealth,
Well earned or else through sheer stealth.
Why bother, shut the ears to those pitiable groans,
Why consider it peremptory to nurse those moans?

Those who foster life and labour to rescue,
Disregarded and ignored, still continue to pursue.
Such sane voices are often muffled and nipped,
Their dreams crushed, their efforts ripped.
Oh! Pandemic stricken man realize your ambition,
Reflect upon your deeds and uncover your mission.

Or to curb the ones who finish nature or else life with grudge,
Perhaps the earth requires direct intervention of a divine judge.
To remind the lost mortals that the world is illusory and impermanent,
Time is ever fleeting and life transient.
So why not let events in this Orchard be naturally dealt,
Let there be dignity in life as well as in death.

Chapter 1

Last evening had brought unexpected and bizarre state of affairs for Wali causing huge crisis in his life. He had no time to contemplate peacefully to decide his future course of action. It was an emergency to be tackled immediately and urgently.

He had heard of such things happening to others but had never dreamt of having to live through them himself. Today was certainly unlike any other. The day was a stark contrast to the simple life of honesty and dignity he had always led. And dignity was what he now wanted to preserve, whatever the cost.

The cost could be heavy. Many lives were at stake. If it were only his own, perhaps he wouldn't be perturbed to such an extent. But he had to save the others come what may, and that would entail defying danger. Never before in life had he to take such risks and never before in life had he been so unnerved. Never had he experienced such dread and dismay, never had he had a reason to lie hidden in a desolate corner.

He had spent the past one hour in complete seclusion. Seated on the stepladder of the houseboat moored in the most isolated spot, Wali had done nothing for the last sixty minutes but gaze impassively through the ripples of the lake water; through the vegetation growing wildly on the bank; through the colours of the aquatic flowers; through the solitude and silence and through the occasional disrupting tweets and chirps with the most disconsolate expression. The serene and pristine environs around him had been utterly unsuccessful in lifting his spirits, having gone completely unnoticed. In disparity to the peaceful ambience, there was turmoil within him. The inner recesses of his mind were desperately fishing into the depths of his faculties; fervently formulating, assessing, rejecting and accepting solutions that would help him to wriggle out safely from the awful trap he had unwittingly got caught in.

Only when the rays of the noon sun fell on his hands inducing warmth in them, did his attention get diverted for a moment to gaze at the cloudless sky and wonder when the monsoon rains would arrive in the valley. They were already delayed this year. Some rain was required for the orchard, for the unripe fruit to turn juicier. Did that matter now? Probably, he wouldn't get to taste this year's main crop at all.

The realization instantly sent him back to his brooding, and rightly so, for such were the circumstances and no man in his position could have readily reconciled with them. The morbid billows of deception he had suffered the previous evening had left him aghast. It had caused such intense fury within him that with each passing hour, his anger was aggravating; the sort he had never experienced before. He had always been a patient man and seldom could affairs make him angry. His once in a blue moon felt anger would be like a rising and ebbing wave, subsiding as quickly as it would reach the crest. Today, the peak had stretched beyond limit.

He wasn't used to handling so many emotions together. Time and again he took deep breaths to calm down the furore in his heart, without much success.

The sudden choppy movements in the still waters of the equally breezeless environs, now made him raise his gaze with apprehension. He didn't have a complete view of the lake from where he was positioned. Only a narrow water channel along the bank, the drooping willows and the towering, teeming reeds hiding him and the nesting sites of a variety of water birds formed his vista.

He needed to check the cause for the turbulence; he decided on an impulse and stood up. His tall lean stature, only an inch less than six feet, sagged a little today unlike his normal stately posture. A tinge of grey at the temples of his thick curly brown hair, that had added grace to his imposing personality till recently had taken only a few hours to add on years. His expressive brown eyes appeared almost feral due to a blend of fear, fury and a night of sleeplessness. Till yesterday, he had looked at least a decade younger than his fifty-four years, but today his taut jaw and deep scowl made him look a lot older. The last few hours had all of a sudden snatched away his lighthearted carefree air and substituted it with a most harried demeanour.

He walked down the narrow passage of the houseboat towards the front deck in quick urgent strides for a broader view of the lake but stopped short of the edge of the dwelling wall. A few steps more and he would be completely exposing himself. That would not be a sensible thing to do.

From here too he had a limited view, only till the curved bank of the alcove. Beyond the bank, he could behold the vast marshland overgrown with reed at the end of which the land suddenly rose into lush green Zabarvan hills with undulating peaks and ridges. A few poly-bags and discarded bottles of mineral water floated close to the bank, an unsightly view, which would have normally angered Wali. Today they were overlooked as his sight was fixed on the prow of an approaching boat, which was rounding the curve and was becoming visible at too slow a speed for the edgy man.

Wasim couldn't have returned so soon, Wali considered. He had barely left an hour ago and couldn't possibly have finished the required tasks.

The boat drew nearer. He could now see the back of the oarsman in his shabby brown woollen *pheran,* and then was revealed the body of the boat with its bright yellow canvas covering for the roof and the two sides. Colourful trimmings adorned the canvas. It was a *shikara*.

It was surely not Wasim. Why would he hire a *shikara?* But then he wasn't even sure whether Wasim would be using the waterway today or he would come back the way he had left; from the hidden passage running through the reeds. He had forgotten to ask him.

The advancing *shikara* sent his heart quivering with anxiety. Who would be interested to venture into this remote part of the lake if not the villains he was trying to avoid? Should he hastily withdraw from sight before being discovered, he considered. But he also knew that the people he wanted to evade wouldn't hire a *shikara*. It was too extravagant and ornate for their objective. It was an ordinary inconspicuous boat he should be wary of. He therefore stood rooted to continue his scrutiny and began to relax as a few head tops covered with sun hats and caps and several pairs of sunglasses began to be unveiled for his inspection.

The *shikara* continued its voyage in the direction of the houseboat. He could now distinguish the foreign tourists who were enjoying a leisure cruise on the lake. One of them aimed his camera at Wali and he instantly turned away his face. "Why does he want to take a picture of an unhappy distressed man?" He thought with irritation. An instant later he wished he too could be boating around with the least worry in his mind. He yearned to change places with the cameraman. He wished he too were clicking photographs of an enchanted land, capturing in his camera some cherished moments forever.

And he wished for more. He wished that time could be reverted and these appalling moments be deleted from his calendar, these last few hours ousted from his life. In just a few hours, his life had turned exactly upside down and now he was a tormented man. He wished to be left alone and allowed the uncomplicated life he had been living.

He felt a pang of envy for the cheerful tourists. Though, they were more than welcome.

For years now there hadn't been many tourists to the Valley. The aggression against the hapless had been keeping them away. Kidnapping and subsequent disappearance of six foreign tourists was the final blow to the state tourism. Wali had noted it gradually declining and then almost disappearing. The earnings from this industry fell drastically, hitting the common man hard.

There was a time, when the Valley used to be free from this strife; the houseboats and the *shikaras* did roaring business not only in summers but almost the entire year. It was also the most popular place in the country with the Bombay film industry of the seventies and eighties. If it hadn't been scared away, perhaps the valley would have continued its importance instead if being replaced by the European and South East Asian destinations.

When the Bombay film crews used to come to shoot a movie, a number of houseboats would get hired for days on end and the lucky owners of the boats got really well paid. Wasim's late father, who was Wali's maternal uncle was the original owner of this houseboat and had named it Haven. It was such an irony that it was in this Haven he had presently taken refuge to avoid being followed and tracked.

It was a comfortable living space: a medium sized bedroom with attached bath, slightly larger sitting cum dining room and a small kitchenette. The sitting room was tastefully furnished and decorated with walnut wood furniture; silk carpets, papier-mâché items and brass filigree lampshades, though the faded colours had now begun to indicate their antiquity. Even the expensive chandelier hanging from the ceiling had been dulled by moisture and years.

Wasim had scarcely earned any profit from the houseboat for the past fifteen years; hence, there had hardly been enough money for its renovation. Once upon a time, it was the most sought after houseboat.

Once, this houseboat had been hired by a film director from Mumbai. Wali was in college then and on being informed about it by Wasim; he had rushed to spend an entire day away from studies to watch the shooting of the film in progress. He had received the privilege of watching the shooting from a close proximity, in the box-seat of the open air auditorium of nature, unlike the big crowd that had gathered at the bank and vied and scuffled for a good viewing spot. He now remembered that a song was being filmed around this very houseboat, and perhaps this was the very spot that he had occupied along with Wasim to watch the actors at work. Shammi Kapoor and Sharmila Tagore were the main actors and after a few shots when it was declared their rest period, he had been introduced to them by his uncle. The next day he had boasted about the event to no end in front of his college mates.

He even recalled the name of the movie now; Kashmir Ki Kali.

His uncle was quite well off then. Poor Wasim was now struggling to make both ends meet.

Wali sighed deeply recalling those carefree happy days. But then life had been, more or less, easygoing for him. It had been a calm sea without major upheavals. He couldn't even commit to memory when his youth had ended and when he had stepped into his middle age. And never even in his dreams could he imagine that one day, all of a sudden, he would be caught in a raging inferno that would threaten to reduce his life to cinders instantly.

Reaching a water channel halfway between the bank and the houseboat, the *shikara* had begun to change its course. Wali's gaze followed the waning stern of the *shikara,* which was now being rowed around a curve into the inlot.

He was once more returned his much needed solitude and he was thankful for it. In the present circumstances he was distrustful of any human company, familiar or unfamiliar, and was more relaxed without any.

He didn't mind non-human company though, even of a head with amazing resemblance to a snake protruding out of the waters, which his vision had next caught swaying to and fro in close proximity of the houseboat. He knew that the deceptive outline belonged to a darter. It was swimming in circles, hunting for its prey. He watched it with indifferent interest as the bird suddenly dipped into the waters. A moment later its serpent like blackish brown neck was out again, this time with a struggling fish caught tightly in its pointed dagger bill. The fish was shaken off, tossed up in the air and once again caught between the mandibles. As it began to swallow its prey head first, Wali's mind too began to infer the equivalent circumstances he was trapped in.

This reflection of the being trapped in a vicious clasp, the ambiguity of his fate in the immediate future and the danger lurking over the lives of his loved ones began to render him feeble. He had been constantly wavering between the weak and strong moments over the past few hours. The parallel between his situation and a fish being swallowed alive with relish affected him so acutely that he felt his energy draining. His fasting since the morning in addition to his stressed out state of mind now rendered his head spinning. He closed his eyes to orient himself. Holding on to the railings, he tried to recover. This feeling of extreme weakness was utterly unfamiliar. The wheels of deceit had taken just a trice to crush all vigour and stamina of, till recently, a robust man.

"There is no place in this world for weaklings," he reminded himself. "Those who lack the power to resist get swallowed whole by serpents like Shakeel. Shakeel is, beyond doubt, a venomous serpent in human garb that has come to prey on us." The speculation made him clench his hands. A slight tremor in them dismayed him. This susceptible state was worrisome. He needed to preserve his strength or else that treacherous Shakeel would destroy him.

Reflexively, he straightened his drooping shoulders and continued to stand holding the railings of the houseboat till the spinning and quivering settled down. He opened his eyes, which instantly began their scrutiny of the expanse. There was a kind of lull all around with the *shikara* completely out of sight and the darter having swum away to a distant hunting ground. With narrowed eyes, he repeated his plan in his mind. He was nervous about having hatched it in a hurry. Nothing should go wrong; even a slight slip could cause him heavy penalty. That made him realize he was taking risks by exposing himself thus and for so long. It would be safe to remain completely out of sight, lest his hunters had decided to keep track on his activities. Wasim too expected it and had instructed him to be cautious.

He instantly backtracked to his original concealed spot.

"Why is Fate so fickle?" He probed, seated on the steps once again. "Why my life had to derail from its smooth course at a stage when I expected undisturbed and peaceful existence? Why a big bundle of troubles had to land on my unburdened shoulders, that too with a force of an avalanche? I have now been hurled out of my stability and thrown onto a road that leads nowhere; I am at a complete dead end. Groping in the dark, the only escape route I have been able to unearth too is a dark tunnel comprising of a single lane. Though, there is a faint distant glint of light at the other end where I see some hope, yet the passage that leads to it is dangerous and sinister.

"Why has the writer of my story suddenly and uncannily transformed the happy narrative of my life into a tragedy?"

"Will I ever be able to reclaim some parts of my happy story? Will my life ever be the same? Will I ever have direct control over my life or will I be trampled by my enemy and finished forever?" The assault of such frightening queries left him highly rattled. At this instant, he didn't have answers to most of the questions, but he knew for sure that it would either be the concluding chapter of his existence tonight or the beginning of a complete new chapter hereafter. In either case; he would stand to lose. His lone concern was if he would be able to save those who were dearer to him than his own life.

Tonight, he would be facing the hardest test for survival. "If I fail tonight, the doom of my family will be inevitable. I will have to take them as far away as possible from this place before the Sun shows itself on the eastern horizon once again. If I don't, I will have no choice but to comply with Shakeel's demands tomorrow morning and then; I, Wali Mohammad Khan, will never again rest in peace."

The thought of meekly accepting the terms laid by some repugnant creatures was so alarming that he received a renewed jolt that brought another bout of restlessness. He got to his feet; as if in preparation for his flight at night. But it was only the first quarter of the day and many hours before his plan would be put through its test. He began to pace restlessly in the limited range that was at his disposal; from one point of his confinement to the other.

His parched throat soon sent him to the interiors for a glass of water. He needed it as much to soothe his anxiety as to quench his thirst. He walked into the kitchen. Picking up a glass from the cabinet, he opened the refrigerator but found it empty. So was a pitcher kept on the counter. He wasn't sure if the water in the tap could be consumed. He stood in front of the sink double minded, hesitant to fill his glass. Then he remembered that along with the tiffin carrier, Wasim had also left a thermos flask on the dining table.

It was a large flask and he found it filled with water till the brim. He filled the glass with his unsteady hands, spilling some water on the table. Shaking his head dolefully, he wiped the table with his handkerchief. Why he was losing control over himself, the thought bothered him.

He drained the whole glass in one go. Leaving it on the table he walked into the bedroom, aimlessly, for no particular reason. He had hours to kill and in his present mental state, it was really a hard task.

There was nothing much of interest in the bedroom except a comfortable double bed and presently it couldn't lure the restless man. He moved towards a curtained window of the room and shifted the curtain aside to peep out. The glistening waters of the vast lake were a welcome sight. He could definitely discern more activity on this side, with a number of boats and *shikaras* plying back and forth, though at quite a distance from the docked houseboat. He could also spot boats loaded with vegetables or with indigenous craftwork and trinkets plying in search of prospective buyers. He roved his eyes further which halted at the famous Char-Chinar; the clump of four *chinar* trees on an island in the middle of the lake. The clump was lush green but would shortly be transforming into flaming hues of yellows, rusts and reds in autumn. He loved the *chinars* in their fiery shroud. Each autumn spent on alien soil was bound to set nostalgic yearnings in his heart; yearnings to return to the land of these stately *chinars*.

Beyond the lake, his vision travelled up the low hills that surrounded the valley and then abruptly stopped at a point on a small hillock. He was pleasantly surprised that from the window he could partly see his two-storied freshly whitewashed house with a slanting green roof, half hidden by the surrounding terraced orchard of his fruit trees.

The sight sent a current of sudden gnawing pain in his heart.

"The trees are laden with fruit and would be ready to be plucked and sold in about a month and a half," Wali thought with sadness. "Will I be able to come back in time to see to the proper packing of the fruit?" He had his doubts. He could have depended on Abdul for it. Abdul was his most trusted man and had worked with him for more than two decades now. And never once had he given him any chance to doubt his integrity.

But Abdul too would have to leave the town now. He wasn't aware of the situation yet, and Wali felt uneasy thinking how he would react to the idea of being uprooted from the soil of his native land. Yet, his life would be in grave danger if he stayed.

Wali knew that on the family front, it wouldn't be too difficult for Abdul to leave; having lost his wife a few years ago and his two daughters happily married and busy raising their families. Only once in two years did he take ten days off to visit his daughters and grandchildren. He spent the rest of his time with Wali and his family and had become more or less like a family member.

Wali remembered those early days when he had recently purchased his orchard and Abdul, a young sturdy man then, was his first employee. Wali had almost exhausted his resources in buying this land and couldn't afford to hire more help. Abdul had slogged day and night along with him to plant the orchard. Wali had been impressed by his sincerity and diligence. And Abdul hadn't changed much, except that he looked an old man now; a man wrinkled in the sun and baked in the toil.

Wali's orchard was his cherished treasure; his life's ambition. He had even quitted his job to devote his fulltime attention to his orchard. He had painfully and carefully selected each sapling of the plantation of four hundred fruit trees. He had to wage a continuous battle against hail, frost and pests to save the delicate saplings. He had nurtured the trees of his orchard like his own children, showering them with fatherly tenderness and devotion. The first time the trees had borne fruit, he couldn't contain his happiness at the finest fruit that the orchard had produced. It was like the pride of a father whose child had brought him laurels. And like a loving and obedient child, never had his orchard failed him. Year after year it had given him considerable earnings. "And now a swarm of locusts has suddenly come to settle on my trees with the intention of gobbling it down... threatening its instant ruin. My treasured orchard...my labour of years will simply be wasted."

"I cannot let that happen!"

"I will have to hand over the safekeeping of my orchard to Wasim. But he is a busy man. It is not right to burden him with added responsibilities at his age. A manager will have to be appointed. Perhaps, Wasim can give the orchard on contract, though it could mean quite a loss. These contractors are so deceitful, always out to make extra money by cheating. But there is no choice." Wali took the decision.

The realization dawned upon him now that it would also be impossible for him to run his export business, at least not for as long as he would have to remain in self imposed exile. And how long would that be, he had no idea. "It can be from a few months, a year to my complete lifetime," Wali thought gloomily. What would happen to his handicraft artisans now? He could in no way inform them of the circumstances. The thought set out another worry. He would be held responsible for keeping them in obscurity. "It will be like deserting them and leaving them in a lurch. They have been dependant on me for comfortable earnings; for their livelihood. But I am totally powerless. I can't even forewarn them of my intentions. As a matter of fact, I cannot reveal my plan to anyone other than the few most trusted people." And he wondered what his craftsmen would think of him when they found him suddenly missing. "I hope they will understand and forgive me and manage some alternate arrangement without wasting time awaiting my return. Wasim can talk to them after I am gone."

"With my export business almost closed now, I can't allow to let the orchard slip out of my hands too. A regular income from the orchard will at least keep me financially independent. I must remember to check with Wasim how much he would be able to help me in this matter."

"And the house! What will become of my house?" The thought produced an immediate painful lump in his throat. He had got this house constructed on Abba-Jaan's insistence exactly twenty-three years ago on the outskirts of the town. Sakina was expecting their second child that time; their Meher.

It was quite a secluded area then, though it wasn't much inhabited even today. They were able to get the property at quite a reasonable rate. Abba-Jaan had sold a small piece of land he owned in the ancestral village. He had also pooled in his savings; his gratuity and the provident fund. He had recently retired as the District Educational Officer and had received the retirement benefits. Moreover, they were required to vacate the government accommodation they had enjoyed till then and take on a rented house. Abba-Jaan had then taken the decision to construct their own house. "We need a bigger house now Wali," he had said. "My grandchildren will need some space and then what am I going to do with the money kept in the bank? You are my only son and my asset. I have full trust that you will not let your Ammi and I ever go hungry. What else do we want in life? Perhaps we would like to go for Haj one day. I will keep aside a little for that and the rest will come once the orchard begins to bear fruit."

Wali too had used the entire funds he had saved from his first job as the supervisor of a carpet factory and the house of their dreams had become a reality. It was the largest property among all their friends and relatives and a comfortable modern house.

Wali moved away from the window and came to sit on the bed. Memory of Abba-Jaan had brought tears in his eyes. He missed him so much. Never before had he felt such intense need of his presence by his side. "My father was an epitome of strength and courage, and I, his son, a pathetic specimen of spinelessness. A vile scamp has easily emasculated me…made me powerless like a trapped animal in a snare. Would he have dared so in front of Abba-Jaan? Wouldn't he have been immediately shown the door, thrown out like a rat held from its tail? And what have I done? Found myself a hole to hide instead of challenging my foe?"

Prior to this day, Wali had never had a reason to indulge in self reproach, but the appalling events of the previous evening had thrown him completely off balance. His helplessness and susceptibility had sent his confidence tumbling downhill. His brimming emotions now found their way out in his unrestrained tears. A stream began to flow unchecked; the drops of pain fell onto his listless hands lying on his lap. For once, he didn't try to stop them. His hands, immobilized by the jolt he had received the previous day, refused to do the needful. He continued to sit inertly till the painful lump in his throat was eased.

He got up to wash his face, only to come back to peep out of the window and gaze at his house once again. "Abba-Jaan died a little too soon. I am about to relinquish almost all my assets without any surety that I will ever get them back. Am I heading in the right direction? I desperately need my father's advice and he is beyond reach. I wonder how he would have reacted to a situation like this."

A deep frown matched his intently labouring mind. "It is surely a tough decision to dump it all and run away. Would Abba-Jaan have a better solution to escape from this predicament? Is it somehow possible to ignore those villains, spurn their directives yet come out unscathed?"

He tried to look at the gruelling problem from different angles, but he couldn't unearth any solution other than what he had planned. "Last evening, an impulsive and instant reaction would have been stupidity, especially in front of a person like Hashim, whom Shakeel has almost certainly brought along as an intimidating component." Wali's instincts had warned him against any confrontation with the treacherous men. "I may be doing the right thing. Wisdom lies not in challenging the mean minded but to outsmart them."

The notion returned Wali a fraction of his self-esteem.

He would have to go away taking his family to a safe place. He would have to go to Salim. He had no choice.

But he had certain reservations about going to his son demanding permanent shelter.

Letting the window curtain fall back, he returned to sit at the bedside once again. "If I were not guilty of treating him shabbily, perhaps I wouldn't have had any qualms about going to him unannounced. And I have treated his wife, Subina, even worse. Abba-Jaan was so progressive in his thinking and I have been such a contrast." Wali couldn't shake off the vapours of penitence which had begun to soak him wet again, just like they had done this morning, when Wali had had this enlightenment for the first time.

"Hadn't Abba-Jaan told me often enough and after each episode of communal violence or racial hatred that religious walls were purely artificial walls? How often had he said that; we are all His children… He is the supreme Father… If He wanted any differences in us, He would have made us differently; but there are only similarities among the human races and colour is no difference. It suits the region one comes from; though easy mobility has now amalgamated different races in today's world and created the confusion… Remember, that these artificial walls of separation are created by none other than man himself… Only man can have such a petty mind to fight over our Holy Father; over the way of remembering Him. The ultimate aim is to bow before Him… how you do it is your choice…In His court no one is superior, no one inferior. Considering one's religion greater is a poor opinion."

How right was Abba-Jaan, Wali reflected.

"And despite teachings like that all my life, I have acted on a whim, like a fool." Repentance was like fetters, tightly closing on him.

"A person should avoid doing things he is going to regret some day, for nothing is more painful than repentance. Or else, make amends before it is too late. If not, you will carry the bundle of those horrible feelings of remorse with you to the grave." Wali recalled the words that Abba-Jaan had spoken just a few months before he had suddenly died of cardiac arrest.

"Is it too late for me to make amends?" He wondered. "*Allah*, please allow me time to atone my sins. Let me compensate by giving Subina the importance she deserves in our family," Wali yearned. His hands, which had lain listlessly on his lap till now, became restive with guilt.

Subina had always conducted herself in such an upright manner. Only he had been blind till today. No...he had pretended to be blind. He had known about her noble qualities all the while. He was also convinced that at this hour of need, she would welcome her husband's family with open arms. He had a kind of assurance that she would provide them with shelter when they were being rendered homeless.

Wali's eyes were once more brimming with tears. The pangs of conscience set off more depression in his already low spirits.

With nothing to do but wait, his time boarded a slow moving vehicle for the first time in life, slow at the time when he was desperate for it to go fast forward, if only by a day to divulge the destiny planned for him.

Alas! Time could not rush with the speed he desired. Many idle and restless hours lay ahead. Sitting alone in his hideout, he began to be haunted by the events from his past. Snippets of memory began to come in flashes; rankling memories, at times sprinkled by some pleasing flickers. Some of these visitations were from the recent past, others from days long gone by. He didn't resist; instead floated along the gentle, soothing, jolting, jerking, cascading currents of his reminiscences.

Chapter 2

"What festivities were in progress! Such hustle bustle...sounds of lively wedding music... animated conversation...bursts of laughter...clatter of the crockery... exuberating aromas of the feast...and I had refused take part in the celebrations. It was a foolish thing to do, to have missed once in a lifetime occasion." Wali's conscious mind presently registered what had always been there in his subconscious.

He had missed the previous night's celebrations of the *mehndi raat* too when henna had been applied to Salim's little finger before wrapping it in a paper currency, thus declaring him the groom to be. Close relatives and a few of Salim's friends had attended the function and there had been music and dancing till late night. He had joined in only for a short while, at the dinner time and then had merely sat impassively, refusing to communicate with anyone, exhibiting total lack of interest. Meals over and he had instantly retreated to his room, though, he had kept awake for hours listening to the sounds of the revelry.

On the morning of Salim's *nikah*, the house was bursting with guests. Everyone seemed to be in jolly mood except Wali. "With whose permission has Salim invited so many people especially my friends, when I will not even be present at the venue of the *nikah*?" He had groused in front of Sakina, having noted the influx of the invitees from the window of his room. Sakina, who had made this tenth trip to their upstairs bedroom since the morning to check on him, to see if her pleadings since the morning had had any effect on his stringent stance, was apparently disillusioned and her fallen face was the testimony to it.

"What has happened cannot be reverted. Most of the invitees have arrived and they can't be asked to depart now." Sakina had made an effort not to sound annoyed, though her endurance had probably reached its brimming level after months of unremitting clash of opinions in the house. She certainly didn't want it spilled over now and mess up things further. Hence, softening her tone she had tried pacifying her husband, "It is our son's *nikah* toady and all we need to do is to pray to *Allah* that everything goes well in his life." She had then continued, "And why don't you join the guests downstairs? Refreshments are being served and you are surely being missed. Wasim Bhai too has arrived and has been inquiring about your whereabouts." Announcing the arrival of his favourite cousin, she had thrown the final bait to lure her husband to join in the celebrations of their only son's wedding.

But today even this didn't seem to work. "I don't feel like meeting anyone. I am fine in my room. It is Salim's show, so let him handle it." He had spoken rather brashly. Ignoring his grousing Sakina had once again begged of him, "If you don't want to join in now, it is alright. But at least get ready to go to the *dargah* for the *nikah*."

He had remained unyielding to her request, "What kind of *nikah* is this where the bride's relatives are missing and Salim's friend is acting as her guardian? It appears more of a staged show than a *nikah*. I don't want to be a part of it and become a laughing stock of the people," Wali had voiced irritably.

Meher had entered their room at that crucial point; as a result she had overheard his grumbling. "Abbu please, be a little cooperative. And you aren't even dressed. We are leaving in ten minutes. Even Salim Bhai is ready and all set for the occasion."

"I am not stopping anyone from going. But I will be more comfortable staying back at home," Wali had reiterated.

"That is not possible, Abbu. You will be the main witness at the *nikah*. You can't ditch Bhai at this last moment! Now come on Abbu ji, got dressed. Look, Ammi Ji has even ironed and kept your clothes ready. You can't act stubborn like a child. Now hurry up. We are not leaving without you." Meher had then held both her father's hands to pull him out of the chair he had been glued to for the past one hour.

He had stood inert, still not making any effort to get dressed. Finally Meher had spoken exasperatedly, "Abbu ji, stop sulking. It is a very important day for

Bhai Jaan and you cannot act a kill joy on this happy occasion. Come Ammi ji, let him get dressed. Abbu, we are waiting for you downstairs. Be there in ten minutes." Meher had almost commanded him before walking out of the room holding her mother's hand and almost dragging her out with her, leaving her father no chance to brood further. He had finally relented, exclusively for the reason that he didn't have the heart to upset Meher.

"Meher had been right. I had really behaved like a stubborn child that morning," Wali now realized. "Three years have passed since then, but till today I have never regretted my conduct. It has taken me three years and a terrible jolt to come to my senses," He moaned softly.

It was three years ago when his relations with his son had taken a plunge into cold waters exclusively due to his inflexible stand, and in all these years no efforts had been made by him to improve them. But today, along with being an unsettling day, was also the day of his awakening. "I am guilty of being a biased…narrow minded chauvinist. Isn't this the sole reason why it is a painful proposition at present to knock at Salim's door to seek refuge? But, when I was the one to start the cold war, I will be the one to end it now," decided Wali at this juncture.

The roots of these snagged relations had appeared a year after Abba-Jaan's death. Salim had recently graduated from the regional engineering college. Wali was the proud father of a son who had earned a professional degree and had grown up into a handsome young man. He was two inches taller than his father and endowed with quite attractive features. He had his mother's soft grey eyes, but his curly brown hair and streamlined nose were undoubtedly Wali's. He had the strong square jaw-line of his grandfather. His healthy ruddy complexion seared in the sun was proof of his long periods of outdoor activity. But it was his captivating smile that had lately become cause for concern for his father. Wali was worried that his son might draw unnecessary attention from the members of the opposite sex. And his anxiety was justified.

With studies over, Salim was looking for a job. Meanwhile, he had been loitering around a little more than what his father liked. Wali wanted his son to help in the business or look after the orchard till he found himself a job. But Salim would disappear for hours every day soon after breakfast, only to return when the Sun would declare the closure of its business in this part of the hemisphere. Wali was worried that he should not get into wrong company, for lately there had been plenty of hawks around to mislead and trap the youth of the valley.

Then one day the secret of his long hours absence from the house got exposed.

It happened the day one of Wali's prospective clients had come from Delhi to explore the business possibilities with him and had shown keen interest in handicrafts manufactured at his cottage industry. The outcome of the meeting had been quite positive and Wali was pleased at the prospects of exporting decorative items of *naquash* and brass filigree work to some European countries. After the business dealings, he had decided to entertain his client by taking him around to see the important landmarks of the town.

After a short half an hour *shikara* cruise on the Dal, Wali had chosen to visit the Nishat Bagh that evening. They had taken a leisure walk through the gardens, enjoying the gentle breeze fanned by the giant palmate leaves of the *chinars* and getting soaked in the moisture rising in whiffs from the fountains in the water channel that ran through the centre of the entire length of the famous Mugal gardens. The enthusiastic visitor had made Wali walk right up to the last terrace which was originally the twelfth terrace of the garden and the most exclusive and impressive one. It was here that Wali had stopped to point out the magnificent view of the snow clad peaks of the Pir Panjal range of Himalayas, when his eyes had got drawn towards a familiar figure half hidden behind a clump of *chinar* grove. He had stopped on his track, shocked. It was Salim sitting on a parapet there. He had his back towards the pathway and was totally unaware of the trouble he was in, being unmindful of the presence of his father behind him. The reason for the shock for Wali was not his son but his companion, a girl, obviously very young, which was apparent from her youthful slim figure. Both of them seemed in high spirits in each other's company. From his position Wali could clearly observe their bare feet dangling and moving around playfully in the water pool which had a large fountain in the centre. Salim had casually placed his arm around the girl's shoulders and both were lost in their own world. Wali watched with disbelief as Salim brought his face close to the girl's and whispered something in her ears. Wali immediately knew that the relationship was not merely friendly but rather intimate. The girl laughed with levity and Wali went red with rage.

How could his son be so shameless as to openly flirt in a public place? Didn't he have any concern for the family's reputation? And what kind of family did the girl come from? She seemed least bothered about the bad name her impropriety might fetch her family.

Wali would have reprimanded Salim there and then if he didn't have an important client accompanying him. He had then noted his compatriot looking at him in wonder at the sudden transformation of his facial expressions.

"Is there anything wrong, Wali Sahib?" He had asked.

"No...no, I was just thinking of something. In fact, I just recalled an important matter that must soon be attended to," Wali had immediately covered up. Thereafter, he had lost total interest in becoming the sightseeing guide for his business guest and had eliminated most of the destinations yet to visit from the list he had in mind. Instead, he had returned home as soon as he could reach his guest to the hotel of his stay.

On reaching home, the first thing he had done was to complain to Sakina. "Do you know what your *sahibjada* is up to? Since he has in hand a plenty of time to waste, he is indulging in romance."

"What kind of romance?" Sakina had asked innocently.

"Kind of romance? Are there different kinds of romances? A variety of them like a number of dishes on a menu card?" Wali had shouted at Sakina. She couldn't comprehend the reason for her husband's ire, nor the rationale of it being aimed at her. It had instantly brought tears in her eyes for she was not used to being shouted at.

Noticing Sakina's anguish, Wali had tried to control his voice and had continued, "You know, he is seeing some girl. He sits with her openly in the most popular and frequented places, with his arm wrapped around her shoulders, whispering, God knows what in her ears. He has no consideration for the prestige of our family. What if any of our relatives or friends had seen him thus? They would have said 'Wali and his wife have no control over their children. They are going astray.' Would I be able to show my face to the world in that case?"

Expecting Sakina to be highly dismayed by the disturbing news, Wali had then waited for her reaction, but her expressionless visage had put across no communiqué and he had continued vociferously, "Perhaps, some of them already know that he is monkeying around with girls and are poking-fun at us behind our backs." Sakina had now begun to look rather hurt than distressed. Was it the upsetting news or his shouting that was the cause, Wali was confused. But he had lowered his voice further and had then spoken more softly, "You better check what is he up to, and who is this girl he is meeting."

Sakina had merely nodded in agreement to comply with his request.

That evening when Sakina had come to their bedroom after finishing her chores, she had said, "I think it is time to think of Salim's marriage. He talks about being in love with some girl called Veena."

"Veena?" Wali had jumped out of his bed. "Veena, a Hindu girl? And these Hindu girls can only be as shameless as openly sitting in public places with unfamiliar young boys. So…He will marry a Hindu girl? Has he gone out of his mind?" After a short pause to digest the information, he had declared, "No one in our family has ever married a non Muslim. And no one in the family has ever challenged the tradition."

Sakina's flustered expressions depicted her apprehension that she would now become a scapegoat to be milled between the two headstrong men of her life. And to escape the milling, she had decided to choose the simplest mode to deal with the situation; silence.

Therefore, for a while Wali's rapid angry breathing was the only sound audible in the room. It was an added reason to discourage Sakina to initiate any immediate discussion on the topic. For an unduly long period, she had quietly sat cosily inside her quilt and watched Wali's furious pacing in the room. She had been sensibly waiting for his anger to subside.

After an extended, oppressive silence in the room which Wali had refused to break, Sakina had gathered courage to speak. "Why don't you start looking for a suitable match for Salim? Ammi-Jaan was saying the other day that children's marriages should be performed in time."

"I hm,…" was all Wali had replied.

"And Ammi-Jaan was also saying that Meher is a young girl now. We should look for a match for her too," Sakina had said after a pause.

This time Wali had immediately retorted, "My Meher is no ordinary girl. Moreover, she is very busy and doesn't have time to be tied in wedlock. She is in the middle of her education. Don't even think of distracting her from her important studies. Right now it is Salim for whom we need to look for a proper match."

The next day, he had spread the word around that he was looking for a match for his engineer son. Proposals began to arrive. Each evening, after dinner,

Wali and Sakina would spend a few hours scrutinizing them. Time began to fly in consultations at home with Ammi-Jaan and with other relatives, especially Wasim and his family.

Meanwhile, Salim got a job with a construction company and became busy in his routine. Wali was happy that he would now have no time for his love life.

Two months later, there was a proposal for Salim from a good and decent Muslim family. The father was an executive engineer with the Public Works Department. The girl was convent educated and a graduate. It was considered by the elders to be the most suitable match.

It was again Sakina's duty to talk to her son and make him agree.

That evening, it was as if hell broke loose in the family. Salim rejected the proposal outright. He wouldn't even listen to it. If he married, it would be Veena or else no one.

Sakina pleaded to her son to abide by his Abbu's wishes, but to no avail. When Wali had received the feedback of Salim's response, he had scolded him at the dinner table that night. "Why are you bent upon lowering my prestige among the family? When I was your age, I couldn't even dream of going against my parent's wishes. We were a generation of duty bound offspring, and here is my son who is least bothered to know what his parents would like. He wants to choose his own rapids… paddle his own canoe. The current education has not modernized but completely blinded today's youth…turned them into insensitive beings."

Salim's inflexible exterior and his total lack of response had annoyed Wali further and he had then shouted at him, "Did I send you to a professional college to become a Romeo?"

Salim had continued to play dumb, refusing to react or reconcile.

"You are marrying the Muslim girl chosen by us and that is my decision," Wali had then loudly emphasised.

As a reaction to Wali's directive, Salim had adopted the policy of non-violence to protest and had staged a walk out on that night's dinner.

The confrontation had made Salim even more self-willed. He lodged his remonstration by refusing to eat food at home or speaking with anyone. He continued his silence and hunger strike for ten days. That made Sakina jittery.

After all, hers was a mother's heart.

On the tenth night of Salim's revolt, Sakina would not stop shedding tears. Wali's attempts to reason with her went abortive. She was inconsolable. "My Salim has lost tremendous weight and his life is in danger," she had wailed. "What kind of hard hearted father are you? It doesn't matter to you if your only son dies of starvation."

"To die of starvation, one needs to starve. So, why would Salim die? And why do you think he has lost any weight? Can't you see he is as healthy as ever? Do you think he hasn't eaten a morsel all these days? You should know your son better; he is a big pretender!"

Sakina's large eyes had looked intently at her husband, apparently wanting to verify the extent of truth in his statement.

Wali had continued more volubly in his endeavour to convince Sakina of his judgement, "He must have been feasting in different restaurants everyday. I personally think he has put on weight with all that oily restaurant food. The only worry I have is that he may spoil his digestion with overeating. And you better not get swayed by his tantrums."

Though he had firmly put down Sakina's pleadings, he himself had begun to feel the strain.

Then in a few days, Meher had come home from her hostel and taken the matter in her hands. Wali was suspicious that it was Salim's doing. He had probably written to his sister and requested her to help him out in this matter and there she had presented herself. It was another issue that her obligatory presence had coincided with her autumn break.

The next morning of her arrival, soon after breakfast she had broached the subject. "Abbu, why are you so adamant about not allowing Salim Bhai to marry the girl he wants as his bride? No one is so rigid these days. What if she is a Hindu girl? Shouldn't the most important eligibility criteria be that she should be a good human being?" And Wali had looked at his daughter with soft eyes. She thought and spoke just like her grandfather.

"Abbu, I have met Veena." Seeing her father silent and meek, Meher had continued with her petition. "She is a very good girl, very soft spoken! She is a science graduate and a very intelligent girl. She has always been topping her class. And, she belongs to a good family. Her father is a professor at the

Engineering College where Salim Bhai has studied. That was where they had met, for her family lives within the college campus. Moreover, she is very pretty. That is why Bhai Jaan is *fida* on her." Meher had spoken the last sentence with a naughty smile and twinkle in her eyes.

"These daughters can turn tough fathers into such weaklings," Wali had silently thought. He could have shouted at anyone at home and intimidated them. But when it came to Meher, he wouldn't utter a word. Nor would he ever refute her request. His daughter was probably his only weakness.

"So, Abbu what do you consider reasonable? Is it breaking your son's heart and making him dejected for the rest of his life or allowing him to lead a happy life with someone he adores? Decide between making him miserable or making him happy," Meher had left no scope for Wali to refuse outright. She had presented her brother's case superbly.

"You should have adopted law as your profession," Wali had suggested with a smile. Seeing a soft smile replacing her husband's frown in days, Sakina had heaved a sigh of relief.

Wali had then conveyed in a much mellowed down tone. "Give me some time to think it over. Such things should not be decided hastily."

He had thought over his daughter's argument all day and night. Perhaps Abba-Jaan would have given similar advice. On top, Salim had turned out to be so wilful. There was no point arguing with him anymore when he would not listen to reason. He had then declared the next morning, "Let Salim choose his future. If he wants to marry this girl, let it be. But don't expect my cooperation."

Salim was apprehensive of the affairs changing for the worse again once his sister would leave, and he didn't want the opportunity to slip away. Moreover, there was a strong chance that if given an extended period for speculation, his father might recant. Therefore, he had decided to tie the knot without any delay.

The brother and sister team had made all the wedding arrangements. The first thing that Salim had done the morning after receiving his father's nod was to rush to get the wedding cards printed. Meher had taken over the shopping responsibilities with Sakina playing only the second-fiddle; her enthusiasm having crumbled due to Wali's disconsolate air. A *kazi*, who would have normally been arranged by his father to read the *Nikah*, had been arranged by the groom to-be himself.

Only Ammi-Jaan's spirits couldn't be dampened by Wali's sulking. She was all frisky and skittish with exhilaration and set about planning the menu for the wedding feast. She had demanded a new *pheran* for the occasion and that was probably the only task Wali had personally undertaken.

A week later Salim was married.

On Meher's insistence, Wali had attended the ceremonies, but only half heartedly. The only time he had come alive during the *nikah,* was to react to the *kazi's* query to Salim if *nikah* to the woman was *kabool* to him, was he ready to accept her as his wife?"

"Think again Salim. There is still time. This may not be the right choice," Wali, who had till then been sitting expressionless and listless next to his son had instantly and animatedly whispered to him. Equally promptly, in a voice clear and urgent had Salim replied to the *kazi's* enquiry three times in succession as required, *"Kabool, Kabool, Kabool."*

Prior to this wedding, Wali didn't remember having heard such hurried acceptance by any groom; it was as if Salim was afraid that the influence being exerted by his father might begin to work. And, with this ultimate opportunity lost, Wali's last bubble of hope too had burst.

Thereafter, his affliction had returned. His glum countenance had continued even at the time of the wedding feast and it was something no wedding guest had failed to notice.

To solemnise the marriage according to the Islamic traditions, Veena had to accept Islam as her religion. Love knows no religious boundaries and she had gladly consented to become a Muslim. Her name was changed to Subina. And she had been rejected by her Hindu family for the same. Her father, Mother or for that matter, no relative from her side had attended the wedding.

Chapter 3

"How we keep nurturing our worthless egos all our lives? We don't even care if in the process we cause deep wounds in others. Our arrogance gets boosted and that makes us highly pleased." In the solitude of the houseboat where there was nothing to distract his thought process, Wali's conscience had currently begun to prick him like a thorn. He was almost ashamed that he had badly slighted the person who should have been treated like a queen of the house. And now, at this time of the dire need, she was the only one they could fall back upon.

"Aren't we supposed to treat others the way we would like them to treat us? Now that I will be at her mercy, in case we reach her house safely, won't Subina have every right to avenge the indignities I had heaped on her?" Wali's latest awareness had added an extra load to his sufferings.

He presently recalled how from day one Subina had begun her efforts to win over his trust and how he had spoilt it all for her.

He clearly remembered her very first morning at their house; her new home, when he was seated at the dining table and Subina had so politely inquired, "Abbu Ji, how will you like the eggs done?"

"Abdul knows. He will make me my breakfast." He had spoken rather rudely.

Then the following days, there had been number of instances when he had tried his best to put Subina down.

"Abbu Ji, let me iron your shirt for you."

"No...."

"Abbu Ji, in my free time I can help you with the accounts."

"No...thanks."

"Abbu Ji, I will get your broken spectacles repaired. The shop is owned by my friend's father."

"No..., I can manage my affairs."

He could very clearly perceive now that at every given opportunity, she had tried to please him. But he had been a downright insensitive man and had refused to be pleased.

And that was not all. There had been some more serious offences on his part. Barely a week following Subina's entry into the family, some relatives and friends had been invited over for dinner. Sakina had expressed her relief to have Subina assist her play the hostess on the occasion and Wali hadn't liked her stance a wee bit. Both of them had been seen in flurried activity the whole day, and he had been out of sorts to see their companionship growing strong in such a short duration. He had considered asking his wife to keep the new comer at arm's-length and not give her so much importance but couldn't gather courage to do so for the fear of scorn. He had then decided that the demonstration of discontent would have to be his private one man show.

That evening, dinner was over and Subina was serving dessert when her mother-in-law had proclaimed light heartedly, "The saffron *kheer* has been prepared by Subina. The effort the girl has put into its preparation, I am worried she might have outdone my cooking expertise." And when Subina had come to serve her father-in-law, he had refused curtly saying he wasn't hungry anymore. The guests had earlier perceived his unhappiness on his son's wedding day; therefore on this occasion too, all of them had cast glances at him conveying that they had well understood it to be a deliberate move. Wali too had caught the meaningful, though momentary flashes of smiles and had felt smug at having achieved what he wanted; to humiliate Subina.

Although, he had discovered that the best line of attack at Subina's unwanted entry into the household was to simply give her a cold shoulder, for nothing would be more hurting than rejection, a few days later, he had been given another opportunity to get even with her for having charmed his son into marrying her. For, that was his strong belief.

One afternoon, as he had entered the house, he had found Subina in the parlour sitting next to his bookshelf reading a book she had picked from it. He had immediately found an excuse to exhibit his anger and had rudely ordered her not to touch his things. She had politely apologized and hastily left the room. He had tried ignoring it, but knew that she had departed with tearful eyes.

In his heart he had felt ashamed of his behaviour, for the books did not particularly belong to him. They were the property shared by all the members of the household. It was his deliberate move to make her feel small.

In contrast, Sakina was a picture of contentment those days. She seemed to be doting on her new daughter and had even begun to put on weight due to reduced activity as Subina had taken over the strenuous household responsibilities. Their lively conversation too would be very noticeable to him, especially when Subina was very formal and reserved in his presence.

Looking at them, Wali would be reminded of the early days of his married life when he had so often observed Ammi-Jaan and Sakina chatting together the same way. There had never been any bickering between them, which otherwise was a common occurrence in many households. There would be constant soothing laughter around, a worthwhile reason to yearn for the comforts of home each evening, after the day's hard work.

Ammi-Jaan too had received her share of attention from the young bride and had very soon formed a positive opinion of the newcomer. She had therefore tried to convey her judgement to Wali. "Wali, our Salim is a sensible boy. He has selected his wife wisely. One rarely finds such prudent girls in the modern times who are so humble and respectful."

But he had felt let down by his son and blamed Subina for having wooed him away. That was the anger he was carrying around within him. And the exhibition of that anger was exclusively targeted at Subina, for she was at home most of the time and too polite to react insolently. Wali wasn't sure if Salim would have tolerated his insults passively. Then Salim was his own son, close to his heart.

A few months later, Salim had declared his intensions of leaving for Delhi, where he had been offered a good job. Wali was pained. "It must be Subina's doing. She must have made him apply for a job away from home," he had groused that evening in front of Sakina.

"What has happened to you? You can't even think straight these days! You should be happy that your son has got a good job. His pay will almost be double. He had been sending applications to various companies for a long time and had received a few job offers too. But this is by far the best offer he has received. Subina has got nothing to do with it. In fact, she is upset and apprehensive about going to a new place. She will be so lonely the whole day when Salim will be away at work. She was revealing her anxiety to me this morning," Sakina's tone had made her annoyance apparent.

"What is the use of his double salary? Won't his expenditure double up when he will have to run a separate household?" Wali had presented another argument.

"It is good for them to be away from us for some time. At least they won't have to see your annoyed expression everyday. I wonder when you will learn to accept the changes which have occurred without your consent. It has been months of your moping now and I think that's more than enough. And what is wrong with the girl? She is so sweet tempered and respectful. Putting aside all that, you must accept that she is our family member now," Sakina had entreated, and Wali had chosen to ignore. All he had then asked was, "When are they leaving?" Being told that they would be gone in just fifteen days, Wali's mood had plunged to its lowest ebb. He had refused further discussion on the topic, diverting his full attention towards the newspaper he was reading, burying his face deep into it, though, he hadn't read even a word more that day.

Wali and Sakina had gone to see off the couple at the bus station, but even while bidding them farewell, Wali had not divulged from his stringent expression, which had become his integral feature in the presence of his daughter-in-law.

"Abbu ji, do come to visit us in Delhi. It will be a good change for you and Ammi ji. Meher is also there. We can all be together then." Subina had extended the invitation to him before leaving.

He hadn't even responded to her offer.

But once they were gone, Wali was upset for months on stretch. He had missed his children. The house appeared empty without them.

Salim had been writing to him off and on but Wali's would reply very infrequently.

Chapter 3   35

He would rather talk once in a while on phone to check on their welfare but didn't have the patience to sit down to write letters. Sakina too had been receiving regular letters from Subina. They had rented a small two bedroom house in Delhi and were slowly furnishing it. The second bedroom was for the parents, as and when they would choose to come. Every month they would buy something for the house and Sakina would get full details about it.

Salim always had praises for Subina in his letters; perhaps it was an endeavour to make his father soften his sternness towards her. In one of his letters Salim had written:

Dear Abbu ji,

Salaam

After one whole month of wait for your letter, I have decided that there is no point waiting anymore. Your very infrequent writing to us suggests that you are extremely busy. I can well understand that running a business as well as looking after the orchard all alone may not be easy for you. Sometimes I think I should have stayed home and helped you in my free time.

My daily schedule is quite hectic. The office duties are quite demanding but I enjoy my work. My seniors appear satisfied with my performance and have hinted an out of turn promotion.

You will be happy to know that Subina has passed her B.Ed. examinations securing a first division. Whatever task she undertakes, she does that with full dedication. She had applied for job in a number of schools and yesterday, she was offered a well paid job in a prestigious school located near our house. I am happy that her complaints of boredom are going to end now, as she will get busy in her teaching assignments from the next week. I am sure she will prove an excellent teacher as she has well in-depth of knowledge of her subjects.

Running a house in big cities turns out to be quite expensive, but with two incomes, it is going to be comfortable now.

We get the pleasure of regular visits from Meher over the weekends. Due to her late hours and heavy load of studies, she prefers to stay in her college hostel despite repeated requests from Subina to shift with us. Though on her visits, she gets her fill of home cooked food and that induces her to be back the next weekend. She is doing well. Subina is taking care of her needs and shops for her when required as Meher has no time for it herself. You and Ammi ji needn't worry for her at all.

We are anxiously waiting for you and Ammi ji to visit us. Winters will be the best time because you can escape the severe cold and snow of the Valley.

With respects from us both to you and Ammi ji

Your son

Salim

Wali had right away scoffed off the idea of Subina becoming a career woman. Not that he had any problem with the modern working women proving their efficiency in every field, but this case was different. Here the offender was Subina and how much she tried, in Wali's opinion she could never do the right thing. Here was another chance to lash out at her.

"Now the daughter-in-law of the house will go out to work and neglect her house." He had complained to Sakina.

"Why? Won't Meher work once her studies are over or do you plan to make her sit at home?"

For once, Sakina's statement had him completely bowled over.

It was more than two years since Salim and Subina had left, and Wali had not gone to see them even once. They both had visited home twice, on long annual leave of about a fortnight each. And Subina had still not conceded defeat in her endeavour to appease her father-in-law. Her own parents had not forgiven her yet, and had completely washed their hands off her. At times, it was quite obvious that she sought a father figure in Wali. And for once a sensitive man had continued to put on a stern exterior, refusing to alter it. Although, in their absence he had missed his children each hour, he had still refused to take off his mask of austerity. Perhaps, he was finding it difficult to compromise.

Some men have big egos, but Wali had a giant one.

"We made Subina convert her religion," Wali's solitude now set him to ponder for the first time, "How superficial is our outlook. She complied with our wishes to make us happy. She obviously knows only that way of saying prayers which she must have learnt from the time she was a little girl; the way children do through emulating their elders. Now she has made efforts to learn verses from the holy Koran and perform *namaz;* when none of the religions have been her choice. She was born in one and married in another. But can we really change her inner thoughts? Isn't true religion the purity of the inner faith? Hasn't she proven that she is beyond the intolerant walls of prejudice created in the name of religion?"

"She would have been Abba-Jaan's favourite. And what a heartless fellow have I been!" Wali faced a series of regrets as his conscience began to register his past offences.

"*'Don't touch my things.'* Are material possessions more precious than a blissful heart? And haven't those books been gathering dust lying on the rack untouched? When have I had time to read all these years? And once out from school Salim and Meher have been too busy for extra reading. And when the books would have acquired usefulness once again, I stopped Subina from touching them. Now, they will continue to lie forlorn and unwanted on that rack."

"*'I am not hungry for the dish cooked by a young girl.'* How much effort the poor girl might have put into preparing the dessert, to impress the members of her new family, especially her grouchy father-in-law? How could have I taken pleasure in humiliating the young person in front of the outsiders? And, hadn't I gone hunting for the leftovers of the *kheer* in the middle of the night? How pretentious can one become at times?"

"*'If my daughter in law adopts a career she neglects her house.'* If my own daughter works, I am a proud father. Why? Hasn't Subina worked hard to earn those degrees? Should her labour of years be allowed to become a futile waste? Should her ambitions and expectations be stifled?"

"Today, I am desperate to arrive at her doorstep for safe sanctuary. Only if…only if, we manage to reach her house! *Allah*, you have every right to punish me but… not this way. *Khudah, rehem kar.* Have mercy on us!" Wali lamented.

He was swept into a whirlpool of awfully lonely and helpless feelings and wished his son to be with him as support. Alone, he was so vulnerable; together they would have exerted efforts to trounce the enemy. The next moment he wondered if things would have actually been better if Salim was with him. It immediately dawned upon him that their prospects of escaping successfully were perhaps far better with Salim being away.

"*Allah* is really merciful. Had Salim and Subina been with us, the situation would have been even worse. More lives would have been in danger and the escape would have become more risky. Moreover, last evening when Shakeel and his obnoxious friends had laid the demands I was able to restrain myself, but had Salim been present he would have found it impossible not to openly exhibit his anger. Being young and impulsive, he would have certainly pounced on Shakeel and then God alone knows what could have happened. It is by providence that Salim is in Delhi. At least we have a safe place to go to now. And then I am not absolutely without help; Wasim Bhai is there like a lifeboat ready to come to our rescue."

"Despite the help; things will not be easy. I will be taking tremendous risks tonight… almost walking on thin ice with the possibility of it cracking anytime… sitting on a barrel of gunpowder which may explode anytime. *Allah*; be with us. Protect us and save us from all dangers." He silently prayed.

The thought of the lurking danger once again brought him his edginess back. Why hadn't Wasim come back yet? Wali had estimated that it would take him at least four hours or may be more to finish the tasks. Only half of that time had elapsed. Wali knew he required patience, but isolation in the middle of the lake along with the anxiety for the successful execution of the plan was slowly getting on to his nerves.

He got up from the bed and walked back to the sitting room for a few sips of water.

Chapter 4

Wasim had offered to take care of everything including withdrawing money from the banks, while Wali remained in hiding. He had felt awfully guilty about making Wasim do the running around, particularly when he was recouping from a viral attack, but Wasim had rubbished his suggestion of accompanying him to carry out the tasks. It would be foolish to take risks when the men were most likely to shadow him to discern his intentions and the whole plan would fall flat if the men developed even a fragment of suspicion, he had argued. As such escaping right from under their noses was a Herculean task, but putting them on a high alert would be like trying to swallow a shark.

They had jointly decided in the morning that money should be withdrawn from both the banks as a large withdrawal from one bank could raise queries. Their perception was that as Wali had lived in the town for ages and his sphere of acquaintances was large, even an innocent remark could become dangerous as words spread around fast. Nothing would be more uncalled for than a simple enquiry by the teller at the bank if Wali Sahib was planning a trip somewhere. And God forbid, if someone overheard the remark, it could spread like a wildfire. There could be contentions that Wali had compromised with his son and was visiting him at Delhi. The tales could reach as far as his home and that would be disastrous. Moreover, nosy visitors to his house could complicate matters further.

Fortunately, he had accounts in two banks; on Abba-Jaan's suggestion. "It is safer in case a bank suffers liquidation," he had said. "At least you would not lose your entire savings if something like that ever occurs." Today it was definitely safer that way, Wali had realized in the morning.

And it was fortunate that he had a brother like Wasim to help him, who was there like an island in the vast sea of troubles, some surety towards safety when danger was closing on his family and him. He was perhaps the only one who could assist his family to wriggle out of the present predicament.

It was even more fortunate that Shakeel had inquired about Wasim at the time when Wali's anger was at its peak. And on the spur of the moment, he had lied that Wasim wasn't in town. Wali wasn't a liar, but in this case he didn't want that Shakeel should have anything to do with his brother. This unintentionally blurted out statement had turned out to be valuable for the plan that he had subsequently hatched. After leaving home in the morning he had headed straight for Wasim's house, for he was the only man Wali could completely trust.

Although, Wasim was two years his senior, they had practically grown up together and had always rendered unconditional support to each other. Wali didn't have a real brother, but Wasim had always proved to be as protective towards Wali as a real brother, right from the time when they were in school, warding off the bullies when they were out to trouble his little cousin.

Memories of his school life now wafted in, bringing with them a profound feeling of nostalgia. Choosing to sit on an easy chair this time, Wali rested his head on the backrest and stared at the ceiling, as if the roof was the screen on which the scenes from the forgotten past had suddenly come alive.

The scene to flash in his mind was the one when he was barely ten years old and he saw himself shivering and hiding behind Wasim.

He and Wasim studied in the same primary school. Wali was in the fourth standard and Wasim in the sixth; the senior most class of the school. Although, their paths crossed often but Wali was a shy and lonesome child, while Wasim was quite gregarious; always surrounded by his group of friends.

Considering him to be grown up enough to learn to handle money, Abba-Jaan had begun to give Wali pocket money once a week, on every Monday, and that would be the day to visit the school tuck-shop. Soon his routine was noticed by the biggest bully of the school, Tariq, who was in the same class as Wasim, and troubles for Wali initiated at once.

Tariq was the largest and probably the oldest boy of the school, having earned that benefit due to his two years sojourn in most of the classes. He was also the only one in school with cracking voice and the first crop of beard on his chin. Therefore, he seldom missed any opportunity to flaunt his special privileges. And it was no secret that he came to school to harass and trouble his victims than to tackle his books. To add efficiency to his purpose, he had his own gang of faithful scamps. They would ever be on the lookout to rob the helpless youngsters and then utilize the loot at the canteen.

Tariq soon acquired the knowledge about Wali's weekly stipend and began to wait for him outside the tuck-shop every Monday. As soon as Wali would appear, he would then be surrounded by the bully and his cronies and ordered to hand over the money. In the beginning, Wali was too scared to resist and meekly complied with their demand. He was fearful of reporting the matter to Abba-Jaan since he was of the firm belief that such a complaint would bring about an immediate discontinuation to his pocket money apart from the unwanted publicity Abba-Jaan's visit to the school would draw for him. He had then tried changing the day of his visit to the canteen, keeping his coin safely at home for a few days. Success eluded him as the ringleader's spies soon discovered the change of his schedule.

When Wali had had enough of harrying, one day he decided to remonstrate. He refused to hand over his pocket money to Tariq and held his coin tightly in his fist pressed to his back. The boys then applied their might to snatch away his treasure. That initiated a scuffle and soon little Wali was pushed to the ground where he lay pinned down. He was no match to the big boys in physical strength but at the moment his resolve was unmatched. Lying on the muddy ground, he had refused to open his palm which held his 10 paisa coin. Tariq had then stood on his unremitting tiny hand and tried crushing it with his boot. Wali had screamed in pain. It was his good luck that Wasim and his friends were passing by and had heard his shrieks; otherwise Wali could have suffered some serious and lasting injuries on his hand. They had rushed to Wali's aid, especially Wasim, charging at the wicked boys like an angry bull. Seeing the opponents, the wild unruly herd had fled. Wasim had bellowed at the retreating bullies to keep off his brother or else he would take serious action against them.

And Wali now remembered how he had clung on to Wasim, sobbing, shaking and hiding behind him, considering him as his wall of protection.

But it was not the end of their troubles.

The following Sunday afternoon Wasim and Wali had gone fishing on the bank of the lake. They had enjoyed the quietude barely for half an hour when Tariq and his cronies appeared on the scene. They had obviously been on the lookout for them. Before the two boys could react, Tariq had pushed Wali into the lake. Mission accomplished, the wicked boys had taken to their heels.

Wali had never known fear and desperation as great as he felt then. He didn't know how to swim and had immediately begun to drown, swallowing mouthfuls of dirty water in the process. Wasim was only an inadept swimmer himself, but, without a second thought he had instantaneously jumped into the water and frantically flinging his arms and legs had managed to reach him in no time. Wali now remembered how he had clung on to his brother for survival, and how Wasim had strived to keep both their heads above the water till some adults had spotted the struggling pair and rescued them.

And this time the news of the bullies' conduct couldn't be kept hidden from Abba-Jaan and an appropriate action had been taken by the school headmaster after the complaint was registered with him. Wali had, by no means, missed the absence of Tariq from school.

And he had felt exceptionally close to Wasim ever since.

Although, there were many instances when Wasim had gone out of the way to help him, but, there was one which had touched Wali the most. It was when he had gone to Delhi for Meher's admission. He had fallen short by a few thousand rupees, having completely overlooked carrying cash to be deposited towards the hostel expenditure. Not wanting to bother Abba-Jaan, he had requested Wasim to send him the money through a common friend who happened to be coming to Delhi.

Till then, he had had no idea of Wasim's pitiable financial condition. It was much later, through the same common friend that he had come to know how Wasim had mortgaged his wife's jewellery to arrange the funds and had also warned the man against revealing it to Wali. The friend had later mentioned it to check if Wali had returned the money as he had felt Wasim was in need of it.

Wali had delayed to return the borrowed sum and had rushed to do so with interest, the day of this discovery, feeling ashamed to have carelessly deferred paying back the debt. Though, not even once had Wasim asked for the money to be returned. That was the dignity of the man. Thereafter, Wali had insisted upon helping Wasim financially, at least to support his son's education till his son finished his college. After completing his graduation in science, Wasim's son, Imtiaz had secured a job as a medical representative in a known pharmaceutical firm and had begun to earn well. That had helped in the desistance of the family's impoverishment.

Today, Wali was confident that Wasim would once again go to any length to help him at this hour of need. That was why this morning, after leaving home, he had headed straight for his house.

"*Asalaammu alaykum* Bhai Jaan, I haven't seen you for a long time," Wali had greeted his brother the moment he had opened the door.

"*Valaikum asalaam* Wali, Come...come, what a pleasant surprise to have you visiting us at this hour. You couldn't have chosen a better day to visit us. I have been getting bored sitting at home all these days. But you have come rather early. I hope all is well."

Wasim was an attractive man with very regular features, and age hadn't been able to snatch away his good looks. Though, he was not half as handsome at present as he was in his youth. Moreover, he appeared somewhat despondent now; his eyes totally lacking the sparkle they once had, as if, his interest in existence had got lost somewhere during the journey of life. But Wali's visits had always and genuinely cheered him up.

"Why have you been sitting at home Bhai-Jaan?" Wali had asked.

"Oh, I haven't been keeping too well lately. I had caught virus and was running fever for the past five days. I haven't stepped out of the house all these days. Only last evening the fever broke, but I thought it wise to take rest for another day," Wasim had answered.

Wali had stood still for a while. There was a faint smile playing on his otherwise ashen face which was particularly noted by Wasim.

"What is the matter Wali? You look pale and your smile too is quite troubled. But why are you smiling thus?" Wasim had asked.

"Bhai, I had never known an illness to turn to ones advantage till this moment."

Wali's reply had brought bewildered frown on Wasim's face and he was genuinely puzzled at the strangest statement he had ever heard. "I don't understand what you mean," he had said.

Wasim's wife, Ayesha had entered the room at this moment and that had prevented Wasim from getting an immediate answer to Wali's mystifying statement.

She was a small and thin woman who looked much older than her age, having greyed prematurely. Wali had noted the usual dismal expression on her face; an expression of a person for whom life has not been fair. It had instantly softened on seeing him.

After the exchange of pleasantries, Wali had wanted secret audience with Wasim without further delay. He wanted to discuss things with Wasim alone to decide the course of his actions. Therefore he had said, "Bhabi-Jaan, I am in a dire need of a hot cup of *chai*, if you don't mind." She had immediately gone to prepare tea.

"Bhai-Jaan, I have a serious matter to discuss with you. I have come at your door seeking help today." Wali had initiated the discussion.

He then revealed the appalling circumstances to Wasim which had him utterly shocked. He was so angry that he wanted to head straight for Wali's house to strangle Shakeel there and then. Wali had to pacify him. "Bhai-Jaan, this is not a time to exhibit anger. You can imagine how I felt when Shakeel laid his demands. My whole body shook with anger but I controlled myself, well knowing the consequences of a rash action. We have to scheme carefully so that we can disentangle ourselves from the net that Shakeel has thrown to entrap us. I have chalked out some ground plan. Now listen carefully to what I say. If you think there is a loophole, feel free to make suggestions."

Subsequently, both the men had talked in hushed tones, much to Ayesha's curiosity. She had served them tea and then well realizing the reason for the oppressive silence in the room that her presence was not welcome, had sat in the adjacent room. They had been talking so softly that she could barely understand a word. Only Wasim had come to her once to tell her not to answer the door. She was to pretend that they were not at home. He had then proceeded to put a large lock on the main door and had come inside from the backside through the door that opened into the kitchen, fastening the latch into position and then pushing the door to make sure it was well secured. He had next proceeded to draw curtains of all the windows of the house. He had never before done anything like that and it had made Ayesha even more curious. That was an hour ago and Ayesha was worried. She knew something serious had happened, but what? Then Wasim had asked her to join them. He had requested her to sit beside him and listen carefully.

"Ayesha, some terrible circumstances have suddenly erupted and Wali needs our help. I cannot give you the details now but we are to leave for Anantnag, to your Parent's home, early tomorrow morning. Fortunately, Imtiaz and his wife are already away and that makes things easy. I am going out with Wali now. When I come back, I will discuss the affairs with you. In my absence, do not answer any knock on the door. Simply ignore it. It is very important. Think it is a matter of life and death."

Ayesha was rightly alarmed.

"In your free time pack the luggage we will need to take with us, for about fifteen days, but make sure no sound leaks out of the house. You mustn't meet any neighbours either. Let them all believe we are away." Ayesha had nodded in agreement. "And could you please pack us some tiffin now? We definitely won't be able to come home for lunch. Lots of things need to be taken care of." Wasim had thus concluded his instructions.

It was enough to frighten Ayesha. Although, she was extremely keen to know what the matter was, she had chosen to restrain her curiosity. She had quietly gone to the kitchen to pack them tiffin, but her discomfort was immense. Things had not been normal in the Valley for a long time now. What could have befallen such a decent family? Wali Bhai was a gentleman and seeing him so shaken was very painful. Also, Sakina was her dear friend. They had always been there for each other at any hour of need. Her son Imtiaz and Salim were good friends. And her Rehman! If Sakina hadn't visited her almost every day to talk her out of her grief, she would never have become normal. She had a very deep wound but Sakina had done her best to heal her.

"*Ya Allah*! All should be well," Ayesha had prayed loudly as the men had left the house secretly from the back door.

"Yes, all should be well," Wali now thought rising from the chair and slowly and inadvertently walking into the other room. "If Shakeel comes to know that Wasim has been behind all the help given to me, he will not spare him. Have I done the right thing to endanger my brother's life too?" The thought at once troubled him. He slumped onto the bed and resting his head on his interlocked hands, he continued to reflect. "Wasim will have to leave the town for a few days as planned. Fortunately, Ayesha's parents and brother are well off. Their shawl factory brings them good earnings and they wouldn't mind having the couple over for a few weeks."

But tonight, Wasim would have to come out in the dark of the night to help them, and ever since Rehman's death, he had been refusing to go out of his house in the evenings. In these last two years, he had not even once stepped out of his house after six, as if the danger was lurking around only at that time, but tonight he was ready to shed his dread to help his brother, Wali thought with gratitude.

Six O'clock! That was the hour Wasim had received the dreadful news two years ago. His teenaged son, Rehman, had been shot in crossfire between the security force personnel and the terrorists at the Lal Chawk. The traumatizing news had dazed Wasim out of his wits. He had become numb and immobile on the chair he was sitting, unable to react. Fortunately, Imtiaz was at home, who had rushed to see if his younger brother could be saved. When he had reached the site of shooting, Rehman had already been taken to the Hospital. Imtiaz had rushed there only to receive the news of his brother's demise. He had been brought dead to the hospital as the bullet had pierced right through his right temple causing an instant death. The body was handed over to the family, the next day after the post-mortem.

Wasim and Ayesha had been devastated. Wali knew that with Rehman's death, a part of both of them had died. Wali had seldom seen Wasim smile after that. He used to be so full of life prior to his son's death. But after it; he was a man crushed under the wheels of misfortune.

Once Wali had suggested, "Wasim Bhai, we should have enquired as to whose bullet killed Rehman. Were the army responsible or the terrorists were the murderers?"

Wasim had answered, "How does it matter whose bullet killed my Rehman? He is gone, and that is the reality. He won't come back, so what is the point in finding out now?" He had continued after a pause, "But the one who wields a gun and aims it at the innocents is a cold blooded murderer. Therefore, I hate anyone with a gun. I hate armed men, whether the terrorists or the men in uniform committing excesses."

Wali had made frequent visits those days to help his brother overcome his grief. One day, when Wasim had somewhat come to terms with the tragic loss he had said, "What is this ongoing struggle for? Freedom of land? Freedom from whom? This land belongs to *Allah* alone. We humans are allowed only transitory abode...like all the other creatures of this planet. It is He who sustains us with the food that grows on this land and we pay for our stay through our labour. So why do we fight for more land when we need only a bit of land to kneel to pray, to pay our respects to the One in heaven above. Or, we need at the most six feet of land to lie prostrate to rest...a land which can give us night's peaceful sleep."

Imtiaz, who was equally upset at the untimely death of his younger brother, had said, "What harm had our Rehman done to them that he had to die so young? Their fight is with one kind of people, people who are in power...the politicians...but the sufferer is the peace loving common man like you and me. And those extremists too target the poor, for the unprotected people can't retaliate. They don't have commandos of some special task force guarding them or bullet proof cars to travel. And what difference does it make to the politicians if common people die of the terrorists' bullets as long as their power is intact?"

"That is true," Wasim had continued, "The common peace loving man is getting pulverized in this conflict. If you are spared by the militants, the army and police victimize you. How many innocent Rehmans have been sacrificed in this ongoing conflict? And these vicious men want nothing but power, power to rule over their brethren. The boundaries they intend to create are artificial...man made. The land, the water, the air; all belong to *Allah*. We should all be grateful to Him for allowing us to enjoy this beautiful world that He has created for us. And we should all follow His Will; to share among us the fruits He has given us. Instead what are we doing? Spoiling nature? Destroying the gift of life? Killing each other? Defiling His creation?" Raising his hands in invocation he had said, "*Ya Allah*! Instil some sense in these wayward men and show them the path of true virtue. End this violence before it escalates into something more serious and destructive."

On a few occasions, Wali had invited Wasim and Ayesha over to share meals with his family. But last year, when Wali had invited the couple along with the other friends to celebrate completion of twenty-five years of his marriage, Wasim had not come. Wali had well understood the reason. Wasim would accept only the luncheon offers but reject all dinner invitations.

"Why was he ready to overlook his fear of the dark and help me tonight?"

Wali wondered now. "Would it be his way of settling scores for the murder of his young son?"

This morning, Wasim had brought Wali to his houseboat, claiming it to be the perfect hiding place in the present circumstances. They had chosen a hidden shortcut to walk to the houseboat. The passage was lined with thickets of reed and bush.

"Wali, I usually take this route instead of the regular road to reach my houseboat. It saves me solid ten minutes of extra walk. Moreover, it is a deserted path, only used occasionally by children. Today it is the safest way to reach my houseboat, unobserved by the prying eyes."

They had reached the houseboat after about fifteen minutes of walk. The boat was lashed to a large iron hook embedded on the bank. They had climbed up the stepladder of the stationary houseboat that had at once come alive acknowledging their presence, rolling gently on the waters, happy to have some company. After scaling the wooden steps, they had reached the narrow passage that ran all around the boat, in the centre of which was a small-enclosed house with a slanting roof. Right in front of where the steps ended; there was a carved wooden door with a window on each side of it. The door and the windows were tightly shut.

"Wali, you wait here. I will go to the other side and unlock the main door. We should not be seen on the boat today but surely you should not be seen here at all. On no account should anyone have even a speck of suspicion that you are here, so it is better that you remain at the rear side only." Saying so, Wasim had gone to the front side alone while Wali waited for him to open the back door.

Meanwhile, Wali had stood observing his surroundings. Very little part of the lake was visible from that side. The area was deserted. "A good hiding place," he had thought with satisfaction.

Wali had come on the boat after a very long time, perhaps after a few years. The condition of the boat appalled him. Decay was obvious at various places and the wooden planks forming the passage had grown mouldy. The carved wooden railing was almost falling apart. Though lying idle for years, this houseboat had been hired for the first time this summer for about fifteen days by a tourist group from Japan. He had felt happy for Wasim and at the same time had wished for the conditions to improve in the valley. Peace was what they all yearned for. Freedom from strife would renew tourism and if the industry caught up once again in the Valley, the houseboat owners like Wasim could look forward to striking it rich all over again. Till then, Wasim would have to manage with his shawl business.

It was Wali who had suggested to Wasim to begin a shawl business. The shawls could be procured from Ayesha's brother's factory at Anantnag and Wasim could be the middleman for exporting the shawls to various states within the country. Since Imtiaz often had to travel on business, he could also make the shawl delivery to various retail outlets. Delhi was a lucrative and ideal place for such business as Kashmiri shawls were in great demand there in winters, and Imtiaz often travelled to Delhi. Wasim had followed Wali's advice and had begun to make decent profit to run the household comfortably. He often had to undertake business trips himself but given a choice, he would avoid them as far as possible. Since the opening of his business, there had been considerable improvement in his financial condition, though, he never had the kind of capital that he could think of renovating the houseboat.

Dismayed by the state of Wasim's boat at the moment, Wali had made a silent resolution, "If I survive today's ordeal and come back to my native land one day, I will refurbish this houseboat as a small gift for my dear brother." Therefore, currently he had found an added reason to get the better of his enemy; to live to restore the lost glory of the houseboat.

Wali could hear the lock being unfastened. Then he had heard Wasim struggle with the latch of the back door. The latch had made screeching sounds, as if it hadn't been unbolted for quite sometime. After some efforts, he had managed to open the door.

"I need to change the rusted latches of the doors. They are really giving me trouble," Wasim had remarked. He had then invited Wali, "Come in Wali and make yourself comfortable. I think I should leave immediately. There is no time to waste. And you better stay inside." Then as an afterthought he had added, "It may not be very comfortable sitting inside for a long time, especially when your mind is not at peace. There could also be stifling heat in the afternoon, but don't open the windows. I think you can go out in the rear passage except remain at the back. Hardly anyone comes to this side. But the front side has an open view. There will be *shikaras* and boats passing by. And if people aren't nosy, they are curious."

Wasim had then drawn a curtain of the rear window aside to allow in some light, and that had brightened up the interiors, though Wali's mood had continued to be bleak as if he was lost in a dark isolated cavern. He had a claustrophobic feeling, and dreaded the prospects of spending hours alone in that closed space. He didn't want to be left alone. He would rather accompany Wasim, but had seen legitimacy in Wasim's argument that their activities would be under scrutiny. While, Wasim had once again gone to the front to place the padlock back, Wali had stood where he was, moving only his vision around a bit but hardly seeing anything. Depression had begun to invade his spirits.

"The lock should make it clear that no one is on the boat." Wasim had said on entering the room again from the back door.

Pointing at the tiffin carrier that he had brought along and now placed on the table, Wasim had instructed him, "That is for you. Eat your lunch whenever you feel hungry, don't wait for me. I doubt I will be able to come back for lunch." On reaching the door he had turned for more directions, "Wali, be vigilant. As Shakeel has full knowledge of the existence of this houseboat, don't lax your attention. And in case any danger appears here, just disappear into the undergrowth. The tall reeds make a good hiding place. Don't worry about leaving the back door unlocked. Avoid taking any risks. If you ever feel unsafe here, the best step would be to go back to my place and wait for me there. If I don't find you on the houseboat, I will presume you have gone to my house."

Wali had nodded with complete understanding.

Wasim had continued to stand at the doorway, tapping his forehead with his fingers, trying to bring to his mind any matter that needed to be considered. Then he had suggested, "Wali, if you give me Salim's number, I will give him a call from the STD booth and inform him of the circumstances."

Wali had instantly reacted, "No...no Bhai, it is better if he doesn't know anything. Otherwise, he will catch the first possible mode of transport and land here. That will make things more complicated."

"I will only inform him regarding your plan of visiting him," Wasim further proposed.

Wali had once again rejected the idea, "No Bhai that will make him wonder why I hadn't called him myself from home to inform him of my programme. He will then try to contact us through telephone and if the fact becomes known to the men somehow, they will get suspicious. So let it be. If we reach his place,

Chapter 4   51

it will be a surprise for him, but if we don't reach on time, he will unnecessarily get worried. And if we are unable to make it Bhai, then….."

Wasim had immediately interrupted him, "Wali, let us think positive. *Inshah Allah*, we will defeat our enemy. And do not worry much. Pray for *Allah*'s blessings. If it is His will, we will be safe and relaxed within twenty-four hours." Saying so, Wasim had left to execute the important matters on hand.

Chapter 5

Wali fumbled to take out his spectacle-case from the pocket. For the first time in life, he had been rendered so nervous that the tremor in his hands was unremitting. Putting on his reading glasses, he looked at his wristwatch. It was almost two o'clock. The banks closed for transaction at two. Wasim should have completed the bank work by now. He wondered if he had been able to contact Nusrat, for it was exceedingly important.

Nusrat had a vital task to perform. She was to get them the bus tickets to Jammu. Wasim had suggested that they should take a taxi for a comfortable journey, but Wali had preferred taking a bus. He would feel safe getting lost in a crowd of passengers, especially when they were going to undertake a night journey for the first time. Alone they all would feel vulnerable, more so at the time when their nerves were already suspended on tenterhooks. Moreover, a taxi would cost more and Wali needed to be careful with his money now.

Being an independent businesswoman, it wouldn't be difficult for Nusrat to procure the tickets. Wali could have bought the tickets on the spot but circumstances were different today. They were to be sure of the availability of seats on the late night bus and the exact departure timings. They couldn't linger on at the bus-stop.

Nusrat was to be instructed to go in a *burqa*. These days the modern working women were not very particular about donning one. Hopefully, Wasim would remember that, for it was really important. A *burqa*-clad woman would escape being identified. Although Shakeel was an idiot and perhaps, would not think on this angle, but the accompanying men appeared sharp, especially that eagle eyed Hashim. He might think of keeping vigil at the bus station. Only Shakeel would recognise Nusrat, and they might send Shakeel to spy on his activities while the rest kept watchful eyes on the inmates of the house. Therefore, each task must be performed with utmost caution; Wali and Wasim had premeditated it all in the morning.

"What if Nusrat is not at home? Ever since her husband has become bed ridden, poor woman has to run all errands single-handedly. It never occurred to me that she could be out when Wasim reaches her house," Wali now thought with growing anxiety, for in their preparations for escape, there was no scope for wasting time. Then he tried to pacify his qualm. "Wasim will go to her house only after visiting the banks, which will be her lunch time. She has to feed Feroz and that is when she should be home."

Nusrat was the only woman who could be taken into confidence at the moment, thought Wali, thought she would have been the last one considered suitable for the job a few years ago.

"How much has Nusrat changed from the time I first met her," Wali recalled. Despite all the present tension, memory of his first meeting with Nusrat brought a faint smile on his face.

He had met Nusrat on his visit to Sakina's hometown soon after their marriage. On the afternoon of their second day of stay, Sakina and he were relaxing after lunch when Sakina's aunt along with her young daughter had paid them a visit. The girl had a childish face and her two ponytails tied high on each side of her head, made her look even more babyish. Wali had refused to believe that she was in her teens. Her large eyes were the most expressive of her features, and they competed with her mouth to gabble.

This restless young girl had barged right into their bedroom and wouldn't let them rest. She kept hovering around them, continuously talking. Wali had never before met such a chatterbox and for a while, enjoyed her prattle that suited her childish looks. But she spoke so much and endlessly on relevant and irrelevant topics that Wali's head had soon begun to ache. He had teased her, "Nusrat, I pity the man who will marry you. You have been here for just half an hour and my head is splitting. Your *shohar* will have his head come apart into two portions if you continue to talk like that forever."

A few years later she was married to a young and very soft-spoken man, Feroz, who ran a cloth business with his father in Srinagar. Having lost his mother at a very tender age and being the only child, had perhaps caused him to become a reserved person. Wali and Sakina were introduced to Feroz by Nusrat when she had visited them soon after settling down and Wali had instantly noticed their contrasting natures. He had immediately taken a liking to the simple suave man with exactly the opposite temperament to Nusrat.

When Sakina had suggested that they should return their visit, Wali had agreed reluctantly. But he had also set his condition; "I will sit only with Feroz. If Nusrat insists on sitting with us and chattering continuously you better distract her, or I will be left with no option but to immediately depart. Don't allow the situation to reach the extent that I may need to swallow an aspirin, for you know well how I hate popping in pills."

"What if Nusrat speaks too much, she has a heart of gold," Sakina had protested on behalf of her sister.

But once in Nusrat's house, there was no escape from her non stop jabbering.

In the following year, on Sakina's insistence Wali had agreed to visit them once in a while, perhaps to return their three visits with his one. Before long, he had begun to notice, to his discomfort, that Nusrat often picked on her husband. She thought it funny to openly declare his shortcomings. Her *shohar* had phobia for water and big women, he snored like a hurricane, his multiplication was poor and his unfortunate wife had to recheck the ledger etc. etc. followed by girlish giggles; as if her comments were the finest examples of witticism. And each time Wali sympathised with poor Feroz, who would never protest being slighted. Finally one day he told Sakina, "Nusrat needs to learn to control herself. If she doesn't, her marriage wouldn't last long. And the culprit would be her non stop wagging tongue. Feroz often appears embarrassed, for she doesn't even for a second stop to think what she should openly articulate and what she shouldn't."

And true enough, as soon as their initial romance was over, the bond between the spouses began to fall apart. In the second year of their marriage, after their son was born, their relationship had begun to slide down rapidly. Sakina, being close to her cousin sister, received regular update of their souring relations, and worried for her sister, she often discussed the issue with her husband. As a result, Wali was well aware of their prevailing family problems and knew that things could become irreparable if not immediately rectified. At the same time, he could do little about it, for interfering in entirely personal matters was not his cup of tea.

Meanwhile, Feroz's father died after a brief illness, and whatever little control Nusrat had over her garrulousness was gone, her tongue having acquired complete freedom. Feroz started to remain irritated. He began to remain out of the house for as long as he could, coming back only for meals. That became a matter of more and continuous bickering, and finally they could hardly see eye to eye. The house turned into a battlefront. Having exhausted his patience, Feroz began to retaliate furiously to Nusrat's taunts and then things would go out of control. A number of times Feroz walked out of the house to escape the verbal onslaught, but how many times could he be sheltered by his friends!

When the first time he had openly complained to Wali about his wife's querulous nature, Wali had tried to convert it into a light hearted matter by saying, "Oh yes, I know Sakina's sister well. Her mouth seldom closes. The real problem will arise when a queen bee discovers it as an ideal place to construct her clan's hive. But then, good for you. You can have easy access to honey."

"Bhai Jaan, you are joking. It is not honey that can ever exude from her mouth but words more bitter than quinine. I am getting fed up with her habit," Feroz had grumbled.

On their next chance meeting one late evening in a market, where Wali had found him sitting on the roadside parapet with an obvious morose expression, he had instantly judged that he was trying to escape from Nusrat's vocal assault.

"Feroz, what is the matter? Your gloomy countenance gives me an impression that *Khudah* has placed the whole burden of the earth on your head. Is all well between you and your Nusrat?"

At Wali's enquiry, he had instantly opened his Pandora's Box of grouses, "Bhai Jaan, that woman has made my life hell. I sometimes wish I were deaf; then her non-stop complaints wouldn't have made any difference to me. If I go home early she finds some excuse or the other to fight, and if I go late, she accuses me of being unfaithful. Now tell me what do I do? You are the only one I can turn to for advice. For others, I have become a laughing stock."

"Send her away to her parents' home for sometime," Wali had casually suggested.

Feroz had immediately quipped with disdain, "She has just returned last week after visiting her parents, after spending fifteen days with them. What peace I enjoyed for fifteen days! But the moment she arrived, her nit picking began with the usual intensity right at the bus stop, for I was a little late in reaching to pick up her highness. She uses her vocal chords to the maximum of their abilities and that becomes even more discomforting. It was highly embarrassing to notice that people were openly laughing at my plight. Then, with her one foot still out of the door, she picked up another fight with me for having stopped to talk to our neighbours and not giving her attention. Once inside; she hasn't stopped fretting till today over things totally insignificant. Bhai-Jaan, she is an impossible woman. I would have divorced her but then she is the mother of my son, who is more precious to me than my own life." Then softening his voice Feroz had continued, "Well, she is quite caring, a very good mother, it is only her tongue which is out of her control." Feroz had thus expressed his woes and views and Wali was rather relieved to notice that Feroz still had some regard left for the foolish woman.

Wali always wanted things to improve between Nusrat and her husband, though he had become even more apprehensive that it was a matter of a few years before Nusrat would be shown the door. He also knew that it was purely because of the soft and tolerant Feroz that their marriage had lasted that long, for had it been someone else, Nusrat would have been in serious trouble by now.

Wali had next suggested, "Send her to her parents' house for a long holiday, say for six months. When she misses you, she will realize your importance."

"What? Send her away for months? What about my meals?" Feroz had appeared alarmed.

"Why, cook them yourself," Wali had given a simple solution.

"But I am a lousy cook and I come back quite late from my shop. Where is the time to cook?" Feroz had sounded genuinely distressed.

"Eat them at a restaurant then," Wali had further advised.

"Restaurant food has never suited me. It is fine to eat out for a short while but not for six months. Moreover, Nusrat is a wonderful cook. I haven't eaten as good a food as she cooks!"

So, that was what was keeping their marriage from breaking, Wali had thought with amusement. This was a true case of a woman finding her way to her man's heart through his stomach; rather through his taste buds.

"Tolerate a doze of few bitter hot words before being served a plate of delicious food. I see no other way out," Wali had said with finality.

A few days later Wali had had the chance to witness Feroz's plight in person.

Winters were at its peak and three feet of snow had hidden the earth under its white rolling cover. Wali wouldn't have been out in the freezing temperatures if he could avoid it, but he had to go out on an urgent errand. He needed to make arrangements for the comfort of his craftsmen engaged in the filigree work. A consignment was to be sent the following month and work was going at a very slow pace. He had been intimated about an accidental dropping of a worker's *kangri,* causing a small fire in their dwelling. The earthenware pot kept in the *kangri's* cane basket had smashed, spilling out the smouldering coals on the poor man's *namda* which had then caught fire. If the flames hadn't been controlled by the neighbours rushing in to help, probably the fire would have spread. Ever since, the workers had become wary of using the *kangaris.* Now in the bitter cold, with their hands frozen, they were unable to proceed at their usual pace.

Wali was, therefore, going to install a large coal stove in the workspace of his four craftsmen. And Feroz's and Nusrat's house chanced to be on the way.

Having finished the task for which he had come, Wali was returning home. As he was walking past their house, he decided on the spot to stop by and say hello to them. In addition, a hot cup of *kahwa* would be the most welcome thing in the bitter cold. He was about to knock on the door when suddenly, cutting through the deep silence, Nusrat's acid words had reached Wali's ears; the sharp pistol shots were being fired at poor hapless Feroz.

"Now may I know why you were talking to Mehbooba? And don't tell me, you were not. I saw with my own eyes. When I peeped out of the window, I found you engrossed in an intimate conversation with her. You were not even bothered by the cold outside. That woman too has no shame. Taking liberties with other women's Husbands! A shameless slut!"

"That is enough Nusrat," came Feroz's subdued response. "I was only enquiring about her husband's welfare. He is not keeping too well lately."

"I know about all your excuses. Worried about other people's welfare! Have you ever enquired if I am well? Last night, I had such a terrible headache and did you bother?"

"Her husband is more seriously ill. He is down with pneumonia."

"So what? Even I had cold last week. It could have become worse and changed into pneumonia."

"Nusrat can never be defeated in a verbal combat." Wali mused as he instantly dropped the idea of visiting them. Taking an about turn, he walked away quickly to escape hearing more of the wrangling or being caught eavesdropping the most intimate conversation.

With each passing year, Feroz had begun to appear more subdued and mute. He seemed to have resigned to his fate; of being tied to a sharp tongued woman. He became withdrawn, stopped complaining and stopped sharing. But Wali had also noted that he never shirked from his responsibilities of a father as well as a husband; and continued mutely suffering his wife's verbal attacks.

With such adverse circumstances at home, Feroz underwent a harrowing experience at his workplace.

One day, a frail teenager visited Feroz's shop and pleaded to be given a job. His parents and an older sister had been killed by the terrorists at their village, though he had managed to escape by hiding in the forest. He had no means of livelihood now. Taking pity on the boy, Feroz had employed him immediately. An extra help was definitely required and since he had made some profit lately, he could afford to hire the boy.

The youth had hardly worked in the shop for a month when one evening three men visited Feroz's shop. Taking them to be his customers, Feroz politely requested them to be seated since he was attending to the other buyers. The men patiently waited till the moment he was left alone with them, and then one of the men revealed a gun hidden under his blanket.

"You have dared to employ a Hindu boy in your shop. When we are making efforts to purge our land of these pests, you are sheltering them. For this disregard, you will have to pay a penalty. We will come after a week to collect fifty thousand rupees from you. Meanwhile, boot the boy out and keep your mouth shut. If you reveal about us to anyone, you and your family will get into some serious trouble." Threatening him thus, the trio had left.

Feroz was initially quite shaken by his creepy visitors but by the next day, he had refused to swallow the warning. He had discussed the matter with the owner of the adjacent shop and came to agree that it could have been just an empty threat. Many lawless elements were trying to take advantage of the prevailing conditions and the visitors could be just one of them. Also, throwing the poor helpless boy out in the streets would be a heartless deed. Therefore, he decided to ignore the matter.

But, it was no empty threat. A week later, just before the nightfall, the group was once again at his shop and Feroz had nothing to give them except twelve hundred rupees he had with him that time. Seeing the boy still working in the shop, the men were even more infuriated. Unfortunately, there was nobody else in the shop at that moment. At gun point, they ordered Feroz to pull down the shutters of his shop. Then he, along with the boy, was taken to the back lane through the rear door. They were made to stand next to the wall and one of the men aimed his gun at them. Feroz pleaded with the vindictive group to spare their lives. He promised them that he would somehow arrange and deliver fifty thousand rupees the very next day.

But the men were relentless and ruthless. They shot the boy through his head. The dead boy slumped against Feroz, soaking him with his blood. As the sticky fluid soaked through his shirt, Feroz's head spun with nausea and he almost fainted. Shivering uncontrollably, he closed his eyes waiting for his turn next, but the men had no such intentions. Who would spread the tales of their barbarity if they killed Feroz? Before leaving, one of the men had said, "Your foolhardy persistence is responsible for this death. Therefore, you are the real murderer of this boy."

Their statement had given Feroz a terrible jolt. For almost half an hour after the departure of the malicious men, he had not found his voice nor had he been able to move an inch. But when at last he found his voice, he couldn't stop screaming. Only administration of a tranquilizer had him under control.

This experience had come as the final blow and made Feroz lose his mental balance. For the next few days, he washed himself every so often and kept uttering, "Only fifty thousand rupees, only fifty thousand…." Nusrat neither understood what was wrong, nor bothered to check. She continued with what had become her hobby; nag her husband to no end.

Never again did Feroz go back to his shop. For a week after the traumatic incident, he suffered a massive stroke. It rendered the young man silent and bedridden. Forever.

And the shock of such adverse circumstances had stirred Nusrat's slumbering conscience for the first time in life. Unaware of the facts, her initial notion was that she was the offender for her husband's condition. She grasped that she had been cruel to her man and had always troubled him unreasonably. But, he was also the one she loved so deeply. Now, the fate had rendered her alone and unaided, and she judged it to be a divine punishment.

But when the facts were revealed, she had held herself even more responsible for the distance created between them. She had made Feroz go into his shell and stop sharing his troubles with her. If she had been more sympathetic, may be, he would have shared his woes with her. And had he talked it out, perhaps, he would not have fallen ill.

Unfortunately, for the deeds done, 'ifs' come a little too late.

Nusrat was left to take care of her eleven year old son, Ali, single-handed. He was at an age when a father's hand in a child's upbringing was of utmost importance. Ali had to be educated. Feroz required a daily doze of expensive medicines. How would the finances be managed? She was shattered. Sakina and Wali gave her months of counselling sessions but she was inconsolable. She wouldn't stop blaming herself for Feroz's condition.

Then about a year later, one day she came to see Sakina in earnest. "Can you believe *Baji*; Ali was seen smoking by our neighbours. I am such an ill-fated woman! If his Abba was in the condition to control him, he wouldn't be going wayward. What do I do now? My son is getting into bad company and I don't know how to control him. He has stopped listening to me at all. I have received many complains that he doesn't attend school regularly. I need Wali Bhai's help. He should talk to Ali; perhaps he will pay heed to his advice."

At that moment, Abba-Jaan and Wali were sitting in the drawing room, chatting. As Nusrat's agitated pleadings had fallen into their ears, Abba-Jaan had become silent. It was apparent from the tender expression in his eyes, that his soft heart was sad for the helpless woman.

Abba-Jaan had then got up with a resolution and said to Wali, "The poor woman appears in dire need of advice." Wali had followed his father into the parlour where the two sisters were engrossed in conversation, but as Abba-Jaan had walked into the room they had fallen silent. After the initial greetings, he had addressed the distressed woman, "Nusrat, we all realize what hardships you are undergoing, but what has happened is a thing of the past now. Today is more important. Tomorrow needs to be taken care of. I know, fate has been quite unkind to you but you have to come to terms with it now. The future only belongs to those who get up after a fall, those who keep walking despite the pain. For, that is the simplest way of getting healed, of keeping hopes alive. Moreover, you are the lone guardian for your son. Think you have to play two roles for your son now; of a mother and a father. Be in control of your life. It is not too late yet." And Nusrat had looked at Abba-Jaan with eyes filled with the tears of gratitude.

Abba-Jaan had continue, "You will have to take your son into confidence. Perhaps till now you haven't realized the plight of a growing up child, whose father is as good as a vegetable and mother drowned in her own pain and remorse. Let the boy know that you need to carry on in life under all difficulties, and carry on with strength. Ask your son to look after the business in his free time. Keep him occupied. Make him feel responsible. And as far as you are concerned, don't let go off your husband's business. See what you can do about it and begin from tomorrow. If you need any help, we are always there for you."

Abba-Jaan's ways were so simple and effective, thought Wali. His advice had had a tremendous effect on Nusrat. She had there and then realized that she had to take up from where Feroz had left.

The very next day she raised the shutters of the shop, which had lain closed for one full year. She had then begun to learn the tricks of the trade. Along with her son, she began to take care of their business. In no time, both mother and son seemed in control of their lives. Ali's performance in school improved, so did the financial condition of the family.

It is amazing to note how circumstances alter personalities; how adversities can kill habits with a single stroke. The transformed conditions of her life had changed Nusrat eternally. She had become a silent and resolute woman. She had also come out stronger and dignified. At times, Wali couldn't believe that she was the same Nusrat he had known a few years ago.

This morning when Wali had made up his mind to leave for Delhi, he had also realized that it would be risky for him or for any of his male acquaintances to go to the bus station to buy the tickets. He had ransacked his brains as to who could be trusted with the task, someone Shakeel didn't know or some woman who could go covered and manage the secret errand efficiently. And he could think of no one but Nusrat. Yes, Nusrat was the only one who could help them out of their plight.

And she could be fully trusted.

Chapter 6

"What will happen if Nusrat is unable to get the tickets? What if all the seats for the night bus are booked?"

All of a sudden Wali sensed stifling heat in the room, the cause for which was only his agitated state of mind. He got up with the intention of opening the window to bring relief to the seemingly heated room. Shifting the curtain aside a little, he stood watching his house again. "Hope all is well there," he thought with concern. He had given strict instructions to Sakina, not to come out of their rooms today. Meher was still sleeping when he had left in the morning. Hopefully, she had followed her mother's advice.

He undid the latch but stopped short of opening the window. He remembered that the houseboat was to appear unoccupied. An open window would be contradictory. How could he forget that? What was happening to him? He had never been so forgetful, so absent-minded. His mind was a whorl of confusion. He slid the latch back and drew the curtain. Feeling dejected with himself, he came back to sit on the armchair.

Back on the seat, his mind instantly strayed away from the present. Wali now remembered something more of the day Nusrat had left after Abba-Jaan had spoken to her. The plight of her helpless aunt had not gone unnoticed by the then fifteen year old Meher, and she had declared with resolution that evening, "Abbu, Ammi, I have decided to become a doctor. Next year when I will be choosing subjects of my future study, I will take up pure sciences. And Feroz uncle will be my first patient. You will see I will make him walk and talk again."

Was that the time when the decision of sending Meher to a medical college was taken? Or was it prior to that? Wali's mind began to probe. His thoughts transferred him further back, into the long past, to the time when his Meher was still in her mother's womb. They had recently shifted to their newly constructed house and Sakina was in the eighth month of her pregnancy.

"Perhaps, her mother had taken that decision long long ago." The thought made him sentimental. It was the time when they were at the peak of their youth. His Sakina was so charming and innocent, so tender, Wali thought with affection. Life had been so beautiful.

Overpowered with emotions, Wali recalled a young Sakina; an extremely attractive and graceful young woman with delicate features. Her flawless and transparent complexion added to her daintiness. She was of average height but carried herself well and thus appeared reasonably tall. She was more or less the same even now, thought Wali with a fond smile, except a few added layers of fat.

Salim was a little boy of three and Sakina was about to deliver again. The work in the house along with looking after an overactive little boy, would sap energy out of her completely. Late one night, when she had put Salim to bed and finished her chores for the day, she had finally come to rest. She had lain down on the bed, but being in a particularly foul mood had refused to respond to Wali's lively chitchat. When Wali had insisted upon knowing the reason for her annoyance, she had complained to him, "No one in the house is bothered about me. Work... work the whole day. Am I considered a superhuman? I do get tired. By the evening, my body aches and you don't even care."

Wali had patiently heard her complaints and then had answered with a smile, "Let me know from tomorrow, Mem Sahib, what work is to be done. I will do all the chores you order me to do."

"*Ya Allah*! How can I make my *shohar* work in the house? What will people say? What will Abba-Jaan and Ammi-Jaan say? Men are not supposed to work in the house. As such they work outside the whole day, earning for the family. Household work is meant only for the women folk." Sakina, with very traditional views, had strongly stressed.

"Why, don't you know that most men share equal housework with their wives in the western countries?" Wali had informed her.

"They must be shameless women, making their men do double the work. And what do these lazy queens do themselves the entire day?" Sakina had enquired. Naturally, she was too tired for brain work at that moment.

"They also work outside along with the men. They do all kinds of jobs and earn equal wages. Therefore, the household work too is shared on equal bases," Wali had answered.

"All women work outside? All of them work in the offices and in businesses?" Sakina had shown surprise.

"Why don't we have countless women workers in our country? Don't we have a woman Prime Minister of our country? " Wali had put forth his argument.

Forgetting her tiredness, Sakina had plopped up into sitting position, as she had now got interested in the discussion. Although political debate seldom fascinated her, neither had she been participating in the frequent ones at home between Wali and his father, but she had cultivated positive opinion of the then Prime Minister Indira Gandhi and that had aroused her immediate curiosity. Alert once again, she had said, "Well, that is a different matter. Indira Gandhi is an exceptional lady and I really admire her. She must be a very strong woman to have not only survived but accomplished great success in the male dominant world."

"Oh yes, she is strong for sure. Only a person with her kind of strength could have declared the internal emergency in the country to suppress the voices of the politicians opposing her authority. Only a woman of her power could have lost the elections due to her assertive governance and then made a comeback, for there was no one to substitute the kind of charisma she possesses." The way Wali had spoken, with a playful smirk on his face, it had confused Sakina. She was unsure whether he was praising the strong lady or was being sarcastic. Wali had very clearly read her confusion but then decided to change the subject. "But, she is not the only strong and the only working woman. Thousands of women in the country are working these days. What about the lady doctors in the hospital where you go for your checkups? Aren't there thousands of lady doctors in our country?" Wali had continued to enlighten Sakina.

That had made her silent for a while, as if she was pondering over the issue. Then she had remarked, "You know, these lady doctors look so smart, so confident and dignified in their white coats. And those instruments, what are they called?"

"Stethoscopes," Wali had provided the answer.

"Oh yes, stethoscopes around their necks make them look so professional. If I have a daughter this time, I will make her study to be a doctor," Sakina had made a decision.

A few months later, Sakina had given birth to a baby girl. When Wali had held his little daughter in his arms for the first time, his heart had burst with emotion. The beautiful child with crystal blue eyes had completely captivated his heart. He had loved her deeply from that moment, and a strong bond had been immediately formed between the father and the daughter. Meher had found a special and everlasting place in her father's heart. Somehow, he knew that his daughter would make him proud one day.

"Probably, Meher's mother had a strong hand in influencing her to take up the medical profession," Wali now thought. But Meher was always a good student. Each time he had gone to her school, her teachers had nothing but praise for her. Wali's heart would then swell up with pride and he would wait for the next opportunity to go to Meher's school. When Meher was in the senior school, even her principal, Sister Maria had begun to notice her.

One time during a parents-teachers' meeting, Wali had met Sister Maria in the school corridor when she was on a round. She had stopped to talk to Wali. "You have a very promising daughter, Mr. Khan…a very bright girl." She had said with a sweet smile. "She is sure to score a high grade in this year's board examination; I won't be surprised if she tops it."

"Oh sure, she is working quite hard for it," Wali had added shaking his head enthusiastically.

Sister Maria had continued, "But that is not all. She is our best all rounder. She made us proud by winning the rolling trophy for our school in a recent Interschool debate. And what a good sportsperson she is! I had watched her play the table-tennis tournament. Our school team won exclusively due to her superb game. She can go to great heights with your support, Mr. Khan. I know that in many families daughters' education is not given priority and girls are married off young. I request you not to commit the blunder of letting her potential go waste."

Wali had continuously nodded with beaming smile lighting up his face and then bloating with pride and choking with emotions, he had responded, "Yes Sister that is exactly what we have in mind. For me and my wife, our daughter is as important as our son. Her grand father too is an educationist. You need not doubt us concerning her higher education."

"May God be with you. Let Him bring you success in your endeavour. Let Him make this lovely child reach the pinnacle of success in life and make her parents proud." Sister Maria had thus prayed holding her rosary and Wali had been so touched by her gesture that he had tears in his eyes.

Meher had worked exceptionally hard in the last year of her school. She was full of determination to enter the medical profession. At times, Wali would be worried at the extent of her diligence, and he would advise her to relax. Sakina would be worried that Meher was not getting enough sleep and that it would tax her health.

But when he was in high school, Salim had been the exact opposite of his sister. Wali had once visited his school on the day of parents-teachers' meeting and had to listen to a long list of complaints. He had come back home highly depressed. Thereafter, he had always avoided any visit to Salim's school. Sakina was very conveniently handed over this job. "You have pampered your son, now you face the music," Wali would tell her.

Salim's temperament matched Wali's, which was what Abba-Jaan had always insisted. Most of the time, he would take life easy. Regular strolls in the main market, an occasional movie with friends and every Sunday in the cricket field were the regular features of his high school life. Salim would listen to only Abba-Jaan's advice and in the final years at his school, Abba-Jaan had taken special care to make him study. Salim did well in the school leaving examinations and managed to enter the regional engineering college, much to the satisfaction of all at home. "He is not hard working, but he is bright," the grandfather had proudly commented.

Abba-Jaan had further said to Wali, "Your son is just your copy. When you were young, you were exactly like him; totally carefree. But he has done what I wanted you to accomplish; get into a professional college. Just like Salim turns a deaf ear to you, you wouldn't pay any heed to my advice, and landed up taking a graduation degree in political science. Fortunately, you didn't go into politics for that was the last thing I would have approved. My savings came handy to buy us the orchard at the time when you were to be settled in job."

"Abba-Jaan, frankly I hate being subordinate under anyone. I have been the happiest looking after our orchard independently."

"Yes, with God's grace, you have done well as a horticulturist. Perhaps you are cut out for it. We have to accept what the Power above has in store for us. We are mere mortals who neither understand His plans nor can change them."

Abba-Jaan had declared his grandson's entry into a professional college a day of celebrations at home. What a feast Sakina had prepared that night! And the beaming smile had become the permanent feature of the proud mother for days to follow.

But Meher was different, with entirely contrary disposition. Her aspirations couldn't be matched. Then she had done it too! The day the results of the All India Pre-Medical Tests were declared, Meher had managed a high score and a sure place in a good medical college. Sakina and Wali were on the top of the world once again. Abba-Jaan had glowed with happiness. Ammi-Jaan had commented, "My granddaughter is my precious jewel. I am totally relieved of the worries for my old age ailments now, for we have a doctor in the family."

"*Bari Ammi*, I am not yet a doctor. It will take another five years to become one," Meher had informed her.

"Then I will keep my ailments at bay for five years," Ammi-Jaan had playfully suggested.

The only hitch for most family members was that Meher had opted to join a medical college at Delhi instead of the regional college. That meant that she would have to stay in a hostel. That was painful for Wali and almost unacceptable to Sakina. Only Abba-Jaan had strongly sided with Meher's decision. "If she has to study medicine, then it should be from the best institute available," he had asserted.

When they were alone in the room, Sakina had addressed her anxiety, "Why can't Meher join the medical college here? I have heard it is quite a good one. If she will stay at home, she will be more comfortable and we will be at ease, without any tension and worry to know if the child is well...if she is getting good rest...and proper diet. Salim has also studied from the regional college. Moreover, it is not safe to send a young girl to unfamiliar surroundings. They get easily influenced by others. And you see what the outside world is like. Haven't you seen on television the kind of dresses these young girls wear these days? Quite brazen! I don't want my Meher to become like that."

Wali would have sided with Sakina, but under the present circumstances, when Meher and her grandfather formed a stronger team, he had no choice but to be in agreement with them.

"Who says Meher is going to be influenced by all that? Our daughter has a mind of her own. Plus, after all the hard work she has put in, we can't become hindrance to the success she still has to achieve. Let your daughter go and pray to *Allah* to take care of the rest." Wali had thus calmed her.

The days prior to Meher's departure had gone in hectic preparations. Sakina had got busy shopping for her; getting new *salwar suits* stitched for her. Occasionally the mother and daughter were found arguing over the designs of the suits and Wali had wondered what difference it made if the shirt was a few inches shorter or longer. How could women argue over things like that? He also wondered why Meher had all of a sudden become so particular and choosy about what she wore. She was not bothered about it earlier. She had always allowed her mother to choose her clothes. But then it was after years that she was seen to be relaxed and contented, after having achieved what she had sought.

As the time for Meher to join the college approached, Wali was tense with anxiety. But he had put up a brave front and not openly reveal his nervousness to any one. He knew if he did so, Sakina would have become jittery, Meher would have lost a bit of her confidence and Abba-Jaan would have been annoyed.

He had accompanied Meher to Delhi. He was anxious to settle her in her new environment comfortably and had found the hostel facilities satisfactory. Meher was to share a medium sized room with another girl and that had pleased Wali, for his daughter wouldn't have to live alone in her room. A company was fine for safety. Moreover, her roommate appeared quite a decent girl. In addition, the girls' hostel had strict vigilance. He had met the hostel warden, a middle aged stern looking female, and was pleased on that front too. The stern lady had assured him that the girls in the hostel were absolutely safe under her reign. That had relieved him of a part of his mental worry.

On his return trip, Wali had felt utterly at loss. Since there was nobody to see him, he had shed a few tears as well. He knew the house would appear so empty with Meher living so far away.

They were trying to come to terms with the fact that Meher would come home only occasionally now, once or twice a year during the holidays, when barely on the tenth day after Meher's departure they had received a frantic call from her. She sounded quite upset and kept crying on the phone. She was homesick, she said. She hadn't slept for days as the senior students made the freshers do chores at all odd hours. She was being ragged at every given opportunity and at times the ragging was bad.

"How bad is it?" Wali had enquired with concern. But Meher wouldn't say beyond that. She had kept sobbing. After the call, Sakina had cried her eyes out for solid half an hour.

"What are some neurotic sadistic women doing to my daughter?" Wali had wailed too. "I am going tomorrow to bring her back. She can study here." He had then declared. Both Sakina and Ammi-Jaan had seconded his declaration.

As soon as Abba-Jaan had returned from his evening walk, Ammi-Jaan had loudly and happily proclaimed the resolution that had been passed unanimously in his absence. He wanted full explanation as to why such an option was under consideration. Then he had said, "Do not take any irrational and hasty decisions. This ragging business, however bad, will be over in a month or two. Meher has always been an overprotected child. She may not be used to the harsh treatment, which of course is unjustified. Why can't the colleges control this degrading practice, I can't understand. But Meher will have to endure it. For, if we become weak and allow sentiments to come our way now, we all may repent later. Meher too will not be happy once this period is over and she sees logic."

He had been absolutely right. Meher had soon got adjusted to the hostel life and the tough medical studies, so had the rest of the family to her being away. Her mother was secretly proud of her daughter studying to be a doctor in one of the best institutions of the country. It was as if her wish had come true. Wali had realized it the day Nusrat had come visiting them and Sakina was heard telling her, "You don't worry Nusrat. Once my Meher becomes a doctor, she will take care of your Feroz. You never know, he may get completely cured. You just wait and see!"

But tragedy had struck the family a few months later. Abba-Jaan suddenly died of cardiac arrest. He was seventy five but appeared much younger than his age and had been a robust man till the end. The heart attack was sudden and shocking. "Not really his time to go!" grief stricken Wali had considered. He couldn't imagine his life without his father. For him, the voice of wisdom was gone forever. Would he be able to take over the responsibility of the family with the kind of far-sightedness and perception Abba-Jaan possessed? Wali was not sure. He had learnt a lot but there was yet a lot more to learn. Abba-Jaan had left a void in his life.

One learns to accept the circumstances where no option is available and

Wali was no different. Life went on for the family, even without the driving force. Time is rightly the best healing power that dulls the pain and at times the memories too.

Years had begun to flow by with rapid pace. Wali began to be totally immersed in his export business and in his orchard. Sakina was taking good care of Ammi-Jaan and Wali was quite unburdened in that regard. Salim was well settled in Delhi and in his heart Wali had gradually begun to pardon him for marrying a non Muslim girl.

Just a few months ago, Meher too had come back home, having finished her basic medical studies and her internship. She now wanted to do specialization, but had expressed her desire to first work and gain experience. She also wanted some rest after years of rigorous routine. To live close to her parents was an added attraction. She had therefore applied for the state medical services. Within a month, she had received an offer to join Pehalgaon hospital and had happily accepted it. She would be able to visit home often, may be over the weekends, she had declared. She was also true to her words and had been paying regular visits to see how Feroz uncle could be helped to lead a better life, although she had expressed her inability to do much now as the brain deterioration was irreversible. Yet, she had seen medical miracles occurring and hoped some improvement could be expected through proper treatment. The concern and presence of a qualified doctor had acted as a new leash of life for Nusrat's family.

Days had been progressing smoothly to Wali's contentment. His children had made him proud by being successful both in educational and professional fields. He was earning comfortably well. Ever since his business had burgeoned, he had been planning to buy a car. Till recently, a large chunk of finances was required for the education of his children. With that burden over, he had examined the latest models of cars and studied their practicality in a city. He had had a few discussions regarding this matter with Meher on her visits home. He had divulged his enthusiasm about relearning to drive. He had learnt driving when in college but hadn't followed up. He wanted to teach Meher to drive too. A doctor should definitely know how to drive, he believed. And finally last week, he had had a Maruti Zen booked. He had made the down payment too.

When Meher had arrived home on a short leave two days ago, the first thing he had done was to immediately call up the Car Booking Agency, requesting them to deliver the car as soon as possible. Both he and Sakina wanted Meher's choice of colour for the car. Day after tomorrow was the day when the car was to be handed over. That day was never to come now, Wali considered dejectedly.

He would have to cancel the booking. He doubted if he would ever be able to buy a car in his lifetime.

Right now, he didn't even have time to cancel the booking.

Chapter 7

Today, all of a sudden Wali's world had crashed. All his hopes...all his aspirations smashed like a fragile glass into splinters! A terrible apparition had visited him at his doorstep causing all his dreams to slide away from his grasp.

"Why Meher's visit had to coincide with that of the vicious visitors? It would have been better if she wasn't here. Or is it really so?" Wali was unconvinced. His dilemma had turned him into a befuddled man and at the moment, he wasn't sure of so many things.

He hadn't looked at the clock for the past hour, busy that he was toiling in the world of his memories. Waking up to his present once again, the ticking time now made him agitated, for the needles of the clock indicated that it was already three pm. Then he remembered that Wasim was to meet Abdul around this time. If things had gone smoothly, they should be here in about half an hour.

His self imposed, solitary confinement had begun to grate on his nerves and he couldn't restrain himself from going out for another exploratory tour. He was relieved that in all these hours on the houseboat, he hadn't been visited by a single human being and that had now boosted his confidence. He stepped out without hesitation to see if Wasim could be spotted approaching. Like a child, he was now getting impatient for his return.

Standing at the head of the steps, barely seven metres of the passage through the reeds could be sighted. Beyond it the brushwood obstructed the view completely. And those seven metres were presently absolutely deserted. Walking down the narrow passage of the houseboat, Wali reached the front deck yet again. The evident absence of any living soul in the area emboldened him and he stood holding on to the railings to scrutinize the surroundings as far as his eyes could behold. There was no sign of the person he was seeking. Only a few water birds revealed some sign of activity in the vicinity. Disappointed, he was about to retrace his steps when a faint haunting sound of flute reached his ears, piercing his heart like an arrow, causing a strange kind of pain. A nostalgic pain! His eyes searched the landscape seeking the origin of the music. Who was playing the flute so melodiously?

He could discern tiny pearly dots moving up and down on a far off green hill. The sound was surely coming from that direction. Probably a Shepherd was whiling away his time playing his flute, while his sheep grazed on to the green nutrition. Wali once again longed to exchange places; with the shepherd playing the flute this time, only he couldn't play the flute so melodiously. He wished simply to lie under a tree with the least worries of the world in his mind. He wished he could be as relaxed, as carefree and as far off from this place as the shepherd.

He closed his eyes to imagine lying on the velvety grass. But he couldn't shake off the feelings of being constrained by tethers that had bound him tightly and painfully. He was, as if, besieged by a whole lot of obnoxious forces and breaking them was the most perilous task.

A draught of cool breeze brushed against his face and he inhaled deeply without opening his eyes. Perhaps it would help to ease his mental strain. The air smelled of the waters of the lake. And it smelled of his land. His Land! His beloved land. A serene vision flashed through his mind; of the wild flowers in the spring, when they too appeared like scattered pearls of different colours; of the crystal lakes of turquoise waters shimmering silver in the sunlight; of the innumerable tiny brooks erupting from the icy slopes and of the pure elixir commencing its journey, sprightly dancing to its own music. And he envisaged the majestic peaks in white patterned caps watching this play of nature from their lofty heights.

This was the land of his ancestors; the land where he had grown up; where he had spent his entire youth, his middle age; where one day he wanted to be buried for his final peace.

He had known no other land so divine all his life and now he was being forced to part with it. In a few hours, he would be far away from his *zameen*…this *jannat*… and then God alone knows when he would be able to come back. Would he ever be able to return?

The distraught reflection made him open his eyes in dismay. He regarded the overwhelming tranquillity of the vast glistening blue lake and the surging green mountains surrounding it with wistfulness. If he would have ever dreamt about abandoning his land, it would have been the worst kind of nightmare, he considered. Today, the worst nightmare was about to become a reality.

The cause for distancing him from this *jannat*, this paradise, was none other than that rascal Shakeel. Wali had been so kind to him. And look what had he returned his generosity with? The ungrateful villain!

Wali couldn't help grinding his teeth in anger and frustration. He wished that a debased person like Shakeel had never entered their lives.

He walked back with heavy footsteps of a tired man and once again sat on the stepladder of the houseboat facing the wildly growing reeds.

His memory renewed its voyage to his past and to the time when he had met Shakeel the first time.

Sakina had been quite ill those days. She was expecting their third child when one day, in the fourth month of her pregnancy, she had slipped down a few steps and that had caused a miscarriage. She was in excruciating pain and Wali had rushed her to the hospital. The doctors had managed to save her life but the unborn child had been lost. There was tremendous internal damage and probably Sakina would not conceive again, Wali had been informed.

He was miserable at the loss of an unborn life, which was a part of him. The thought that his blood had circulated through the little being which was lost before it could open its eyes to the world was very painful. Yet, Wali was thankful that his Sakina had been protected by God.

When they had come back home, Sakina was still quite weak. There were two bouncy children to be looked after and Ammi-Jaan was finding it difficult to manage alone. There was energetic Abdul, but he was also required to run Wali's errands and take care of the orchard. He could help in the house only in his free time.

Seeing Ammi-Jaan struggling with the children and the housework all alone, Sakina was haunted by guilt feelings. Therefore, she was up and about much before she should have. Shortly after having sprung back to her normal routine, one evening when she had come to the bedroom to rest for the night; Wali had noted her pale and fatigued face. She was carrying a glass of warm milk and a hot water bottle to aid her to sleep well. What she did next was quite bemusing. Wali had watched in horror when she had casually tossed the glass of milk on the bed and carefully kept the hot water bottle on the table. He had hopped out of the bed to escape being scalded by hot milk. Sakina had gone red with embarrassment as well as annoyance. Changing the bed linen at that hour was of course an added bother.

He had then realized that something was seriously amiss. Sakina was getting so tired by the evening that she was losing control over her responses.

From the very next morning, he had begun to hunt for an all time help for her. He had gone to the market one of those days and had found a helpless boy of about twelve sitting outside the grocer's shop. He was clad in tattered clothes and was sitting on the steps crying and shivering in cold. Wali had enquired from the grocer about the boy.

"He had come into the shop asking for a job fifteen minutes ago and I had refused. I already have two employees and I can't have a platoon of them." The shopkeeper had answered with irritation, not knowing till now that the boy was sitting and mourning the job refusal right outside his shop.

Wali had immediately decided to employ the boy in his house. It was as if his prayers had been answered. He had then talked to the boy who told him that he had come all the way from Kupwara region. He was an orphaned boy and his father's cousin, who had provided him with food and shelter till now, had recently decided to abandon him. He had worked as a labourer for a few days, earned some money and boarded the bus that brought him to this large town. He had come here with the hope of finding some suitable employment but now he was a disillusioned boy. He had been to various places in the town but everyone had refused to employ him. Nobody wanted anything to do with an unfamiliar boy with unknown background. His money too was finished. He was hungry as he hadn't eaten anything for the last two days. But despite that, his pride had stopped him from begging. He would rather die than beg.

Wali was quite impressed by the boy's sense of dignity. "What is your name son?" Wali had asked.

"Shakeel," The boy had answered.

"Look here, I can give you employment if you promise to work hard and honestly. You will have to work in the house, helping the ladies with the chores. You will be given monthly wages along with shelter and food. If you agree to the terms, you can come with me right away." Wali had made the offer.

The boy had immediately and willingly grasped the opportunity. Together they had marched back home. Initially, Sakina had exhibited no enthusiasm at the prospect of a whole time help for her, as she had found the boy quite untidy.

"From which zoo have you brought this specimen?" She had inquired the moment the boy was outside the hearing range. "He doesn't seem to have had a bath for days and is stinking badly."

"Give him a bar of soap, toothpaste, a toothbrush and send him to take a bath. He should be fine after that. Give him Salim's old clothes. He will easily fit into them. He can live in the outhouse with Abdul. I have brought him to help you in the household work. If you teach him properly, he may learn to cook as well. To begin with, let him do the cleaning. He is an orphan and we can provide him with shelter. And give him something to eat first. The boy hasn't eaten for days," Wali had explained.

And Shakeel had become a permanent and willing employee in the house. He appeared happy and well adjusted to his new duties. Salim too had found a playmate and both of them could often be seen together in the evenings playing; mostly cricket, which was Salim's favourite game. Every member of the house treated Shakeel well. He was well fed and it soon began to show in his healthy glowing complexion.

One day, after Shakeel had been with them for about six months, Abba-Jaan proposed to send him to a nearby school. "Let us educate the boy. He can help in the mornings and the evenings. As such there is hardly much to do the rest of the day. Let him utilize the free time in studies."

And Shakeel had been admitted to a local government school. He was spared many chores to allow him time to study. Salim too took upon himself the task of helping him with his studies in the evenings. Though Salim was an enthusiastic teacher, Shakeel turned out to be a bad pupil. He showed the least interest in learning. However, the family was determined to be successful in their mission. Whenever Abba-Jaan or Wali would find the boy sitting idle outside, especially during examinations time, he would be ordered inside to learn his lessons. Soon it was found that instead of obeying, he was slipping to the other side to hide among the fruit trees. When the first examination results were declared, Shakeel had failed. Abba-Jaan had insisted upon continuing his education. Though, the following year he had managed to pass just on the margin, the year after that he had clearly projected his disinterest in studies by flunking again.

Abba-Jaan had then gone to Shakeel's school to talk to the headmaster and had found out that for quite some time the boy had hardly been going to school. He had been stealing away and perhaps loitering around with some other errant boys. He would always return home at about the closing time of the school, giving the impression that he had been to school.

Abba-Jaan had been infuriated and when he had confronted the disobedient boy with the evidence of his misconduct, Shakeel had nothing to say in his defence. He had simply lowered his eyes to avoid meeting Abba-Jaan's angry ones. When Abba-Jaan had strongly reproached him for evading school and had insisted that Shakeel take a vow of never missing school again, he had immediately responded. "When I don't want to study, why are you forcing me to go to school? I work in the house and isn't that enough. I was brought here only for that. Nobody told me then that I would have to go to school as well. On top of that, the school is not a pleasant place to go. The masters are so rude and never hesitate to thrash the students and I can't take that. I am not going to school from tomorrow." That was his final declaration.

One can help only the person who is ready to take a few steps himself. How could Shakeel be helped when he had simply refused to budge?

That night Abba-Jaan had stated at dinner, especially addressing Salim and Meher. "He is a silly boy, who doesn't realize that there is no substitute for education. Education obliterates ignorance. It opens doors to a wide world of literature, numbers, science and technology, of the wonders of our earth; of archaeology, geology, oceanography, astronomy, anthropology…, it opens the shut doors of mind and makes one see reason. If you have to go through a few years of hard work for it, it is worth it."

Wali had commented, "Shakeel is a fool who thinks we are out to trouble him by sending him to school."

Abba-Jaan had still been persistent and in the following days, he had tried to lure Shakeel to continue his studies a number of times by asserting various benefits of being educated. But all the pleadings had no meaning for the one who was as stubborn as a mule. The more had the members of the house tried to put sense into his head, the more had Shakeel become adamant, not realizing that it was out of concern for his well being that his benefactors were trying to help him. He couldn't be forced to go to school against his wishes. Hence, that was the end of the efforts at schooling the helpless boy. The efforts had only been successful in enabling him to be able to read and write.

With nothing else to occupy his idle brain, very often Shakeel had begun to disappear in the afternoons for hours. It was understood that he too deserved some free time, so he was given the liberty. And all members of the household were busy in their hectic routines to have time to check where he was going.

Chapter 8

"Shakeel was a perverse youth with totally misplaced interests and this was something we should have realized then," Wali reflected presently. "In place of hypothetical conclusions, as soon as Shakeel had begun to be rebellious and opinionated, we should have verified the background of his associates. It was a big blunder on our part to have freely allowed such associations instead of strictly restricting his loafing. Better than imposing restrictions, as soon as he had begun to depict his true colours, he should have been shown the door. Deeming his behaviour as normal adolescent idiosyncrasy was a misconception. The knaves do not deserve compassion, and Shakeel is the best example for it." Wali's awareness was like a match lost by a good player all because of the faltering decisions.

The first signs of Shakeel's defiant behaviour had appeared after he had completed three years in the household. It was the time when the communal disturbance and terrorism had begun to reach its vicious feelers around the far and wide corners of the country and the globe.

Wali had recently purchased a coloured television with a larger screen to replace the old black and white one. It was kept in the living room; the common place shared by the family to relax. After returning from his evening walk, Abba-Jaan would switch on the television to avail the report of the events in the country and the world, and at times for some light entertainment. Anyone with some free time in hand would join Abba-Jaan. Wali would habitually come to spend an hour or so with his father before dinner. Then invariably, the contemporary world scenario would initiate the father and son duo into long discussions. Ammi-Jaan and Sakhina would be more interested in music or entertainment than such conferences. Therefore, the moment the political debate would initiate, they would find excuses to escape either to the kitchen or to their rooms to execute some on the spot invented tasks. Salim and Meher would have very little time left from their busy study schedule, neither were they encouraged to waste their time in front of the entrapping gadget. Only once in a while, generally on a holiday, were they allowed some free time in front of the small screen.

But Shakeel was the only inhabitant of the house who would ever be keen not only to watch the television but to poke his nose in the adults' discussions. He would consistently hop into the room the moment Abba-Jaan would switch on the television and station himself on the floor carpet next to Abba-Jaan's chair with the pretext of massaging Abba-Jaan's tired feet. Everyone knew that it was an excuse to watch the television. Since Shakeel would make sure to have finished the assigned work by then, having adjusted his work timings accordingly, there was no reason to raise any objection. Then to show off his rudimentary awareness, Shakeel would often be found passing uncalled for comments. Taking him to be an immature juvenile; his silly quipping was quietly put up with.

However, his misshapen ideas had begun to be notably exposed at about the time when the Babri Masjid issue was becoming the scorching hot politically stimulated topic of the day. Abba-Jaan, Wali and Shakeel had followed its development from the rudimentary stage to being turned into a highly controversial issue by a staunch Hindu party, who proclaimed their rights to build a Ram Mandir in place of the centuries old mosque. They had experienced the buried skeletons of history being excavated, after they had been lying dormant for almost five hundred years. The rationalists, like Abba-Jaan, well understood that it was a gimmick to win the forthcoming elections by aggravating religious sentiments. Others, like Shakeel, were getting caught up in the trap. And, Wali had witnessed a battle between the two extremes; between the sagacity and the idiocy.

One day, Shakeel was as usual sitting and massaging Abba-Jaan's feet while the news of the Political party's call for the *Kar Sevaks* to congregate at Ayodhya to knock down the Mosque was being telecast. Clips of some demonstrations by the party workers at various towns and cities were incorporated for the right impact.

"They dare not touch our *Masjid*. If they do, they will need to be given a good lesson," Shakeel had spoken rather assertively.

"What kind of lesson?" Abba-Jaan had asked in a voice intoned in surprise, his attention having fully drawn towards Shakeel at his extra vocal incursion.

"Kill them!" Shakeel had voiced even more aggressively, encouraged by the attention he had received.

Abba-Jaan's expression had immediately undergone an alteration. His face was red with rage. "What did you say? Kill them? Kill them for those pieces of stones? Kill people as if taking life is a child's game?"

After a pause to gain control over his anger, he had continued in a softer tone, "Silly boy, keep in your mind; *Allah* does not live in those pieces of stones with which we construct our mosques or temples. He lives in the hearts! Heart of each being! And you talk about the destruction of those hearts? Don't ever utter such nonsense in front of me again. There has been no dearth of mad men on the earth; who have done nothing but escalate violence. And remember, violence only shatters lives of people."

Shakeel had continued to sit stony faced, showing no reaction. Abba-Jaan had then further stated, "These politicians intend to sway the gullible into ethnic violence, and if most people begin to think your way, they will be successful in what they intend. That is exactly the game they are trying to play; create rift among people. What have hard working people like you and I got to do with these issues? For us, all men are like brothers."

"You are not a true *Mussalman* if you speak in favour of the *kafirs*." Shakeel had then rudely proclaimed before walking out of the room in a huff.

Both Abba-Jaan and Wali had been stunned at his behaviour. There were certain ethics of conduct expected by the inhabitants of the house, but Shakeel appeared to be all set to break them.

Though, Wali had the knowledge of his rude conduct towards the ladies lately, as Sakina had complained about it a number of times. But being disrespectful towards the master of the house was unheard of; rather outrageous. Wali could never speak loudly in front of his father, and this chit of a boy dared to be impolite to Abba-Jaan?

That had initiated Wali's vexation as well as his concern regarding Shakeel's behaviour. He strongly suspected that the boy had picked up some undesirable company; and these elements were filling him with extreme ideas. He had then decided that he needed to counsel the boy; to instil some sense into him.

For the past few years, their valley had been turning into a hubbub of terrorist activities, and soft targets like Shakeel were being specifically picked up for recruitment in the insurgent groups. Since Wali considered the young orphaned boy his responsibility, he wanted to do everything within his power to prevent the youth from being drawn into radicalism.

The whole of the next day he had waited for an opportunity to talk to Shakeel, and had caught it in the evening when he had found him returning quite late from somewhere and trying to sneak in on tiptoes. He had confronted him at the doorway of the servant quarter. "Shakeel, I want to know where you have been out till this late. What are you up to lately?"

"Oh, nothing really," Shakeel had tried evading his employer with a curt reply. He had then turned to go inside, totally ignoring his master, and that had caused Wali's anger to rise.

"I am not going to put up with your disorderly conduct, Shakeel. And I know about the stupid ideas you are stuffing your brain with. It is not for a boy of your age to get involved in politics. Already, many an inane youth of the valley are getting misled into unlawful activities. Make sure you keep away from all that and choose your friends carefully."

"OK," Shakeel had uttered quite impolitely before making another effort to march in. That had caused Wali to lose his cool.

"Where are you going when I am still discussing the matter? You better learn to be courteous. Moreover, it was no way to talk to Abba-Jaan yesterday. I will not stand any disrespect towards my father." Wali had perhaps, for the first time raised his voice to scold Shakeel.

At this rebuke, Shakeel had stopped to turn and face Wali completely. "I know how to choose my friends. And if speaking out my views loudly appears rudeness to you, then it is not my problem." With these offensive words he had strode into his room haughtily, shutting the door with a bang. Had it been Wali's own son, he would have immediately punished him for the uncalled for behaviour. But in the case of his young employee, he was hesitant to take a similar action.

Though, the obstinacy of the boy had astounded as well as enraged Wali to such an extent that he wasn't able to sleep well that night.

The next morning, when Wali was alone with Abdul in the orchard, he had discussed Shakeel's conduct with him; with the perception that being closer to Shakeel, Abdul might manage to put sense into the boy's head. Abdul had declined outright to negotiate with the boy. "*Huzoor,* he is the most pig-headed creature I have ever encountered. He wasn't like that initially, when he had come to live with us. He was a nice and obedient boy then, almost a submissive mouse running to do errands to please us all. But lately, something has turned his brain lopsided. He has completely gone mad. May be…, may be we should admit him in a mental asylum." Abdul had then given a broad grin, apparently pleased at his ingenious idea. He had then continued with a subdued chortle, "It has presently occurred to me that it is surely the best means of getting rid of the foolish youth."

Wali had mildly chided Abdul. "Abdul, be serious sometimes. The matter is grave. I have a feeling that Shakeel is getting involved with some radical group and the change we see in him is their doing."

Abdul's smile had vanished instantly. "Quite possible," he had responded in a bland tone. Then after a minute of a puckered brow and some hesitation which indicated his reflection whether it would be fine to reveal the matter to his master, he had pronounced, "*Huzoor,* I have full knowledge of the directions this scatterbrain is heading for and I have tried discouraging him a number of times. But the dumbbell not only turns a deaf ear to me, but at times is shockingly rude. Many a time, I have considered bringing his behaviour to your notice, but then didn't want to bother you with insignificant troubles. Now that you mention it, you can well imagine how he is behaving with me…a mere servant, if he could speak like that with you and *Barae Huzoor*, not caring to show respect to his masters. You are right. This is clearly the doing of his peer group. He is, without any doubt, mixing with the wrong kind of people."

Wali's voice had revealed clear exasperation, "But Abdul, I fail to think of a way to discipline him. I can stomach it if he is discourteous to the mistress or me. But imagine, he is impolite with Abba-Jaan as well!"

"The puffed-up cock has no consideration for his elders. He has no business to be impolite with the people who feed him and provide him with shelter. And *Huzoor* with me too he is most of the time downright offensive these days, especially since he has realized that our ideas do not match at all. In fact, it is the toughest task to suffer his company these days, even for those few hours we are together in the rooms at night. *Huzoor,* what really worries me is that he may meet the fate of my nephew if he continues to follow this trail."

"What about your nephew, Abdul?" Wali couldn't help asking.

As a response, Abdul had slowly walked towards a jutting rock on the hill wall and proceeded to sit on it, as if his legs had suddenly refused to support him. His distressed face indicated how painful was the memory of the incident he was about to recount.

"*Huzoor*, he too was a high headed youth, passing through the age when the youngsters begin to consider themselves too smart to heed to the wisdom of the experienced. His father, my elder brother, had great dreams for him, for his boy was quite bright in studies. He wanted to educate his son and see him become an achiever. But the young boy got into wrong company and was completely swayed off his feet. He turned rude and disobedient overnight. One day, about five years ago, he ran away from home. We came to know that he had gone across the border to join some training camp there. The distraught parents kept waiting for one whole year for any information regarding his whereabouts. Then; all of a sudden one night, he came home in secrecy and utter urgency. He had come to see his parents despite the lurking danger, he had declared. The urge to meet his mother had brought him home despite risks involved, he had claimed." Shaking his head in disgust Abdul had continued, "That was a great favour he had done for the poor parents who had become half their sizes ever since their son had disappeared without a trace. He had come with some presents too, a calculator for his father and an imported wristwatch for his mother." Abdul halted a moment to smile ironically, as if scornful of the insignificant material things.

Abdul continued his poignant narrative, "Early next morning, he left for an undisclosed destination on an unknown mission. His visit did nothing but brought troubles for the family. A day later, my brother was picked up by the police for questioning. What he underwent at their hands...*Allah* alone knows. When the innocent man returned home after spending a week with the protectors of the law, it was another being...with broken body and shattered spirit. Then; a few months later, we received the news of the youth's demise. He had been reportedly shot dead in an encounter with the army somewhere near the border, though his dead body could never reach home. The news of his death was brought by a similar errant youth from a neighbouring village, who was a member of the same band. They couldn't stop to pick up his body due to the heavy firing by the army, the lad had reported."

Abdul had continued to sit with his head dug deep into his chest, overwhelmed by the sore memories. Wali stood with his arms folded across his chest, listening pensively to the tale quite similar to the ones he might have heard or read about in the papers so very often.

After a brief silence, Wali had said, "Abdul, you never mentioned this incident prior to this day." Abdul had raised his head to look straight at Wali, "*Huzoor,* what is the need to reveal such upsetting affairs? And how could I disclose that my own nephew had joined the terror campaign? What would you have thought of me?"

"It wasn't your fault, Abdul. Don't I know you well?" Wali had said.

In reply, with a subtle nod, Abdul had lowered his head once again. Wali had continued to probe, "How is the boy's family now? The incident must have upset them a great deal."

"*Huzoor*, I did mention to you about my brother's demise year before last. He was the unfortunate father of the young boy. He passed away much before his time and his son was the cause for bringing about his early death. His son had chosen to disregard his wishes to become a terrorist. As if, that wasn't enough suffering on its own, he had to undergo unimaginable torture at the hands of the law keepers. All these woes added and he developed a heart problem. His son's death was the final blow. He couldn't bear the shock of his only son gone in the prime of his youth." A sob had escaped Abdul's lips. "And the poor mother has gone crazy… sits at the doorstep the whole day… with the imported watch in her hand…counting hours and days…still waiting that perhaps one day her beloved son would come back home. When I had gone home last year, I went to see my sister in law. Initially she simply stared through me, and when her eyes did show some signs of recognition, she softly asked me if I had brought any news of her son's wellbeing. It shattered my heart to see her thus." Abdul sighed and became silent. Only his tearful eyes spoke of his grief.

Wali had then slowly shaken his head dejectedly. When he had spoken, his voice was barely above a whisper, "Abdul, this is not just a single tragedy, but a misfortune that has ambushed our entire cherished land. And what are these wilful youngsters achieving through these subversive activities? When will they realize they are being trapped for these futile acts? Why don't they understand that the outcome is going to be nothing more than a human tragedy transpiring to shatter lives day after day?"

After this discussion, Wali had felt even more anxious to prevent Shakeel from setting out on similar path. But despite days of contemplation, he had failed to find means of controlling the errant boy. At times he would be so annoyed with Shakeel's conduct that he would consider acquiring someone else to work in the house and ask him to leave. But he didn't have the heart to order the youth out, thinking he had no family to fall back upon. The lingering fear at the back of his mind that Shakeel might decide to join the prevailing terror-campaign as a full-fledged recruit once he would be on his own, further prevented Wali from dismissing the boy from his job. He had mollified his perplexity by giving the reasoning that it would be such a pain for Sakina to train a new servant all over again, especially when Shakeel had become quite adept at his work. He had, therefore, decided to endure his behaviour, expecting a change in him once he would leave behind his adolescent years.

Salim was a few years younger than Shakeel, and it had become an added matter of worry for Wali that his young son might pick up uncouth habits under the influence of the haughty and uncivil youth.

As far as Meher was concerned, Wali had been totally unperturbed. He had specifically noted that she had begun to keep her distance from Shakeel and could no more be seen in the company of the boys for their usual evening game of cricket.

In any case, she couldn't be much interested to be always made the fielder, perpetually ordered by the boys to run around to fetch the ball. Wali had often found her arguing in her soft ways and then managing to bat, but that would be a rare privilege. He had frequently seen her after such a dispute, clomping away in protest down to the hillside. She would then occupy herself by collecting wildflowers and foliage and making some necklaces and bracelets to wear around in the house. Wali smiled recalling her new found hobby those days. Her mother and grandmother too would receive similar gifts and then it would be amusing to see the ladies donning vegetation jewellery to please little Meher.

Then Meher had gradually begun to withdraw from the cricket game and Wali had wondered at the change. Probably, she was deliberately avoiding Shakeel, her maturing understanding having registered the crankiness of his behaviour. Or, was it her mother responsible for her withdrawal, who was trying to wean her daughter away from the young-males' domain? Wali had explored. But he also knew that Meher's interests were absolutely different; she was too young to take interest in politics and most of the time would remain singularly absorbed in her studies. Her persistent aim was to retain the top position that she secured each year in her school examinations. In addition, Wali deliberated at the moment, Meher was made of soft and prudent stuff which could not be infiltrated by anything ungracious. She had always been politeness personified.

But having found a handy playmate and companion of almost his age, Salim often spent time in Shakeel's company and the first step that Wali had taken in that regard was to subtly put a stop to their outings together which especially took place on holidays. "One never knows," Wali had thought, "Shakeel might introduce my son to his extremist friends and they may try to influence my son too. After all, he is young and vulnerable, therefore, needs to be shielded from choosing a wrong path; the path so menacing."

Fortunately, with the mounting study pressure, Salim had begun to find less and less time for jaunts with Shakeel. That had provided some relief to Wali. He had also noted that Abba-Jaan too had begun to painstakingly keep his grandson occupied in study or suitable discussions, and had realized that his father had probably been following a similar course of perception. Though, this topic had never been discussed openly, obviously to avoid sounding discriminatory.

Then with Wali's attention diverted towards these irritants at home; a few months later, on a cold December day of the year 1992, the Babri Masjid had been demolished.

Shakeel had been watching the news along with Abba-Jaan and Wali, the evening of the dismantlement of the mosque by a provoked unruly mob. Abba-Jaan had switched off the television vociferously stressing, "I don't want to watch madness prevailing in the country. It is nothing but an ugly face of frenzy… mob hysteria… instigated by some selfish politicians! And look at these politicians! Instead of espousing a future vision of a progressive society…instead of making promises of amelioration, they pick up an issue some five hundred years old to make it a platform to fight elections and then incite people into such madness."

Shakeel had stomped out of the room, evidently in utter rage. Though, this time he had spared them any comments, they had grounds to be seriously worried for him. The suction pump of terrorism was, as such, gleefully sucking in even moderately secular mindset, thanks for the propaganda from across the border and the excesses committed by the men in uniform, but now such transpirations were sure to add fuel to fire and Shakeel would be the easiest

Chapter 8

target marked for enrolment.

This time Wali too had felt resentment at the disregard shown by the provoked mob towards their faith. Once Shakeel was out of their hearing range, he had set free his opinion in front of his father, "Abba-Jaan, I agree what is happening is pure vandalism by the fundamentalists, but at the same time why is it being allowed by the people in power. Why should the fanatics be licensed to hurt the feelings of minority communities, that too by raising issues from the past history? Why has the state of affairs been permitted to aggravate to the present situation when it should have been nipped in its bud by banning the party for their non-secular idealism? Aren't these secular double standards, where leaders themselves provoke citizens against each other? Shouldn't such leaders be held responsible if they manage to provoke susceptible people like Shakeel into joining extremism?"

Abba-Jaan had nodded in agreement, "My son, you are absolutely right in feeling this way. The present day politicians are nothing but opportunistic hawks. This Hindu party has thrown a dice to gather the Hindu votes and the hysteria that you are witnessing presently shows that they have been successful in their gamble. Such are the men who do not allow the common Muslims to develop a sense of belonging in a state declared secular by its constitution. Our community is losing faith in the present day leadership and feeling more and more alienated. That is the sole reason why the demand for separatism has become all the more strident in our valley."

"Then holding plebiscite appears the only solution. Let us be independent. It may also result in eliminating terrorism from the state." Wali had passionately stated. Abba-Jaan had silently and thoughtfully gazed at him, making no comment.

"However, the Indian Government has evaded the issue despite the promise made in 1948, surely because of the fear of losing the valley to Pakistan," Wali had further expressed.

"Wali, holding plebiscite has lost its relevance after the elapse of nearly half a century now. If ever the plebiscite is held, there will be three possibilities: accession to Pakistan, declaration of an independent state or its continuation as a part of the Republic of India. I have contemplated for hours over the issue and have come to certain conclusions that obviously may differ in majority opinion. Firstly, I feel that whatever will be the outcome of the plebiscite at present, it will cause all the more chaos. Before settling down to governance the winners may try, by hit or by trick, to eliminate the opponents and all those who might have risen voice against their policies some time or the other. After all it is a power game where the mighty always have the upper hand. Next, should it be acceptable to us to become part of the country that has not found its own political stability even till date and the country promoting terrorism as means of settling scores? Finally, will it be economically viable for us to clutch on to the small area that our valley is comprised of, without any solid industrial support? How will the jobs be generated within the state for the entire populace? Do we have enough capital and means of self-sustenance? Therefore, won't it be profitable to be a part of the stable and growing economy that stands on a solid platform provided by its industries? I think it will be in our interest to flourish in cooperation rather than perish in opposition."

"But Abba-Jaan, don't instances like the demolition of the Mosque become impediments in the efforts towards mutual cooperation?"

"Of course, they do. But who are the people who create such impediments? The egocentric politicians, who want to make personal profits by creating rifts! And who are the ones who will get victimized? Only the common man! Therefore, doesn't it become imperative for the rational people to raise their voice to expose the designs that are causing friction amongst the communities?" After a period of quiet during which both the men pondered over their discussion, Abba-Jaan had commented, "And you are right in feeling worried for Shakeel. I too am quite apprehensive regarding this boy, who appears all set to be drawn towards the escalating militancy in our state. He is surely in touch with some extremist group. You can plainly read that in the signs of his rebellion."

Since Abba-Jaan had articulated such a declaration for the first time, Wali had instantly enquired, "Do you also feel…"

Their discussion was halted at this point, for Shakeel had entered the room to announce dinner.

The next day, Shakeel had disappeared for the entire day. When he had come back late in the evening, having taken the day off without any prior permission, Wali had tried investigating the reason. Shakeel had informed his master in the usual rude tone that he was with his friends discussing issues. Ignoring his insolence, Wali had warned him again not to sway away from sanity under the influence of some vicious brains. Although, he had taken special care to speak in rather a gentle tone this time; for he had decided after a period of reflection that if he wanted the youth to see reason, he would have to handle him tactfully. He had also concluded that Shakeel was passing through a difficult age; when the peer pressure can easily blind rationality, when brawn rather than brain works more efficiently. Therefore, he had decided that patience was probably the only effective tool under the present circumstances.

But, the fast spreading flames of the communal fires set off by the politicians were slowly embracing Shakeel and the similar wavelengths into a tight grip of insurgency. Wali and the like-minded people could hardly do anything about it.

Abba-Jaan and Wali's analytical discussions too were becoming longer. They were united in their opinion that; as planned by the power hungry and politically vested parties, the demolition of the Mosque was turning into a sensitive issue. The politicians had very successfully played with the sentiments of their fellow countrymen. They were quite clearly adopting the policy of Divide and Rule, a mischief which the British had played at the culmination of India's struggle for freedom, and that had led not only to the country being cut into pieces but bathed in horrific bloodshed.

Abba-Jaan had repeatedly communicated to Wali that the nation was once again passing through very difficult times and Wali had often heard him entreating the divine power (for who else would listen to a common simple man) that the saga of untold miseries recorded in history should not be repeated. He was heard imploring that the people be spared the nightmarish experience called ethnic violence.

In the following month and a half, his fears had begun to turn into reality. The law of the unruly ruled the streets of many Indian cities including Mumbai. The irate Muslim mobs descended upon the streets to protest demolition of their religious place, followed by Hindu mobs attacking more places of worship. Both the groups dismantled more sacred structures, assaulted each other and caused more senseless bloodshed. The police joined in with guns to shoot at the mobs. By the time the frenzy subsided, only in Mumbai thousands of lives had been snuffed out.

Thereafter, began the exodus of thousands of Hindus and Muslims from the grounds they had called home and where they had lived for generations, but now that home felt unsafe and unprotected. They could no more live in the vicinity of each other, for the weak thread of trust had been broken.

And the ones who had fractured the belief in brotherhood, watched the scattered splinters from a safe distance.

Meanwhile, an uncanny quiet had descended over Shakeel and the rest of the country.

Abba-Jaan and Wali had discussed with anxiety that this chain reaction could spread far and wide unless someone in power was able to constraint and pacify the agitated people and arrest the situation which was going out of control. And sure enough, the repercussions of the horrendous act were soon felt in the neighbouring countries of Pakistan and Bangladesh, where the innocents Hindus and their places of Worship were targeted fiercely. "How could the politicians be so callous as to have completely overlooked this foreseen impact of their deed? Or is it that they don't care If the Innocents suffer?" Abba-Jaan had queried.

There were many who cared and were crying hoarse to put stop to the prevailing madness but the sane voices were few and were getting drowned in the tumult of the mass hysteria.

"Wali, how many innocents have met with unnatural and terrible deaths? How many have been rendered destitute? The responsibility of all these murders lies entirely with the political party that has raised the dispensable issues. They should be the ones to be brought to trial and convicted," Abba-Jaan had vehemently stated.

Although the situation had been brought under control after the army and the Rapid Action Force were deployed, it was not the end of the unrest in the country but the beginning of the worsening situation.

For; the innocents' bloodshed was followed by the bloodshed of more innocents by the equally eccentric terrorist forces. Numerous blasts shook Mumbai, particularly its Stock exchange a few months later.

The same evening, when the news was being watched as usual by the threesome, Abba Jaan had voiced, "Wali, I completely fail to understand what purpose will be served by such terror attacks, by this fanaticism."

Shakeel, with a wily smile playing on his lips had immediately quipped, "Are we bangles clad women that we should keep sitting quietly and watch our holy places destroyed and our men killed? Some of our brothers have successfully exhibited our strength today."

"You call those murderers your brothers?" Wali had annoyingly articulated, causing an immediate scowl on Shakeel's face.

For quite sometime now, Abba-Jaan and Wali had had more reasons to appear serious and worried. Their Valley, known for its natural beauty and tranquillity, too was being soaked with innocents' blood. The target had been the Hindu community; the soft spoken, peace loving people with whom they had shared the land for ages. The Pandits had caused no harm to anybody to deserve the horrific treatment. They had been forced to abandon the homes of their ancestors and run for their lives. Divisive forces had been at work in the Valley now for years and nobody dared disapprove these acts of terrorism vociferously. The few audacious voices were silenced with equal ferocity. Many were considered police informers and eliminated mercilessly. The moderates had been the helpless spectators to the absurd hostilities.

The villages had been repeatedly attacked to wipe out all those who did not follow the tenets of Islam. "Haven't the slayers themselves gone against the tenets through their violent acts against the helpless victims?" Abba-Jaan would echo this frequent reflection. "Now where will those poor families go? How will they survive without shelter and means of livelihood? This is no way to treat your fellow men," he had sounded his dejection after each episode of violence.

Unfortunately, there were only a handful people who were beyond the influence of the incitement; those who possessed the rationalistic vision of Abba-Jaan.

He had expressed, "It is a pure political game! The infiltrators from across the border and some of our men bought by Pakistan have formed a nexus to create rift among us. But by creating communal disharmony in a nation that has more Muslim population than in its own country and by continuous harping about the Kashmir issue, Pakistan is not doing us any favour, it is offering us nothing but troubles, merely accumulating difficulties for the common man. The hate campaign will pointlessly cause shattered families and added miseries. The people blinded by hatred fail to perceive the political game."

Wali now recalled that the rising insurgency in the state had attracted worldwide attention, which till then was being ignored as personal headache of the Indian Government, when six foreign nationals were taken hostages by a terrorist faction. The act of terrorism had achieved exactly what it had sought; Attention.

"When the freedom fighters are treated badly, a strong retaliation is the only option left. I think it is a brilliant idea to pressurize the Indian government to release our comrades languishing in jails," was the comment made by Shakeel that evening, when the news had made the headlines.

"Brilliant idea or the daftest thing to do? And are you so close to those people that you call them comrades? Won't an act like this now keep the tourists away from the valley?" Abba-Jaan had scolded Shakeel.

"We don't need the foreigners coming and spoiling the mindset of the native people," Shakeel had said.

Wali had then informed him in a tough tone, "If you are strong, nobody can change your mindset. And tourists are vital for us as they bring in capital and our people gain wealth. Tourism, being an important industry, is an essential lifeline of our state known for its natural beauty, especially when the affluent tourists from the western nations visit the valley in large numbers."

Shakeel had narrowed his eyes as if trying to weigh the pros and cons of the argument in his mind, but hadn't made further comments.

Wali recalled further that how the days of search for the lost tourists had ended tragically. Out of the six persons abducted, only one could escape successfully, one beheaded body had been found, and even till today, the fate of the others was not known.

Sitting alone in his present hideout, Wali now reflected how the ruthless talons of terrorism had continuing to grip India in its clutches without any respite. Abba-Jaan was right that it was all due to the negative policies of the neighbouring government, which knew that it wouldn't be possible to win a full fledged war with India. They had already tried it thrice. The time was for continuous vexation and torment. The only way to trouble a fast growing economy was to keep it bleeding. The terrorist movement in their state was thus the result of meticulous planning. Infiltration was easy because it was on the border. Its high mountainous terrain was favourable too, most of which remained unguarded. Such reckless ventures had then resulted in the Kargil War, which at one point had threatened to escalate into a full-fledged war, but had luckily stopped short of that. Nevertheless, it had been quite damaging, causing destruction on both the sides and snuffing lives of many young brave soldiers. In the end what it had achieved was nothing more than generating more hostilities between the neighbours.

Wali was presently reminded how day after day; year after year his discussions with his father had centred on the prevailing political scene.

Soon after the Kargil war, one day he had brought some information home to discuss with his father. "Abba-Jaan, it is rumoured that the fighters from across the border were not only infiltrators but also the regular Pakistan army personnel fighting along. And it is also alleged that along with more than five hundred young soldiers and officers of the Indian army martyred, a complete regiment of the Pakistan army has got wiped out in the operation. Now think of it, what has been achieved by initiating such a combat except unnecessary loss of life? No one can ever gain through violence; instead, all stand to lose. And those who send their armies for such abortive combats need to understand that."

Abba-Jaan had nodded in agreement before adding, "The wars are decided at some high profile meetings of the manipulating politicians and the young are sent to die at the battle front. Do the inciters ever wield weapons and fight like soldiers themselves? The present day politicians are proving to be the biggest mischief-makers. The class of committed politicians is, as if, fast disappearing. The current political game is all about Power and Money. Whether they are the politicians of our country or of Pakistan, they are all the same; sheer opportunists!" Abba-Jaan had angrily commented. "The sole reason for all this trouble is the corrupt politician."

"Corrupt politician? Why would a corrupt politician want war?"

"Firstly, to sell the weapons and make profit. It is disgusting the way the corrupt minds work; making profit by digging graves of the brave martyrs. And then they want to divert the attention of their respective citizens away from their dirty deeds. These unprincipled political demagogues are the ones to trigger hostilities, even create cross border rivalries. There are more selfish motives behind their operations than to make easy money; like aiming the downfall of the political foe by swaying the public opinion away from the popular leader. So, conflicts are born out of nowhere."

"But who wants conflicts? Who wouldn't crave for peaceful democratic existence?" Wali had posed the next query.

"I'm sure the people of Pakistan would want that too. Common sensible citizens throughout the world want peace; they want to extend their hands in friendship and end hostilities."

"You are right Abba-Jaan. I'm sure there are always better and peaceful ways of solving disputes."

"Of course, there are. Violence and terrorism are not the answers to the differences. It is only the power-hungry who wrongfully inflames people and disallows harmony," Abba- Jaan had added.

"Abba-Jaan, I too find no justified reason for any war and feel that it is mere aggression against humanity. In fact, why should wars be fought when there isn't any winner, everyone is trounced with massive loss of life and property on both sides. It is always a great setback for the world economy, except, as you said, the profit made by the few handful corrupt and debased humans. Throughout the history of mankind, wars have brought about nothing but ruin. Battles have been fought, but has the senseless destruction left human beings any wiser?"

Abba-Jaan had shaken his head in disgust before speaking, "Yes, that is true that man hasn't learnt much from history. Many civilizations are lying buried under the rubble of plunder, and aggression is still raging. When the monster named over-ambition strikes a man it blocks his common sense, murders in him the sentiments of mercy and compassion and turns him into a brutal beast. That was the disorder suffered by Gonghis Khan, Hitler, Mussolini and the likes. The fascism emerged as a monster trying to guzzle the world into its insatiable belly. Two world wars have been waged with catastrophic results. What had been gained through the trail of destruction and torture unleashed by the Nazi forces? Only that at its peak, it resulted in more horrors; in the wreckage of the Japanese cities."

"Throwing of Atom bombs on helpless people was a display of vulgar barbarism," Wali had added rather fumingly, "It was the worst decision of the twentieth century; the worst verdict against humanity. This flexing of the nuclear muscle power has been on the increase since then, instead of its immediate rejection due to the horrendous results revealed in its unimaginable devastation. The race to acquire the nuclear technology has become the fastest race of the times, irrespective of how deadly it could prove for the mankind. When today's deterrents will become tomorrow's offensive weapons, survival will be at stake. But do they care? Millions of dollars have gone into developing these lethal weapons; in a world where many go hungry to bed. The policies of the major powers are so arbitrary; the countries emulating their nuclear paradigm are declared rogues. The superpowers must realize that weapons of mass destruction need to be completely obliterated from the face of the earth and they should be the ones to pave the way."

"You are right, Wali. But you see, with the nuclear weapons gone, the control of the superpowers will be terminated and they are not going to like it. Presently, the world is made to abide by the dominion of the superpowers for its survival. After the fall of the USSR, there has been only one superpower, the USA, whose hegemony is being witnessed ever since; whether it is the hegemony as hard power, structural power or the soft power. Many of the terrorist factions are nothing but the brainchild of the superpowers. They have been raised for continuous conflicts in the areas where their dominance will then prevail. Conflicts are also necessary for the arms dealers who have close nexus with the politicians, for who will spend billions of dollars on arms without the existence of conflicts? Many countries have been invaded with the excuse of creating balance, and hasn't it resulted in creating more imbalance in the world? But who will bell the cat?" Abba-Jaan had stated.

Wali had added, "But we also know that hegemony of one super power does not last forever. Power is highly seductive. There are always others ready to grasp the opportunity. What do we know; tomorrow it may be India or China dominating the world. The question is: Does the world need such supremacy. Abba-Jaan, in your opinion, is socialism the answer to the world problems today?"

"I believe that the need today is of an equitable society based on a balance of capitalism and socialism, without the hardliner communist ideas. Anarchy and dictatorship need to be shown the ultimate doors. Profits should be divided on the basis of the intellectual or the manual contribution made. The world needs to shun all kinds of violence for its salvation. More important, the policy of nuclear disarmament is urgently required, with mutual agreement of all the nations. We cannot allow the bestial acts be repeated against humanity. The countries have to conduct themselves with responsibility; realize the need for friendly collaboration, more so as the planet is precariously balanced on the nuclear warheads today. We don't want another future Hitler who may take the world to the brink of a nuclear disaster, to its complete annihilation. And the powers should never forget that whenever there are efforts towards dominance and unjustifiable suppression, there are bound to be revolts, uprisings by the suppressed lot. History is the testimony to it. Therefore, instead of dominion, the aim should be at an egalitarian society, where no one is homeless, no one hungry and no one illiterate."

"Accurately spoken, Abba-Jaan. If this muscle flexing is halted and the people throughout the world cooperate for mutual benefit with the wealth equally shared by all, perhaps no one will have any excuse to indulge in subversive activities. When there wouldn't be any snake, why would a stick be required? Terrorism will then automatically decline."

"But were there any signs of respite?" Thought Wali now.

Wali evoked at present, that contemporaneously to what was happening in the country, the world scenario too was getting hot and turbulent. For the common man throughout the world, it all was getting more and more perplexing. The political game was neither tangible nor conceivable. It was only ambiguous!

A large number of terrorist factions had emerged and were continuing to emerge. The terror campaign was penetrating unimaginable corners of the world. Kenya, Tanzania, Yemen... And the number of innocent victims of the terrorist strikes ever on the increase. Hijacking of planes, school children taken hostages, blasts in the busy shopping centres, buses and trains... people were nowhere safe. Wali had often wondered what would be the end result of this madness! Were we heading for a major disaster? He had often discussed it with Abba-Jaan, who would shake his head in distress. "Perhaps a divine intervention is needed, for degeneration is setting in the civilization. The mind is becoming so depraved that people kill the defenceless without flinching, without even flickering their eyelids! Solutions are not found by digging more graves in an already blood stained soil. They are not found in the blasted pieces of innocent human flesh." He would say.

Soon the entire globe was to be shaken by a terrorist strike of unimaginable magnitude which would leave the world stunned, and Wali livid at Shakeel's arrogance.

September 11 2001; Wali now remembered that it was almost a year before Abba-Jaan's demise, that the tallest buildings in the USA, the World Trade Centres at New York, were targeted by the terrible insane forces. Thousands of people were inside the buildings and hundreds in the planes with which they were hit. It was the biggest terrorist strike in the history of mankind and Wali presently hoped that something so appalling may never be repeated.

Wali could so clearly recall to his mind the events of that evening, when he had noted Abba-Jaan hurriedly returning from his evening walk.

There had been hectic activity in his orchard the entire day as the last crop of apples was being plucked, packed and sent to the major metropolises for sale. He had returned home for a cup of tea and with the setting in of the evening he was at that moment walking again towards his orchard to conclude the day's activities and disburse wages to his daily labourers. Seeing Abba-Jaan's tall, majestic figure returning in haste, Wali had stopped on his tracks, apprehensive that something had gone wrong as Abba-Jaan had never appeared in such urgency. He had then rushed to assist his father thinking he might need help.

Abba-Jaan had momentarily halted and breathlessly spoken, "Wali something terrible seems to have occurred. While on my walk, many people asked me if I had watched the latest news bulletin. When I asked them what had happened, they simply told me to switch on the TV and watch myself. Some people appeared quite pained at what has happened but there were others donning cynical smiles. " He had then hurried on, uttering to himself, "I wonder what has happened. I hope it is not another monstrosity."

Wali had followed him back home in an equal flurry. Abba-Jaan had straight away switched on the TV. There was no need to change the channel. The news channel was on. The scene that Wali saw on the small screen had shaken him completely. Both Abba-Jaan and Wali had stood rooted to the floor, speechless, in deep shock.

The terrible disaster was being shown repeatedly. A Plane was heading straight for the upper floors of the building and then the chaos...the fire, the dust and the destruction!

Was it an accident?

The other building was still standing tall, but within minutes it too was struck by a second plane and burst into a huge fireball. The people were running in all directions, incoherent, incapable of comprehending as to what tragedy had befallen them.

Two planes had targeted two towers. It was no accident! It was clearly a deliberate act. The long hands of the vice had entrapped and engulfed the unsuspecting innocents.

The fire brigades were then shown speeding towards the site of the tragedy, the brave firemen leaping out in earnest and rushing inside the buildings in urgency, definitely with the objective of rescuing as many trapped victims as they could. And then both the buildings collapsed, one after the other. Abba-Jaan drew in a quick breath. Wali watched aghast. What had happened to those firemen? Would they survive? What about the people who could not be evacuated?

Then Wali had become aware of another presence in the room. While their attention was focused on the television, Shakeel had quietly sneaked into the room and now stood watching the catastrophe being projected again and again. Wali had immediately noticed a sardonic smile playing on his lips and that had made him furious. How could he be so insensitive? The sane do not smile thus when tragedies befall on others. He wanted to order him out of the room; instead, he had chosen to remain silent to avoid more ugliness in an already unpleasant atmosphere.

Shakeel was the one to break the silence. "Sets them right! They think they are very high and mighty! Now they have been taught a good lesson," he had said.

Irritated by this cheeky comment, Abba-Jaan had said crossly, "Whom are you talking about teaching a lesson, Shakeel? To those innocents who had gone to the offices in those buildings to earn their daily-bread through sheer hard work, or those brave men on duty whom you saw entering the buildings to save lives of the trapped people? Many of them might not have harmed even a fly all their lives! What will anyone achieve by killing the innocents?"

Shakeel had then replied rather loudly and curtly, "That country needed to be taught a lesson. Their conscience needed to be woken. They can't dictate people like me and meddle in our affairs."

Wali had felt his anger rising at Shakeel's impertinence. "The fellow has such nerve as to repeatedly speak harshly with Abba-Jaan! Who does he think he is? Is he some VIP taking care of the world affairs?"

He had then verbally pounced at Shakeel. "Is it right to kill innocent people to hurt the conscience of the men in power? Don't murderers and the power hungry belong to the same ilk; the people without conscience? Do you think those men responsible for this disaster have any conscience? Do they feel any remorse to see that they may have killed thousands of unknown and totally harmless people? It could have been my son there or your own brother working in that building. There may have been many hard working well-educated youth from our valley there. Have you pondered over that? No man with ethics will ever undertake such depraved acts of violence. And could you tell us why you are talking about raising the conscience of some people so far away? Do you even know in which part of the globe does this place exist? You are simply being swayed by wild ideas of some aggressive minds. Use your own discretion Shakeel, rather than getting influenced by the others, by the violent people bereft of morals." Wali had still more to say but having spoken it all in an enraged huff he was now breathless, although slightly easy for having vented out his anger.

Abba-Jaan had then taken over, "We may have our reservations on the policies of the American government, we may have reasons to disagree with their dominant stance and their self appointed constableship of the world, but targeting the innocent citizens of any country is an unpardonable crime against humanity."

But Shakeel was quiet only for a moment, then like any fool who thinks he is the most knowledgeable person on his meagre store of knowledge, he had said, "It is a holy war…and people do die in holy wars." It was obvious that he was in no mood to relent. And it was quite evident that he was unyielding as he had evidently had some discussions with his like-minded friends.

Abba-Jaan had then tried explaining to him, "Holy wars are not fought with the innocents. If one has the full conviction that fighting is the only solution, then have the courage to fight like a soldier and not like a coward."

"They are not cowards. Those men have even laid down their lives for the cause," Shakeel spoke with aggressive vehemence.

Abba-Jaan anger was obviously on the rise now, so was his voice. "Laying down one's life to inflict pain on others is not commendable. Instead, sacrificing your own self to alleviate the pain of the sufferers is the true service towards humanity. If there is a cause for a struggle, then instead of the suicidal missions against the unarmed innocents, one should prefer to be a martyr in a battlefield. Otherwise, will a person be anything but a cold-blooded killer? And the slaughterers don't belong to any religion. For, no religion teaches violence against the guiltless. No holy scripture teaches that it is fine to wash your hands with the blood of the sinless."

Wali had then added, "Shakeel, do you even for a minute realize that with the intention of shaking the strongest country in the world, these fanatics do not mind shedding gallons of innocent blood! They don't care for the young lives snuffed in their prime, the children orphaned, the young partners gone, and the old parents left to shed tears till the last day of their lives? Who will wipe the endless streams of tears that will flow from the eyes of the people shattered by such tragedies? All this has no meaning to you and those vicious men?"

There was silence in the room. Only the sound of the heavy breathing of the men was audible, angry breathing; each man incensed to defend what he strongly believed. Then Abba-Jaan had said, "*Ya Khudah*! Why don't you give equal sense to all? Why have you put these evil hearted amongst us, who neither rest in peace themselves nor allow others to rest in peace? I am worried that the day is not far when the grudge of a handful will bring about the downfall of the human race. "

As it had happened on some previous occasions, Shakeel had stomped out of the room in an obvious anger. And Wali had instantaneously realized his mistake of assuming that Shakeel was now a mature man. It was hard for stuck-up people like Shakeel to change. The surprise element for Wali was that despite having attended uncountable discussion sessions between Abba-Jaan and him, Shakeel had not picked up even a speck of the doctrine of respect and forbearance. Instead, his source of influence lay somewhere else; with the people steeped in violent flames of brutality.

Probably, their discussions were beyond his understanding, totally going unregistered in his brain. For him, the direct and aggressive language of the extremism was perhaps more comprehensible.

Chapter 9

As of now, Wali concluded that this terrorist strike had emboldened those who deem violence their voice, for whom all are enemies except the brutes similar in temperament. And the world was to continue to suffer unjustified attacks. Tunisia, Bali, Israel, Morocco, Egypt, London........ Leaving Wali wondering each time; what lay ahead? When would the world begin to feel safe again?

In addition, there had never been any dearth of political vultures taking advantage of the volatile situation in the home country. The Ram Temple issue had been broiling on, now for years, courtesy; the opportunists. The politicians had managed to involve a large chunk of simple-minded people to build a shrine; an act that was destroying the secular fabric of the country, at the time when the need was of uniting people as one fraternity against divisive forces. And it brought the next disaster a few months later, in the form of the Godhra train incident. The compartment bringing back the *kar-sevak*s from Ayodhya had caught fire, killing scores of them. Was it an accidental or deliberate tragedy, why would the opportunists wait to discover? It was a providential chance to be exploited. The repercussion was the Gujarat riots. The target was the Muslim community in the Hindu dominated and a Hindu Party ruled state.

One morning as Wali had picked up the newspaper at the breakfast table, he was aggrieved to a see a picture on the front page. The picture itself spoke volumes and required no account. It was a photograph of a tearful terror-stricken man pleading for his and his family's life to be spared. A murderous mob, not seen in the picture, had surrounded his house. Wali had no idea whether the man had survived or was butchered heartlessly, for the news item hadn't mentioned it, but his indignation at the sufferings of an innocent man was intense. He showed the picture to Abba-Jaan, who had immediately responded by loudly exclaiming, "*Ya Allah*, what kind of heartless butchers are these, who have no mercy for the innocent man begging for his life!"

Shakeel, who was serving breakfast had overheard the remark and had rushed from the kitchen to peep at the newspaper. Seeing the picture, he had first confirmed if the man was a victim of Gujarat riots and then had sarcastically remarked, "See now! You are always trying to shield these butchers who kill our Muslim brothers. I have always known that the *kafirs* deserve to be dealt with stringently. They need to be shown no mercy. And to protect our religion, we should now be ready to fight."

"Shakeel, you must realize that communal riots, the acts of terrorism in the name of religion, defeat the very purpose for which the religions were initially conceived. The great prophets of the world wanted to unite people into a fraternity of brotherhood and not divide them. Fighting with each other will serve no purpose, only bringing the original culprits; the politicians to trial will. For, they are the ones who instigate brother against brother and are the serious criminals."

"What brothers are you talking about? *Kafirs* can not be considered our brothers," Shakeel had proclaimed loudly.

Abba-Jaan had replied calmly, "Shakeel you know, the people involved in this violence have similar judgment as yours, which is why they are implicated in such evil. They are filled with malevolence and view people not as brothers but as enemies, simply because of difference in religious beliefs. They are also the ones who view life as something so valueless that it can be wiped out without any remorse. Don't you think that somewhat similar events have occurred against Pandits of our valley? They too were butchered mercilessly."

Shakeel had replied insistently, "Our valley has different problems. It is a conflict between the natives and the outsiders. It is about our land."

Abba-Jaan had simply shaken his head in disgust, well realizing that it was useless to argue with an irrational person.

In the days to follow, newspapers and TV channels were full of reports of rioting and carnage. The unrest was spreading on relentlessly from town to town, from village to village and a large part of the state of Gujarat was caught up in pointless ethnic violence. As the reports of the atrocities committed against the innocents by the rioting mob and the connivance of the top politicians began to be exposed by the media, Wali had noted that Shakeel had begun to appear grim. It was as if something was cooking up in his mind. His outings too had begun to become longer.

May be Abba-Jaan had noted it too, Wali thought now, for one evening he had again discoursed on the issue of virtues, to put forth his ideas especially to enlighten Shakeel. Despite years of such relentless efforts and continuous snub by the conceited youth, Abba-Jaan had not accepted defeat.

Wali now recalled that it was a Sunday evening and Salim and Meher too were present in the room. Abba-Jaan had spoken addressing the youngsters, "It is just a mob of disoriented, misled people. Religion is just an excuse. Neither *Allah*, nor *Bhagwan* permits shedding of innocent blood. These people belong to no religion. Only *shaitan* can live in such hearts."

Encouraged by the vigorous nods by Salim and Meher, he had continued in an earnest, "Children, you must remember that the differences in religious doctrines or holy rituals do not make us different. We belong to the same species. We look alike so obviously we have a common descent. Therefore, we human beings are supposed to live like brothers and be ever ready to lend helping hand. We are supposed to be humane and not slit each others' throats. "

While Salim and Meher had again nodded in agreement, Shakeel had interrupted viciously, "I don't know about all that. But the fire to take revenge is burning hot in my heart. How can we sit idle, when our Muslim brothers are being burnt alive, being butchered like carrots? If I come across any of those murderers, I won't spare them. I will slit their throats, cut them into pieces; the way they have treated the Muslims in Gujarat. I will wage a holy war against them."

His morbid statement had shocked both Salim and Meher, who being unaccustomed to these kind of expressions, had glared at him with distaste.

Abba-Jaan's tightened lips and shut eyes were indicative of how pained he was. He had then said, "If others are murderers, should you also become one? Should you shun your sanity and tag on to the violators of peace? You are harbouring some foolish notions in your mind, absolutely immature thoughts! It is the doctrine of peace and amity we need to pursue. Young lad, remember, satisfaction is never experienced by taking lives; it is felt deep down in the heart by saving one. I too was instrumental in saving a life once, though not directly, and that has always given me an immense feeling of contentment."

"Is that so?" Shakeel had simply said. He had shown no interest in knowing the facts.

"Abba Ji, tell us about it," Salim and Meher had instantly voiced.

Abba-Jaan had then sat surrounded by keen ears, narrating his experience of the partition days.

"It happened shortly after the declaration of independence in August 1947 and splitting of the country into two segments. As soon as the division of the country was affirmed, exodus of the Hindus from Pakistan and of the Muslims from India began. You must realize that it is not easy to depart from a home where you have lived all your life; it is not easy to quit the land of one's ancestors; never to return. Imagine; if tomorrow we are asked to abandon our house forever and go to an unknown land, if we are made destitute overnight, what would be our condition? But the people, persecuted by the deadly waves of political rivalry, were given no choice. It is an irony that certain people in power are allowed to decide a course without realising the adversity of its effects. And what can a common helpless man do, except follow the natural instincts for survival?

So, the people abandoned what belonged to them once, to go to strange and unknown lands. The migration of the people should have been a peaceful operation but then there are always mischief makers among us who can cause harm of unimaginable proportions.

We all could feel the extremely volatile situation prevailing, created entirely due to the political differences, and feared that it was ready to explode with tiniest of sparks. That was exactly what happened."

Wali had watched his children listening wide eyed and had thought how easy it was to persuade the young minds. That was why they required the right kind of exposure and unfortunately how much the family members were trying, Shakeel preferred the wrong influence.

He now recalled that Meher had interrupted to enlighten her grandfather about her knowledge of the events. "*Barae Abbu,* we had a long chapter in our history book on India's struggle for independence and also the causes and impact of the partition. It sometimes makes me angry to think how the foreign rulers had exploited the indigenous population." She had said.

"Yes *Bachh*, those were really the sinister days. First it was the years of the British oppression and then once the partition was declared, the ethnic violence marred the joys of being the citizens of independent nations. That was the saddest and the darkest period of the Indian history when people of the same nation were provoked to kill each other. The bloodbath that had followed the declaration of independence was the episode drenched in treachery."

Wali too had listened with interest the incidence Abba-Jaan had then narrated to them. He also remembered how Shakeel had simply sat with expressionless face.

Abba-Jaan had continued. "I was studying in a college at Lahore. Lahore used to be the educational centre of North India before independence. Then, turbulence that had set in the country with the demand for a separate Muslim nation began to be more and more violent. Even after the declaration of two separate nations, people were incited into nonsensical violence which was getting out of control. Considering the prevailing tense situation, I decided to come back home for a few days. It was just after the declaration of independence in August that I had boarded an afternoon train at the Amritsar station to go to Pathankot. In the same compartment was seated Mr. Prem Chand Wangu, a gentleman known to my family. He told me that he had come to drop his wife and children at his wife's parents' home. His father-in-law was running a carpet business at Amritsar.

I was happy to have some company for the journey. Travelling alone was not a very comfortable proposition, especially when the atmosphere around was negatively charged. I had read reports of unimaginable carnage of hapless people and butchering in the trains and buses. Therefore, having someone of Mr. Wangu's age as my companion; gave me considerable sense of security. We both chatted throughout the journey. I talked about my college and my future plans. Mr. Wangu talked about his business. Soon we were discussing the situation in the country. It turned out that both of us were against this division of our country by political aspirants. We agreed that it had simply happened because there was clamour for power. Jinnah had become a serious contender to the post of the Prime-Minister of the newly self-governing country. So Pakistan was carved out to accommodate him as the head of the

Muslim dominated nation and Pt. Nehru as the Prime Minister of the Hindu dominated India.

By the evening, we had reached Pathankot. We needed to take a bus from there for further journey. As soon as we came out of the station, we confronted a crowd of troubled people.

They were all standing in front of a shop, listening to the news on the radio. We too got curious and inquired from one of the persons in the crowd about the important news. We were told that terrible rioting had started off at Amritsar. Mobs were let loose in the city. Muslims were hunting and killing Hindus and vice versa.

The news was really bad. I feared that this rioting could soon spread like a wild fire to the yet peaceful parts of the country too, if our inexperienced leaders did not control the situation.

For Mr. Wangu, there couldn't have been worse news. He began to perspire. He muttered more to himself than to me that he had just left his family in the city where now people were killing each other. His children were small. His wife was young and beautiful. God knows what the butchers would do to them.

I stood with him, helplessly looking at his condition. I had no words either to console him or to soothe him. But I could understand his plight.

Then Mr. Wangu made up his mind. "I am going to Amritsar to bring back my family," he said with determination, and with long strides he walked back to the station. I followed him, now seriously viewing whether he was taking the right decision. My mind was telling me something else. I began to analyze the situation.

Mr. Wangu was really walking fast; I was finding it difficult to match his pace and had to run to keep up. He appeared absolutely resolute.

We reached the ticket window. Mr. Wangu inquired from the clerk when the next train would leave for Amritsar. He was told that it was about to leave in fifteen minutes. "Give me one ticket and make it quick," he sounded desperate.

At the very moment, when the clerk at the window was preparing a ticket for Mr. Wangu, the stationmaster had reached there and had overheard Mr. Wangu's request.

"Where do you want to go?" He confirmed of Mr. Wangu.

"I am travelling to Amritsar," Mr. Wangu informed him briefly.

"Mister, I have just had a talk with my colleague at Amritsar and I believe that the situation there is not good. Ethnic rioting has broken out. The unrestrained mobs are running wild, attacking and killing hapless victims."

"That is why I must reach there. My wife and small children are there. I must bring them back from there," Mr. Wangu said.

"Are you sure you want to go there now? Wait till tomorrow. May be, by then the situation will be brought under control," The stationmaster suggested. He then added, "Well, it may not be right on my part to dissuade one person when the train full of passengers is ready to depart to the same destination. If it were within my control, I would have cancelled the train's departure but I am no authority and have to wait for orders from the high command."

"Then why are you dissuading me?" Mr. Wangu had spoken rather angrily.

"Simply because others have already purchased the tickets and you haven't," the stationmaster had quietly replied.

Seeing Mr. Wangu's hesitancy, the clerk tore down the ticket he was holding in his hand till then. Through his gesture, he clearly told him that going to Amritsar would be foolishness.

I too was waiting for such an opportunity, for there was a powerful compelling voice in me urging me to help the man take the right decision. If I had voiced my advice earlier, Mr. Wangu would have dismissed it; considering it to be an opinion of a young immature mind, advice of a person who didn't know what a wife and children meant to a man.

I said to him, "Yes sir; that is right! Even I think it is not the right time to go. Situation appears really bad."

He replied, "I do not care about the situation. I must bring my family back. They are not at all safe there."

Three of us gazed at Mr. Wangu, wondering how to make him change his mind.

Then somebody came to call the stationmaster and he left. The clerk got busy with some other customer and Mr. Wangu became entirely my responsibility.

I had realized by now that Mr. Wangu's decision was unwavering but I too felt strongly that I would have to discourage him from putting his hand in a lion's cage.

"Think sensibly sir. Your family is not on the streets. They are safely inside their house." I put forth my argument.

"Houses can be attacked. When there is mob fury, anything can happen." He said to me with apparent fear in his voice.

"Still, the question is who is safer, your family inside the house or a lonely man on the treacherous streets?"

"What do you mean?" Mr. Wangu now cooled down a little.

"I mean, it will be difficult for you to reach the house from the station. You will be at more vulnerable position on the street, that too all alone. The question is; will you be able to reach the house with blood thirsty mob let loose?"

"So what do you suggest? That I should not go to bring my family back? I should leave them there, among what you just said; the blood thirsty mob?" He was a highly agitated person at that moment and rightly so.

"I only suggest that you wait and watch the situation. Do not take any decision in a hurry. We can stay in Pathankot tonight. In the morning the circumstances will be clearer and then you can take further decision."

I thus offered to stay with him for the night, rescheduling my programme.

That had some effect on Mr. Wangu. He reluctantly agreed to wait till the morning. We found a guesthouse close to the station and hired a room for the night.

I could sense Mr. Wangu's restlessness throughout the night. He didn't sleep a wink. Nor could I!

'Why were people becoming as brutal as to become murderers of the innocent? Why was there so much religious intolerance? What made people burn with hate at those they had never known in life? We gained independence from foreign rule after years of struggle, what for? To slit each others' throats, bathe our land in blood? Are we mature enough to handle problems of the independent nations, when we are behaving in such beastly manner? Would we be able to take our country on the path of development and advancement?'

Chapter 9

Such questions kept haunting me throughout the night.

Early in the morning, we went back to the station. The sun hadn't yet risen and most of the town was under the protective custody of slumber. Yet, I felt a strange disturbed calm at the wee hours, as if it was a facade of peace, soon to be shattered by bloodcurdling hollers. I was frightened of the artificial quietude, expecting sword-yielding crowd to be chasing me soon. I can't explain what a terrifying feeling it can be!"

At this point when Abba-Jaan had become quiet, Wali had noted a sad forlorn look brush past his face. He had also noticed the pale and drawn faces of Salim and Meher. The children appeared as frightened as if they themselves were experiencing the charged atmosphere of the partition days. Abba-Jaan, without doubt, wanted to acquaint the children to the menace of religious intolerance, to the futility of the pointless bloodbath. But Shakeel was definitely unperturbed, though at the moment it was clear from his expression that he had become interested in Abba-Jaan's narration, as if it was a fairy tale.

Abba-Jaan had continued to tell his story, "We entered the Pathankot Railway Station once again and directly marched to the ticket counter. A different clerk was on duty at that time. Mr. Wangu inquired about the timings of the next train to Amritsar. The clerk was about to reply when we heard a voice from behind "Weren't you here yesterday evening?"

We both turned towards the source of the inquiry.

The stationmaster was standing behind us. He appeared quite serious and upset. Perhaps shaken! We looked at him. After a long silence he said, "You wanted to buy a ticket for the train that left in the evening for Amritsar?"

Mr. Wangu nodded.

"I have just received some terrible news from the stationmaster of the Amritsar station. He was so upset that he couldn't even speak clearly and was initially totally incoherent. Then he somewhat managed to communicate to me the tragic reports regarding what happened on that train at night."

My heart skipped a beat. Mr. Wangu was standing so still that it appeared he had stopped breathing.

Then the stationmaster said, "You are a lucky man. What a narrow escape you have had sir!"

We looked at him not really understanding what he implied. I presumed that the train had probably derailed.

"Sir, you have escaped from the jaws of death. You know what transpired on that train? Butchering! Cold Blooded murders! A Muslim mob boarded the train at some station. The moment it reached a deserted place, they began their carnage. Each and every Hindu on that train was killed. People tried to hide under the berths, they ran into the toilets, but there was no escape. They were pulled out and murdered. Some even jumped out of the running train to escape from being hacked by the knives and the swords. Not a single Hindu reached the city. It is good that you heeded our advice…God has saved you."

We were stunned. I looked at Mr. Wangu. He was silently crying. My eyes too were brimming with tears. Killing innocent people was a deed that reeked of insanity. How could the normal people do something like that? How could they? I kept asking myself.

The stationmaster continued, "My colleague said there were streams of blood flowing in the compartments of the train. He had to fulfil his duty of inspection of the train and he couldn't walk inside. Dismembered bodies were lying everywhere. Many people had been beheaded. Many had their throats slit."

The man was now choking with emotion. He continued to inform us, "The stationmaster sounded terribly disoriented. He mentioned about going on leave. He can't stand this madness, he told me." And the shocked stationmaster of the Pathankot station took out his handkerchief to wipe his eyes.

Mr. Wangu was openly sobbing and I was holding on to him, to console him. My legs were shaky and I too needed support.

"Do you think my family is all right?" He turned to ask me.

I had no words to keep him going. I simply gazed at him. "Let god take care of all," was all I could manage to say

"Those were such terrible days. Insanity prevailed over sensitivity…over sensibility."

There was a painful silence in the room. The listeners of the story had been really touched by Abba-Jaan's narration of the horrendous incident.

Then Abba-Jaan had said, "The only satisfaction I had at that time, and have till date is; that I could desist an innocent man from undertaking a dangerous

Chapter 9

journey, thus saving him from a sure and horrible death."

Wali now remembered noting how both Salim and Meher had appeared deeply moved. Meher had secretly wiped her tears with her *chunni,* though her action had not gone unnoticed by her father. And Salim had sat shell-shocked. Wali also recalled that directly addressing Shakeel, Abba-Jaan had then said, "On the contrary, if I hadn't stopped Mr. Wangu that day, I would have never forgiven myself. Each time I recollect that incident, I shudder with horror at the thought of cruelty of some human beings towards their own brothers." He had then become quiet, as if lost in his memories.

Salim had then interrupted his thoughts, "Abba ji, what happened to Mr. Wangu's family? Did they survive the riots?"

"Yes, Mr. Wangu told us that the family had taken refuge in the Golden Temple area which was considered safe. Anyway a curfew was imposed from the next day and slowly the situation was controlled. As soon as it was safe, Mr. Wangu had rushed to bring back his family."

"You also stayed with him till he left for Amritsar," was the next inquiry by inquisitive Salim.

"No, the station master offered that Mr. Wangu could stay with him till it would be safe to go to Amritsar and I took a bus to go home."

"How come I have never met Mr. Wangu?" Salim now wanted to know.

"He left to settle in Amritsar a year or two after the partition, to join his father-in-law in the carpet business. He had come to visit us before leaving, to express his gratefulness for my wise advice that had saved his life. That was the last time I met him. And we have never heard from him again," Abba-Jaan answered.

"Then when did you go back to your college?" Salim had asked next.

Abba-Jaan had then informed, "I never ever could go back to Lahore. I had to complete my graduation through correspondence course."

And then Shakeel had got up to go, Wali now recalled. On reaching the door, he had halted. Turning towards Abba-Jaan he had said, "Saving the life of a *kafir* is no big deal." Having voiced his debased opinion, he had walked out of the room.

Shakeel's reaction had stunned all. Abba-Jaan's expression indicated how much he had been aggrieved by the boy's attitude. He had said with certain alarm, "This boy is becoming arrogant. We all are so polite to him. We care for him like our own son. And he goes out and picks up wicked ideas. Wali, be careful, I don't know if we can trust him anymore."

Turning towards Salim, Abba-Jaan had added, "*Bachh*, remember one thing in life. No religion is greater than humanity. You are young and with an impressionistic mind. Never get swayed by wrong ideas. Be strong. Remain sensible and control your sentiments. Fanaticism in any form is destructive."

And Salim had uttered just one sentence which was enough to satisfy both his grandfather and his father.

"I am your grandson Abba ji and Abbu's son," he had articulated softly.

Chapter 10

Wali now recollected that Meher had been so touched by Abba-Jaan's narration that it had rendered her speechless. The pain for the human-sufferings at the hands of some brutal mortals had been so apparent in her large soft eyes that Wali was unsure if it had been the right type of exposure for her. The very next day he had realized that at times such revelations are instrumental in bringing out the sensitive as well as the stronger side of a young person's personality.

For, the next day Meher had shown her father the poem that she had written the previous night on a piece of paper torn from her school notebook.

Wali recollected that he had preserved her poem in his wallet, as a prized gift from his growing up daughter who was beginning to possess her own perspective of the prevalent world. Thereafter, he had been so engrossed in his life's toil that he had hardly ever reflected upon it.

It should still be in his wallet, he recalled, for each time he had changed his wallet, he had carefully preserved those momentous sentiments. He now eagerly took out his wallet from the pocket of his *pheran* and after a brief hunt, he managed to find a pale and worn out paper. He stood up with a purpose and walked inside the boat. Carefully opening it, he spread the paper on the table and put on his spectacles. Drawing the chair closer, he sat down to read the poem.

MAKE THEM SMILE AGAIN

Our verdant orchard may have been set on fire,
The innocent blood may have drenched its mire,
A tragedy may have been set up by the dreadful forces,
The bleak future may be what this violence endorses.
But, why this minority should be allowed to succeed?
Why the caring and concerned shouldn't rise and accede?
To save the orchard from ruin and blaze,
And to bring relief and smiles on masses in daze.
There is still time to cure this orchard's blight,
That has been eating its very roots with delight.
Let us halt the pollution of minds and our land,
Let us curtail the destructive forces with firm hand.

Wali read the poem a number of times, becoming more and more convinced each time what a mature poem it was for a young school going girl to write. He also realized how relevant and appropriate her opinion was even today.

Carefully folding the sheet of paper and keeping it safely once again in his wallet, he reflected that the disparity in human thought and action had always caused conflicts, except that the world had stood the test of times due to the presence of sizeable goodness. He was also convinced at the legitimacy of the conclusion of the poem. "Meher is absolutely right; firm hand is required to rein in people like Shakoel who are bent upon having the world wounded."

Wali recalled further how exulted he had felt at the creativity and reflections of his young daughter that he had instantly directed her to take her poem to her grandfather, well knowing how proud he too would be of his granddaughter. But she had refused saying, "No Abbu ji, I wrote this poem only for you, for you are strong and in position to curb the destructive people. I have brought something else and more suitable for *Barae Abbu*."

She had then shown him a book of poems, which she had brought from her school library. They both had then marched to Abba-Jaan's room to show the poem to him.

Meher had stated to her grandfather, "*Barae Abbu*, I had read this poem when I was in the seventh standard. Yesterday when you were narrating the incident of how you had saved Mr. Wangu's life, I recalled this poem. It is just appropriate for the people like you, who are so concerned about bringing about the feelings of brotherhood and compassion in the world. People like Shakeel are just the opposite. They believe in bloodshed. He is no more than a stupid and ignorant fool."

Abba-Jaan's eyes had twinkled and his face had lighted up by a large grin at this recognition by his granddaughter. Then Abba-Jaan and Meher had read the poem together. And Wali had been the listener.

He had been able to gather the beautiful meaning of the poem. He could now remember just a few lines though. He tried recalling them. The protagonist of the poem, Abou Ben Adhem had suddenly woken from his sleep and was taken aback seeing an angel in his room. The angel was writing in a book of gold; "The names of those who loved the Lord". Abou wanted to know if his name was in the list. A negative answer saddened him. He then made a request that his name may be written, "as one that loves his fellow men". The angel visited Abou again the next night and showed him the names of those who loved the Lord; and "Ben Adhem's name led all the rest."

How accurate Meher's conviction was, Wali now thought. His Abba-Jaan surely deserved to be with *Allah*, for he truly loved his fellowmen; irrespective of religions. Wali walked out to look up at the crystal clear azure sky and speculated, "May be, Abba-Jaan is watching over us from somewhere up there." The thought gave Wali some solace that perhaps tonight he would have some help from above.

Recollection of those happy days and the statements made by his son and daughter brought tears to Wali's eyes now. Salim's one sentence had said it all. He had always been so upright. He had paid the least attention to politics, something that usually becomes a pastime of majority of young men. It was more creditable, since the political scene was becoming hotter and hotter in the Valley with the increase in insurgency and the terrorist strikes. When many young men were being misguided into adopting extremism, Salim had been singularly engrossed in his professional studies and had never given his parents a chance to be alarmed at his conduct.

"Why is it always the bad experiences that jolt us out of our slumber and make us register so many things in life which we have begun to take for granted? In routine, why do we forget to appreciate our endowments and count our blessings?"

It was Wali's day of awakening. "I have treated my son unjustly. When he has to spend his life with his partner, who am I to interfere in his plans? As a father it is my duty to guide him, not make life miserable for him. Moreover, all through his growing up period he was taught, especially by Abba-Jaan, that religions are not meant for dividing but for uniting people. It is I who should be blamed for floundering Abba-Jaan's beliefs." Wali closed his eyes tightly and shook his head in disgust.

After Abba-Jaan's death, Wali had become so busy that he seldom had time to sit down to reflect upon the wisdom that he had collected unconsciously through the journey of life. Abba-Jaan had been the source of most of the wisdom that Wali had treasured. Sitting alone now, his memories were rushing out like restrained school children spilling out to explore new horizons. His memories were becoming instrumental in understanding the rationality of existence. They were also easing up the path he was about to tread. They were revealing to him the futility of violence and hatred in the world.

"What is the use of the sight if you are blind to the plight of others? What is the use of the tongue, if you remain a mute witness to injustice? What is the use of a human life if you have never rendered help to a needy," Abba-Jaan's words uttered to Meher after reading the poem rang clear in Wali's ears now. Despite all that education, he had remained blind and deaf, Wali thought with regret. He should have at least raised his voice against terrorism, which was slowly engulfing the sanity and defiling the tranquillity of his beloved land, Wali apprehended.

He was finding it strenuous to stand on his weak legs for long and now came to sit on the steps again, to mull over the fact that Abba-Jaan had become exceptionally quiet for the days following the Gujarat riots and Shakeel's reaction. Most of the time he would be frowning, engrossed in deep thoughts. Then a few days later, instead of proceeding for his walk after the evening *Namaz*, he had asked Shakeel to follow him to the sitting room. Wali too had followed his father out of curiosity.

Sitting down on his favourite easy chair, Abba-Jaan had said, "Shakeel, something has been troubling me and I want to talk it out with you. I am discussing things with you as I would do with Salim. So listen carefully."

"Yes *Barae Huzoor*, my ears are always open for you," Shakeel had answered with enthusiasm and had sat down cross legged on the floor besides Abba-Jaan.

"Your eyes too need to remain open," Abba-Jaan had said with a polite smile.

"But my eyes are wide open. Look!" Shakeel had said opening his eyes wider till they almost popped out.

The boy has no manners; glaring at Abba-Jaan like a blockhead, Wali had silently thought.

"I am not talking about these two restless eyes you have on your head. I am talking about the inner eye; the eye of your spirit!" Abba-Jaan had stressed.

"Is there an eye inside the body too? Are you implying that I have more than two eyes, one hidden somewhere? How come I can't see with it?" Shakeel was genuinely amazed.

"This is the eye which makes us see reason. And lately you have been very unreasonable."

Shakeel had begun to understand what Abba-Jaan implied and had immediately become stiff.

"The other day you had been talking about holy war or jihad. I have called you here to explain the meaning of jihad. This is a holy word which has been misinterpreted by many. Son, jihad is a holy war which is not fought with the innocents. In fact, it is not fought with others but own self."

Shakeel had begun to laugh uncontrolled. "Why must I fight with myself? You mean I must injure myself, cut my arm or commit suicide?"

Abba-Jaan was finding it difficult to maintain his cool, but he did. And Wali thought how difficult it was to give advice to a stuck head.

Abba-Jaan had continued, "Jihad is not a war against other religions or people with different faiths. It is the battle with one's own vices. It is a battle with anger, jealousy and hatred we breed inside us and we should try to eliminate them from our lives."

"Is it not a battle with injustice and inequality in the society? Is it not a fight against slavery?" Shakeel had argued heatedly.

Abba-Jaan had answered calmly, "Yes, absolutely! Once you have overcome your own vices, you become capable of helping others and you have every right to fight against injustice."

"That is the war our men are fighting. The war is for freedom from slavery," Shakeel had declared forcefully.

"Freedom from slavery? Aren't we free people? Are we restrained or restricted from doing what we want to do? Our Valley is free. We are nobody's slaves. We live in a democracy; a government of the people, and not ruled by any dictator," Abba-Jaan had stressed.

"My land is not free. The war is for the freedom of my land!" Shakeel had insisted.

"It is less for the freedom of any land, more for power. Some weak minded have got sold in the hands of people with vested interests; those who aim at the authority and profit of a high position. It is a politically motivated issue. What have people, who indulge in day to day hard work, got to do with politics? You better be careful Shakeel and shun your extremist ideas. It is not proper to be so obstinate. Remember, we need harmony in the society, not turbulence."

"There is bound to be turbulence when there is dissatisfaction. And there is bound to be war and violence when freedom and justice are at stake." Shakeel was so vocal that he appeared akin to a highly motivated soldier in a battlefield, ready to slaughter those he considered his enemies.

"No, that is not true," Abba-Jaan had expressed with equal intensity. "Justice and equality can also be won over by non-violence. Freedom can also be achieved by peaceful means. A simple man once proved that; by getting independence for the entire nation through non-violent means."

"Won a war without fighting?" Shakeel had shown genuine surprise.

"Yes, fought against suppression and injustice without lifting a finger," Abba-Jaan had said.

"Who was he?" Shakeel had now got interested.

"Haven't you ever heard of Mahatma Gandhi?" Wali had intruded in the discussion for the first time. "He was the one to draw the masses together to raise voice against the British. He was beaten and jailed a number of times for initiating the Non-Cooperation Movement. He went to jail with fortitude, and offered himself for more suffering if that could alleviate the sufferings of the native population from the British oppression. The British finally relented and agreed to negotiate with him. That man got the support of the entire nation and finally won freedom for his country from the foreign rule. If freedom can be won by peaceful talks, what is the need to indulge in violence?" Wali had spoken slowly, lucidly, as if he was conducting a class on Indian history for Shakeel's benefit.

Abba-Jaan had added, "True! Violence begets only violence. No solutions are ever found by trying to destroy each other, but by… "

But before Abba-Jaan could even complete his sentence, Shakeel had interrupted, "Oh! That Gandhi fellow? I once read about him in my schoolbook and I don't believe in his way of life. He was not impressive at all. He looked a pauper."

"He was a simple man; a saint," Abba-Jaan had said.

"He was nowhere close to being a commander who can lead his army against the enemy. Moreover, Muslims did not follow his policy. For them the leader was Jinnah. Even I know about all these things," Shakeel had interjected.

"Who says Muslims were not Mahatma's followers? What about the prominent Muslim congress leaders during the struggle for freedom? Maulana Abdul Kalam Azad was one of those who were never in favour of the partition," Wali had informed Shakeel.

And Abba-Jaan had added, "Have you ever heard of Khan Abdul Gaffar Khan from Baluchistan? He was known as the frontier Gandhi. He believed in and followed Gandhi's philosophy of non-violence all his life, though after partition, he lived in his home province in Pakistan. There may be many more who have spent their lifetimes preaching the doctrines of peace and tolerance. "

"Such ideas might have worked with the British and in the olden times. But the times have changed now and such beliefs are outdated." Shakeel was not the one to surrender.

A frown had immediately appeared on Abba-Jaan's face. He had then stated with exasperation. "Shakeel, I don't know how to make you understand. I am getting worried for you."

Shakeel had reacted with utter disrespect, "You don't need to worry on my behalf. I know how to look after myself." Saying so, he got up and marched out of the room.

Abba-Jaan had watched him go and then had said to Wali with obvious irritation in his tone, "Wali, I am very apprehensive regarding this boy. I am quite sure he is getting involved with the terrorists. Some people like Shakeel are so ungrateful. They rather pay attention to the strangers than to the people who care. They have no regard for their mentors. They have no consideration for those who try to protect them from adversities. They are *namak haraams*." Wali had nodded in agreement. After a short pause, Abba-Jaan had continued, "The ideas this boy has picked from his peers are now almost irrevocable; sticking to him like leeches. At times I see such conceit and unrest on the face of this empty headed fellow that I have started to wonder if it is time to let him go."

"Yes Abba-Jaan if you so desire, I will begin to look for another servant from tomorrow," Wali had proposed.

"Wali, what is the guarantee that the other person will be any wiser. Unfortunately, more and more people in our valley have begun to believe in aggression as solution to all the problems. I wonder when people will attain some perception to let this mindless violence end. Or, they will destroy everything; including themselves."

Chapter 11

"Abba-Jaan was absolutely right; some people can never mend their ways. Shakeel has turned out to be the biggest ungrateful scoundrel I have ever…ever known in my life." Wali's hands automatically turned into fists and despite the fact that he was a non-violent man; he wished he could clobber Shakeel into a pulp that very moment.

"It was my fault that I didn't pay heed to Abba-Jaan's advice and gave notice to Shakeel at that very moment. We had put up with him beyond endurance and that has given him wrong ideas. He probably began to consider himself indispensable big-wheel. That is the reason he has returned now with hideous intentions."

"Instead of sacking him from his job, we allowed the polluted scum to arrogantly resign and honourably depart. I should have kicked him out," Wali now felt a strong sensation for the first time in life, a sensation to physically kick the man who was presently the cause for his anguish. "I should have kicked him out when soon after the Gujarat riots, he had asked for three days' leave and I had reasons to suspect him of treason."

Wali had expressed his desire to know the reason for the request for leave, for ever since Shakeel had joined the household; he had never taken leave for more than a day, and that included the unsanctioned ones. A few times, when he had suffered from illnesses, he had been well looked after at home and exempted from all work till he recouped his health. Moreover, he had always mentioned that he had no home other than this, no relatives he would ever want to visit. Then what was the motive behind the sudden requirement of the leave?

Initially, Shakeel had given no direct reason other than he wanted to visit some places with his friends. Wali was in no position to refuse since it was the first time Shakeel had made such a request, but had insisted upon knowing his destination. Then half-heartedly, he had allowed him three days' leave to go to Jammu. But, he had serious grounds for worry when he had caught Shakeel using the telephone the evening prior to his departure.

Wali had left home to walk down to the orchard around five that evening. It was also Abba-Jaan's walk time. The women folk were in their rooms, as usual, before launching the dinner preparations. Wali had remembered on the way that he had to make an urgent call and had immediately backtracked. That was barely after five minutes of his departure. As he had entered the parlour, he had found Shakeel talking to someone on phone, telling the person that everything was in order and the job would be smoothly executed. Then seeing Wali, he had become flustered and had hurriedly put down the receiver. Wali had asked no questions but the discomfort on Shakeel's face had left him uneasy.

Shakeel had left early morning the next day. A day later, there was a terrorists' attack on a famous temple at Jammu, leaving scores of devotees, who were in the temple at the time of the attack; dead, injured or maimed for life.

When Wali had heard the news, he had become troubled. Was it a coincidence that Shakeel's visit had concurred with the attack? Not wanting to worry the other members of the house, Wali had remained tight lipped but his mind was in turmoil. "Although they have had reasons to suspect him, is Shakeel in reality leading a secret life unknown to them? Has he stooped to the level of becoming a murderer? Should he allow Shakeel to continue to live in the house or he should be shown the door immediately before he incurs serious troubles for the family?"

At the same time, Wali had felt deeply concerned towards the boy who had been living with them for years. "No doubt, he has been discourteous as well as obstinate and his ideology is surely perverse, drenched with bigotry, but is he capable of undertaking such violent assignments? Does he have that kind of nerve? Perhaps my distrust is baseless. If Shakeel was guilty, he could have easily given me a wrong name of the place he was to visit."

But his suspicion could also be well founded. "He has been telling someone on a sly about execution of some plan. Moreover, he had become so confused and red faced when suddenly caught red-handed? What other plan could it be if not this that had rendered him agitated when caught discussing it?"

Chapter 11

Wali's dilemma was great but he had decided to wait to get hold of some solid evidence of Shakeel's seditious activities, before pronouncing the verdict.

Shakeel had appeared extra cheerful after coming back from his jaunt. And it had left Wali wondering further whether his joviality was due to the change of scene he had had or was it something to do with successful execution of some vicious plan.

Wali had begun to become more and more convinced that it would be quite soon he would have to ask Shakeel to leave. He had discussed it with Abdul who had similar views. Abdul had volunteered to provide extra help at home to compensate for the shortage of a hand. But he was of the strong opinion that Shakeel should be thrown out without delay. "Enough is enough," Abdul had voiced.

Wali had then begun to wait for the right opportunity.

However, Wali was spared the task of ordering Shakeel out. A few days later Shakeel had himself approached Wali to intimate him of his decision to quit.

It was after he had served them breakfast that morning. When the other family members had left, Wali was the only one present in the room engrossed in reading the newspaper. As Shakeel was clearing the table, he had stopped to declare his intentions. He had addressed Wali, "*Huzoor*, I have served you and your family for many years now. I have decided that it is time for me to move on. I will be leaving immediately."

Raising his eyes from the newspaper, Wali had simply nodded in agreement.

Wali's lack of reaction had astounded the conceited Shakeel and his eyes had clearly revealed his wonder at the indifference, as if his pleasure of seeing surprise and anguish on the face of his master had been cruelly snatched away from him.

"Where will you be going?" Wali had then asked form behind the newspaper.

"Right now I am going to visit my village. Thereafter, I will go where my fate will take me." And he had become silent, refusing to tell any more.

Wali too had thought it wise not to probe further. Secretly, he had felt mighty relieved.

When Wali had disclosed Shakeel's desire to quit the job to others at home, Sakina had exhibited obvious distress while others had remained unconcerned. Abba-Jaan had simply said, "Let him go. Perhaps that will be in our best interests."

Wali had become double minded for a while before conveying the final acceptance of Shakeel's resignation. The main reason was Sakina's distress.

He had evaluated the situation. "It will definitely be difficult for Sakina to run the house without a help. The whole family has become used to Shakeel running various errands. But stopping him wouldn't be right. He seems to have made up his mind. Moreover, his delusive behaviour called for an ultimate decision. It is perhaps a gifted opportunity to let him go. Abba-Jaan too wants that, and porhaps he is right. Shakeel's staying on will perhaps endanger the safety of my family."

"Since children have grown up and are quite independent now, Sakina will have to do with whatever help Abdul will be able to offer in the mornings and evenings. I am not in favour of hiring an unknown person as a servant in the house anymore. Times have changed from when you could easily trust people."

That evening he had intimated Shakeel of his decision, "Look here Shakeel, we can't stop you from going if that is what you have decided. You have served us for a long time. You have grown from a boy to a young man here. We will be sad to let you go. Let *Allah* be with you wherever you go."

And Shakeel had disappeared from their lives for a long time.

Chapter 11

Chapter 12

Wali had presumed that it was a good riddance but it was not intended to be so.

"Why has he come back now?" Wali thought angrily. "It would have been better if he was gone, never to return, gone out of our lives forever."

With agitation ruling over the better senses of the restless man, he now got to his feet and walked halfway towards the front deck, stopping short of exposing himself entirely. He keenly peeked around for any approaching boat that would bring Wasim and get him reprieve from this torturous wait. There was lazy late afternoon hush over the lake now. His eyes fell on the avenue of tall *chinar* trees in the distance. They were so beautiful and majestic. So Sturdy! No storm could shake their roots, thought Wali. But the storm that Shakeel had brought had uprooted him completely and thrown him flat on the ground. "I wish I could be as strong and sturdy as the *chinars*," he sighed deeply. "Will I ever be able to stand tall like a *chinar* after the present storm? I am not even sure if I will survive this storm." In the warm afternoon, a shiver ran through Wali's entire body.

He reiterated his resolve, "I have to undertake the venture, irrespective of the risks involved. I will not buckle under pressure nor will I compromise. My gamble will be to make my adversary complacent, catch them napping and then prevail over them."

This reflection made him revise the plan step by step that he and Wasim had formulated that morning. He then previewed Wasim's schedule for the day in his mind. After winding up all the work, Wasim was to meet Abdul at the grocer's around three in the evening. If he reached there after four it would be too late, for then Abdul would have left. He had conveyed that to Wasim in the morning and Wasim knew well the importance of meeting Abdul. It was extremely vital to discuss the plan with him, and it could only be done at a place away from the house, away from the spying eyes. It was now past four o'clock and that was a reason to be anxious. Wali was worried that Wasim might have been late to reach or might have not been able to locate the exact place of meeting and as a result could possibly have missed contacting Abdul.

Was that why it was taking Wasim so long? Wali's patience was almost giving way. He was rightly agitated for soon he should be heading home. If he took long to return, the wicked men posted there might get suspicious.

The realization immediately made him edgy. His position still restricted his field of view and he was tempted to walk to the front and have a good peep. He had to remind himself again that even one wrong move could prove disastrous. He retraced his steps and halted at the door. Inside, it was hot and suffocating now. It was pleasantly breezy outside and he stood holding the railing, letting the cool air brush against his face.

"Everything around is pleasant. It is only in my heart that there is misery. Will I ever get peace and my happiness back again?" He searched for some ray of hope, for he had always been an optimistic man. Though, his optimism had received severe jolt the previous evening, he was desperate to hold on to whatever was left, even the tattered threads.

"If winter comes, can spring be far behind?"

The quote that Abba-Jaan had often uttered now rang in Wali's ears. He recited it loudly but this time it failed to give him much reprieve.

Abba-Jaan was a voracious reader. English literature was his favourite subject and that was the reason he had earned his honours degree in that subject. Wali seldom had time to read books. Business kept him occupied. Therefore, Abba-Jaan had taken over an added responsibility to keep him informed by discussing prose or poetry that he would read. He had once read out this beautiful poem by some English poet, whose name Wali could not immediately recall. Also, he hadn't understood the complete poem having found it quite complicated, grasping only the part Abba-Jaan had explained. Wali had gathered that the poet had talked about some stormy winds being harbinger of life. "The West

Chapter 12

Wind" by Shelley, the name cropped up after a little labour.

"Will there ever be spring for me after the present cold storm?" It made Wali wonder. The winters which had now come into his life were extra intense and threatened to overshadow the spring forever. Such were these winters that they were swallowing the warmth of his optimism, leasing an ice age into his life.

He closed his eyes to visualize the spring season.

"Spring! Beautiful spring of my Valley! Will I ever be able to see the beautiful spring of my land once I am distanced from it?" The query almost choked him with emotion.

The spring was the most beautiful in his orchard. When the cherry, apple, plum and apricot trees began to blossom one after the other, beginning from the early spring, it was like paradise on earth. The sweet fragrance reached as far as the interiors of the house exhilarating his spirits. Then, he always slept with the windows of his bedroom wide open despite the midnight chill. During the daytime, he forever tried to find excuses to spend the maximum time in his blossom-laden orchard.

But, for him the storm presently in his heart was worst than the severe winters of his land. In fact, he did not mind the winter season at all. It was as enjoyable as any other season. Nature added spice to life with its ever changing seasons. Besides, how would spring be appreciated if winter was missing?

When the whole landscape would be covered with snow, it ushered in a peaceful silence so particular of the season. The noise of the hectic business activities would subside and it would appear as if people had stopped working. But the forced imprisonment due to biting cold outside turned advantageous. Considerable work would be going on behind the closed doors. People earned more profit in the winters than they did in the summers. Handicraft workers produced more articles. The carpet making, the *pashmina* shawl weaving, the embroidery work, the famous *jamavar* work and the decorative articles made of papier-mâché, the *Naquash* work of intricate designs on oxidized copper/silverware, the basket weaving; it all went on at a fast pace. Wali's artisans too produced maximum objects of art in winters. So winter had never been depressing for him, Wali considered.

Perhaps once, only for a short while! Wali's memories now transported him to a time, long ago, when Meher was a small baby of three.

It was mid January, the peak winter time. It had been snowing non-stop in the town for the past two days. Heaps of snow had collected outside which was almost four feet deep, Wali now recalled. One night after dinner, Abba-Jaan and Wali were watching the evening news. Salim and Meher were playing close by. Since the room heater was on, Wali had time and again warned the children to be careful and had instructed them to play in the opposite corner of the room. Then the power had gone off. All of a sudden, it was dark in the room. Little Meher had got frightened and had rushed to be with her Abbu. On the way, her foot had got entangled in the wire and she had fallen. The fall had produced a loud banging sound. Wali had jumped from his seat and dashed to pick up Meher, her cries being the guide for him in the dark. Picking her up in his lap, Wali had tried to soothe her. But her screams were alarming. Wali had patted her on the face but the strange sticky wetness had him paralyzed. He knew it was blood.

Sakina had rushed in with a battery lantern. The sight they all had encountered in the faint light got them terribly scared. Meher's face was covered with blood. She was badly hurt. Wali had panicked. Meher's screams had brought Ammi-Jaan rushing in too. Both the women had taken Meher to the bathroom to wash her face. Wali had followed them. Abba-Jaan had stood glued to his position in shock; unable to decide how to help the child. Little Salim had been so frightened that he had sat in a corner of the room shivering. Abba-Jaan had noted him thus and had picked up whimpering Salim in his lap.

After the blood had been washed, a large gaping wound on Meher's eyebrow was detected. They had guessed how the injury had occurred; her head had probably hit the corner of the side table and that had caused a serious injury. They had applied some antiseptic and bandaged her head, but that would not be enough. The child had lost lot of blood and needed immediate medical attention, Wali had realized.

"Wrap the child in a blanket. I am taking her to a doctor." He had ordered. Putting on his warm *pheran* and covering his head with a fur cap, he slipped into his snowshoes. He then collected the sobbing child once again in his arms. When the door was opened, he had encountered a raging storm outside. Abba-Jaan had offered to accompany him, but Wali had refused, well knowing that it would not be possible for him to hurry along.

Not caring for the inclement weather, Wali had stepped out into the dark blustery night, with a torch to guide him. The icy winds had immediately cut across his face like sharp razor blades, and in an instant reaction, he had pulled the blanket over little Meher's face. Trudging through the deep snow, he had to struggle to keep on the footpath. It was difficult to locate the path, especially in the dark, as it had disappeared under piles of snow. The whole landscape was plain haunting white, all other shades having been engulfed by the cold mantle. It was due to sheer practice over the years that Wali knew his way; and kept trotting down the hill without stumbling into the dell.

The blizzard sent the snowflakes right into his eyes, piercing him like needles and almost blinding him. He slipped a number of times and each time he would tighten his grip on his little child, protecting her in his bear hug. Soon he was exhausted. His arms were stiff. His legs had begun to ache due to immense exertion. But his determination and love had kept him going.

Meher had been sobbing initially in short hiccups of a frightened little rabbit. Soon she was fast asleep, probably due to the warmth and assurance of her Abbu's hug. Wali finally managed the cumbersome journey in about forty-five minutes and reached the nearest dispensary.

There was no electricity in the dispensary. The doctor on the emergency duty had examined Meher in the faint light of a lantern. She had a serious wound; a centimetre long cut, almost splitting her eyebrow into two. Her eye had been saved. The wound would need stitching. The doctor advised Wali to wait till the electricity was restored, since it was a delicate operation.

They had waited for about half an hour after which Meher had woken up. Finding herself in strange unpleasant surroundings without her mother, added on to the pain and she began to howl once again. Wali was finding it difficult to pacify her. Her shrieks made the doctor take the decision to commence the stitching right away. Calling his assistant, they laid terrified Meher on the operation table and gave her a prick of local anaesthesia. Wali had held her little hands. He couldn't bear to see the stitching of the wound and had turned his face away. Meher had kept on bawling, almost uncontrollably, asking for her Ammi. Her painful cries were heartrending and had shaken Wali out of his wits. It was all too much for him and his hand had begun to shake. Finally when the wound had been stitched and the doctor had got busy winding up, Wali had sat down on a chair and sobbed quietly.

He had wept, for the sufferings of his child had been even more excruciating for him than his own painful wound would have been.

The doctor had said something about keeping vigil for certain signs like dizziness or vomiting within the next twenty four hours. They were expected if there was an internal injury to the brain. The statement had kept him worried for the following fortnight, though Meher had been playing and running once again from the next morning.

That was the worst ever winter for Wali. And at present; some wicked beings had turned the current pleasant summer into something worst than those agonising winter days.

Chapter 13

Wali recalled how the sight of his little Meher suffering was unbearably painful for him. She was a helpless baby then. Even today, when she was a young woman, her pain would be as unendurable for him as it had been then. He had to do everything within his power to keep the evil from hurting his family.

"Today is the test of my strength, for there haven't been such adverse circumstances ever in my life. And I am determined to pass this test. Being the sole protector of my family, I will allow none to hurt the people dear to my heart. I will protect them even at the cost of my own life. As for now, no treasure can surpass the value my family hold for me!" Wali had repeatedly tried to gain strength through such assurances today and this was slowly fetching the desired effect.

A bronze winged jacana fluttered out of the reeds, breaking Wali's train of thoughts. He spotted the metallic greenish bronze wings catching the sunrays to glimmer iridescently. His gaze followed the bird inadvertently as it sat on a patch of water hyacinths that had spread a charming lavender carpet. But today neither the graceful gait of the bird nor the lovely flowers were successful in raising any emotions in him. Instead, he spotted some bladderworts growing in a corner close to where the bird was strutting around looking for food and they became the centre of his attention.

He looked intently at the plants. They at once directed his memories to a walk with Meher on the waterfront boulevard of the same lake, when she had pointed out these insect eating plants to him. She was in her final year at school and biology was one of her favourite subjects.

He had accompanied Meher to the market that evening, as she wanted to buy a book. It was a beautiful summer evening and they had decided to take a walk after the purchase was over. Then, the magnificent sunset had made them stop. How could they not marvel at the awe-inspiring phenomenon of nature? "It happens every evening but can anyone ever ignore the glorious event?" He had stated, pointing the horizon to Meher. She had watched the sunset dumbstruck, as if watching it with her Abbu was all together a novel experience. Once the sun was veiled by the mountain range, he had turned to go and had noted Meher hunting for something in the wild vegetation growth at their feet.

"Have you dropped something, Meher?" Wali had asked.

"No Abbu ji, I am hunting for a clover with four leaflets," Meher had replied.

"But, as far as I know, clovers have only three leaflets," Wali had informed her.

"Very rarely one can find a four leafed one too Abbu, and if you do, you are going to be lucky. With my exams beginning soon, I need good luck," Meher had informed him, at the same time carrying on with her incessant search.

"Nonsense.... Clovers can't give you luck. Only your hard work will," Wali had stressed.

It was then, that Meher had spotted the bladderworts and had pointed them out to her father. They both had then got engrossed inspecting the carnivorous plants. He had been amazed to know that there were many species of insect eating plants on the earth and one of them was the native of this very lake and growing right in front of him. That was the first and the last time he had inspected the bladderworts.

When did he have the sort of time to spend on such frivolous activities, especially after the children had left? Today, when he had time, everything appeared rather dreadful, including the bladderworts.

He now keenly watched an insect entering the trap door of the bladder growing on a leaf of one of the tiny plants. It was attracted fraudulently, and Wali knew that it was now trapped forever. It would be turned into an absorbable juice and assimilated by the plant. A life gone into oblivion!

His perception having altered through hours of introspection, this time he didn't compare the carnivore with the debauch man. Instead, he fancied he could be a bladderwort for a day, a giant one, to happily gobble down an insect with the name; Shakeel. That would be the termination of all his problems. But finding it an unappetizing thought, he immediately withdrew his sight from the vegetation growth. 'To fight a criminal, one doesn't become a criminal," he mused.

A flock of ducks flew past hurriedly on some urgent business and drew his attention towards them. His gaze followed them, this time his heart longing to join them in their flight. The flock took a U-turn around the houseboat and disappeared from his sight. He looked up in search of more company and spotted a few kites leisurely gliding high up, a few dark dots distinct in the cobalt sky. He saw them as deceitful beings, so full of pretence of being on a pleasure excursion, in reality waiting to pounce upon their prey. That reminded him that he too had left behind a few deceptive kites in his house and his present actions were focussed on the endeavour of not letting them prey upon his family.

He grimaced at the realization that today he had no control over his reflections. Every thought converged onto the treacherous gang he had left back home. But had they all stayed there throughout the day? It was not possible. Some must have been stationed outside his house as the self appointed sentinels, while the others might have ventured out and most likely were currently immersed in their efforts to unearth his whereabouts.

This insight immediately made him survey his surroundings with watchful eyes; to detect any undesirable company. An uncanny stillness prevailed as usual. But this inspection made him conscious of the altered look of the lake. For a while, Wali gazed at it unable to comprehend why it looked different to him now. Oh, yes! The light falling on it had lost its fierceness and he hadn't even realized it. The dazzling white light had given way to a pale one with a tinge of golden. Wali's eyes now sought its source. The sun had commenced its journey across three-fourths of the sky. The evening was setting in.

"Just the right kind of light for photography," thought Wali. Long ago Sakina's brother, who lived in the Gulf, had gifted him a Nikon-70 camera. Wali had developed photography as a hobby ever since. He must have clicked hundreds of family photographs. His landscape photographs were mostly clicked in the golden light of the late noon. It was the light he loved. He had almost complete record of Salim and Meher growing up. He had never missed any important occasion.

Perhaps once! He reflected with deep pain in his heart now. He had refused to take out his camera during Salim's wedding. It was the most immature act to sulk like a child; the thought echoed yet again.

The photographs! He had completely forgotten about the photographs. If the golden hue hadn't reminded him of them, he would have perhaps lost them forever. Once back home, he would pack his entire collection, he decided. They would help him to recapitulate the time gone by. They would be the memoirs of his whole life and he would live the evening of his life through his sunny days. At least his past would remain with him; a happy past, for the future was uncertain now.

And he would take his camera too. Salim could use his camera. Otherwise, he didn't have much to pack. He would carry two pairs of day clothing and perhaps two pairs for the night. That would be enough for his needs. Moreover, he should have a light baggage in case the women needed assistance and in case they needed to sprint down to save their lives. But he should remember to pack some warm clothing for the winter too. He would have to do his packing himself. Sakina would have no time. She would have to do her own packing, after overcoming the shock. She and Meher too would have to pack the bare minimum, only what they would be able to carry easily. Ammi-Jaan will have to be packed off earlier, again with only essentials.

"It is not going to be easy for the women to leave their house, especially Sakina. She is so attached to it. Over the years, she has collected a whole lot of souvenirs from the places she had visited and other pieces to decorate the house so charmingly. Now she will have to leave her cherished collection behind." Wali's heart ached thinking of the sacrifice Sakina would have to make. He dreaded to face her and Meher once back home. Ammi-Jaan would perhaps be more accepting due to her mature outlook. He needed tact and time to make them understand.

He should be heading back home soon. He has been out for hours now and the chances of his vicious guests getting suspicious were on the increase.

But Wasim had still not come back. There was definitely something wrong. He had been gone for more than five hours now. He shouldn't have taken that long. Had he been discovered and captured by Shakeel and his wicked mates? Wali's mouth went dry at the thought.

He walked inside on the remedial mission. He had been drinking water the whole day to soothe his nerves. The tiffin carrier was lying untouched next to the thermos flask. Wasim had instructed him to eat the food that Ayesha had packed for them. But Wali had not felt hungry. He had had butterflies in his stomach the whole day and hunger had simply eluded him. Water had been his only requirement since left alone in the houseboat. He picked up the thermos flask but didn't notice its lightweight. Only when he tilted it to pour water, he found that it scarcely contained a few sips.

"There may be a mineral water bottle somewhere in the kitchen. Wasim surely would have bought some when he had customers over." With the thermos still in his hand, he walked towards the kitchen. He had barely reached the door of the kitchen when he heard some voices from the front side of the houseboat. The houseboat shook unsteadily as someone plodded up the wooden ladder.

"Thank God, Wasim has come back," Wali thought with relief. He forgot all about being thirsty and anxiously began to walk towards the rear door to greet Wasim, well knowing that he would come from that side. Then he stopped on his track.

Somebody was fiddling with the front lock. Why would Wasim do that? He had himself locked the front door to make it appear that the houseboat was moored and not operational. He had said so before leaving, then why was he opening that door now. "I should peep out and remind him not to open the door," Wali decided and took two steps towards the window closest to the main door. He was about to shift the curtain when he heard a voice saying, "The door is locked."

His hand froze in its position and a shiver traversed through his whole body like a bolt of electric current.

It was a familiar accent but it did not belong to Wasim. "Then where is Wasim? Has he been made captive and these men now have the knowledge of my presence on this houseboat?" Terror had Wali fixed to the spot.

Then somebody, sounding totally unfamiliar and distant, obviously inside a boat in the lake said, "I told you Wasim is not here. I haven't seen him in the last few days. Come back now. Let me take you back to the shore."

"Wasim is safe," Wali closed his eyes in relief and breathed slightly easy.

"No, wait. Check the place thoroughly." It was a stern voice from the same distance. Wali had also heard this voice before.

"Should I break the lock?" The first voice inquired.

"Why would you break the lock?" The voice full of surprise asked. He was seemingly the boatman.

Wali's heart skipped a beat. He turned to rush out. Perhaps, he should leave the boat and hide in the reeds.

"Don't be silly. You can't attract attention. I don't know when you will learn these simple facts. Check the other side." Wali heard the distant stern voice commanding.

He became immovable again.

"All right, all right. I will inspect the other side as well. But I tell you there is not a soul on the boat."

Subconsciously, Wali might have expected this to happen, but now that Shakeel had reached the houseboat, he was shocked beyond reckoning. Had he come in search of him? No, perhaps he had he come to investigate if Wasim was really out of town. He knew very well that Wali was very close to Wasim and in case any help was required, Wasim would be the first person Wali would contact. The stern voice unmistakably belonged to Hashim. Wali was now sure that Hashim was leading Shakeel around. He was the shrewdest, the most dangerous of the gang and the most hazardous for the safe execution of his plan.

Wali now heard Shakeel's footsteps fading down the passage. The boat rocked unsteadily as he strode on to reach the opposite side of the boat. He was coming to check the rear side, and the back door was ajar. It had remained open ever since Wasim had left. Wali was standing in the centre of the room. In two quick leaps he now reached the door, put the thermos flask on the floor, and quickly shut the double-leafed door. He then tried to push the latch in position. But it was stuck. Wali pushed harder. He shouldn't make any sounds but this old latch had become rough due to corrosion and languor. Wali frantically tried to shove it in place.

Shakeel would have reached the far end of the boat by now. It was the time to try the hardest, for he was the farthest from this point. He might not hear the sound, Wali hoped. He had to take the risk. If Shakeel found him here, the plan he had been hatching and following for the past many hours would be completely smashed into bits. He would immediately know that Wali had no intentions of gratifying him, instead he was surely setting up some scheme to hoax him and his companions. That would be catastrophic. That would be the end of everything that he was trying to preserve; his life and the lives of his loved ones. He couldn't allow that to happen.

Wali regretted not having followed his first impulse. Perhaps, there was still time and he was now tempted again to dash out right into the reeds and hide there. Wasim must have expected such a visit and that was why he had made similar suggestion. But the next moment, he considered the tremendous risks involved in that action. There may not be enough time and Shakeel might spot him dashing out. Moreover, the open rear door of the houseboat could set the men wondering. That would also be an invitation to them to inspect the interiors. His bag with all the important papers was inside. Now there was definitely no time even for a short journey of ten steps to go and fetch it. If it was discovered by these men, it would be disastrous. His best chance, therefore, would be to remain hidden inside, he hurriedly concluded.

He now set in motion the hardest and intense efforts to bolt the door by moving the large rusted latch up and down a few times. His nervousness was on the rise. His almost uncontrollably trembling hands were rather becoming a hindrance in securing the door, and with each passing second, executing the simple task was becoming harder. His hands had become clammy. Additionally, the little too prominent scratching sounds dismayed him and he halted his efforts. He desperately looked around to locate something, perhaps some oil to aid him to reduce the sound.

Caw....Caw...Caw...scratch...scratch...a crow hopped and cawed simultaneously on the railing right opposite. May be there were two birds for the scratching activity was quite frenzied for a single bird. "But what dear birds," Wali thought as he renewed his efforts to conceal his presence on the houseboat. He now clenched his teeth and directed the complete energy of his system onto his hands well knowing it was now or never. This was the last fraught attempt of the man for survival. And the providence surely supports the one who makes sincere efforts. The latch slid into the socket and the crows had provided the right kind of cover up.

"From where had this rescue team arrived?" Wali seriously mused.

Shakeel's footsteps were once again clear, approaching the back door now. Wali looked around in frantic movements of his eyes, to see where he could hide, where he would be totally concealed. Then he noticed, just in time, that the rear window's curtain was drawn aside. It had remained so after Wasim had pulled it aside in the morning. If Shakeel peeped in through the window, which he was most likely to do, he would be able to see him in the room clearly. And there was no time to find a hiding place now, for the sound of approaching footsteps were just a few metres away.

Wali decided to stay next to the door, and pressed himself as flat and as close to the door as possible. He would have to take this stake that it was probably the best hiding place. Unless Shakeel peeped from the extreme corner of the windowpane, he shouldn't be able to see him. Wali desperately inspected the room once more, shifting his eyes around to see if there was anything that might give Shakeel a clue of his presence inside. His black bag was well hidden under the bed. The tiffin carrier lay unopened on the table. Wali felt slightly comforted.

Then he spotted his spectacles lying on the table. Although, it was a very small item, but a person with a sharp mind would surely note it and perhaps wonder about its presence there. Shakeel definitely did not belong to the sharp-minded category, but Wali became worried that he might recognise his glasses he had with him throughout the previous evening. It was too late now even to rush to the table to collect them.

The footsteps, as expected, stopped at the door. Shakeel tried to push open the door and the door shook. So did Wali with it. He prayed with his eyes closed that the old latch should not give away. There was a harder push now. Wali too received a jerk. Thankfully, the latch did not divulge. The door was next shaken, as if the person expected to get an easy access into the interiors once the door fell apart. Along with the door, the houseboat swayed. Wali fought to maintain his balance. In the process, his foot struck the thermos lying on the floor and it began to topple. Wali leapt instantly to save its fall, for the sound produced would have surely made the devious person suspicious. Wali picked up the thermos at the nick of time and as he straightened, he received a mighty jerk from behind as the door was kicked hard. He almost lost his equilibrium. Another such jerk would have surely sent him crashing to the floor but fortunately the quaking stopped at this instant and the footsteps moved on. Wali instantly recovered his balance and then repeated the squeezing act. He once again stood fused to the door; as flat as possible.

As Wali had anticipated, the sound of the footsteps stopped at the window. Undoubtedly, the villain was peeping in. Wali tried his best to remain motionless. He held his breath and waited nervously. Minutes passed like hours. Lack of any sound indicated that the scoundrel was taking an undue long time to inspect the interiors. Why wasn't he moving away? Had he noted his glasses lying on the table? Or could he see him and was waiting for him to make a wrong move?

Time passed into perpetuity. Wali's heart was pounding so hard that he now got worried Shakeel might hear its thumping sound. To top it, he was finding it difficult to keep his shuddering body in check and remain absolutely still. At last the pounding sound of the footsteps occurred again and then began to recede.

When Shakeel had reached the other side of the houseboat, Wali was still glued to the rear door, as its extended attachment. He heard his crass voice say to the boatman, "O.K. let's go. There is no body here. Perhaps Wasim is really out of town."

Wali relaxed his taut body and began to breathe somewhat easier.

"I told you so. You were just wasting your time." It was the boatman.

"I was making sure. We had an important business matter to discuss with him. Never mind, there is always the next time," Shakeel tried to explain.

The houseboat tilted a bit to one side and slowly steadied itself. Wali subsequently noticed some faint lapping movements in the lake. And then, once again there was total silence.

He became aware of his shivering legs now. He needed to sit down but waited for a few more minutes before moving back into the room. Once the long stillness soothed his qualms, he walked away from the door on his unsteady legs. When he sat down on the chair, he realized that his whole body was shaking. He was angry at himself for being such a weakling. Never before in life had he felt so panicky. No one had ever been able to frighten him to such an extent. He wished he could bash up Shakeel, for that villain alone was the cause for his trepidation. Instead, he pounded his fist on the table a number of times and uttered under breath, "That one time poor boy... in pitiable condition...hungry and destitute... whom I had picked up from the streets and given shelter...who was never mistreated... that helpless urchin today has turned out to be such an ungrateful scoundrel... such *namak haraam*!" There was nobody who had ever seen him so angry and there was nobody to see him so at the moment. And if somebody had seen his blazing eyes at present, the person would have immediately grasped the extent of his anger and would have remained at a safer distance for self preservation. Unfortunately, he was in no position to exhibit his anger in front of those who truly deserved it.

He had never ever been provoked to such an extent that it could make him sick. "I shouldn't have provided protection to this debased serpent," he thought, and Wali had labelled him thus for the second time today. Why wouldn't he; it had been less than twenty four hours and this man had made life hell for him.

Life before that had been so peaceful. He and Sakina were aging gracefully. They had fulfilled major duties of life. He was planning to take Ammi-Jaan and Sakina for Haj. It would have been possible in a year or two. Life had been almost free of worries. Minor worries are the part of life. But today a major crisis had come visiting him, shattering his tranquil life into fragments.

Lately, he had been looking for a suitable match for Meher. Sakina had been pestering him regarding this issue. But it was not so easy to find a match for a girl who was not only extremely beautiful but very intelligent. On top of that, his Meher was highly qualified. Only a more qualified doctor would have been suitable for her. He had conducted a futile search among the circle of his friends and acquaintances. Then recently he had taken his petition to *Maulvi* Sahib at the Hazratbal mosque, as he was the person who would be in contact with a large section of the town's population. *Maulvi* Sahib had promised to keep it in mind and inform Wali if he found anyone suitable for his highly educated daughter.

But now things had taken a terrible turn today. He, along with his family, was hanging from a thin string, and if it broke, they all would plunge into darkness forever. Therefore, it became mandatory for him to fight his battle for survival suspended from that thin string.

It had all begun yesterday evening, when this rascal, Shakeel had emerged form nowhere to torment him. It was as if the door of hell had opened up to let out some evil spirits.

Chapter 14

The whole day Wali's mind had been meandering through the streets of his memories and now it had reached the most recent events; the most dreadful and disgraceful ones. As these events began to unroll in his mind, he began to pace the room in an agitated state. He wished it was all a dream, though a horrifying dream but a dream nevertheless, which would vanish the moment he would open his eyes. Unfortunately, it was a harsh and bitter reality. Last evening was the most unfortunate evening of his life; an evening which had initiated a quake, had him caught in a maelstrom and badly shaken.

Wali had been habitually taking evening round of his orchard ever since he had planted it; to keep regular check on it. Besides, it gave him good exercise. Although, he didn't have to worry about the routine tending, for loyal Abdul's supervision was absolutely reliable, but one had to be alert for early signs of pest or disease infestation. Any carelessness in that regard could incur heavy financial losses. A few years ago, the Leaf-curl as well as the Brown-rot diseases had affected a large measure of the fruit crop and Wali had promised himself never to allow such infestation recur in his orchard.

The previous evening, Wali had been happy to see his healthy trees once again richly laden with fruit. He had also gone through the accounts of the year's sale of the orchard produce. The cherry crop, as well as the peaches and the plums had already been harvested and sold. The Gilas Awal number and the Gilas Misri varieties of cherry had been much in demand in all major states of the country and had brought him considerable earnings. The Quetta peaches too had sold well and so had the Santa-Rosa and the Green-Gauge varieties of plums.

But the main produce of his orchard was the apple crop with two hundred and fifty trees of mixed variety. The famous indigenous species like Hazratbali and Kesari had also been harvested and profitably marketed. Others were yet to ripen. Amri variety was always in great demand. Orders came from as far as the central and Southern India. But the Red Delicious and the Golden varieties sold the best, especially in the metropolitan cities. And this main apple crop was still unripe. Wali had inspected a large part of the orchard and expected a bountiful yield of the core fruit crop too. He was confident that the key apple sale would help fill his coffers this year too.

He had thus returned home in high spirits, least expecting that this happiness and contentment was to be short lived and would soon be squashed like a rotten fruit under the boots of some vile beings.

His nightmare soon began.

He had barely removed his *pheran* when Abdul came to inform him of some visitors. He was quite surprised. He wasn't expecting anyone that evening. Moreover, it was close to the dinner time and nobody paid visits that late. Not Uninvited.

"Who has come visiting at this hour, Abdul?" He inquired.

"*Huzoor,* there are couple of men whom I don't remember having seen before. They asked for you, so I came directly to inform you of the visitors. If you so desire, I can go back and demand their identity." Abdul offered.

"No...no...I will check myself," Wali declared.

Putting on his slippers and hurriedly throwing a shawl over his shoulders, Wali went to the door to receive the visitors. There were four men standing outside. In the fading light of the approaching night, their features were not clearly visible. He couldn't place them nor recollected having seen any one of them before. On top, they appeared clandestine figures, slovenly encompassed in woollen blankets.

"How can I help you?" Wali had asked. At the same time, he had mounting worry in his mind. Things were not right in the Valley. He must be wary of the strangers. What were these sneaky looking characters doing here anyway? What business could they possibly have with him?

Then one of them, the shortest one barely five and a half feet tall, said, "It seems Wali Sahib you haven't recognised me. You have forgotten me pretty soon!"

Wali still couldn't identify him. Though there was faint familiarity in his voice, yet Wali couldn't discern at the moment where he had met this person. In the nightly shadows, he tried peering at his face but encountered total lack of allusion. Seeing him silent, the same man spoke again, "I am Shakeel, Wali Sahib. You have forgotten your Shakeel."

Now the veranda lights suddenly came alive. It was probably Abdul who had done the desired job. The features of the man standing in front of him currently became clearer.

"Oh Shakeel…! How could you expect me to recognise you? It has been ages since I last saw you. You sound so different. On top, your face is hidden behind your newly acquired feature; your beard. And why have you wrapped yourself in a blanket? Winters are yet far away." Wali had spoken it all with a friendly laugh. Then turning towards the others he said, "You all must be Shakeel's friends. Come in please."

They instantly responded to the invitation and eagerly followed Wali inside his house.

Having invited them in, Wali was uncertain where the guests should be seated. They all appeared quite unkempt and emitted foul smell of people who hadn't bathed for days. It seemed that their blankets hadn't ever been washed.

Usually, the labourers and the small businessmen were received in the veranda outside. Some garden furniture was installed there for the purpose. But then such visits invariably took place during daytime when it was warm enough to sit outside. There was only one formal sitting room inside the house where the close family friends were entertained. The present guests couldn't be taken there, for Wali was sure Sakina would be unhappy if her upholstery was soaked with the fusty reek of the visitors.

Wali had, therefore, slowed his pace to think of a place where Shakeel and his friends could be taken. Perhaps the parlour adjoining the main sitting room would be fine. Though Sakina had decorated it too with some fine furniture, but it was less ornate and good enough for these smelly beings.

Shakeel seemed to have read the uncertainty of his mind and before Wali could proceed towards the parlour, he traversed ahead of him and led all to the main sitting room. Wali was considerably annoyed but was left with no choice other than to follow them.

The only sign of soberness that Shakeel had revealed was to remove the mud plastered dirty shoes outside the sitting room before entering it, the act which had fortunately been followed by the rest.

Once inside the sitting room, the guests immediately proceeded to remove their blankets. Each one was carrying a backpack, which were then kept in a corner of the room. They began making a big pile of the foul smelling clothing in the corner. Wali stood aside and politely waited for them to finish. Then, to Wali's surprise, they also removed their *pherans*, which they were not expected to do if they had planned a short stay. As soon as they had done that, Wali's eyes instantly caught sight of the prominent possession with each person and had him startled. All four men had rifles strapped across their shoulders. Wali instantly became tensed and speechless. He wasn't sure if he had done a wise thing of allowing these odious men inside his house.

They unstrapped their rifles next. The senior most man, who appeared to be in his mid thirties, examined the room, obviously looking for a place to keep his rifle. The others waited. Then the man came upon a decision and the others followed his example. They placed their rifles side by side on the floor, leaning them against the contrasting white washed wall. The presence of the four rifles was well pronounced and quite unnerving. Despite his vexation, Wali watched the proceedings passively, though he had begun to feel mild jitters.

If the visitors had come with the intention of a simple social call, what was the need to carry guns? Some warning bells began to ring in Wali's mind but presently he was helpless. He had barely invited them in and couldn't ask them to leave straight away. But, he would try to remove the visitors from his house as soon as possible. The best stance would now be; to offer them tea, exhibit a friendly guise and then ask them to depart.

"Please, make yourselves comfortable," he politely offered. Shakeel immediately occupied the exquisitely carved walnut wood chair with an expensive cushion woven from the finest silk. He would have surely known that it was a prized family heritage and meant only for important guests. Wali watched the proceedings helplessly as the others plonked themselves on the cushy sofas.

Wali then sat down on a simple side chair.

Once seated, Wali studied Shakeel more minutely. He had thinned quite a bit. The chubbiness on his face was gone, and it had become quite gaunt. He was scruffy unlike the times when he worked in the house and neatness was a strict requisite. On his skinny face, his aquiline nose had emerged like a hooked beak of an eagle. His dry fractured lips were almost repulsive. Wali had always considered him to be a tolerably pleasant looking fellow but now he seemed to have lost whatever charm of youth he had in his brutishness.

"What has he done to himself? Doesn't he realize that he was much better off living here?" Wali silently considered, having observed it all in a glance.

He opened the conversation, "Shakeel how could you expect me to recognize you. You have changed quite a bit. You have become a man from the boy you used to be when you lived with us."

"Yes, Wali Sahib! Time has flown. And you are right. I have changed," Shakeel replied in a pompous tone.

Wali was faintly irked by Shakeel's manners. He was treating him as an equal, addressing him by his name. The previous respectful way of addressing him as his master; *Huzoor*, was missing. But he chose to ignore it, for his concentration was focussed on scheming a way of getting rid of the group as fast as possible.

Wali instantly proceeded to achieve the desired by calling out to Abdul. He immediately responded. "Abdul, do you mind serving some tea to our guests?"

Abdul nodded and then turned to go but something made him stop. Wali too glanced at Shakeel wondering why he hadn't greeted Abdul with whom he had shared the living space when he lived in this house. He noted that Shakeel was looking down at the carpet, totally ignoring Abdul. But Abdul now peered openly at Shakeel and then instead of giving a smile of recognition he frowned, perhaps after noting him posted on a high chair next to his master.

"If I am not mistaken, you look quite like someone I once knew." He opened the conversation with slight caution.

"Is that so Abdul Bhai?" Shakeel now looked up and answered with a self important smile. It immediately brought bearing of recognition on Abdul's face and he at once became bold.

"That person was a mischief maker. I wonder if you are the same person who would bother me all the time with his rowdy behaviour." Abdul went on deliberately.

Wali wondered why Abdul was instantly and directly attacking Shakeel. This was not expected of him, despite the fact that Abdul was a straightforward man.

"Wow Abdul Bhai, you have a remarkable memory. But surely, I wasn't rowdy." Shakeel was immediately defensive. His expressions clearly depicted his annoyance and he sheepishly glanced at his friends to perceive their reaction. Only the youngest member had a gleeful smile at this war of words. The other two wore quite stern masks, Wali noted.

"Not only rowdy but also snooty. And except for the messy beard that you have grown, I can see that there isn't much change even now," Abdul insisted upon continuing with his annotations.

Wali knew well that Abdul could be quite blunt if he chose. If he didn't like something, he wouldn't hesitate to give his opinion. Wali presently understood that Abdul was probably annoyed by Shakeel's conduct of acting important by totally disregarding his presence now as well as at the time of his arrival. Even though Abdul was the first to meet Shakeel, he had totally given him a cold shoulder. And that was what had almost certainly piqued Abdul.

Before this exchange could turn unpleasant, Wali once again reminded Abdul to prepare tea for them.

Wali noted the way Abdul shifted his glance from Shakeel to the chair and then making a face before leaving the room. He derived that Abdul hadn't liked Shakeel's attitude of overlooking the protocol, and sitting on a chair higher than the one on which sat his one time master. In addition, he possibly hadn't liked the idea of serving the person who was once a junior helping hand in the house.

Doubtlessly, the first impression that Wali had formed of his foursome visitors was exclusively negative, but as a gracious host, though a reluctant one, he chose to keep them amused till they decided to leave.

So, turning his attention back towards Shakeel he said, "You have not introduced your friends to me. Are they all from your village?"

"No, they are from different places in the valley. Yet, my friends are more like my brothers." Shakeel pronounced the word brothers prominently and Wali knew this was in reaction to Abdul's recent comments, whom he now probably considered his adversary.

He simply nodded.

Shakeel then continued pointing first at the oldest looking member of the group, "Hashim Bhai has come to our Valley on a mission from ...."

And Hashim immediately interrupted. "Aren't names enough, when we are all from the same Valley and belong to the same religion? Shakeel, you need to tell only names."

Wali was quick to grasp that he was the gang leader, since he was also the man who had decided where to keep their rifles. He was now becoming convinced that they were members of some outlawed militant outfit. They surely didn't appear to belong to some religious faction. And donning rifles; what other mission could they be on except for spreading mayhem?

So as expected, after leaving his job at their house Shakeel had become a militant! That was why their identity was to be kept secret. This inference increased Wali's worry manifolds. This Hashim fellow, who looked quite stern, was perhaps from across the border. He was the tallest man of the group, a little above six feet in height. And he was a fellow from whom most people would like to distant themselves. His thin lips were shut tight inside bushy dark brown moustaches and beard. It appeared they hadn't opened into a smile for ages and were therefore jammed. His narrow piercing eyes were icy cold and full of malice. His shallow complexion was pockmarked, which added to his severity. Wali would have to be wary of what he talked to him.

"This is Ahmed and this is my close buddy Shaukat," Shakeel completed the introductions, keeping them the briefest possible this time.

Wali wasn't sure at this instant if those were their real names. But he wasn't interested in knowing them either. Though in the brief period, he had reviewed the personalities of his guests minutely.

Ahmed had a long red beard. He was wearing a turban and appeared to be about thirty. He was a burly man of medium height. His small eyes were restive and his nose was stubby, as if somebody had boxed and flattened it. There was a scar running through the entire length of his left cheek and Wali was convinced that it was made in a knife attack. He seemed a little easier going than his senior, for he smiled and nodded at Wali on being introduced. Yet his eyes were unsmiling. They were definitely not the eyes of a merciful man. However, he was better of without that smile, for his scar became prominent and his left eye flickered when he smiled, adding brutishness to his appearance.

Shaukat was an inch or two taller than Shakeel, but he was a juvenile. He hadn't even grown beard. He was still soft and immature; not more than seventeen or eighteen. He had quite regular features; in fact, he was the most pleasant looking person in the cluster of uncouth blokes. "What is this young boy doing among a bunch of cruel looking men?" Wali wondered. He was also too young to be given the responsibility of handling a rifle. Such youngsters were quite capable of making use of the power of gun in an immature way, impulsively, committing drastic mistakes, Wali considered seriously.

Wali peeked at Shakeel once more, more intently this time and realized that he too had acquired that rugged appearance that comes with a lot of outdoor activity. But the fact that he had undertaken some perverse jobs was clearly revealed by the savage look in his eyes. It was definitely a group of wild and spiteful men, barring the youngest member, who was perhaps a new recruit. As a result, he made such a stark contrast to the other members of his group. His eyes still radiated smile and warmth still exuded from his person. He hadn't yet committed a serious crime, concluded Wali.

"When did you come to Srinagar? Was it recently or you have been here for long?" Wali tried to keep up the conversation.

"Wali Sahib, we have just arrived here. Yours is the first house we have come visiting directly after alighting from the bus," it was Hashim answering the question.

'Oh, I see," was all Wali managed to utter in face of his dwindling spirits. He had begun to anticipate barrage of more undesirable revelations. He began to sense some strange distressing iciness in the room. He had never felt so uncomfortable in any company all his life as he was presently feeling.

Abdul brought in tea and he was grateful for the interruption. All of a sudden, he wanted Abdul to remain in the room with him but couldn't find an immediate reason to convey it to him. Abdul left after serving tea, strangely without uttering a word this time. He was in no mode to demonstrate sociability towards the group, Wali realized.

Over the loud slurping of tea, the crude sound which invariably all the guests made, Wali tried to continue polite talk.

"So Shakeel, what do you do these days? Are you working close to your village or…?"

"Not at all close to my village." Shakeel interjected and for unknown reason they all laughed.

"Well Wali Sahib, my work takes me to far off places. One day I am here and the next day miles away. I travel from place to place, at times across the border."

Wali knew what he was implying and therefore he chose not to make further inquiry.

But Shakeel continued to give him more information, for that was the task he had come for. "Wali Sahib, I am not a mere servant in somebody's house anymore. I have a big bank balance."

The two senior visitors now smiled knowingly at Shakeel's statement. Shaukat nodded vigorously in agreement.

Wali immediately flinched. He could clearly grasp how he must have acquired a big bank balance. He changed the topic.

"Where are you guys staying?" He asked next.

"We are your uninvited guests, Wali Sahib. How could I think of staying anywhere else but with you? Ever since I left a few years ago, I never came back to this town. It is my first visit here in years. And I have come specially to meet you."

"Oh, is that so?" Wali said and was tongue-tied for a while, his depression having multiplied manifold at the information. They planned to stay with him. He could not refuse. These were not the men one could afford to offend. You never know how they would react. They might not hesitate to take extreme steps. He would have to be careful… be diplomatic. He had no choice but to accommodate them for the night. Hopefully, they would go away tomorrow morning. Seeing the men's eyes on him, he then loudly said, "Sure! You can stay the night with me. I will ask Abdul to clean the outhouse and arrange for four beds. But right now it is time for dinner and I will inform the mistress of the house to have enough food ready for all of us." Saying so, Wali left the room.

He went straight to the kitchen where Abdul was preparing some curry. "What is Shakeel doing here, *Huzoor*?" Abdul instantly asked in an undertone. "And I don't like his company. *Huzoor*, ask them to leave."

"Abdul, it is not so easy. They have expressed the desire to stay here for the night," Wali informed him.

"Stay here with us? No *Huzoor*, impossible. Ask them to go somewhere else, perhaps a guest house," Abdul sounded adamant.

"Abdul, we cannot annoy them. They may get irked with us. We can't take that risk," Wali tried to explain.

Abdul then nodded with the most worried expression on his face. "*Huzoor*, they are carrying guns. Are they terrorists? Has Shakeel become a terrorist?" He wanted confirmation from Wali of what he suspected.

"Abdul, it is better to overlook certain things. Just be careful you don't utter anything which may annoy them. Avoid confronting Shakeel too. I don't think he is at all reliable now. It is better not to talk much. After the dinner is ready, prepare their beds in the outhouse. Perhaps, you can sleep here tonight, inside the house," Wali suggested.

"Yes *Huzoor* that is a good idea. I will sleep inside the house. I won't be able to sleep a wink in the company of those horrid gunmen," Abdul declared vehemently.

That would be a good arrangement, Wali thought. Making Abdul sleep inside the house would be safe for him as well as for the ladies of the house. As such Abdul was a big mouth. It would be very difficult for him not to speak out his mind when left alone with Shakeel, and he would also be ever ready to give a piece of his mind to the rest of them too, especially when his tongue would be free to waggle in Wali's absence.

Wali nodded giving his approval and proceeded to find Sakina.

As he reached the staircase to go to his bedroom upstairs, he heard a faint sound of laughter coming from Ammi-Jaan's room. "So as usual, the women are at their gossip session," Wali thought with certain fondness and walked into Ammi Jaan's room. She and Sakina were engrossed in some interesting chitchat and appeared highly amused at what they were discussing. "Bless these women," he thought. "They have always lived together like a mother and a daughter."

Chapter 14

153

He politely apologised for interrupting their conversation and requested Sakina to follow him as he needed to discuss something urgent. Sakina immediately collected the knitting material spread around and followed Wali who led her to their upstairs bedroom.

"Sakina, that good for nothing Shakeel has come back," Wali informed Sakina as soon as they stepped inside their bedroom. Sakina didn't react to the statement. Her facial expression revealed what she probably wanted to say, "So what? There was no need to climb all those stairs to give this information." Wali then continued, "He says he has come to meet us. And he has not come alone. There are three dangerous looking men with him. I think they all belong to some terrorist outfit."

This statement had an impact of a thunderbolt on her. "*Ya Allah!*" She sounded highly alarmed. "Get rid of them quick. I don't want them in my house." And she was quite vocal in her reaction.

"Sakina speak softly. I don't want them to hear our conversation. And that is precisely why I have brought you up here. They are unreliable men. We should not annoy them. And it is not so easy to get rid of them. They have expressed their desire to stay with us. I have asked Abdul to arrange for their stay in the outhouse. Abdul will stay inside the house tonight."

"Will they go away tomorrow morning?" Sakina immediately wanted to know, reluctantly accepting the situation since her husband had already committed himself. But the fear in her voice was more than obvious.

"I am sure they will. Now see to it that dinner is served to all. There is no need to make it elaborate. Keep it simple," Wali advised her.

Meher, who was in her room till now, walked in with a book in her hand. When she found her parents talking in undertones, she immediately got curious to know what was happening.

"Why Abbu and Ammi, what are these secret talks going on. Can I interrupt them?"

"Nothing really of importance Meher, except that fellow Shakeel has come to meet us. He has come with some friends and will be staying the night with us," Wali casually informed her.

"Oh, so we have some guests tonight. Ammi Ji, if you need any help let me know, though I think Shakeel can give you a helping hand as he has been doing earlier. By the way what does he do now?" Meher asked.

"I haven't asked him that, nor am I interested in knowing. His friends appear rather sneaky characters and I want them out of the house as soon as possible," Wali replied.

"Well, I too would like to keep my distance from the sneaky characters, though if Ammi Ji wants then I can come down to help," Meher offered again.

It now suddenly occurred to Wali that he should keep both the ladies away from the fellows; especially the women's eyes should not fall on the rifles that the men had kept on display. That would unnecessarily alarm them. "I think Abdul can help your Ammi in the kitchen. And there is no need for anyone of you to come to the sitting room. Stay away from these unwanted guests. Both of you needn't be bothered about their presence." Wali almost ordered them.

"Abbu, who is interested in that half witted Shakeel? I rather stay in my room and read my book. As such I have come home to laze around and renew my energy for hectic hospital schedule. Since I am not really required, Ammi ji, I don't mind dinner being served in my room." Meher then retreated to her temporary indolence.

Sakina followed Wali downstairs to go to the kitchen so that she could help Abdul to prepare extra dinner. "Sakina, as soon as your work is over, go upstairs. Eat your dinner with Meher and stay in your rooms. Let the winding up of the kitchen work be done by Abdul tonight," Wali instructed his wife.

Having done the groundwork, Wali walked back towards the sitting room. As he neared it, he heard voices indulged in some fervent discussion. He couldn't understand a word, for the discussion was in undertones. As Wali entered the room, the murmurs instantly died down.

"They are up to something," Wali was convinced. He hoped that it was nothing to do with him. It couldn't possibly be, for he was a simple peace loving man. He was totally against any violent means for solving disputes and Shakeel knew it very well.

He sat down in his original seat. There was silence for a while. Wali's mind probed to find some topic to discuss. What could be discussed with these unknown men of completely unknown pursuit? One discussed the topics of common interest; about professional matters and perhaps politics. But with

Chapter 14

these men, who surely indulged in some shady activities, such discussions would be risky. It was better to follow what he had advised Abdul, "Speak as less as possible." When they would take offence to some casual statement was unpredictable. If he had judged right, they definitely appeared a bunch of reckless fiends with nefarious designs. Yes, he could discuss about weather. But then weather cycle this year had been as normal as possible. The latest climate issue was the Global Warming. But that subject would be quite alien to them. And then why would these gun-toting men be interested in the environmental issues?

Thus, Wali's search for a topic was going waste and he was unable to find a way to end the prolonged and embarrassing silence.

Then to his relief Shakeel broke the silence. "So Wali Sahib, how is everyone? I see no activity around. When I was here, the house used to be vibrant and spirited. Where are the dwellers of the house? I don't even see Abba-Jaan."

"He had never addressed Abba-Jaan as such. It was exclusively my privilege," Wali thought with contempt. Loudly he said, "Abba-Jaan is no more. He left for heavenly abode more than four years ago, shortly after you left."

"Oh! That is sad," Shakeel said.

Wali thought that Shakeel didn't appear sad at all. In fact, he was clearly relieved. He appeared to relax immediately. He had been always scared of Abba-Jaan, despite his show of insolence just before leaving, for he knew Abba-Jaan would not tolerate any nonsense. If he had been present in this room, he would have probed the type of work the men were engaged at, and specifically the reason for carrying the guns around. Perhaps, having seen the guns, he would have refused point blank to provide them any shelter even for a night.

"Am I a weakling?" Wali wondered with dismal spirits, "For, I couldn't gather the courage to refuse them lodgings in my house."

There was return of the disconcerting silence in the room. Shaukat was keeping himself amused by wandering his vision around, looking at the various pieces of adornment, most of which were handpicked by Sakina. Wali noticed the other three men exchanging glances time and again.

Then Shakeel further inquired, "And how are the mistress and your children?"

"They are fine," Wali said with a kind of finality, for he wanted to avoid discussing his family with them.

But Shakeel did not relent. "I don't see anyone around," he said again.

"The mistress is busy with Ammi-Jaan. It is her dinnertime and she needs to be looked after. She is old you know," Wali answered.

"And the children? I don't see Salim Bhai around. Is he in town?" Shakeel next asked.

Good he is not around, Wali thought with certain relief. He realized that even if Salim was in town, Wali would have tried his best to keep him away from Shakeel and his shady cronies.

"Salim is working outside the town," He told Shakeel. For unknown reasons, Wali did not want to provide Shakeel with more information regarding his son. He also noted Shakeel nodding his head and smile.

"Did he complete his engineering studies?" Shakeel continued his conversation.

"Yes...yes, he did," was all Wali was ready to say.

There was once again silence. What more was there to discuss with a man who had once broken all bonds with them and had preferred to follow some wretched ideas than to indulge in hard and honest work, thought Wali. Moreover, before he had left, Shakeel's conduct had also been doubtful. He had become impudent and conceited. And Wali thought that Abdul was right in his judgement; Shakeel hadn't changed much in that regard.

Meanwhile Shakeel was looking down at the carpet in deep thought. "What is he thinking?" Wali wondered. "He is hesitating to speak about something. There appears to be some specific purpose behind his visit?" Wali began to get even more worried.

Then Shakeel once again looked at Wali.

"And Meher? I heard she is a doctor," Shakeel now inquired.

"That is right. She completed her studies a few months ago. She is working in a hospital," Wali said proudly. After the utterance, he realized that Shakeel hadn't even addressed Meher as sister, something he had been doing when he worked in the house. Wali was annoyed that he was taking too many liberties.

Chapter 14

For the first time, one of Shakeel's friends intruded. He was Shaukat. "A doctor is the most useful person in society, especially when a doctor is required to dress the injuries or extract the bullets embedded in a body."

And Hashim immediately glared at him followed by producing an artificial cough. Wali grasped the gesture immediately; he realized that the cough was a warning signal to indicate that the person had spoken the forbidden words. Wali dismissed his statement as an immature thought.

"I believe Meher is here these days," Shakeel then asked.

"Yes she is. But how do you know?" Wali was slightly taken aback.

"We had visited Pehalgaon before coming here. We had come to know that Meher is working there, in the government hospital. There we were informed that she had gone home on a few days leave," Shakeel explained.

"Why did you need to visit the hospital? Is every thing all right?" Wali asked with curiosity. He immediately presumed that probably Shakeel or one of the accompanying men was in dire need of medical help and Meher was perhaps the only known doctor who could help them.

But before Shakeel could answer, Abdul entered the room to announce that the dinner was ready. Usually water and basin would have been brought into the room for guests to wash their hands. But Abdul announced loudly, "There is a tap outside. Shakeel I'm sure you remember where it is. Whoever thinks it is important to wash before eating may go out for that purpose."

When the four men left the room, Abdul quickly brought a *samovar* and a towel to help Wali wash his hands. He was still frowning and resentment was writ large on his face. Wali was slightly amused at his infuriated countenance, which was a contrast to his usual jollity, though he didn't comment on it. But Abdul was not the one to keep quiet.

"Does Shakeel think I am his servant? He is sitting with you as if he is an important guest. Can't he come to help in the kitchen?"

All Wali had said was, "Shhhhhhhh…," for he had heard the men approaching.

Once inside, the men were led to the dining area that was an extension of the sitting room, but a level higher. They sat cross-legged on the floor cushions with low individual tables in front. Abdul brought large steel plates with small steel bowls arranged in a semicircle. The lentils, mutton curry and dry vegetables had been filled in the bowls. Frowning Abdul efficiently served everyone. He then brought a plate of rice and served a portion to all.

They ate in silence for a while.

Then Ahmed spoke for the first time in his gruff voice, "The food is really good. For a long time we have been eating whatever has been available. Only when you eat hot home cooked food, you realize its value. Isn't it Wali Sahib?" But he sounded so bland that Wali took it as a formality and didn't find any need to reply except giving a lukewarm smile.

"Oh Yes! Your servant is a very good cook Wali Sahib, or has the delicious food been cooked by the mistress?" It was Shaukat this time. His compliment sounded absolutely genuine and Wali couldn't help responding.

"Well, it is a joint effort of the both, I am sure," He answered.

More silence followed.

On Abdul's next entry into the room with a few glasses of water, Shaukat demanded, "Bhai, serve me some more rice. My appetite is insatiable today."

Abdul immediately quipped, "Be careful about how much you eat. The mistress and I have yet to eat, so don't gobble down everything. Hmm,...But you can see the rice plate lying there. Some rice is left in it. Help yourself." And he left the room.

"Abdul has never been that rude with anybody. He wouldn't mind cooking more rice but had never ever refused to serve anyone. He really appears irritated. He has been badly put off by the coarse guests. But then he had never gotten along with Shakeel even in those days when Shakeel resided in this house. There had always been regular wrangling between them." Wali silently ate and thought.

When the dinner was over, Wali received immediate indication of overstuffed tummies of the men as the after dinner silence was interrupted by a few loud burps. The room stuffed with the unwashed smell began to become stuffier and Wali looked for an excuse to leave the room for some fresh air. He got up to call Abdul but he had barely taken two steps towards the door when Abdul came on his own to remove the used dishes. Wali then Proceeded to open the window facing the compound. Below the window were the four guns still

Chapter 14   159

on display. Wali stood a metre away from them, avoiding any physical contact with them lest they made him feel defiled. Bending double, he reached for the latch from a distance and managed to open the window. Fresh air instantly rushed in, bringing him relief.

As he turned, he noted the four stiff figures staring at him. The men hadn't liked his close proximity to the guns. Wali guessed the rifles were loaded and immediately moved away, at the same time irked at their attitude.

He now wanted to dismiss the men for the night right away, when Shakeel said, "Wow Abdul Bhai that was a good dinner. Now if you could brew us some *kahwa*, it will be great."

Before Abdul could refuse point-blank, Wali said, "Yes Abdul, *Kahwa* is a good idea." It had immediately occurred to him that perhaps this digestive brew was an absolute requirement of the men who obviously had overeaten.

The men then got up and went out to wash once again. Wali too went to the kitchen to see if Sakina and Meher had eaten or if there was enough food for Abdul. Abdul had prepared two plates and was taking dinner for the women upstairs. Wali peeped into the rice vessel which had sufficient rice left for Abdul. Satisfied, he retreated from the kitchen.

When he came back to the sitting room, Shakeel and his friends hadn't returned. Perhaps they were enjoying the pleasant breeze outside, Wali concluded.

When Abdul came in with a pot of *kahwa*, they still hadn't come in.

"Abdul, call the guests in, otherwise *Kahwa* will become cold," Wali requested him.

"*Huzoor,* your order can't be refused, otherwise Shakeel and his friends can drink ice cold *kahwa* as far as I am concerned." Making this statement, he left unhappily to look for the guests.

Wali considered retiring for the night now and not entertain the guests anymore; instead he sat browsing through a magazine, unable to make up his mind. Perhaps, he hesitated leaving the frank and blunt Abdul alone with them.

Abdul came in after more than five minutes. "*Huzoor*, they are coming. I had to go hunting for them all over till I located them in the orchard. I wonder what they were doing in our orchard. Why should Shakeel take them there? It is not his father's property."

"They were perhaps taking a walk after overfilling their stomachs. Don't be bothered about them. Hopefully they will depart tomorrow, so let us tolerate them for a night," Wali suggested.

"It was alright if Shakeel had come alone to visit us, having realized the importance of the people who had once sheltered him. But, what was the need to bring along a bunch of scoundrels?" Abdul pronounced the next critique.

Before Wali could respond, the men were once again heard en route to the room and Wali gestured at Abdul to keep quiet.

Abdul served them *kahwa,* unsmiling and reproving.

Wali had always found this hot sweet and spicy beverage with the predominant flavour of saffron very soothing. He took a deep sip. Abdul started to go back towards the kitchen but stopped at the door and turned to address Shakeel. "Will you be here for breakfast in the morning?" But without giving him time to respond he continued, "We eat breakfast at nine. If you are planning to leave before that, then *alvida,"* Saying so, he marched out towards the kitchen.

Wali couldn't help smiling at his candour.

Shakeel now addressed Wali, "Abdul Bhai is very keen to know when we are leaving. Well! We don't have much time and we can't stay for long but it all depends on you now Wali Sahib."

"Depends on me? How?" Wali was fittingly surprised.

"Wali Sahib, I am here on a business with you. But before we discuss it, I would once again like to remind you that I am not the same Shakeel you used to know once. I have saved quite a bit of money. I am planning to buy some land with it later. Right now, I barely stay for more than a few days at a place. So money is safely stacked in a bank."

Wali listened to him quietly. It was none of his business if Shakeel had a bank balance. Neither did he care if had one. He did not want any business dealings with him either. If he was planning to share his business with that money then he should forget it. Or, were they going to threaten him into submission? He became alert. He should be careful how he handled these men. He must to be polite and apply tact to evade them, he reminded himself again. He couldn't afford to be blunt like Abdul, for these men did not take Abdul seriously and overlooked what he uttered, taking it to be non serious jabbering. But each word that he would utter would be weighed and construed.

Chapter 14

"I am happy Shakeel that you are doing well and have a bank balance now. How did you exactly hit upon your treasure?" Wali asked with a crack of smile, in an endeavour to turn the conversation light hearted.

"I am in a militant outfit, in the Liberation Army. And we get well paid for it."

Hashim coughed as a warning but Shakeel paid him no attention.

Wali squirmed uncomfortably on his seat. Here was an open declaration that it was ill gotten money. Shakeel had obviously been paid for committing some murders.

"I don't know what you are doing is right Shakeel. But I don't want to discuss all that now. You know my point of view quite well." Wali's voice had acquired sternness despite his reluctance to do so.

"Those were your father's views. What about your own views?" Shakeel asked rather impolitely.

Wali was irked by his effrontery. He measured the question for a few moments and then spoke slowly and politely, "Abba-Jaan was my father and bound to have his influence on me. I am proud to say that my father was man of great vision and much above petty discrepancies prevalent in today's world. I may not have reached his loftiness of thought yet, but I think and feel the same way as my Abba-Jaan and you also know that very well. I think we are in this world to share love and peace, not wage war."

Hashim and Ahmed stiffened at Wali's soft retort and Wali noted it unmistakably. He received unpleasant stares from them. They were surely irked, for words like love and peace were not part of their vocabulary.

Nevertheless Wali continued to iterate, "The world is so beautiful and this beauty becomes manifold with care and affection, with good relationships shared by all."

Shakeel exchanged glances with Hashim and Ahmed. Hashim nodded. Wali watched passively without speculating its meaning.

"Wali Sahib, I am here exactly for that purpose. I want to extend my hand in relationship." Shakeel now grasped the opportunity.

"What is he uttering?" Wali wondered. "One extends a hand of friendship. Shakeel must make foolish statements."

"We were never enemies Shakeel," Wali said aloud with a smile.

There was a complete silence in the room now. The irritating slurping sounds had all of a sudden ceased. Shakeel kept his cup of *kahwa* on the table. Others were holding their cups as if trying to warm up their hands. Wali picked up his cup to take a sip. He realized that four pairs of eyes were on him now, as if stabbing through him. He suddenly felt alone and extremely uncomfortable. The atmosphere had suddenly turned sinister as if something foreboding was about to take place.

He focussed his attention on Shakeel and giving him another weak smile, waited for his response.

"Wali Sahib, I am here to ask for the hand of your daughter in marriage," Shakeel now said loudly and with overconfident assertion.

The smile froze on Wali's lips. He was stunned. His heart skipped many beats. Had he heard the right words? He gasped. He quickly took a sip of *kahwa* to overcome his shock and he choked on it. He had a bad bout of cough. His eyes began to water. His mind was in a confused state. There was a painful constriction in his chest. He wanted scream at the rascal and ask him to get out of his house.

Then his eyes fell on the lined up rifles, right in front of him. They were the deadly AK47 rifles. Now for the first time, he realized that it was a deliberate act. They were position there prominently with certain intention. Shakeel was not making a request. It was an order. The guns were in fact pointed at his temple. Those men were cold-blooded killers. Their hands were stained with blood, blood of the innocents. They had killed before. They wouldn't hesitate to kill again. He was surrounded by a bunch of ruthless murderers.

Wali's hands and feet had gone absolutely cold. His heart had begun to pound as if it would jump out of his chest. The overwhelming silence of the quartet screamed at him. The stillness of the atmosphere warned of an impending storm. Their vicious stares reeked of blood.

"*Ya Khudah*! This illiterate rascal has eyes on my Meher. My beautiful and bright child! I have to protect her from this evil man. How could he dare to dream of marrying my daughter? This cannot happen. But if I refuse now, things will go out of control. They will probably kill the entire family and take Meher away by force. Had he visited Meher at Pehalgaon for that purpose? Think Wali think! Think how to deal with these scoundrels?"

Chapter 14

Wali couldn't help shaking his head in disgust even while applying tremendous efforts to gain self-control; for he knew that he couldn't exhibit his revulsion openly.

His daughter was one of the most stunning and winsome young women in the entire town. God had perhaps carefully chosen the best genes from each member of her lineage and endowed Meher with them. She was tall and lithe, her features stunning; delicately soft like her mother's. Her complexion was real peach and cream like the heroines of the romantic novels. Her chestnut brown silky hair fell in thick wavy locks. Her almond shaped blue eyes dripped with intelligence and innocence. She was a princess who deserved no less than a prince as her life partner. And here was the most foolish, illiterate and unsightly man aspiring to marry her and marry her by executing pressure.

"How could this repulsive rascal even dream that he is in any way a match to my beautiful Meher?" Wali controlled his impulse to pounce on Shakeel and strangle him.

He felt forlorn and unprotected. He envisioned himself as a helpless easy prey, surrounded by a pack of snarling wild hounds ready to shred him into pieces, though he wished, he were an untamed bull who could gore them all with his horns and pound them under his hooves.

The cough gradually subsided. It had subsided long back. He had been pretending for some time. He had been buying time to think of an appropriate answer. He now looked up. All eyes were still fixed on him. All features were grim. Wali's eyes were red due to the exertion, so was his face red with anger, but his features were now controlled and well masking his inner rage.

"Shakeel, you just now told me that you have an unsettled life. Your work takes you to different places, then how can you marry? You need a settled life to be married," Wali's voice was distinctly shaky.

Shakeel looked at Hashim, as if seeking an answer.

"Once a woman is married, it is for her husband to think how and where to settle her. She remains no more under her father's authority," Hashim said in a stern voice.

Wali was desperate to find some excuse to put off the proposal. His mind had, as if, stopped working. Threat was looming large over his Meher, over his entire family. "How could Shakeel stoop so low? How could he even dream of getting accepted as my daughter's husband? The very thought is disgusting…downright abhorrent. Doesn't he realize that?"

Loudly he said, "My daughter is highly educated. She can't be married off without her consent."

It was Hashim speaking again, "Then it is left on you to make her consent. But what is the need to ask for her opinion? Your decision, as her father, should be the ultimate word and as a dutiful daughter, she has to accept your verdict. Women should not be given the freedom to make choices."

"These men are mean. Shakeel too has been totally brainwashed. And on top of that, he has foolish aspirations. How could a murderer dream of marrying such an intelligent and qualified girl as my daughter? And here I am, totally helpless. These brutes have tied my hands behind my back."

Wali broke into another cold sweat. Beads of perspiration were apparent on his forehead, noted by all the members of the malevolent group, but he was unmindful to them. He was frantically probing his brain to find a solution. "If Abba-Jaan were alive, he would have thrown these rascals out. No! It is good that he has been spared this torment. I am exercising extreme control but had he been alive and present at these current discussions, he would not have been able to control his anger and these men could have reacted fiercely. Discretion is required to handle these men who know only the usage of one language: Violence."

"Such things are not decided in a hurry. I need time to think it over," Wali's voice was much controlled this time.

"How much time do you need?" Hashim asked.

"A few months at least," Wali replied quite firmly. He would plan something meanwhile to wriggle out from this mess, he hoped.

"We don't have time, Wali Sahib. We do not know about tomorrow and you request for a few months!" Shakeel laughed mockingly. His urgency was obvious. He knew that either he should have his way now; forcefully, or it would be never.

"Wali Sahib, we can give you at the most one day. You can make whatever arrangements you want to, tomorrow. The *nikah* will take place day after tomorrow," Hashim said with finality.

Chapter 14

"Not so soon. How can things be arranged in a day?" Wali almost cried.

"We do not need elaborate arrangements. Keep the ceremonies simple. There is no need to inform your relatives presently. They can be informed of the marriage later, if you choose to do so. Only one *Maulvi* is required who will read the *nikah*. Few ornaments and clothes can be arranged for the bride. The wedding rituals will be performed in the morning. We will be leaving with Shakeel's new wife after lunch, day after tomorrow," Hashim sounded business like. They had planned it all elaborately.

Now Shakeel quipped in, "There is no need to invite even Wasim Sahib. I know you are very close to him but it will be better if he is not present at the time of the *nikah*."

"He is scared of Wasim, for he is strong and direct, and is a man of action. Shakeel doesn't want any support around me. He wants me to be alone and helpless." Loudly he lied in his anger, "He is not even in town. He is away at his wife's parent's place."

There was once again painful silence in the room. Only Abdul's voice could be heard from a distance. He was singing in his quarters, loud enough to reach them in the sitting room. Wali wanted the singing to stop immediately. It was not an occasion to rejoice.

He must be making arrangements for these rascals' conveniences without a clue of their intentions, thought Wali with bitterness. His desperate requirement of Abdul to be there by his side returned. At least, he would have someone who would be on his side against these heartless villains.

"And one thing more Wali Sahib; since you won't have any time to arrange for any wedding gifts for your son in law, it will be better if you gift him a part of your orchard. That will also give him an excuse to visit you often," Ahmed commanded this time.

Hashim continued, "Yes, half of your property should be transferred in Shakeel's name. Half you can keep for your son. It will be an equal distribution. It is Shakeel's wish that your son should not be deprived of his right, more so as he is also his childhood friend."

Wali used immense willpower not to gnash his teeth in anger. "The scoundrel is acting very charitable, as if a large hearted man is doing us a great favour," he considered sarcastically and waited stern-faced for more scandalous demands.

Hashim continued, "We know you have some handicraft business too. You will immediately begin to send fifty percent profit from it on the address I will give you before leaving day after tomorrow. That will be for the sustenance of your daughter and it will keep you satisfied that your daughter isn't starving."

Wali's anger was almost uncontrollable now and he could hide it no more. "My daughter is a qualified doctor. She is capable of earning her own living." His resentment was apparent in the way he spoke; slowly and bitterly, stressing each word separately.

Hashim answered with ferocity, "She will only be doing voluntary service under our command from now on. Doing a regular job is out of question."

There was once again silence in the room. Wali's dilemma was immense. He was going numb with shock. He was now speechless. "So these scoundrels have come well prepared. They must have done a meticulous planning of how to entrap us. Let them take away my property, my whole orchard, but please God make them spare my daughter."

Hashim continued, "We do not have time presently to make the property deal. But we expect you to keep the papers ready and the deal can be finalized on our next visit. We may come back after a few months or a year. That is not yet certain. Our life is full of uncertainties."

"So for months or a year I wouldn't even know how my daughter was being treated, where she was living and under what circumstances, or whether she was alive," Wali thought with immense agony. He had a painful lump in his throat now which made it impossible for him to speak any more.

Neither could he think any more. He had no notion how to escape from this predicament. He definitely must have appeared shocked and distressed for Hashim continued, "Wali Sahib, let me warn you. We are not used to taking refusals. Nor do we tolerate any deception. If you try to be smart, you and your family will get into serious trouble. And it is not an empty threat. I am sure you understand that, given that you appear an intelligent man."

Wali looked at Shakeel. This time Shakeel lowered his eyes. He couldn't meet Wali's eyes anymore. He had brought these dangerous men to the house with wrong intentions. He was using Hashim's shoulders to fire his gun, since he couldn't do it himself. And fire the gun on the people who had once sheltered him? Wali couldn't recall even once when anybody had been harsh with him. Only Abba-Jaan had openly condemned his ideas. Had they committed drastic mistake in treating him as one of the family? Had that given him ideas of acquiring real place in the family, that too forcibly? Wali was, for the first time in his life, feeling remorseful for treating someone with kindness. Shakeel did not deserve it for he was a born scoundrel, Wali was sure of it now.

Wali was seething with anger. If circumstances had been different, he wouldn't have hesitated to strangle Shakeel with his bare hands. He would have killed him to save the honour of his family. But all he did now was to shift his glare away from the repulsive character.

"*Huzoor,* the sleeping arrangements are done." Abdul now entered the room and brought some respite from the painful discussions. But, he stopped at the door and looked from one man to the other. The intense silence and tension in the room was easy to perceive. He looked at Wali's pale aggrieved face and knew instantly that something was drastically wrong. But he didn't know how to help him so he chose to follow his master's advice and swallowed his observation.

To Shakeel he said loudly, "Come on Shakeel. Bring your friends. It is time to sleep. In fact, it is much beyond the usual sleeping time for us. My master is tired and needs to rest."

The four men immediately got up. Picking up their belongings and their guns from the sitting room, they followed Abdul.

Hashim stopped at the door and said authoritatively, "Wali Sahib, we are happy with your cooperation. But kindly remember; tricks will not be entertained!"

His impertinence made Wali gnash his teeth in frustration. Who was he to threaten him thus? But the shocking proceedings had by now gagged him and rendered him mute.

Abdul, who was waiting in the corner for an opportunity to talk to his master, looked at Hashim in surprise. He apparently seemed offended by the statement and opened his mouth to say something but Wali preceded his speech. "Abdul, show them the sleeping quarters. Thereafter lock the house. I am going to sleep," he ordered him loudly and dryly.

Abdul quietly left along with the men. Wali noticed him looking at him from the corner of his eyes before going. He was very grim. "My expressions must have revealed a lot to him," Wali realized.

Sure enough! Abdul had noticed his master's drained out face. He had noted his fearful eyes. And he knew something unpleasant had occurred after he had served *kahwa* and had got busy eating his dinner and setting the beds in the quarters.

Wali knew that Abdul would come back to him to inquire about the reason that had caused him such open anxiety. Wali was in no mood to speak to him or to anyone at the moment. He needed to think. Think and plan. Till he had decided the course of his action, there was no need to put others in distress.

Wali walked out of the sitting room. His feet automatically took him to Ammi-Jaan's room. This was his daily routine. To give Ammi-Jaan a goodnight hug. But this time he stopped at the door. He couldn't face Ammi-Jaan today. She would immediately guess something was wrong. Wali turned back to go directly to his room.

"Is that you Wali?" Ammi-Jaan called out loudly. "Come in. You are very late today. I have been waiting for you."

Wali had no choice but to face his mother. He swallowed hard, took a deep breath and entered the room. Before Ammi-Jaan could say anything he spoke, "Ammi ji, I have a bad headache today. I don't feel too well."

"Take a painkiller. And Wali, you are working very hard these days. I am noting it for quite some time. You must relax occasionally; otherwise you will soon get stressed out," Ammi-Jaan said indulgently.

"Yes, Yes I will." Saying so, Wali left the room without hugging his mother. He was afraid to do so, for he wasn't sure if he would be able to control his emotions once the soothing arms of his mother embraced him.

Wali slowly walked up the stairs to his bedroom. His shoulders were drooping. His legs were unsteady. He needed to hold on to the railings for support, something he never needed to do prior to this day. It had taken some vicious men just a few minutes to wring the entire strength out of his body and presently, he felt like a squeezed cloth ready to be hanged on a clothesline. No, it was worst than that, he was being readied to be a sacrificial lamb. He was a cornered prey, soon to be shredded into pieces and that too shockingly by the man who was under his obligation. What an ungrateful rascal Shakeel had turned out to be!

He halted outside his room. Despite exercising immense control a sob escaped his lips. "Allah, please save my Meher. Save us form these evil men," his wounded heart implored silently.

He leaned against the wall and fought to attain normal expressions. It took him quite sometime to gain control. When he finally entered the room, Sakina was in bed, cosily wrapped in her quilt. He felt relieved that he wouldn't have to give her any explanations for his troubled exterior. But Sakina had been up and waiting for his return. She raised her head to have a good look at her husband and noted a lot at a simple glance.

"You took a lot of time. There was no need to entertain Shakeel and his friends for so long. And look at you now. You look so tired, absolutely pale. You are surely unwell. Can I get you some medicine or perhaps a glass of hot milk?" She asked with concern.

"No…no, don't bother yourself, I am fine. You go to sleep," he said softly, forcing his voice to sound as normal as possible.

Before Sakina could notice more and probe further, Wali turned his back. He aimlessly picked up a magazine lying on the table and toyed with it. That was to give Sakina an impression that nothing was amiss and he was his normal self. Then changing his clothes he slipped into the bed, still trying his best not to reveal his grievous expressions to Sakina. Once in bed, he instantly turned his back towards her.

"Sakina, please switch off the table lamp," he requested her in a mild tired tone.

Chapter 15

Sleep had totally eluded Wali the previous night. The salacious demands of his visitors had made his blood run cold. It was as if he had been brought to the edge of a cliff and asked to make preparations to celebrate the coming event; of being pushed down the gorge into the turbulent waters. He was desperate to save his neck but was at loss how; being surrounded by a gang of armed ruffians. The situation certainly couldn't have been trickier!

He wanted to toss in the bed in response to his agitated mind. But then Sakina would have known that something was amiss and he did not want to put her in distress at the moment. Passively lying on a side, he was feeling as if he was buried under a heap of rubble and slowly getting suffocated. His mental pain was far severer than any physical pain he had ever experienced. He tightly held on to the bedpost. His eyes were tightly shut to endure the immense ache inflicting him.

His heart was crying bitterly. "I have read *namaz* regularly. I am a devoted man. I have led a simple and honest life. I have never committed any sin knowingly. To my knowledge, I have never inflicted physical or metal pain on anybody. Then why is all this happening to me? Why am I being tormented? What am I being so severely punished for?"

He wanted to cry loudly but he couldn't even sob. Sakina would get alarmed. He shed silent tears. By the time his tears had dried, he felt completely drained out.

An evil eye had fallen on his beautiful Meher. She was in extreme danger and her father was so helpless. He had to do something. But he couldn't find a loophole. Some dirty parasites had suddenly appeared to suck their blood. A maniac had come with lewd desires. Wali had never in life felt as furious as he felt presently. His pride, his dignity, his self respect had been hurt. More than that, these fiends were out to wound his Meher and that was something he couldn't endure. The whole affair was shameful.

"The power of weapons has clouded the idiot's brains and he has no sense of how sordid is his aspiration," thought Wali.

"A large bank balance; Nonsense! Shakeel said that he had earned through a well paid job. As if I don't know where the money has come from! It is dirty money, earned through dirty means. Through committing, God knows how many sins! It is swathed in blood," Wali cringed at the thought.

"All my life, I have believed in mercy and compassion. I have always respected God's creation. I have thought it my duty to save the weak and the helpless. Today, I myself have become a helpless victim at the hands of some merciless men. They are bent upon ruining an innocent person. I cannot allow them to spoil and destroy a promising life. I cannot let them take away my Meher by force, use her and then throw her forlorn on the streets." Wali began to make up his mind. The determination of a man, though wounded and shaken, had begun to replace the dread.

"This depraved man has attacked me in my house. It is a serious challenge. What should be my reaction? How should I prevent my life from being smashed into fragments? What would a man do in such a situation to defeat his enemy? "

Wali's mind searched earnestly. The loophole had to be discovered when survival was at stake.

"If I don't obey them, they will murder us all in cold blood. I am sure of that. The rifles have been brought precisely for that purpose. I cannot permit that to happen. How can I see my mother killed in front of me even if I had only a few seconds to live? My spirit would never rest in peace. I am a husband. I have taken vows to protect my wife. I am a father. I must shield my child from the butchers even if it means shedding my own blood." His mind had begun to work in defiance.

"I am prepared to lay down my life for the honour of my family. I cannot allow the half witted stinker to lay his dirty hands on my daughter." Wali was now turning resolute.

"I will not allow Shakeel to touch my child, even over my dead body. I will not let anyone injure my daughter or victimize her. This rogue may have been carrying a gun and gun toting villains along, but he is a coward and has met a staunch adversary head on. I may be the lone warrior in the rival camp but I am not a weakling that I will meekly accept the ignoble demands. I will save my family as well as thwart a deceitful man like Shakeel's attempts of causing us harm." Wali was slowly regaining his composure as well as recovering his iron will.

"I do not have guns, so I can't match the fight with guns. I don't even know how to fire one. I have never in life lifted even a pistol. My fight will have to be different. It will be a fight of wits. It will be a test of my strength," he decided.

He did not have much time with him. Just one day! He would have to think of a way to survive this ordeal. Wali continued to ransack his brain to solve the mind boggling problem he had all of a sudden confronted today, a problem which had erupted like a volcano without any prior warning. Planning required time and that was something he didn't have in hand. He would have to find a way out, to save their honour as well as their lives. Foremost, he would have to hide Meher somewhere, where these villains wouldn't be able to lay their dirty hands on her.

Thirst had him distracted from his thoughts. He got up to drink water. Sakina always kept a glass and a jug of water on the table. He filled his glass and let the cool liquid trickle down his throat. He felt soothed.

He didn't feel like going back to bed. Sakina was softly snoring. He wasn't worried about waking her up. She was a sound sleeper. Only loud and hectic activity in her vicinity could disturb her sleep. He walked to the window and pulled the curtain aside to peep out.

Outside, the landscape was faintly lighted by the crescent moon. His attention was at once drawn towards some movements in his compound and that put him instantly on high alert. He possibly couldn't be spotted in the darkness, he supposed, nevertheless he should exercise safety measures. At once he drew the curtain back and then taking cover behind the drape, he once again peeped through the pane. In the dark of the night, profiles of two men against the straight whitewashed boundary wall of his house slowly became distinct.

Who were the men and what were they doing there in the dead of the night?

He could now recognize the figures, though they appeared somewhat different without their turbans. One was unmistakably the tall and slim figure of Hashim. The other man was of medium height but stout. That could be Ahmed. They were standing there and discussing something in undertones. It was well beyond midnight. Why weren't they asleep? Did they have some pernicious intentions?

Wali now noted the rifles in their hands and instantly stiffened. He was petrified.

Had these men changed their plans? Were they planning an ambush and were lying in wait to take him by surprise tonight? What should he do now? He didn't even have any weapons for self-defence. How should he protect his family? He felt a shiver run down his whole body. He was once again traumatized by his helplessness. "Should I call for outside help? Should I go down and wake up Abdul?" He considered. On the other hand, keeping a watchful eye on them to know their intention was absolutely imperative. Therefore, he didn't move even an inch and waited in suspense for further developments.

He was still glued to the window with uncertainty wringing his heart when Ahmed began to move towards the outhouse. Hashim went to sit on the boundary wall and lit a cigarette. Wali waited for another five minutes. There were no more movements. Only the glowing butt of Hashim's cigarette displayed some intermittent motion, but his body was absolutely still. The red glowing spot gave creeps to Wali, like some fiery evil eye glaring at him from the dark. Hashim's rifle, rested across his thighs, was well defined too. Wali now understood what was happening. They were guarding his house in case the family decided to slip away.

Escape?

"Yes, that is what I will have to do. Escape! I will have to take my family away from the danger zone. I will take them to a safe place, out of the reach of these wolves, somewhere where these terrorists should not be able to locate us. That is the only option to save Meher from their clutches. But where can we go? Where does such a secure place on this planet exist? Who will give sanctuary to a family on the run and for how long? Why…? We will go to Salim. Why didn't I think of that before? My son's house will be the right place to seek shelter in. We won't be under any kind of obligation there. It is the place where our dignity will remain preserved."

And Wali's mind began the toil on a different track. Should he try to slip out right away? That wouldn't be possible. Getting Ammi-Jaan ready to depart suddenly, that too in the middle of the night wouldn't be feasible without any noise being leaked out. Further, the women would demand explanation and the activity inside the house would surely alarm these mercenaries of malice stationed outside.

What was more; such a venture would require proper planning.

He wanted to know what time it was. Ahmed had been on duty till now. Change of guard had just taken place. Hashim had taken over the guard duty from him. Wali looked at the shining needles of the radium wall clock. The time was 3 am. This was perhaps the third change of duty. Shaukat must have been the first guard. What about Shakeel? Was he being spared or he will take over from Hashim at the daybreak? Hashim had taken over at this time, considering it to be the most crucial period. What would be the best time to escape?

Wali went to the bathroom and without hesitation switched on the light. He waited for a minute and then flushed the toilet. Switching off the light, he moved back to the room and next to the window once again. Hashim's head was lifted at an angle; obviously he was looking at the bathroom window. Wali noted the nodding head.

This time Wali smiled to himself.

He went back to lie on the bed once again. His mind was now working fervently. Yes, he would escape with his family from right under their noses. It was a great challenge; to hoodwink the weapon laced terrorists. Certainly the most risky enterprise! At least he could try. "Of course, I will try irrespective of the risks involved. If we manage to escape, it will be our windfall; or else it will be better to die than to accept their immodest demands."

But he would require some help. He would not be able to handle it all alone. And the right person to seek help from was Wasim. Wali had full faith that Wasim would go out of his way to save them. And then there was Nusrat. She could help if it was required.

Thinking of Wasim, made him rationalize why he had lied to Shakeel about him. Wali wasn't a habitual liar. Then why had he lied at the spurt of a moment? Was it a divine intervention?

"A lie is not a lie if it is told to save someone," Wali was convinced. "Perhaps this lie will save them tomorrow."

And he also decided that he was not going to part with an inch of his prime property; which was the result of Abba-Jaan and his lifetime labour. At least, it would never go into the hands of the terrorists. His assets would never be used for decadent activities.

The first person he would contact in the morning would be Wasim, his cousin brother. And Wali began to make elaborate plans in his mind.

Wali was emotionally and physically drained out. But now he was resolute. He waited for the sun to rise, for then would start his real battle.

Chapter 16

Having tired himself by the restless trudging inside the houseboat after his self-imprisonment since Shakeel's traumatic visit, Wali finally stretched himself on the bed. His agitation had somewhat subsided and his breathing had attained normalcy. It was a big relief for him to know that their escape plan had not been exposed and it could still be executed as intended.

Wali once again began to notice his surroundings. The first thing he now observed was the intricate patterns on the roof. The roof, like the rest of the houseboat, was made of cedar wood. It was made of carved blocks of about fifteen square inches each, held together through dovetail joints with patterns carved intricately. There were straight and zigzag lines, there were circles, squares and triangles making abstract and floral designs; to him each block appeared like a labyrinth; an inextricable maze through which finding an escape route was mind boggling.

And he envisaged, "My escape plan too is like a tough maze. I need *Allah's* blessings to come out of it successfully."

The escape plan that had started to form in his mind at night was beginning to take shape this morning and Wali's mind now began to repeat the events of the morning almost in graphic details.

Even before the light of the dawn could fade away the crescent Moon and the morning star Venus, Wali was out of the bed. His feet carried him involuntary towards the window and he once again shifted the curtain slightly to check on the activities in the vicinity of his house.

On any normal morning, Wali would have drawn the curtain completely aside to let the first light of the dawn declare beginning of another day inside his bedroom. Then he would have noted the dew on the grass and the flock of chirping sparrows busy in their morning exercise routine. He would have admired the jutting peaks of the Himalayan Mountains forming a silhouette against the pale pink horizon. This particular season, he would have then opened the window to enjoy the waft of cool fresh morning breeze laced with the odours from his orchard.

But today, he had as if completely failed to remember this routine. Instead, he stood like a thief peeping through a small gap he had made in the window curtain to ensure secure state of affairs outside. The first thing his eyes fell on was a figure draped cosily in a blanket and squatted on the ground. The person was comfortably leaning against the wall and the angle of the head indicated that he was fast asleep. Wali's eyes sought the weapon, whose visible absence surprised him. But an intent scrutiny revealed the jutting butt of a rifle from under the blanket and Wali was quite sure it was Shakeel on duty at the moment. No one else in the group would be as careless as Shakeel, for he was the only one well acquainted with the gentle inhabitants of the house. And, no one had reasons to keep the rifle hidden under the blanket except the one guilty of wielding it against his benefactors.

Wali's judgement was accurate, for to drive away a troublesome fly, Shakeel's hand along with his face soon emerged from under the blanket confirming Wali's speculations.

So, Shakeel was the final change of guards, and was appointed for the least susceptible hours, when the daylight would prevent their captives from fleeing. The way Shakeel was asleep smugly, Wali realized that it would be the easiest to escape from under his nose.

In fact, Wali had another temptation to gather his family promptly and depart right away. But it wouldn't be easy, not without preparing Ammi-Jaan for it. Firstly, she might not agree to go away from her house and then would certainly demand an explanation. The women needed to be made ready to leave. Sakina might like to carry along a few valuables and that wouldn't be possible in a hurry. Some of these dodgy men might be awake now. Breaking through the cordon of the fierce armed guards and walking at Ammi-Jaan's pace all the way to reach the point where a conveyance could be procured was simply not viable.

In addition, was it the right time to escape? Definitely not! They should be able to straightaway quit the town. Hiding here and there till the departure time was very risky. For, where could they hide where these pests wouldn't be able to hunt them out?

The escape would have to be systematically and carefully planned. It would have to be foolproof as far as possible. He would have to discuss it all with Wasim; he decided, moving away from the window.

That gave Wali the reason to immediately proceed to get ready to depart.

When he came back after his bath, Sakina was sitting up but still wrapped cosily inside her quilt.

"Where are you going this early?" Surprise was apparent in her tone.

"Sakina, I have some important work today which may keep me out the whole day. Could you please make me a cup of tea?" He requested her.

"But you shouldn't go out today. You ought to rest."

"I can't do that Sakina. I need to attend to some urgent work."

Sakina had a good look at her husband and then declared decisively, "Work can wait. You need to attend to your health first. And you know, you look even worst than last night. Did you sleep well? Is there something bothering you?" Sakina had probably never seen her husband so worried. It was as if scores of worry lines had erupted on his face overnight. He appeared pale and spent. He was never as distressed as he appeared presently; not even when Salim had declared his intentions of marrying Subina. He had made a glum face and projected a big frown then. It was a display of his annoyance, not genuine grief. But there was definitely something serious troubling him at the moment. What could it be?

"What is the matter? You were fine till the previous evening. Then what has happened to upset you thus?" Sakina insisted when she did not receive any reply from her husband.

"Nothing is bothering me. I am fine. Just have a headache. A cup of tea should cure it," Wali replied elusively, without meeting his wife's eyes.

Though Sakina had felt concerned, she knew her husband well. She was sure that he was worried stiff over something but also knew that insistence on her part would be useless. If he wanted to share things with her, he would do it at his will, eventually. Therefore, she quietly left to make him his morning cup of tea.

While Sakina was away to the kitchen downstairs, Wali took out his folder from the locker of his godrej almirah in which he kept important papers. There was a sheaf of his bank papers. He carefully checked all the passbooks and the chequebooks. Next, he scrutinized the property papers. All were in order.

He then fetched the ledger from the main drawer of his study table. It had the accounts of the payments made, received and yet to be received. He wanted to check the accounts in detail, knowing there was a huge amount to be collected as payments but there was no time for it now. He kept the file atop the folder.

"What other important documents need to be removed from the house, papers on which the vicious visitors should not be able to lay their hands?" He tried to think. "The Certificates!" There was a big bundle of certificates and degrees; the school leaving certificates, the graduation degrees of the entire family and many others. He took out a big packet from the back of the top shelf of his cupboard and checked all the certificates one by one. His own graduation degree could be recognized due to the colour of the paper. "It too has turned yellow and aged," Wali thought pensively. He was in possession of Abba-Jaan's graduation degree too, which had yellowed even more.

Major part of the collection constituted the children's certificates. There were many earned by Meher in school for various competitions; for curricular and extra curricular activities. There were certificates awarded to Salim for excelling in sports. He lovingly read aloud the photocopy of Salim's engineering degree and Meher's provisional certificate for having completed her MBBS studies. Her degree would be the latest addition once the convocation was held a few months later.

Shuffling through the certificates now, Wali apprehended that they were not mere pieces of papers but the most important assets of their lives. They were the recognition of knowledge acquired through hard work over a long period. Everything else could be left behind but not the certificates. For him, Meher's certificate was far precious than all other assets combined, for it was the pedestal for her successful life. It was a surety that she would never live in subjugation, but with dignity.

Wali held Meher's certificate in his hands and once again gazed at it dotingly;

MBBS: Bachelor of Medicine & Surgery; a qualified doctor, with a bright future. How assiduously and with singular dedication, had she worked to earn this degree! And now some daft fellow had come to strangle those well-earned dreams before they could see the beam of light. These vicious men, blinded by the power of weapons and the lust for power, wanted to wipe it all with a single clout. These unlettered fellows had no reverence for knowledge, no respect for the accomplished. That was the sole reason for their indecent ideas.

His decision had now received reinforcement from his reflections, and he realized that the course of action that he was contemplating upon was the only option left with them. "My decision is bound by my duty as a father; as a preserver of my children's aspirations," Wali ascertained as he made a neat pile of the certificates.

At the bottom of the pile, he came across another neat brown envelop; totally unfamiliar. He had no recollection of this packet. He took out its contents. It too was a small stack of certificates. They were the photocopies. He examined the top one. It was a Graduation Degree in Science awarded to Miss Veena Wali.

Wali? Was that her maiden name?

The discovery shocked as well as pleased Wali.

"What a coincidence! And look at this girl! She must have surely noted this parity but never mentioned it to me," Wali reflected with a faint smile playing on his lips despite the present tension. Instantaneously, he also had the retrospection of how shoddily he had behaved with her. "But how could she tell me when I have always slighted her and kept her at an arm's distance," Wali thought pensively.

It was the commencement of the repentance Wali would experience throughout the day.

Currently, he recalled the day she had come with this packet to him. "Abbu ji, Salim has told me that you are the guardian of these important papers. Could you please safeguard my certificates too?" She had asked politely.

Wali had directed her dryly to keep them on the table and without glancing at them; he had kept the packet along with the rest of the certificates later, and then completely forgotten about it. A few days before their departure for Delhi, Salim had got the photocopies made and had taken the originals with him. He had left the photocopies with his father for safekeeping.

"Perhaps, Subina wanted me to inspect her certificates the day she had brought them to me, to impress upon me that she had been a good student, and could be a fine member of the family too. She yearned for a better treatment from me, the treatment that she truly deserved, and how badly I might have disappointed her." Wali's elucidation at the moment added another layer of misery to his already depressed spirits.

But now that he had finally inspected Subina's degree and the other certificates for the first time today, they confirmed the fact that Salim and Meher had time and again tried to bring to his notice and he had casually overlooked each time; Subina had been a clever student and had always scored a very high grade. "Bright girl!" He silently acknowledged and felt sheepish that her potential was being noted by him at the time when she had acquired importance as the one who would provide them with a safe sanctuary. He had justified reasons to be dismayed by this realization.

Picking up the certificates, he touched them to his forehead in a gesture of respect and in restitution. He seriously contemplated, "Her maiden name and my name are the same. I have failed to listen to God's pronouncement, who has been trying to tell me that there is no difference in us due to diverse religious convictions. The difference has never been due to our beliefs, what region we come from or where we were born; but only due to what we become subsequently. It is only owing to the contents of the heart and nothing else. The distinction should be formulated on just one ground; difference between good human beings and the evil ones. Regrettably, foolish people like me reject the goodness, for the synthetic walls of prejudice make us blind to the knowledge of its existence on the other side of the fence."

A feeling of remorse began to swallow his ego. Everyone in the house had accepted Subina. Even Ammi-Jaan was blissful in her company. But he was the only one who had never treated her well. He had been an adamant fool to have ignored such a gentle and intelligent person.

"I had given shelter and attention to that ungrateful rascal Shakeel and rejected an upright girl. I hope I am able to make amends with her in this lifetime. If I don't survive my trial today, I will never be able to tell her how sorry I am for my behaviour. *Allah*, please help me to live to see another dawn so that I may seek atonement," Wali's heart begged earnestly.

He realized that he needed to give full credit for Subina's fine upbringing to her parents. "I admire them who have inculcated such politeness and tolerance in their child. The girl is full of etiquettes and respect. At the time of the present crisis in our lives, I am confident of the warm welcome she will extend to us if we manage to reach her house safely. If I live to see the future, I must visit her parents one day and humbly intimate them of my gratitude."

Sakina had now entered the room with a pot of tea and a plate of biscuits on a tray, interrupting Wali's thoughts. He didn't want her to read the culpability on his face and he once again set in motion his hectic activity. He quickly arranged the entire bundle into a neat pile and then shoved all the certificates into the folder. But the act did not escape Sakina's sharp eyes.

"Where are you taking these important papers?" She immediately asked.

"Sakina, I will talk to you in a minute. Let me first collect all the papers," he answered.

Nothing significant should be left behind on which these men could lay their hands, Wali probed his mind again. Salim's letters! He had forgotten about them. They had his address on them. Leaving them behind could have been disastrous! He ran to the other end of the room, back to his writing table. The letters were in the topside drawer, kept in a neat bundle dotingly. Wali had read each letter at least five times. He picked them up and counted them. There were total twelve letters. He discovered another bundle of letters and these were the ones, Meher had written when she was in the hostel at Delhi. It was straight away added to the bundle in hand. He then opened the other drawers one by one, but found nothing significant.

"Sakina, you had received some letters from Subina." He then said, "Quick, fetch all of them."

Sakina was seated on a chair sipping her tea. Her eyes were following Wali as he scuttled around in the room. "What is he up to today?" She seemed to be asking herself, finding his behaviour quite out of the ordinary.

Mention of Subina's letters alarmed her. "What is the matter? Why don't you tell me?" She couldn't help asking again.

"Sakina, have some patience. I will tell you, but first get the letters," Wali almost ordered.

Sakina got up and fetched the keys of her godrej almirah from under her pillow. She kept her most cherished treasure locked in it, and the letters from her children were surely as treasured as her jewels. She brought a tiffin box which Wali recognized as the one in which Salim used to carry snack to school. Sakina opened the plastic box and fished out a small bundle. She handed the letters to her husband. All the while, her eyes were trying to find the rationale behind the requirement of the letters all of a sudden and so early in the morning. Ignoring his wife's inquisitive gaze, Wali counted the letters. There were twenty-two letters in all. A few were written in a neat feminine hand, totally unfamiliar to Wali but each of these had a few scribbles at the back by Salim too. Others were from Meher. Wali put all the letters in the folder, which was now bulging with papers.

"Sakina, do you have a small bag in which I can keep all the papers safely?" He asked.

Sakina wordlessly marched into the adjacent storeroom and soon brought a small black waterproof airbag. "I hope this will suit your purpose?" She asked and stood next to her husband, observing his movements more closely. Though, the questions she wanted answered were piling on with each passing minute, she kept her patience. Since the matter concerned her children, it was obligatory to probe it. She waited for the right moment.

Wali inspected the bag and nodded his approval. "Yes, it is just the right size," he said as he put the folder and the file inside the bag. They easily slipped into the bag. He closed the zip fastener and kept the bag on the table.

Having finished his tasks, Wali heaved deeply and looked straight at Sakina for the first time since the morning. Holding her arm gently, he led her to the easy chairs. Once both were seated, he filled his cup with tea and took a sip. The hot beverage felt calming. Meanwhile, from the corners of his eyes, he could see Sakina patiently looking at him, waiting for an update on the information he had kept to himself till now. He kept his cup on the table and addressed her, "Sakina, now listen to what I have to say carefully. Something very serious has happened," seeing instant fright in her eyes, he quickly added, "But you needn't worry. I will take care of everything."

"*Ya Allah!* Are the children all right? Are Salim and Subina well?" Sakina closed her eyes and placed her hands on her cheeks in an automatic reaction, having instantly presumed that some misfortune had befallen her children. She looked like a frightened chicken, readied to be sacrificed and seeing her thus, Wali's heart cried for her. What would be her condition when she would know that her darling daughter was the target of the vicious men who had visited them?

How would she react to the news that her home was no more hers, and she was not only being rendered homeless but a destitute? Or, they were about to embark on a perilous venture and he couldn't give her the surety of its successful execution? He couldn't even assure her that this would not be the last day of their lives.

Swallowing hard he replied, "No. . .No, it has nothing to do with them. They are absolutely fine. You need not worry on their behalf. But the trouble has visited us."

Sakina seemed to relax a little. Her hands slowly returned to her lap. "Is it then something to do with the visitors? Is it Shakeel?" She asked. She had had the suspicion since the previous night; when in a glance she had noted her husband distraught and worried, that something had occurred between him and the visitors to upset him drastically.

"Yes Sakina, you have judged accurately. Shakeel and the men accompanying him belong to some terrorist outfit. They are carrying guns and are dangerous. They have laid down some demands," Wali revealed to Sakina. He informed her about the presence of the guns, for he wanted Sakina to remain alert in his absence. Secondly, she had to be prepared for more shocking things, and he decided it would be sensible to make her ready step by step.

"What sort of demands? How could Shakeel come here demanding things? And carrying guns? He can't mean us harm! He has grown up here with us. He was well treated and well looked after when he lived with us."

"It is not the time to trust anyone. Every so often people take advantage of your kindness. Well, I don't have time to discuss all that. I have to go out as soon as possible on some urgent work. So while I am away, do not allow any of these men inside the house, not even Shakeel. Whatever excuse they give to come inside, simply ignore them," Wali instructed.

"You appear very serious. If the matter is so serious why are you hiding it from me? And if the guests are so dicey, why don't you ask them to leave immediately?" Sakina asked.

"Sakina, the men are dangerous and the matter is quite complicated. They are going to be here for one more day. I will tell you everything once I come back after taking care of certain things. You have to trust me. Meanwhile, you and Meher are not to go in front of the visitors. Make that clear. You both have to stay inside with the doors closed and properly bolted all the time. Keep

Chapter 16   185

Ammi-Jaan inside too. Better still, you all stay in her room, together. Shakeel might make a request to be allowed to meet Ammi-Jaan. Simply refuse. Tell him she is not well and is not to be disturbed. But you don't deal with any of them directly, not even Shakeel. Let Abdul be the mediator. He will be here with you for most of the day," Wali directed.

"But Meher and I had planned to watch a movie at the Neelam theatre. Meher had bought the tickets for it when we had gone shopping yesterday," Sakina protested.

"Sakina, please understand! Things are really serious. Forget about the movie. Both of you have to stay inside. At no point of time are you to leave the safety of the indoors, for it could be risky. Meher can read her books or watch TV. The three of you can chat. And make sure these men are kept at bay but well fed." Wali's tone was commanding, laced with slight impatience and plainly conveying to Sakina that this was to be the final ruling regarding their agenda of the day.

He had thought it wise not to divulge with any more information presently, for there was no need to create panic in the women now. He would tell them everything when the time would be right. "Moreover, if I told Sakina the reality now, she would be agitated the whole day," he thought. "None of the women will be able to hide their emotional state and the unwelcome visitors may become extra alert. That is the last thing required for the smooth operation of the plan I have in mind".

"You haven't eaten anything. If you are going out now, I will make you some breakfast." And Sakina got up to go to the kitchen.

"No…no Sakina, I don't have time for breakfast. I will manage that some place." Wali was feeling rather sick at the moment and he did not feel like eating even a morsel.

"And one thing more; prepare an elaborate dinner tonight. Don't prepare a feast, but the way you prepare when we have guests over for dinner." He had given her an important task and knew it would keep her occupied for most of the day.

Sakina did not probe further. She simply nodded her head. But there was plain anxiety on her face.

Wali picked up a biscuit and slowly munched on it. If he did not eat anything,

Sakina would not let him go. He slowly sipped tea from the cup and further cracked his brains to see if anything else needed to be taken care of.

"Sakina, there is some noise in the kitchen. I think Abdul is up," Wali said.

"Abdul has been up for quite sometime now. He was preparing tea for those men when I left the kitchen." And this time Sakina had a clear aversion written on her face when she mentioned the men, for she now knew for sure that they were not trustworthy; they were rather troublesome and dangerous.

"Sakina, could you please ask Abdul to come to the room? I need to discuss certain things with him too," Wali made a request.

Sakina immediately went out to call Abdul. Wali didn't feel like it, but he picked up another biscuit to munch. He felt weak and needed energy; he decided. Despite his appetite having been completely killed by the horrid dealings, he forced himself to eat.

In a few minutes, Abdul followed Sakina into the room.

"Yes *Huzoo*r, what are your orders for today?" Abdul asked as soon as he entered the room. He then stood erect, with hands folded in front, waiting to be provided with the instructions for the day's schedule. Though, the way he scrutinized him, it was evident to Wali that he was inquisitive to know what had transpired between him and the visitors the previous night.

Wali cleared his throat, as if preparing to address a gathering, meanwhile considering the option of revealing to Abdul all or only a part of the dreadful events. No, he couldn't reveal it all now, not in front of Sakina, he decided. Therefore, he deferred discussing things with Abdul for the time being. "Abdul, today you will be on duty at home for the entire day. The orchard need not be visited. The guests we have at home must remain under your continuous scrutiny."

Abdul instantly reacted, "What? That bunch of ruffians is not departing today? If you permit me *Huzoo*r, I will shoo them all out right away. Is it their ancestors' property that they have lodged themselves here as our uninvited guests? And I am not entertaining them anymore. Serving them dinner once was more than enough."

Total lack of expression on Wali's face left Abdul wondering and he fell silent. Wali quietly listened to Abdul's grumblings and then sighing deeply he said,

The Burning Orchard

"Abdul, listen carefully to what I say now. First of all, despite the fact that Shakeel and the accompanying men are most unwelcome to you, you have to be polite to them. At no point of time will you get into arguments with any one of them."

"*Huzoor,* I don't like these men. And they are carrying guns! Yesterday evening when I noted the weapons openly kept in the sitting room, I had a strong urge to direct them all out of the house. If you hadn't stopped me, I would have driven out the wild herd forcefully. How can I be polite to that high headed Shakeel who thinks he is your equal? How dare he bring some crooks and guns here and then sit on a high chair in front of you? He looked such an idiot with his dangling feet which wouldn't even reach the floor, but the highest chair he must occupy," irritated at the unannounced raid of their home by the loutish men, Abdul couldn't help exaggerating.

"Ignore his behaviour Abdul, he doesn't have brains. And if you cannot be polite to them, then talk to them as little as possible. There is no need to openly exhibit your annoyance," Wali advised him.

"But *Huzoor,* I am annoyed at them. And how much I may try, I can't hide my feelings. I am not good at it…not at all. And right now, I want to kick Shakeel and his friends, and send them all rolling down the hill. It will be the easiest deliverance." Abdul wouldn't relent, more so, as he had witnessed their peevish behaviour towards his employer just a few hours ago, and his master's demoralized spirits spoke distinctly that their presence in the house was due to some dubious reasons. To top it all, the impudent conduct of the tall mean looking man had left him wondering about the group the whole night. He was almost sure that these men were involved in terrorism and that was the reason enough to spend the entire night tossing and turning.

Wali silently gazed at Abdul and thought, "I too would love to do just the same, kick them all out of my house." He seriously wished he could, but it was too fabulous a wish, totally impractical. On the contrary, the men were to be kept pleased; at no point of time should they be annoyed while he was away. That could cause unnecessary problems and at the moment, Abdul couldn't comprehend the seriousness of the situation. Therefore, he now directed him in a stern voice, "Pay heed Abdul, they are dangerous men. I will be out of the house for most of the day. I am giving you the responsibility of looking after the ladies of the house. You are not to go to the orchard today. Stay at home, exclusively indoors and make sure that none of these men enter the house at any time. Feed them well. Give them a heavy breakfast and a heavy lunch.

They will remain lethargic and sleepy after their gluttony. And keep your mouth shut all the while. For the sake of the safety of us all, it will be the best that you just do not talk to them. I am sure you understand your responsibility." Turning towards Sakina Wali continued his instructions, "Sakina, the food is to be sent to their quarters. And each time Abdul goes out, shut the door. Unless Abdul asks you to open the door, do not open it. Peep before you open the door to see if things are fine."

Wali noted that Sakina had begun to breathe heavily in nervousness. Her large eyes had dread writ large in them. Abdul was nodding as well as frowning. His normal happy go lucky expression was acquiring gravity. His usually laughing eyes were presently visibly angry. They both had begun to appear dismayed. Wali once again felt apprehensive how well they would be able to endure the gruelling reality.

He was distressed to see their frightened faces and thought, "But it is necessary to warn them. They have to be on the alert. Shakeel may try some tricks and that has to be prevented. Hashim is a hardened criminal. It is quite apparent from his countenance that he has no compassion in is heart. He was the one who had openly threatened me with dire consequences if I tried to be smart. If they get provoked, they could become unmanageable and God knows what they might do. Abdul alone wouldn't be able to handle them. The only solution presently is to keep them gratified. I am leaving the helpless vulnerable women with these criminals hovering around. But at present I have no choice. I have to arrange for an escape."

Wali slipped into his *pheran* and up on his cap. Picking up the bag, he moved towards the door to depart. On reaching it, he suddenly felt very depressed. He was sad and worried for the women; each of whom he loved so dearly. It was difficult to leave them thus. He turned once again to glance at the two scared faces. His heart was spilling over with sympathy. But he felt extremely powerless. The momentary stop also made him recall an important instruction he had forgotten to give. "And one thing more; a very important thing; If Shakeel asks about Wasim Bhai, tell him he is out of station. Tell him that he has gone to his wife's place to see her ailing father."

Wali stood at the door for a while more. He wanted to make sure that everything had been taken care of. He intently looked at Abdul and realized, he still hadn't been informed of the state of affairs transparently. He had completely overlooked the fact that Abdul would be an important confrere in their flight plan tonight. But the detailed discussions would not be possible here, at home. For the purpose, he must give directions to Abdul to meet him at a pre planned location. He mulled over it and quickly arrived at his decision. "Abdul, you will perhaps need to go to the market to buy provisions for tonight's dinner. Leave around two thirty, after making sure the house is secure. Meet me at the Modern Groceries, the store two shops away from our routine ration shop, the Rizvi's Store. I need to discuss certain things with you, away from home. The Rizvi store is known to Shakeel and therefore not safe. Wait for me inside the Modern Groceries till about four. If I am unable to come, I will send somebody. But make sure that neither Shakeel nor any of these men accompany you. Choose a different path to elude them in case you see them following you. Do not mention the name of the shop at any time. But if they insist in knowing your destination, don't make it evident that you are hiding things from them; instead give a wrong name and a wrong place, like … like tell them you are going to the Alamgiri Bazaar which is three kilometres in the opposite direction. Is that all clear?"

In the same breath he added, "And Sakina, be very very careful while Abdul is away."

Both Sakina and Abdul nodded at once. Wali realized that they both hadn't spoken a word for a long time. "It is fine for them to be scared. It will keep them vigilant and on their guard," he considered.

He then said, "For our deliverance, we all need to keep prayers in our hearts. *Allah* will be our redeemer. I will come back as soon as my work is over. But if I am slightly late, do not worry. Just look after yourselves. And carry on with your routine normally, as if nothing is wrong."

Wali stepped out of the room. Sakina and Abdul followed him.

"Where are our guests, Abdul?" Wali asked while climbing down the stairs.

"That kid Shaukat had come to ask for tea. I was in the process of making them tea when you summoned me. I think they are in the sleeping quarters right now. Should I serve them tea now?"

"Yes, this is probably the right time. With the excuse of serving them tea, keep them all in their sleeping quarters and make sure they remain inside when I leave. I don't want them prying over me. I will wait till you go to serve them tea," Wali said.

Abdul immediately complied and walked towards the kitchen.

Wali and Sakina stood quietly side by side next to the main door waiting for Abdul. How much Sakina wanted to know about Wali's undisclosed mission for the day, she remained tight-lipped. But her heart had begun to quiver with fright and worry for her husband. On top, they had terrorists present in their house and that was a reason for extreme unease. She had heard of so many instances of their reckless and merciless ways. She also wondered about Shakeel's hard-hitting demand that was causing such extreme tension and worry for her husband. She was amazed how Shakeel had transformed from a simple boy to someone to be dreaded. It was unbelievable.

Wali could well grasp his wife's anxiety through her fidgety hands that were nervously rolling and unrolling the corner of her *chunni*. Standing beside his highly upset wife, Wali simply prayed in his heart for the safety of his family and the success of his difficult mission, knowing well that it was going to be the toughest day of their lives.

Soon Abdul appeared with a tray. Four large steaming mugs of tea and a plate of biscuits were arranged on the tray. The door was opened to let him out. He stood scrutinizing the surroundings and then nodded to Wali before walking towards the servant quarters. Wali had never seen Abdul so serious in his life.

"Abdul has understood the situation pretty well," thought Wali with satisfaction.

Turning to Sakina he said almost in whispers, "Now close the door after I leave and remember to keep it bolted. If the men ask for me, tell them I left for some work a little while ago, no matter when they ask that. Talk only through the window. But be your normal self. Remind Abdul to talk less. That way he won't commit any blunder. Once again, open the door only for Abdul! And Sakina, you must take care of Meher. She is still a child, immature at times. Make sure she doesn't go anywhere near Shakeel. Make her understand that he is not what he used to be when he lived with us. He is a dangerous man now, so are the accompanying men. I trust you with that responsibility."

Sakina nodded and Wali noted the pain in her eyes. He had repeated the warnings over and over again and that had set her to be highly anxious. She was indisputably worried stiff for him now; having grasped that he was leaving on a perilous operation.

"Take care and *Khudah Hafiz*," Wali said as he opened the door to go. When

The Burning Orchard

he turned for one last glance at her, Sakina's tearful face was pale and upset. She was almost sobbing. He felt as if he was being sent to a war front by a wife who was unsure of his return.

Wali stepped out of the house cautiously and heard the door closing behind him. There was a distinct clicking sound of the door being immediately bolted.

There was no one outside. The servant quarter door could be seen only from near the boundary wall of the compound. Wali took long and quick steps to reach the end of the compound. The footpath descended from here. Wali wanted to get away from the house as quickly as possible, for he did not want to encounter any of the visitors. He looked back once to be sure that no one was following him in person or with eyes. He could now see the broad shoulders of Abdul at the door of the outhouse. He was guarding it well and making sure nobody came out of it. He felt sudden tinge of anger to realize that he was sneaking out from his own house in a sly, like a criminal.

The pathway descended rather steeply for about four metres before taking a hairpin bend towards the backside of the house. On both the sides of the footpath was his terraced orchard. Each day when Wali began this descent, he walked down slowly, savouring the sight of his robust trees, sometimes divine in the beauty of their blooming blossoms, sometimes cheerful when richly laden with healthy fruit. These would be the times when even the strongest branches of the trees would be bent low with the heavy burden of the fruit they bore, yet seemingly so blithe at rendering their selfless service that Wali would be overwhelmed at their modesty. He would then bow to them, thanking them for their generosity. When winters would be at their peak, he would survey the snow laden trees poignantly, feeling sad that they were to bear the hardships of the elements of nature, yet proud at their sturdiness. His trees appeared heavenly even then. Whatever the season, each time he would adoringly behold them, breathe deeply to accept with gratitude what they were offering him in return of showering them with his care. He would smile at them as if exchanging the early morning greetings, touch them lovingly, remove a dried leaf here or a dead branch there and proceeding on.

If the trees possessed the power of observation, and who knows they may, it would have distressed them to note that today Wali hadn't even as much as glanced at them. Instead, he scampered down the path, oblivious of their presence, till he reached the point from where the rear side of the first floor of his house was visible. He stopped there. Something had suddenly occurred to him. He scrutinized the area. The edge of the rear compound was about seven metres from the footpath where he was standing. He tried looking for the path that Salim and Meher used to take when they used to go to school. They would invariably be late and to save time they would run out of the kitchen door at the back and take a straight descend down from this area, rather than leaving from the front door and going around all the way. He had also seen them using this pathway while at their play in the evenings. The path hadn't been used for a long time, ever since the children had grown up. Probably it had been covered by grass now, for Wali couldn't locate it.

"Never mind!" Wali now thought. "The slope is no doubt steeper on this side. The incline is not so gradual, but can be tackled. This is the path to be used tonight for the front side is expected to have guarded patrol. Only Ammi-Jaan will not be able to walk down this incline. For her, some alternate arrangement will have to be planned. Perhaps Wasim Bhai will come out with some solution. Once we manage this slope without being detected, it should not be very difficult after that. The rest till the main road can be covered comfortably fast." Thus making up his mind, Wali scurried on downhill in short quick steps, to reach the venue of his important rendezvous. The time was limited and there was a lot to handle.

Lost in his planning for the evening and cursing the wicked men for his trauma, he had soon reached the market place of the town. The bazaar was rising from the nightly slumber to the slow beginning of a hustle-bustle. Vegetables and fruits were being unloaded from the parked tempos. Some grocery shop owners too were raising the shutters. Most shutters were still down, for the business behind them was the type that would begun at a leisure pace, when the housewives would step out to purchase the necessities and at times the needless, having executed the morning obligations of sending children to school and their husbands to work.

The transformation from a hush to the verve of activity reminded Wali that such was also a place where one was quite likely to meet acquaintances. He had instantaneously reacted to his cognition by quickening his pace as he wanted to avoid meeting anybody. He felt ill, and was sure he looked one too. He had no patience to deal with the unnecessary enquiries regarding his health and affairs. More important, he had no time to fritter away. Therefore, despite being breathless soon, he had not slackened his speed.

Then he had spotted Allahrakha, a business acquaintance, exactly the type of person he wanted to avoid. If one wanted to reach some news to an area far and wide or spread a rumour like a wild fire, Allahrakha was just the right candidate for it. And Wali had to accost him today of all the days! The wisest thing to do would be to avoid him at all cost to stay alive, Wali had seriously contemplated.

He had conducted an examination of the locale in an earnest and had chosen the first narrow lane to detour. He had thrown one last glance at Allahrakha and was relieved to see him focussed on a heated argument with someone. "Thank God he hasn't noticed me," thought Wali, as he slipped into the lane. "For, had I been spotted, I would have been made to run a marathon through the streets, hounded by this man. Allahrakha is also not the one to concede defeat easily and wouldn't have rested till he had known the exact purpose of my visit to this place so early, the reason for my earnestness, my agenda for the day and finally my destination. Such are the rare genus of people born with some special instincts; of excessive curiosity, and are rightly branded Nosy Parkers by the language connoisseurs." A soft smile was playing on Wali's lips as these enjoyable thoughts distracted him for a while, pushing the obnoxious ones to the background.

The lane Wali was now walking on was barely broad enough to allow a small vehicle; two or three wheelers to ply at a time. Old concrete and wooden two storied buildings stood on either sides of the narrow lane, housing the shops as well as the homes of the owners of the shops. The dilapidated wooden structures clearly portrayed the pitiable financial conditions of the inhabitants of the area. "Here lives populace in such poverty, while on the other hand abounds people akin to the visitors I have at home who endorse poverty, who believe in destruction rather than building up for mutual prosperity. It is their activities alone which are causing heavy losses on the finances of the state, and it bothers them the least," Wali reflected.

He continued at a rapid pace as he was in a hurry to reach Wasim's house. He hadn't been able to share with anyone the ghastly events which had occurred after dinner last night; as a result, he had begun to feel stifled. He desperately sought someone to share his anguish with, who would guide and help him at this hour of exigency and who could be trusted better with this depressing secret than Wasim Bhai.

Thus rushing through the narrow lanes, Wali had turned right into an alley to reach the main road again and had almost collided with a *tonga,* having failed to react either to the clip-clop sound of the pony's hooves striking the cobbled street or the jingle of the bells tied around its neck. If the *tonga* driver had not shouted to warn Wali, and if he had not reacted and jumped aside on the nick, he would have probably lay crushed under the hooves or the wheels. The *Tonga* too was brought to an abrupt halt and the driver glared at Wali in anger. He then opened his mouth to perhaps rebuke him but then something stopped him. His expressions softened as he read anguish on Wali's face. Shaking his head in exasperation, or possibly in sympathy, he ordered his pony to proceed.

Once the *tonga* had been safely driven away, Wali had stood still for a while more, recovering his shaken nerve. "What a close shave it was," he had considered. "I better be careful. I still have to rescue my Meher from being pushed into a hellish blaze. I have to reach my family to a safe place. I can't think of quitting till I have accomplished these tasks. My spirit would wander forever if I left the world with my responsibilities unattended. I have to live and live for the survival of my family. I must also exist to see my enemy defeated. Once these tasks are accomplished, perhaps I will be able to face death with more fortitude."

He had now reached the broad main road once again. An auto-rickshaw scooted past, throwing a cloud of diesel smoke on him. He coughed to throw out the unwanted toxic fumes. The advent of modernity had brought its ills to this paradise too. This area of the town was fast becoming polluted like the other big cities in the country.

Wali was instantly raided by the concern that who would rescue the contemporary world from being assaulted by the deadly pollutants; the noxious fumes of the vehicles as well as the contaminated minds? The fact that both the types of invasions were becoming increasingly lethal made him wonder if the world was heading for a catastrophe.

"Will there be any salvage for the ill-fated humanity bent upon self destruction?" Wali desperately wanted to know.

The long walk had made him weary and he stopped for a survey. Wasim's house was still at about fifteen minutes walking distance and he was tempted to hire an auto-rickshaw. He raised his hand to stop one but instantly decided against it. He wanted no one to know of his destination. The secrecy of his mission was a matter of utmost significance today.

He continued to tread on, on his now weary legs. Now and then, he would glance back to confirm that no one was trailing him.

He had the full knowledge of their existence, had casually noted them each day, but today he particularly regarded the army pickets at almost every two hundred metres along the main road. A wall made out of sand filled gunny bags behind which stood an armament on duty; a weapon laced soldier in his full combat gear. Wali was tempted to seek help and he stopped close to one such picket. He was unable to make up his mind and was rightly hesitant. He quickly considered the pros and cons of seeking such an aid. The army would surely facilitate to get rid of the extremists hiding in his house, but would his family come out of it unscathed? He wanted the safety of his family, which these people wouldn't guarantee. His extremist guests too knew that well, which was why they were not bothered about him going out alone to make the arrangements. Though, the arrangements he had in mind did not coincide with their wishes. But, as long as his family members were their hostages, they would remain placated.

He glanced at the soldier on duty and found him standing rigid, closely watching him with suspicion. Naturally, he would be worried stiff of the intentions of the person who stood so near, aimlessly and for so long. Encounters of the paramilitary with the terrorists were the common occurrence in the valley and for these non-indigenous men; every person was a suspect until proven otherwise. And these men were not trained to wait for proofs.

From the corner of his eyes, Wali noted the soldier's right hand move slowly from the gunny bag where it had been casually placed till now towards the gun and then to the trigger. It was a startling realization for Wali that currently he was a suspect and at the mercy of the soldier's discretion. He could press the trigger and claim to have killed a possible terrorist. Such things had been happening. Quite commonly.

Wali controlled his panic and tried to look at the soldier directly as casually as was possible in such a situation. He now realized that the soldier was eyeing his hands which at the moment were in the pockets of his *pheran*. He at once took out his hands and dropped them on his sides, noting at the same time the soldier breathing easy, in obvious relief.

And Wali instantly dropped the idea of seeking help. He quickly walked away, feeling the soldier's eyes penetrating his back.

By the time he had reached Wasim's house, he was almost labouring for breath, something that had never happened before. Prior to this day, he had always been proud of his robustness, but today his confidence lay crushed on all facets.

Chapter 17

Wali was totally immersed in the replay of his recent implausible experiences when a slight rocking of the houseboat jolted him out of his musings. His heart thumped against his ribcage in panic yet again. In an automatic reaction, he jumped on to his feet and waited with bated breath for the reason of the sway to become clear. He conceived that this rocking was different form the previous one, when Shakeel had plodded up the ladder. The boat presently swayed quite gently so the turbulence could be due to the water current set off by some boat passing by or simply by a draught of strong wind.

But subsequently he could discern someone lightly climbing up the ladder leading to the boat. He stood bonded to the floor on the legs that once more seemed to be melting away. This time the footsteps did not stop at the front door. Instead, the soft yet confident strides moved on. The person was coming straight towards the backside. No! There were two different sounds of footsteps. Could they be Shakeel and Hashim again? Had they come to know that he was hiding here? Had they appeared again to take him by surprise?

The footsteps neared the rear door. Wali rushed to stand next to it once more, judging it to be the safest hiding place from his previous experience. He checked the bolt. It was in place. He hadn't opened it ever since bolting it about an hour ago. He hadn't drawn the curtain either and that was probably the correct action. The drawn curtain could have raised some doubts in the mind of the otherwise idiotic bloke, Shakeel.

The tick-tack and the flip-flop sounds now stopped at the door. Someone pushed the door gently followed by a soft knocking. Wali refused to respond; instead he waited, breathing heavily in alarm.

"Wali, why have you bolted the door from inside? Is everything okay?" The most welcome sound reached Wali's ears.

Relief bathed Wali from tip to toe and he smiled to himself for being such a nervous wreck and not once thinking that it could be Wasim returning, though the whole day he had done nothing but wait for his return. He again had to struggle with the rusted latch but the loud scratching sounds naturally didn't bother him. When he had managed to open the door, Abdul's pale worried face became visible behind Wasim's comforting figure. The men entered the room. Wali straight away fastened the door once again.

"Why are you bolting the door Wali? You look quite distressed. Have things been all right?" Wasim asked anxiously.

"It is good to take precautions," Wali said calmly. He then added, "I thought you would be coming from the other side, from the pathway through the reed bush. It seems you have used the waterway."

"Yes Wali, the vehicle I have hired is parked on the main road. So I hired a boat to reach here. Moreover, I was pretty late and knew you would be worried. I probably managed to save solid half an hour by choosing not to walk through the reed bush," Wasim explained.

"I see," Wali said and quietly stood waiting for the men to settle down before he revealed to them his unnerving experience, though he was impatient to divulge what had recently occurred. Wasim slumped down on a chair, obviously very tired. And after resting his cloth bag full of the rations he had shopped for the night next to the wall, Abdul made himself comfortable on a floor cushion. Wali immediately noted distress writ large on Abdul's face and that sent his alarm bells ringing. "Abdul, you appear quite aggrieved? Are things under control at home?" He asked.

"Abdul is shocked…horror-struck, for I have revealed to him the appalling circumstances we have been dragged into. He had an idea that things were not right ever since Shakeel had arrived with his noxious friends, but had no inkling that their intentions were so immoral," Wasim explained to Wali.

Wali nodded slowly in approval, for Abdul had to be made aware of the adversity anyway. That was the exact reason for which meeting him away from home was essential. Wasim had done a great favour by relieving him of the unpleasant task.

Abdul was to play an important role in the escape plan. In fact, without his cooperation the escape would be quite impossible. But first he was anxious to know how the men had been behaving behind his back. "Did the unwanted guests cause any trouble in my absence?" He asked Abdul anxiously.

"Apart from Shakeel troubling me for this and that, the men didn't bother us much. The pigheaded Shakeel though tried a few times to enter the house. First he wanted to meet your mother, and then he offered to help me in the kitchen to prepare breakfast. But he should have known that he can't outsmart me. I can handle ten scoundrels like him at a time, and kept him absolutely on the other side of the door," Abdul informed with a gratified yet weak smile.

That made Wali even more worried. "I hope he doesn't manage that now, when the women are alone," he expressed his concern.

"No, he won't. He wasn't even at home when I left. In fact, he had left along with that tall weird looking man shortly after breakfast, soon after the hard boiled pole had inquired about your whereabouts from the kitchen window and I had told him that you had left only recently for some urgent work," Abdul informed Wali.

"What about the other two men? I hope they won't create any mischief," Wali inquired again.

"I don't think so. Those lumps of stinking flesh were flopped on their beds most of the time. They were in fact taking turns to sleep and to shuttle around and around the house. But we ignored them completely," Abdul answered.

Wali nodded slowly. He understood that one man was perpetually on the guard duty. The same was expected at night. But the knowledge that they were taking rounds of the backyard too was rather disturbing. He wished that they shouldn't establish their picket there too for that would become a great hindrance in the escape plan. Extreme precautions would now be required before their venture tonight.

Slowly walking away from the door with uneasy thoughts troubling him, he occupied the vacant chair. He then informed Wasim of Shakeel's visit to the boat in his absence.

Wasim immediately stiffened and there was clear annoyance as well as agitation in his voice. "What did the scoundrel come here for?"

"Looking for me, what else," Wali could afford to speak calmly now; company of his trusted group had brought him relief and boosted his confidence.

Wasim inquired further with an obvious alarm, "Did he come to know that you were here, on the boat?"

"No Wasim Bhai, I had a narrow escape." And Wali proceeded to tell them about his near encounter with Shakeel. Wasim and Abdul listened with grave attention.

Wasim then said, "I too had a close shave with them, Wali. I almost came face to face with that rascal. It was only because I was on the alert that I managed to evade him and that tall fellow accompanying him. That is why I am so late."

Wali's dismay was apparent. So Shakeel had been looking for him all over the town. It could mean trouble now. It was also not a good sign as the men would become more vigilant tonight, whereas, they needed to be made complacent and unmindful. The escape plan was becoming more and more complicated.

Wasim continued, "I had finished my work at the bank and was about to step out, when I casually glanced through the window. Two men were sitting on the roadside railing scrutinizing each man who left the bank. I couldn't have recognized Shakeel if you hadn't told me about his beard. Yes, behind the beard he was Shakeel. I was quite sure. I then waited, standing close to the window, keeping a continuous eye on them. I picked up a newspaper to hide behind. Then the tall man stood up and gestured at Shakeel to do the same. I thought they might enter the bank and decided if they did that I would hide in the washroom. But they moved away. They had hanged on outside the bank for about fifteen minutes, and left only after making sure the person they were looking for wasn't there."

"They were trying to locate me to keep track on my activities," Wali stated as a matter of fact.

"Yes, I have a similar notion. At the same time if they had seen me, they would have known that you had lied to them and that would have made them realize that something was being cooked up behind their backs to dodge them. Anyway, from the bank I directly proceeded for Nusrat's house. Fortunately she was at home. After absorbing the shock of the tidings, she agreed to immediately go to the bus station to get the tickets. Before she walked out, I thought it wise to peep out to check if all was clear and to my utter shock, I found the scoundrels standing on the road outside Nusrat's house."

"What, they had reached there too?" Wali almost cried with anguish.

"Yes. Initially I felt the earth sliding from under my feet thinking that the scoundrels had come to know of our plans. Then I read the uncertainty on their faces and concluded that they were on Mission Unearthing. Wali you are right, they were on the lookout for you. Since they hadn't been able to locate you, they were visiting the places of your acquaintances one by one. I am sure they must have visited my house too. But Ayesha must have fooled them into believing no one was there. They were quite desperate to know your whereabouts."

"Hmmm…," Wali nodded to agree, but a deep frown had begun to form on his face.

"Well, we had no choice but to wait for them to depart," continued Wasim. "Meanwhile Nusrat served me lunch. However, even after half an hour the leeches were still sticking on. We couldn't wait the whole day. So, Nusrat went out on the pretext of washing her laundry at the outdoor tap. She confidently marched out with a bucket and a bar of washing soap. After washing a few clothes when she turned to hang them on the clothesline, she came face to face with the two men as they had moved closer. She then loudly asked them the reason why they were hanging around. That caused them to look a little sheepish. You know Nusrat's ways. She increased her volume and shouted at them to buzz off or else she would call out to the neighbours to teach a good lesson to the shady characters. I was watching the whole drama from behind a window curtain. Shakeel opened his mouth to say something, perhaps to introduce himself but the tall man pulled him away. They seemed to have retreated but we waited for another fifteen minutes to be sure of the clear grounds. It was only after we were satisfied that the duo had left, did Nusrat leave for the bus station, well hidden behind her *burka*. Meanwhile, I left to arrange for the vehicle and meet Abdul. I think the men must have visited the houseboat after that."

"So they are suspicious about my intentions. Wasim Bhai, it is not a good sign. They will be on a high alert tonight," Wali expressed with mounting worry.

"You leave that to me *Huzoor*. I will not let them spoil your plans. They will reach you over my dead body," Abdul spoke this time.

Wali smiled faintly at Abdul. His lean weathered figure and comforting presence was reassuring. In the last few years, especially after Abba-Jaan's death, Wali had perhaps spent maximum time in his company. The consideration sent a wave of nostalgia in his heart, especially when those good old days were about to be terminated. "Abdul, every thing has gone down the drain. All that hard work we had put into our orchard, the business, all is lost in a jiffy. Could we ever imagine that we were sheltering a pest who would one day be hell bent upon destroying us?" Wali ended with a deep sigh.

Overwhelmed, Abdul slumped against the wall. His shoulders stooped and he hid his face in his arms rested on his knees. His slightly shaking shoulders revealed that he was sobbing. Wali closed his eyes shut and tried to gain control over his emotions. In that complete hush in the room, Abdul's soft sobs sounded akin to penetrating heart rending bawl. "No Abdul, don't cry. Our tears are not so worthless that an insignificant creature should cause them to flow. What is more, it is not the time to lose heart. It is the time to be strong and determined for we need to preserve strength to defeat the wicked designs of these perverse men."

"*Huzoor*, why can't we report them to the police? Let them be caught," Abdul suggested in a controlled voice but without shifting his head from its position. He knew that he couldn't reveal his tearful face to Wali and demoralise him. He well understood that all Wali required today was a strong support.

"Abdul, you know very well we can't do that. They are four of them, with deadly AK47 rifles. My mother, wife and daughter are their hostages at the moment. Ahmed and Shaukat are guarding the house even if Shakeel and Hashim are out. Any approach to the house can be seen and it will be difficult for the police to reach up undetected, especially before dark. Then there will be resistance. Even if these men get eliminated, they will make sure to kill us first. The security force too may not be so bothered about saving our lives. For the most of them, the priorities will be to finish the terrorists and claim the prize; accolades and promotions. Abdul, it is not so simple. Today, it is the matter of life or death for us. We are on our own and will have to tread each step carefully," Wali explained to him.

"*Huzoor,* what will I do once you are gone? *Allah* alone knows when you will come back. All my life I have served you. I have known no other way of life than the one spent with you. You are like a brother to me." Abdul was observed exercising control over his emotions.

"Who said you are going to stay here? Abdul, once the men discover that my family members and I are absconding, they will not spare you. They will know that you were hand and glove in the scheme," Wali told astounded Abdul.

Wasim, who had been listening to the discussion silently, now got up and walked to the window. He stood there surveying the exterior. Meanwhile, Abdul sat with bent head, chewing over the circumstances that were effecting total alteration in their lives. He was agitated as well as angry. But he could also discern that they all were absolutely helpless.

Satisfied of the absence of what he was seeking, Wasim returned to his seat.

"Yes Abdul, you too will have to leave," Wasim informed Abdul.

"Where will I go *Huzoor*? Should I go back to my village? But I can't be a burden on my daughters. They are too upright and will never refuse me shelter. But it could create problems in their family lives. I will have to find some place to live on my own," Abdul loudly considered his changed circumstances.

"Abdul, I do not want to force anything on you. If you want to go back to your village, you may do that. But I think these men will be seething with anger once we manage to give them a slip. Shakeel knows your village. He may reach there to take revenge and to know about our whereabouts. Wasim Bhai and I have decided that you should go to Delhi too. You have served me for a long time Abdul. In your old age, let my son look after you too," Wali said and looked at Abdul with soft pleading eyes.

"But we will come back soon, won't we? Who will look after your business? If the orchard is not maintained regularly, it will get ruined. The fruit trees can catch disease with the blink of an eye. We can't stay away for very long. After all, for how long will these men await our return? Once they are gone, we can be informed by *Bhai Huzoor* and then we will come back," Abdul was suggesting with an eagerness of a child.

"Abdul none of us have any idea when will it be safe to return. These men belong to some terrorist outfit, though we don't know which one. And after today we are going to be on their hit list, to be targeted at the first possible opportunity. These are vicious men and will be broiling to take revenge.

Chapter 17

Shakeel will be the one on constant lookout for us after he would be tricked and humiliated by us. So Abdul, returning soon will be quite risky. We will have to observe the prevailing conditions before taking a decision to return. And that could mean years."

Abdul gently nodded in agreement. His tear filled eyes depicting his aching heart sent a stabbing pain in Wali's heart too. He apprehended how unaided they all were, utterly defenceless. Utterly constrained.

Wali continued, "Now Abdul, for the success of tonight's venture you will have to stay back till after the midnight. That is to give the men a false assurance of our presence in the house. If need be, you must distract them to make it easy for us to slip away. But you should leave the house around midnight, for that may be the safest period. Go straight to the bus stop. Catch the first bus to Jammu that leaves around seven thirty in the morning and from Jammu take a train to Delhi. I will leave Salim's telephone number with you. Inform us from the station the moment you reach Delhi and someone will come to pick you up. Once in Delhi, we will see how things go."

There were three disconcerted minds and total silence in the room now. All the three men were anxious and fearful, well knowing that a night full of risks lay ahead. They had no idea what would be the outcome of the venture. But they also knew that they had to try. Accepting things like cowards and wasting a young intelligent life was just not admissible to any one of them. Meher was dear to them all. They had seen her grow from a lovely little girl to a beautiful young lady. She was now a qualified doctor and they were all proud of her achievements. They would go to any length to protect her.

Then Wali addressed Wasim but spoke more for Abdul's benefit, "We will have to lie low for a while, for months or perhaps years. But *Inshallah*, Bhai we will come back here someday, back to where we belong."

"You sure will Wali. This is the soil of your land and to it you must return one day," Wasim said, in an endeavour to apply balm over Wali's wounded soul.

Wali closed his eyes and made an immense effort to stop tears from flowing down his cheeks. His wounds wouldn't heal so quickly. Then, along with an injured ego, there was the agony of suspense. Eyes red with the exertion, he continued in a shaky voice, "Meanwhile, I leave my assets in your care Bhai. It is left to you to decide what to do with my orchard and my house in my absence." His tearful eyes prompted Abdul to immediately rest his head on his knees once again and shed more silent tears.

"Do not worry on that account Wali. I will safeguard your orchard and your house, till you come back. I will do whatever will be within my power to see that no bothersome elements misuse the property that belongs to you. And I will assure that you regularly receive the profit from your orchard. You will need that money."

Wali bowed his head and touched his forehead with his hand to salaam his brother, a gesture to indicate his extreme gratitude.

"Wasim Bhai, I think we should give some money to Abdul to reach Delhi," Wali spoke after a few moments of stillness in the room.

"Yes Wali, first take your money which I withdrew from your bank. I spent some on the tickets," Wasim took out an envelope from his bulging inner pocket and handed it to Wali.

"Wasim Bhai, what about the vehicle you have hired? I must pay you for it?" Wali asked as he took out a few five hundred rupees denomination notes and handed them to Abdul.

"I didn't pay anything. You know my old friend Hassan, who runs the transport business?"

"Yes yes, I know him well, though only due to business associations. I have sent my consignments a number of times in his trucks," Wali answered.

"Well, I know him since our college days. He is a good man. I had gone to him to hire a taxi for tonight, to transport us to the bus station. But when I explained the circumstances to him, he suggested that I should use his private car," Wasim said. Then noticing a frown on Wali's face he explained, "Hassan is trustworthy. He won't open his mouth. He was the one to suggest that hiring a driver could be unsafe for they couldn't be expected to keep secrets. Since I know driving, I wouldn't have to depend on anyone. He has left his car at my disposal for the rest of the day. That made my trip to Nuorat's house to collect the tickets and to the grocery shop to meet Abdul easy. I will return the car early in the morning. By the way, it is a Maruti Van"

Wali felt relaxed. Avoiding the involvement of an unknown driver was definitely a good idea. Trusting just anyone and entailing a stranger in the escape plan would be, without doubt, unwise.

"Let's now quickly revise our plan. Abdul needs to know it all and there isn't time to waste," Wasim continued. "So here is the scheme from now on. I will drive you both home now, till the main road and we can decide upon the spot where I will park the vehicle tonight. I think I should pick up Bua-Jaan right away. She won't be able to walk down fast and that will slow you all down too. So let her leave as early as possible."

"No Bhai, Abdul and I should not go back together. The men are not going to like that as they will think we had been planning things together. That is the last idea I want to put in their heads. In addition, if any one of them is posted on the road and spots us alighting from a car together, they will immediately be ready to act. You can drop Abdul, after making sure that the area is clear of the spies, and I will go walking. That will give a considerable difference between our arrival times. Moreover, Abdul has to reach the provisions in time and help cook the dinner," Wali suggested.

Wasim nodded his head in agreement, "That is fine. I will drop Abdul then. I will select a spot where I will wait with the vehicle tonight, a spot which will be the closest yet not visible from the house, probably around a curve. I will show the spot to Abdul. On my way back, I will pick up Bua-Jaan. Perhaps Abdul can bring her down secretly till the main road and I will wait in the car. It will be better if she is safely evacuated from the house at the earliest. In case of danger at the time when you will be leaving, you may be required to dash down; and it will be impossible if she is with you."

"Yes Bhai, I was thinking somewhat on similar grounds but completely overlooked discussing it with you this morning. With Ammi-Jaan safe, half of my worries will be over. But how will she leave now, in front of the dangerous hounds? They will be immediately suspicious. It has to be done without their knowledge and that will not be possible at this time, in the broad daylight." Thumping his forehead lightly with his closed fist and considering thoughtfully he then continued, "I suppose it will be safe to evacuate her from the house only at the time when the devils are at dinner."

Wasim nodded again, "You are right. When will you be at dinner then?"

"We usually eat at nine, but I think we can have it early today." Then turning towards Abdul he asked, "Abdul, will it be possible to eat dinner half an hour early tonight?" Seeing him nodding in agreement Wali continued, "We will be at dinner at exact eight thirty. Ammi-Jaan's departure should coincide with that time. The greedy men will remain occupied gorging, so that is the opportunity we will grab when they wouldn't get even a hint of what is going on behind their backs."

"That is decided then. It also means I will have to come up personally since Abdul will not be free at dinner time. That is fine with me. I will come at exact eight thirty, and make sure that the scoundrels are kept immersed in their feasting at that time," Wasim said.

"Wasim Bhai, it has just occurred to me that it will solve a lot of problems if Meher and Sakina too left along with Ammi-Jaan. I will be more relaxed then, knowing all the women are safe. Abdul will serve us dinner and then at the first opportunity, we both may be able to slip out together," Wali suggested.

"No, Wali no! I had considered that option but from what you tell me about the men accompanying Shakeel; they are cunning. They will smell the absence of the women. Once they demand to check the house and subsequently find them missing; they will go berserk. They will not spare you. They will also know where to find the women. Therefore, they have to be made complacent before attempting any venture. They have to be caught napping," Wasim presented his logic.

"You may be right. In that case, I will make sure Sakina shows herself to them once or twice during the meals, to keep the men complacent," Wali thought aloud.

Wasim continued, "Make sure the dinner is served just before I reach, may be at eight twenty five. You will have to keep Bua Jaan ready but you stay with the men. Don't reveal the truth to Bua-Jaan. It will be very difficult to take her away then. She might rush with her stick to hit Shakeel, which of course he rightly deserves. But the current of events may then turn to our disadvantage. Make some excuse…like…like…may be Ayesha is not well and she needs her. I will leave Bua-Jaan with Ayesha at the bus station. Ayesha will have enough time to explain to her the circumstances and make her understand. Then I will come back to fetch you, Sakina and Meher. I will be on the main road by eleven. The last bus to Jammu, for which I have bought your tickets, leaves at sharp twelve. You should be at the spot where the vehicle will be parked latest by eleven fifteen. Few minutes up or down do not matter. But if you do not come by eleven thirty, I will go to the police, for it would mean some serious problems have cropped up and you are in trouble. Is that clear Wali?"

Wali and Abdul nodded their heads. Then Abdul addressed Wasim, "*Huzoor*, if Shakeel finds you in town tomorrow, he may try to harm you. We may have escaped, but what about you?"

"Don't worry Abdul; I will be catching the first bus in the morning to Ayesha's home town. I will come back only after enjoying fifteen days of my in-laws' hospitality. I have informed my son too, who is at his wife's place these days and was to come back day after tomorrow. I called up Imtiaz to ask him to stay on for another fifteen days, giving him a brief explanation of the circumstances. By the time we all come back, things should be fine. These men can't linger on for that long. They are controlled by their higher command." He was quiet for a moment, pondering, trying to bring to mind if some important points needed discussion. Then he said to Wali, "Wali, I will give you a call day after tomorrow to check if you all have reached Delhi safely. I will keep in touch with you regularly through public phone booths. But you should never try to contact me through Salim's personal telephone number. You know very well that a call can be traced. We need to take utmost precautions and cannot afford laxity at any moment of time." Wali nodded slowly.

Wali's anxiety was on the rise as it was now time to proceed back home. His subconscious mind had started a churning in his stomach once again, and his conscious mind had begun to analyse nervously what lay ahead. Soon he would be undertaking his life's toughest test and he wasn't sure how well prepared he was for it. The result would be known within a few hours but the success was uncertain. They had done their best in the short time available to them. He then reminded himself, "But why should I worry so much. The final judgement will be conceded by *Allah*, so why should I bother about the outcome. Whatever will happen should be accepted as His will. He has already provided so much help through Wasim Bhai. Executing the plan would have been impossible without him."

Abdul interrupted Wali's thought process. "*Huzoor*, if you don't mind, may I take the liberty to present my judgment?"

"Yes, Abdul, what do want to say?" Wali asked.

"I have a feeling that this all may just be a hoax set up by this wretched Shakeel. This cluster of crooks may not be associated with any radical group. They may just be a bunch of cronies whom Shakeel has pulled together for his intentions. This militant theory may just be a pretension. They may simply be trying to frighten us into falling in line with their demands, using the opportunity of the prevalent conditions in our state. For, why would they be given permission to undertake such an activity as they are presently involved in? Why would anyone be bothered for an insignificant recruit like Shakeel and help him get his depraved wishes fulfilled?"

Abdul looked at Wali with tenderness that conveyed the possibility of his judgement being accepted and perhaps his master wouldn't have to abandon his home and run away furtively to save his beloved daughter. Perhaps he would agree to challenge the decadent men and escape becoming destitute overnight.

Wali narrowed his eyes and looked intently at Abdul, considering his view gravely. There was surely some legitimacy in his statement. But his own judgement regarding the characters of his guests couldn't be wrong. He had seen all sorts in his life and could smell evil from far. Also, he had spent almost an entire evening with the nasty group. Abdul had spent only a few minutes. Even if they did not belong to any radical group, they were evil. Hashim's threat wasn't an empty threat. Then, what about their loaded rifles? He then spoke more to himself than to Abdul, "No, we can't take the group lightly. Their rifles are genuine AK 47s. And Hashim and Ahmed are no novices in the game. They are the types who don't play games but execute orders. What do you say Bhai?" Wali now turned towards Wasim for his suggestions. "Should we ignore their threat and seek police help?"

Wasim, who had been following the conversation absorbedly instantly voiced, "No, we can't take any risks. If their weapons are genuine then perhaps they mean business. We also know that Shakeel had contacts with such a group even at the time when he worked in the house. Though, Abdul is right. Why would they be given permission to carry out such activities, I too fail to understand. They may not be acting at anyone's behest. Yet, taking risks will be foolhardy. So, let us stick to our plan. More immediately, you all need to shift to a safe place out of the harm's way."

Wali sighed softly. How he wished that Abdul was right and the threat presented by his guests could be taken lightly. At the same time, Wasim was correct at his judgement. It would be foolhardy to jeopardise safety of so many lives.

Wasim then continued, "I think that is about all. It is almost five twenty now and both you and Abdul should get going. Abdul should be home by five fifty and you will reach a little after six. Half an hour gap is good enough difference. Wali let us not leave together. You go first. Abdul and I will leave after five minutes, after I lock the boat. We will then be rowing back in our hired boat till the shore where the vehicle is parked."

Wali slowly walked to the table and picked up his spectacles and pocketed them. "If there is sight left in my eyes after tonight, I will need them," he thought pensively. Without meeting any of the men's eyes, he proceeded towards the door. Highly despondent, with his head and arms, like his spirits, drooping limply like the branches of a weeping willow, he reached the door when he recalled that he had forgotten to hand-over the bag with his personal papers to Wasim. That would have been a serious blunder. He retreated and walked swiftly towards the bed. Picking up his black bag from under it, he entrusted it to Wasim. "Bhai, you keep my bag. It has all my important papers; the property papers, the bank papers, the certificates and the ledgers etc. You can keep the bag in the vehicle. I will take it from you at the station, that is, if I reach there. Otherwise, give this bag to Salim."

Wasim nodded gravely and then shook his head in disgust, "Oh, I too forgot to give you this packet." He handed Wali a large packet he had kept on the table after his arrival. Wali had wondered about it when Wasim had come with it but hadn't enquired about its contents, taking it to be his personal shopping.

"What is in the packet?" Wali asked.

"Oh, it is Nusrat's wedding dress. It was her idea and quite a brilliant one. She said that if Wali Bhai would go home without a wedding dress, the villains would get suspicious. Her wedding dress has been lying useless ever since her marriage. She doesn't have a daughter who could use it. She said that she would be happy if it could help Sakina and her family. She has ironed it and folded it neatly. It looks almost brand new. She also picked up some artificial cheap jewellery from the market on her return trip from the bus-station. She has shown me the ornaments. They look amazingly real gold, and it is a good ploy to fool the rascals. I comprehend Nusrat is quite a clever woman," Wasim informed Wali.

Wali suddenly realized that he had completely overlooked this important task. His hand got lifted to lightly hit his forehead in an automatic reaction of self-reproach. "Bhai, the villains had instructed me to pick up the wedding dress and some jewellery last night and I had completely forgotten about it. After all it is a work supposed to be undertaken by the womenfolk. Nusrat has saved me form a serious fix. I would have been questioned about it and then I would have been in a sorry plight. It was rather thoughtful of her. She surely is a smart woman. Wasim Bhai, when you meet her next, kindly let her know how grateful I had been for her benevolence. We couldn't have managed without her help. May *Allah* bless her and her family. May He cure Feroz of his affliction." Wali had these wishes bursting forth directly from his heart. He stood quietly for a moment and then said, "And Bhai, I couldn't have done without you. Today,

I have no words to thank you. I will never be able to return this debt, even if I survive tonight's risky quest. If I don't, remember me kindly. You have been more than a real brother to me. In my absence, you will have to be a father to my Salim and Subina. Tell them that their father loved them both." And Wali hugged his brother. They stood in each others reassuring arms for a while. It was an emotional moment for them. They had no idea when would they meet after tonight or whether they would. Their eyes were moist; with the tears of love and the fear of uncertainty.

Wali then said, "Wasim Bhai, I am really sorry to have dragged you into these dangerous affairs. I really had no choice."

Wasim answered, "Wali, don't mention it ever again. If a brother stops helping his own brother in need, this world would become an unstable place to live. Moreover, this particular time, I am driving a strange satisfaction by planning to dupe the armed terrorists. I feel as if my Rohman is backing me from somewhere above, asking me to defeat the negative forces. This is my way, our way of condemning terrorism. We are simple peace loving and hard working folks. We shun violence. We believe in world being one large family. Terrorism has done nothing but earned a bad name for our community. Wali you will realize once you go to Delhi. I had similar feelings when I had gone there two years ago. The moment a common non-Muslim person comes to know that you are a Muslim from Kashmir; they look at you with suspicion, no matter how truthful, polite and genuine hearted person you may be. For the world today, we are all branded terrorists; thanks to these misguided minds like Shakeel's."

Wali nodded his head in silence, at the same time wondering if his Salim and Subina too were the victims of this kind of discrimination. Whether, he too would have to face similar treatment from now on.

"What can a simple common man do to voice his opinion? How can the world be made to understand that all men are not the same and all men are not in favour of aggression? Every community is comprised of all kinds. There are many like them; who themselves have become victims of the malevolence. Men like them have no means to make their voices heard. The world listens to either the leaders, good or bad, or the gunshots. No! The deafening sound of powerful blasts gets heard even better."

"Who is bothered about a common man, who can easily be blasted into thousands pieces in a split of a second?"

"In the effort to hurt the conscience of the powerful, the innocent citizens are becoming the easy victims. But neither these ruthless killers, nor a large chunk of politicians have any guilt feelings associated with the sense of right and wrong. The ones with conscience are the sufferers, the scapegoats to be sacrificed."

Such were the thoughts rushing through the minds of men who were at the receiving end right now, the victims of the futile unrest the world over.

Wasim sighed heavily and broke the silence, "All the best Wali! You better leave or your guests will be really troubled. May *Allah* be with you!"

"And *Allah* be with you too," Wali said. He then quickly walked out of the interior of the houseboat closing the door behind him.

He was startled by the transformation in the waters of the lake. Whatever was visible of once a calm blue lake had turned inflaming orange. There were ripples of waves due to the mildly blowing breeze and the whole lake appeared to be on fire; an emanating swelling and surging blaze.

Wali automatically looked towards the horizon. Two thirds of the Sun was visible behind the contrasting dark mountains. The horizon too was painted in flaming colours, though a few grey clouds mellowed down the effect. Wali watched the setting sun with strange ache in his heart. Would he ever be able to see the sunset so glorious? Was it the last sunset he was witnessing from the land of his ancestors?

Or was it the last sunset of his life?

Chapter 18

Wali reached the head of the stairs of the houseboat and straightened his tall frame. Taking a deep breath, he stood erect and dignified for the first time that day. He inhaled deeply the flavours of the waters and the glow of the sinking sun before walking down with firm steps. The fiery energetic colours had, as if, filled him with strength and resolution. Missing the last few steps, he stepped on the land in one leap and proceeded in a hurried trot. He felt the freedom of a prisoner released from captivity and noticed his surroundings with interest. The long dying shadows of the tall reeds shifting side to side with the wind were bidding him goodbye. "*Alvida,*" he muttered softly and at once became aware of their rustling whispers returning his valediction.

Into the deeper bush, he confronted hectic activity revealed through the loud twittering and tweeting of numerous water birds that inhabited the lake. This side was definitely a paradise for bird watchers. Wali had come to such areas numerous times for the same purpose but today he had no time to enjoy the spectacle of the egrets, cranes, herons, kingfishers, ducks and geese, restless in their preparations for the nightly rest. They were about to call it a day and he had the major task of the day's calendar yet to perform. A purple moorhen made its presence felt when disturbed by his thumping footsteps she scurried away with three toddling chicks following their mother. Wali stopped to allow her not to feel threatened and watched the family with interest till it reached the safety of the giant water lily leaves. It reminded him of somewhat similar circumstances he might face while undertaking tonight's operations. No one would be interested in allowing him a free passage then. There would be many to bar it.

After a brisk walk of several minutes, totally engrossed in his thoughts, he unexpectedly spotted two huddled figures and instantly missed a few heartbeats. He halted on his track. Who was hiding in the foliage? Was someone waiting for an ambush? A few precautionary steps ahead he noted with relief; the children signalling him to be quiet by touching their lips with their index fingers. He smiled and nodded at them. They were playing hide and seek, the game that he too had played the entire day today. In addition, he would have one more session of the game tonight, trickier and deadlier.

He passed by a small islet of a single house, inhabited by a lone family. The children playing hide and seek probably lived here. Their small wooden house was completely submerged in a surging vegetable garden. Wali couldn't help surveying the healthy growing tomatoes, beans, bottle gourds, pumpkins and a woman watering her garden through self made contraption of a foot operated watering can which dipped into the lake to lift water when released and emptied its contents onto the garden when the attached paddle was pressed. Would such healthy and fresh vegetables be available at the metropolis, he couldn't help wondering.

This was the beginning of the signs of some habitation that Wali had come across after hours of seclusion. Soon he would be passing through the danger zone; the bazaars and he must stride across unnoticed. He should carefully choose to walk through shadows and dark alleys.

When he came out of the reed-bush, the sun had disappeared behind the mountains. He turned for one last glance of the lake. Only the farthest part of the lake was visible. The orange glow of the waters was gone. It had been substituted by a grey haze. "Just the way the brilliance of youth gives way to old age before the complete darkness. One realizes the swiftness of the passing time only when it is gone, and my time is perhaps gone too. The current dreadful events may also lead me from the grey to the dark." It was an agonizing thought.

The cool breeze had become stronger now. Wali's *pheran* fluttered in the wind. He shivered with cold and put his hands in the pockets of the pheran for warmth. It wasn't very cold, like the real winter cold, but Wali was weak today. He had shrunk in these last few hours. The worry and the fast had both rendered him sapped. Yet, he now had the strength and firmness of a strong willed man. The daylong reflection had given him the clarity of purpose. He was earnest to save his Meher. He was anxious for the safety of Sakina and Ammi-Jaan. Abdul too must remain unharmed. He was ready to make any sacrifice today to save them all. Beyond that, nothing substantial mattered. Material things weighed so trivial for him now, leaving all major assets behind a trifling matter as compared to defeating the threat looming over their heads. He was ready to face the consequences of his actions; for he believed in their validity.

The worried frown, which had remained on his face since the declaration of the heinous designs by Shakeel, was now erasing out. Instead, his lips were held tight together in a firm resolve. Shakeel won't lay a hand on his Meher. He would never send his daughter to rot with this rotten man for the rest of her life; for whatever life he would have allowed her to live.

Abdul's comments returned to Wali's mind now. Perhaps Abdul was right. "I am being unnecessarily panicky, almost paranoid. Why would an organisation back Shakeel's immodest designs? Why the hardened men like Hashim should be assisting Shakeel in his craving? Why has the group travelled all the way just to fulfil what an insignificant mortal like Shakeel had desired?"

The probe revealed something dreadful to him. A brainwave hit him like a thunderbolt and he stopped dead on his track. He realized that Shakeel was possibly a scapegoat who was about to be sent on a dangerous assignment. He was being pleased into docility, being gratified into accepting something that was full of risks.

He felt quite sure of the substantiality of his reasoning. Walking on more slowly now, he contemplated over his latest reckoning. Shakeel probably had been asked if he had any particular desires, for he was to be given a present before being sacrificed on the altar of the desires of some selfish powerful men. Hashim was the hangman trying to fulfill Shakeel's last wish, otherwise he seemed least the type who had the patience for such trivial matters. He would have preferred an easy and quick method like kidnapping. Was that the reason of their visit to Pehalgaon? Then what had made them change their plans? Did Shakeel extend his desire to take his bride honourably? He might still have some remnants of conscience that had prevented him from destroying them till now. No wonder the wild men were behaving with restraint and were being a bit civil.

But for how long this would restrain last, Wali wondered. It was like a cracked dam threatening to explode anytime, ready to bring about ruin. How many more innocent lives would be readily sacrificed along with that dim witted fellow? It was of least importance to the people with vested interests; such people who were behind all the mayhem created in the world today; who would not allow peaceful negotiations as means to solve problems. Why should it matter to those for whom life has never held any value? Power was the most prized passion for them. They were experts at successfully creating inhuman humans who would kill in cold blood. Hashim and Ahmed were such final products. Shakeel was being processed and Shaukat was still raw.

What they would have done with his Meher once Shakeel was gone? He shook the thought out of his mind. It was disgusting, almost frightening to even imagine. Meher had to be rescued at all costs, Wali resolved earnestly.

What if he failed in his endeavour? There was a great chance of the letdown of their escape attempt tonight.

A tragic scene flashed across Wali's eyes.

Booming sound of AK47 rifles and some bodies lying scattered soaking the orchard soil red!

He realized that the episode would in no way be novel for the inhabitants of this strife torn region. The news would be read…tongues clicked…some discussions among the known held and then the episode would be forgotten. The people would go on with their routines totally unaffected by such customary incident.

"But some people do care. Abba-Jaan cared. I care. There may be many more who are concerned." This thought process made Wali recall having read a poem written by a Kashmiri poet; Bashir Athar titled 'An Unclaimed body'. "How beautifully and powerfully has Bashir Athar projected the tragedy that has struck the people of our region!" It had pierced right across his heart to read the fate of many an innocent people accused of being police informers and cruelly done to death by the terrorists.

"Does the same fate await us?" Wali wondered with swelling panic. "A family of police informers…done to death brutally, mercilessly…unclaimed bodies…no mother awaiting the return of her children…no sister searching for her lost sibling."

"But in our case, there will be a survivor to helplessly shed tears over the bodies draped in blood stained shrouds… will anyone help Salim hunt down and punish the guilty?"

The tremor in Wali's hands was returning. His legs began to feel heavy as if he was plodding through mounds of snow. He slowed down, dragging his feet with tremendous efforts but they were reluctant to proceed. If he didn't have responsibilities to realize, perhaps he would have allowed his instincts to prevail; to return to the safety of Wasim's houseboat.

Wali shook his head vigorously to drive away the unpleasant ghostly thoughts. "Death has to come one day, if it is planned for today then let it be," he thought firmly. But he guaranteed himself that he wouldn't give up meekly, without a fight.

He forced the weakness out of his system yet again. He had to. Otherwise, his weakness could crash his plans. And the failed plans would mean just one thing: The End.

Ear-splitting jarring music, concoction of a Kashmiri folk song being played on the radio in one shop and from across the street equally loud Bollywood music reached his ears and sounded like a crass cacophony. It irritated him. Exasperated, he quickened his steps to reach where his reflections could prevail without interruption. Moreover, the markets were overflowing with the shoppers and the amblers and Wali wanted to eschew sociality. He was much happier alone with his ruminations and his planning. In addition, some decadent humans had taken just a few moments to make him lose his trust in fellowmen. At least today, all men were not trustworthy.

He had now crossed the bazaars, through the rear lanes, without any further hindrance and was walking down the main road, endeavouring totally to hide in the shadows of the avenue of *chinar* trees. There were a few people around, but none preferred to walk in the murky spots which were not safe considering the prevailing circumstances in the valley. For Wali, the same obscured areas were the safest today.

The fading shadows reminded him that he was indisputably being missed at home. For his own people it would be a matter of concern, for the posted guards; a frustrating situation. And for him, it was no less than the feeling of proceeding towards a battlefront. Seemingly, he was the front liner in a battle formation and therefore to survive, he must fight the battle with valour. More than valour, it would be his strategy that would salvage them from the current mess. Though, it was now more than affirmed that it was a; Do or Die situation tonight.

He increased his pace and walked with long strides. His decision had lifted the weight off him and infused him once more with driving force. He soon reached the base of the footpath that led to his house. As he began to climb up, he realized that he had been totally absorbed in his thoughts and had overlooked surveying the main road to decide upon a suitable spot where Wasim could wait for them tonight. He halted and turned to inspect the road. The first curve was visible but it was pretty shallow. From his memory he knew that the next one had quite a deep contour. Yes, that would be the most suitable place to park the vehicle in the dark of the night for it to remain unnoticed. It was also not far from the footpath. He would tell Abdul to covey it to Wasim when he would come to pick up Ammi-Jaan.

He almost rushed up the steep footpath. He was in a hurry to reach home now. His family required his presence at home. He didn't want the men to get even slightly suspicious of his designs. On the way, he had cooked up detailed explanation for his day's schedule and hoped it would work. Very shortly, his plan too would begin its trial and he wished it to be successful. It would only be possible if the men were made totally smug. Although, they were basking under the glow of their possession; the deadly AK47 rifles, their over confidence was the weakness he was going to exploit tonight.

He scampered on. He still had a lot to take care of. Sakina and Meher were to be informed of the adverse circumstances and that would be painful. Ammi-Jaan was to be made ready to go with Wasim and that would require tact. Packing was to be done which would take time. And the group of armed men was to be kept in the dark about the activities inside the house. It all needed caution in handling the situation. And time was limited.

The issue that bothered him the most at this instant was the approaching moment to reveal all to Sakina and Meher and their reaction. He had dreaded this moment the whole day and it was so close now.

The day light had almost faded away when Wali reached the spot from where the rear side of his house was visible. He halted now and once again observed the incline in the twilight. Although it was steep but they had lived all their lives around the mountains. He would manage the descent. He was sure that Meher too would easily traverse it. He wasn't sure about Sakina. She would perhaps need assistance.

Wali scanned the area. No one was around. His fruit trees were standing lonely. Green unripe fruits had filled the apple trees. In a month when the fruits would ripen, once again there would be a hue of colours in his orchard; once again it would be exuding wafts of sweet fragrance. And he wouldn't be there to experience the beauty of it all. Well, Wasim Bhai would look after his orchard and that was some consolation. Wali walked on with vigilance now, pushing aside the numerous thoughts that had been invading him one after the other. He was soon to face the dreaded foursome once again and the thought pricked him like a painful sting. He readied himself for the revolting job.

As Wali stepped onto his compound, the repelling faces of all four men came into his view all at once. Shakeel and Shaukat were sitting on the steps of his veranda. Ahmed was sitting on the boundary wall of the compound. And Hashim was pacing up and down the compound in a meaningless way. It appeared to Wali that his house had already been turned into an impregnable fortress by these rowdy invaders, making it hard for the imprisoned inmates to escape. "But escape we will!" He once again affirmed in his mind.

The moment his eyes fell on Wali, Hashim stopped his marching and stood facing him.

"Where have you been the whole day Wali Sahib? What have you been up to?" He asked with certain sternness of a headmaster reprimanding a wayward student.

"I was making arrangements, what else?" Wali answered dryly.

"It doesn't take so many hours to make arrangements. We made it clear yesterday that we do not want it to be an elaborate affair. And we do not want a crowd invited over. Or were you out to invite undesirable personnel?"

Wali remained unfazed. "I haven't invited anyone. I have that much sense. Yet, something needed to done for the occasion," he answered curtly. He wanted to be as brief with them as possible.

"What kind of arrangements have you been making, Wali Sahib?" Hashim's tone was clearly mocking.

"Why, the bank was to be visited as money was required for certain purchases. Shopping was to be done, and that takes time. Then *Maulvi* Sahib was to be contacted," Wali answered.

"We were in all the main market places today. But we didn't see you anywhere." Hashim looked straight into Wali's eyes with a challenge. He was clearly being sceptical.

The Burning Orchard

The inquiry failed to make Wali nonplussed. "Why? Were you spying on me?" He asked with slight contempt, returning the stare. He knew that if he tried to be over friendly, or even frightful at his enquiries, the cunning mind if Hashim might begin to get suspicious. He had to be his normal self, depicting clearly that he wasn't very happy at the turn of the events. He was surely not expected to be happy, especially by Hashim. Any stance other than this would raise clouds of doubt in his shrewd mind.

"No, we were just sight-seeing. Although we expected to see you around, especially at the Hazratbal mosque, for you must have gone there to contact the *Maulvi*. We spent almost half a day at the Hazratbal." Hashim appeared to cool down a little but his tone was still cynical.

"I didn't go to the Hazratbal. I thought of contacting *Maulvi* Sahib of Chashme Shahi Mosque. He is personally known to me and would understand the situation," Wali lied. He couldn't escape telling lies today, he thought. He had already decided upon these answers for he had expected these queries.

"Oh, so you had gone to Chashme Shahi side. That is far! No wonder they didn't see you around. But still you took a long time." Ahmed hopped down the wall and joined his comrade now. Probably Hashim wouldn't know where Chashme Shahi was located, so Ahmed had given a hint of it being far, Wali realized.

"I stayed at the Mosque till the afternoon prayers. I had gone there soon after finishing my bank work but *Maulvi* Sahib was busy and I wanted to speak with him only when he would be alone. That took away most of the day. I went shopping after that," Wali said. Then he immediately added, "Is there anything else that you want to know? Or do I need to give you minute by minute account of my day's agenda?" Wali's tone depicted his annoyance, and it was deliberate.

"Well, what have you got in that big packet? Can I have a look?" Changing the topic Hashim now extended his hand, demanding handing over of the packet.

The mention of packet brought all the members of his gang come rushing. "Petty minds," thought Wali. "Do they think I will be openly carrying weapons, and displaying them at the first opportunity?" Loudly he said, "Nothing much. It is a bit of shopping that I could manage." But he ignored Hashim's extended hand completely.

"I would like to see your shopping Wali Sahib," Hashim didn't withdraw his hand although he was clearly irked by the snub.

"Yes, yes, what have you bought Wali Sahib?" It was Shakeel's inquisitive eyes probing the packet.

Wali opened the packet slightly to reveal the bright yellow embroidered dress.

Shakeel gave a big grin. Hashim wasn't satisfied. "May I take it out?" He sought the permission rather impolitely.

"He is well trained and quite thorough. No wonder he is the leader of this pack of wild hounds," Wali thought with distaste. He quietly handed over the packet to him now. Hashim's patience shouldn't be taxed anymore. It would be risky.

Hashim took all the contents out of the bag. He shook open the dress. Next, the closed jewellery box raised their curiosity. It was opened with interest. The shining elaborate golden necklace with matching earrings seemed to have taken their breath away. Even Wali, who now saw the ornaments for the first time, was impressed at the beautiful design as well as their outward show for they seemed to be made of pure gold. Shakeel immediately took it out and weighed the necklace in his hands. He seemed greatly impressed. "Greedy fool," Wali thought, at the same time noticing Hashim running his fingers around the empty box, pressing the lining to check it methodically. Satisfied, he smiled for the first time and proceeded to dump the dress back into the bag without folding it. The necklace too was carelessly placed and the things were handed back to Wali.

"Well done, Wali Sahib. You have a good choice as well as a sensible understanding. I appreciate your cooperation, knowing well that you have no other choice. We are the men who only know to take, and take at any cost." Hashim was challenging him once again, Wali realized.

"It is foolish to be over confident, man! One must never presume the opposition to be weak. The enemy should always be considered smarter. But how smart may Hashim consider himself, he is going to be defeated in this war of wits," Wali thought silently while he took the set out once again to keep it properly in the box. It was an on the spot made plan, a gesture to mislead them into thinking that it had cost him some real money. It was a deliberate act to make Shakeel feel that it was an expensive buy. It was an act to cool them into smugness.

"I haven't seen the mistress or Meher the whole day today. The house was turned into a barricade by Abdul Bhai. He wouldn't let us in," Shakeel let out his grouse.

"Shakeel you know pretty well that woman of our house do not expose themselves to unknown males," Wali immediately retorted. "But the mistress will be there to serve you dinner tonight," he quickly added. His tactics called for a change as the men were to be made unsuspecting and contented from now on.

"Meher is a modern girl. She too can enjoy the feast with us tonight," Shakeel now made his suggestion.

"I do not think Meher will be comfortable eating with strangers," Wali answered rather gently.

"Well, I am no stranger. Tomorrow, I will be a family member. Moreover, I haven't seen her for a long time. She must have changed quite a bit. Convey my request to her to eat dinner with us."

"I know it will be useless. She wouldn't want to be exposed to strangers," Wali insisted, keeping his voice still under control, though he had begun to get irked.

"When she exposes herself to strangers all the time, being a doctor, she can come down to sit with us too," Shakeel argued.

"Dealing with patients is a different matter altogether. It is a professional relationship," Wali closed the subject with certain degree of sternness in his voice now, knowing well that an illiterate and high headed man like Shakeel would not understand the polite language. "Now if you will excuse me, I need a cup of tea and some rest before we meet for dinner." Saying so Wali walked towards the main door. It had now occurred to him how right Wasim Bhai was. It was essential for these men to see Sakina and Meher around. Otherwise they would be filled with suspicion.

"Abdul hasn't served us the evening tea either," Shakeel said and followed him. Wali did not want anyone of them inside his house till the dinner time but was at loss how to evade Shakeel who was walking right behind him with clear intentions of gaining access into the house.

Wali rang the bell.

"Coming, coming! These uninvited unwelcome guests have made life miserable for me in a day. The whole day I have been at their beck and call. I wonder when they are leaving." The irritated and loud sound of Abdul was clearly heard. Wali smiled to himself. He knew that the act was put on.

The door was opened. Wali was planning to give Shakeel a slip by quickly slipping inside and abruptly closing the door before he could step in, although that would have appeared an obvious and impolite action. But now he met Abdul blocking the way with a tray of tea cups held in his hands. "Oh! *Huzoor*, I am sorry. I thought Shakeel or one of his worthless friends was ringing the bell," Abdul said, more for the benefit of the other listener. And Abdul gave a meaningful smile to Wali. Wali realized that Abdul had been waiting for his arrival to serve tea to the horrible guests.

Abdul shifted slightly to let Wali pass. As soon as Wali was inside, he once again blocked the way. "Shakeel, you are at the right place. Tea is ready. You may have it at your outdoor station or inside the quarters. That is your choice. Now hold this tray and take tea to your friends. I have a whole lot of work in the kitchen. I wonder why the mistress is preparing special dinner when there are no special guests, but only some undesirable elements around." And Abdul gave no chance to Shakeel to speak even a word in protest. He was handed the tray and the door closed with promptness on his face.

"Bless you Abdul," Wali whispered to him, at the same time smiling in appreciation. He followed him to the kitchen; "Make sure the dinner is ready on time. Meanwhile continue to keep these men at bay. I have to talk to everyone about the plan now. I think I will start with Ammi-Jaan, for that will be the simplest task tonight." Abdul seriously nodded. Wali moved towards Ammi-Jaan's room. He stopped on the way, near the telephone table. He must give Salim's number to Abdul before he would forget. Keeping the bag he was carrying on the table, he quickly scribbled the number on a piece of paper from his personal hand written directory. He must carry the directory along, he decided on the spot. It would be the only link with the past once he would leave his house tonight, he considered with sadness, turning the pages and glancing through the familiar names. All those names and addresses seemed so close to his heart, especially at this time when he was being distanced from everything familiar, everything cherished. He kept the directory on top of the bag.

He walked back to the kitchen to give Abdul the phone number. "The phone number is important. I haven't written any name on it. That is precautionary.

Nevertheless, it should not get into the hands of any one of the rascals," He advised Abdul. Abdul nodded and put the slip at once in the secret pocket of his vest.

Wali now became conscious of the dinner preparation going on in the kitchen. The kitchen was filled with food odours and it made him suddenly hungry. "Abdul, make me a cup of tea and bring something to eat to my room upstairs. My empty stomach has begun to protest. "

Abdul sadly gazed at his master's distraught face and nodded. He guessed that he hadn't eaten a single meal the whole day.

Wali then proceeded toward Ammi-Jaan's room. On the way, he kept closing all the doors to avoid any leakage of sound.

Ammi-Jaan was reading a book on spiritual doctrines. Seeing Wali enter, she kept it on the table along with her spectacles. "Wali, where have you been? I haven't seen you at all the whole day," she complained.

"Ammi-Jaan, work kept me busy," he replied.

"No Wali, You must not work that hard. Look at your face. It looks so strained. You look terribly tired. I know you are working non-stop without taking rest and I am worried for you," she spoke with serious concern.

"Hmmm…" was all that Wali said in return. He was at loss how to open the topic. Telling lies to Ammi-Jaan was not easy. He didn't remember ever lying to her.

"Is everything all right Wali? There is something troubling you." Affairs couldn't be kept hidden from Ammi-Jaan for long, Wali thought. It also gave him an opening.

"No Ammi-Jaan, things are not fine. I am coming from the hospital. Ayesha Bhabhi is not well. Remember she had once that terrible stomachache. She had it again today. Wasim Bhai had called me. We took her to the hospital. The doctor has given her some medicines and now there is some relief. But she has been asking for you Ammi-Jaan. She says if Bua-Jaan comes to her, she is going to be all right."

"Oh! Poor Ayesha! What should we do Wali? It is quite late to go now, although I would like to go to see her."

"Ammi-Jaan that has already been arranged. Wasim Bhai wants you to stay at their house tonight. Imtiaz and his wife are away. Wasim Bhai is all alone and he is not confident. He is really worried for his wife. He has decided to come to fetch you. He will be here in about two hours, once he has given Ayesha something to eat." Wali's concocted story had begun to sound convincing.

"I don't mind going but how will I go Wali? Walking that far is not possible for my old legs. I wish your car had already been delivered. Then you could have driven me there."

"Wasim Bhai is bringing his friend's car. You will have to walk only till the main road, Ammi-Jaan. He is going to escort you down. Do you think it will be fine with you?" Wali asked.

"Why don't you come along, Wali?" Ammi-Jaan proposed. She didn't seem secure of going at this time of the evening without her son escorting her.

"I wanted to Ammi-Jaan, but there are some guests coming over for dinner. If I get free early, I will surely join you," Wali didn't want Ammi-Jaan to know about Shakeel, at least, not till they were safely away.

Ammi-Jaan got out of her bed. There was certain purpose in her actions. Such opportunities come once in a while. Otherwise old age becomes a dragging monotony of time.

"Wali, I will pack for tonight. Could you please give me my small bag from the closet? It is on the top shelf. I haven't used it for a long time. Not since your Abba-Jaan decided to join *Allah*," Ammi-Jaan said.

Wali opened the closet. Ammi-Jaan's closet appeared so empty. There was a time when it would be full with her clothing. She was very fond of good clothes. She had an excellent collection of *pashmina* and *jamawar* shawls. But a few months after Abba-Jaan's death, one day she had called Sakina and given her all her prized collection. "You use what you like, *Beti*. There are a few brand new shawls and *pherans*. I didn't use them deliberately thinking Meher would need some when she would get married. You can keep some for Salim's wife, when he ties the knot. The prices of these things have gone skyrocketing lately. Then you may not get products of such good quality. The businessmen want to make extra profit these days and the quality suffers as a result." And when Sakina had objected, she had said, "What am I going to do with all these now. My age to wear fancy clothes is gone."

Wali felt relieved thinking that it was good Ammi-Jaan wasn't attached to her things any more and she wouldn't have much treasure to leave behind. He took out her bag and handed it to her.

"Ammi-Jaan, pack one or two extra changes, that is in case your plan to stay there extends," Wali suggested. "And Ammi-Jaan, can I request you to stay in the room till Wasim Bhai comes. The guests I have are not to my liking and I don't want my family members to be exposed to them."

"There are some people outside the house since the morning and Sakina told me the same thing. Sakina and Meher were in my room till after the lunch time. When they left to rest in the afternoon, Sakina warned me to stay inside. Who are these men Wali?" Ammi-Jaan showed curiosity to know.

"Ammi-Jaan, they appear to be some shady characters and want some business with me. I am not interested and I will try to shake them off. You know well it is not the time to trust any one," Wali replied.

"You are right; the world is changing for the worse. People are becoming selfish. The feeling of cordiality is going away. Instead, people are ready to pounce at each others throat even for minor conflicts. Your Abba-Jaan used to say that the foreign rule had brought all these ills to our country. You are right in being wary of the strangers." And Ammi-Jaan got busy packing.

Wali walked out of her room. He stood outside the closed door and heaved a sigh of relief. One major task had been taken care of. It was less difficult to tell Ammi-Jaan a fabricated story than he had expected. For once he hadn't felt guilty telling lies. It was only to save them all. Ammi-Jaan would eventually know the truth. And he silently prayed that he might be given many more chances to hug his mother. He prayed that his mother should be safely evacuated from the house without any inkling of the goings-on to dreadful men. He fervently prayed that these should not be his last moments with his mother.

As he stopped by the telephone table to pick up the bag and the directory, he stood regarding the old telephone that had served the family for years now. Innumerable business transactions had been conducted through the gadget. It had kept him connected to his children and his friends. "Today, for the entrapped family, this small black instrument is the only means of communication with the outside world," thought Wali. At the same time he wished he wouldn't need to use it tonight, for it would mean using it to summon help. He casually picked up the receiver to put it against his ears and then slowly put it down.

Chapter 19

When Wali walked up the stairs to his room, his brow was creased with deep furrows. He couldn't discard the foreboding fear from his heart. The enemy had laid siege to his house and he was the lone unarmed defender, a warrior without any expertise. To hoodwink the gang of vicious criminals would not be easy. But no matter what; he would definitely attempt to break through the cordon tonight, he reminded himself the umpteenth time. Each new hurdle was making him more and more resolute. With this self avowal once again, he reached his room.

It was close to seven. It had been a long day of worry for him. His head had begun to throb and he badly needed a cup of tea. He had also the most important task ahead of him now.

As he entered his room both, the women instantly looked up at him. It was obvious that they had been anxiously waiting for his return. Meher was posed supine on the bed, reading a book. Sakina was sitting close by; knitting a new sweater for him, despite the protests from his side a number of times that he didn't need a new sweater, for he already had more than he needed. It was better if Sakina had paid heed, he thought, for this project would have to be abandoned now. He felt overwhelming emotions for the tender affectionate women, who were to endure unnecessary mental torture shortly.

He greeted the women with a frail smile, kept the bag on the side table and sat down to remove his shoes.

Sakina immediately noted his distraught countenance and frowned with disapproval. "Work kept you engaged almost the entire day," she complained. He looked up at her. She still had that disconcerting look in her eyes. She must have spent the whole day in anxiety, thought Wali as he took off his *pheran*.

"Abbu ji, is everything all right? Ammi ji was saying that you were worried stiff about something this morning?" Meher asked and sat up on the bed cross legged, waiting for an answer.

Abdul now barged in with tea and snacks and spared Wali from giving immediate response. He too had begun to appear quite fazed. He was in deep thoughts, as if making his own plans. He threw a quick glance at the occupants of the room. Realizing that an easy atmosphere still prevailed in the room, he at once concluded that the women were still in the dark about what had befallen them. Keeping the tray on the table, he gave a meaningful nod to Wali and left as brusquely as he had entered. There was a feverish urgency in his actions. And it was one of the rarest occasions when Abdul hadn't spoken a word.

Wali picked up his shoes and kept them on the floor at the side of his bed, keeping them ready for they would require to be worn again a few hours later. Putting on his slippers, he went for a wash. He didn't have time to spare, yet he dilly-dallied his return. It was now time to reveal the truth to the two women he loved so dearly, and he felt weak kneed. He dreaded their reaction. There was disquiet in his heart, for soon he would be making them miserable with the terrifying news. He wanted to spare them the suffering, but it was unavoidable. The loathsome task had to be undertaken and undertaken immediately.

He went to the window and casually peeped out. Shakeel and Shaukat were sitting on the boundary wall moving their legs to and fro in a gesture indicative of their immense boredom. Hashim and Ahmed were standing a little further away, feverishly discussing something from which the juniors seemed deliberately excluded. Having noted it all, Wali quietly closed the window and drew the curtains close. Next, he walked to the door and bolted it from inside. Then he came back to sit on his favourite easy-chair.

"Yes, things are not fine at all. That scoundrel of a man Shakeel has created immense problems for us," he said finally.

"Problems? How can a trifling boy like Shakeel create problems for us?" Meher asked innocently. Not receiving any response from her father she continued, "Ammi ji was saying that ever since he has come with a group of similar friends, you have not been the same. What is the matter Abbu ji?"

Wali remained quiet.

"And I suppose you have been overworking lately. You look very pale. I think a complete medical check-up is required for you. I will go to the main hospital tomorrow and arrange for it. I have a few good friends working there," Meher spoke in a professional style.

Wali took a sip of the hot beverage. It made him feel a bit composed. He picked up a piece of the home made savoury snack to eat. He put the whole piece in his mouth. Hunger had suddenly invaded his appetite. He slowly munched on, unable to make up his mind how to begin.

"We will think about the medical check-up later. Right now more immediate problems need tackling. Shakeel has come here on a bestial mission. After all, what can you expect from an ignoble being like him," Wali said.

"So he hasn't improved with age! Where does he work these days? And what is he planning, Abbu ji?" Meher asked with childish curiosity.

"And you mentioned that the men are carrying guns!" Sakina now intervened.

Meher continued rather in a casual tone, "Are they terrorists Abbu ji? Imagine that chicken of a boy becoming a terrorist! When he was here, he used to be so timid, even scared of mice. Once, Salim Bhai had chased him all over the place with a mouse held from the tail. And Shakeel had become so scared that he had run down to the main road, screaming his lungs out. He had refused to come back for quite sometime, even till much after Bhai had let the mouse go." And Meher burst out laughing recalling the funny scene she had witnessed as a child.

Wali didn't even smile. He couldn't today, even if he tried. Seeing him so serious, Meher stopped laughing and gave him a quizzing look.

"Abbu ji, if you don't like them, why don't you ask them to march off. After all it is our house and we won't have people we don't want," Meher verbalized emphatically. She appeared to be wondering why her father hadn't followed the simple logic.

"Yes, exactly! I have been musing over it the whole day that why you hadn't told Shakeel and his friends to leave the house yesterday? What if he is carrying a gun? He won't kill us!" Sakina added.

Wali now responded, "Don't be so sure Sakina. And the problem is not that simple Meher. Shakeel is a scorpion with a deadly sting, a venomous serpent. If I had known it earlier, I wouldn't have ever picked him up from the streets and brought him home. He has no consideration for those who might have harboured him once. He is a selfish predator who has come to prey upon us."

There was now a deadly silence in the room. Both the women had begun to appear uneasy.

"Listen to what I am going to say now. Do not react loudly. The sound of our discussions should remain inside this room," Wali cautioned the unmistakably demoralized women. He then proceeded in undertones, "Shakeel has created a mountain of problems for us. He has brought some hardened terrorists along to threaten us, in case we do not accept his demands," Wali said.

"Demands? What kind of demands Abbu ji?" Meher now asked softly, taking care to keep her voice low.

"I feel ashamed to open my mouth my child. But it has to be revealed to you. Shakeel has come here with an intention of taking you away as his bride. The wilful men have ordered the *nikah* to be performed tomorrow morning," Wali fell silent after his statement. His head dropped as if shamefacedly trying to hide in his chest.

Sakina drew in a quick breath. Meher's face lost all colour. Both the women stared at Wali stunned at the revelation. Throughout the day, Sakina had been pondering over what Shakeel and his cronies might have demanded of her husband to cause such agony in him, but she hadn't even come any close to this in her presumptions. She had guessed that men had probably demanded some financial aid, which was a substantial amount thus causing him anxiety and the papers that he had collected in the morning were required for the same. Just a few moments before his arrival, she had wondered why it had taken him so long to arrange for the money. But, this was outrageous, blatantly vulgar.

After absorbing the initial shock that had numbed her to the extent as to defer an immediate reaction, Meher vociferated, "What nonsense! That is impossible Abbu ji."

"That is unthinkable," added Sakina equally vocally.

"Shhh.....speak softly. Walls have ears," Wali cautioned them once again.

"I am not scared of that wretch of a man. In fact, I feel insulted and defiled by his impure thoughts, when I always thought that he had sisterly respect for me when he served in our house. I will go and tell him right away to buzz off." And Meher got up to go.

Wali held her hand and stopped her. "Do not react impulsively Meher. I would have done just the same if I could. Shakeel is accompanied by a fellow named Hashim, who, I think, has come from across the border. He is a real shrewd fellow. Each time I am in his company, I can feel negative vibrations emitted from his being. His very persona is encompassed in cruelty. He is a hardened and trained terrorist, I am sure of it. He won't hesitate to kill anyone if need be. I wonder how many innocent people he has already killed. The first thing that the rascals did on their arrival yesterday was to display their AK47 rifles. The rifles were kept right in front of me, against the wall. Shakeel knows very well that such a proposal as he has made would not only be unacceptable to us; but considered downright disgraceful. He knows we would never agree unless pressurized. And he is aiming guns at our temples to make us agree," Wali said.

Meher slowly came back and sat on the chair opposite Wali. Sakina covered her mouth with her scarf and began to sob after absorbing the first shock. "*Ya Allah!* What are we to do now?" She spoke to herself.

"So Abbu ji, do you mean that I should quietly accept the lewd offer and marry an illiterate fool? I should marry a terrorist when all my life I have been taught to stand for truth and non-violence? All those years of hard work to achieve my aim in life were a waste? No! I will never marry that rascal, even if he kills me," Meher sounded resolved. She looked resolved too. Her playful innocent smile had been obliterated instantly; instead she suddenly looked tired and haggard. Her eyes were emitting embers of anger.

"He won't kill you, *Beti*. He will kill us all if we refuse to comply with his wishes. And then he will take you away by force. That is my understanding of a criminal mind," Wali spoke softly.

Meher looked around in desperation. Then she said to her mother, "Ammi ji, help me pack. I will catch the first bus in the morning to Pehalgaon. As such I was to go after two days. My leave will be over then." Turning towards her father she said, "Abbu Ji, will you accompany me till the bus stop early in the morning? We can leave much before the sunrise, may be around four O'clock. When I am gone, this stupid terrorist won't be able to do anything."

"That won't help Meher. This group of scoundrels had first visited Pehalgaon before coming here. They know you are a resident doctor there. How they got this information, I have the least idea. They probably have a contact here; in this town. Moreover, there was an armed vigilance outside our house the whole of last night and is expecting to continue tonight as well. The men have been lurking around the entire day, some trying to follow me, while others keeping a vigil on the house. The telephone is also not working. Probably the wires have been cut." Wali shook his head in desperation. He did not want to divulge with his plan right away. He wanted to prepare the women, wanted them to become hand and glove in his contrivance on their own will.

Meher looked at her father in a deep shock. The news had shaken her out of her wits.

"Abbu ji, what should we do? Please save me from the terrorists. Abbu ji, Please! They will spoil my life… They will kill me… Marrying one of them is as good as dying anyway… Please Abbu ji, do something," Meher pleaded pitiably. She was shivering all over. Blood had completely drained from her face and she had acquired ghostly pallor.

"Meher, what do you think we should do? Do you think calling in police is a good idea?" Wali now asked.

Meher did not reply immediately. She looked from Abbu to Ammi to Abbu again. Her desperation was obvious. Wali silently waited for her answer. Sakina continuously shook her head and moaned pitiably. Meher was shivering like jelly, her condition no less than that of an innocent captive facing a firing squad. She breathed deeply a number of times and that seemed to help her regain her composure a bit. Finally, she said in a quivering but mildly calmer voice, "Abbu ji, if we call in the police; there will be an encounter. If these men are really hardened criminals as you say, then they will kill us first. I do not mind dying, but I can't see you and Ammi ji being harmed. Nor can I bear *Barhi* Ammi ji troubled, who is as such so helpless." After a moment's silence she added, "Did you say that the telephone wires are cut? How can we contact anyone now? I have left my cell phone behind at Pehalgaon. I forgot to pick it up in a hurry to catch the morning bus." There was plain fear in her eyes.

Her calm once again vanished and she put her head in her hands and began to sob. Sakina sat stiff, her tears no more flowing down her cheeks. She was shell shocked at the events. Their helplessness had begun to turn her into a stone.

"Is there no way out Abbu Ji?" Meher articulated through her sobbing.

The women had undergone enough torture, decided Wali. It was now the right time to reveal his plan, for the chances of it being accepted were the highest at this juncture. If Sakina and Meher refuse point blank to run away like fugitives, it could still be disastrous. But this little doze would perhaps be useful now to make them fall into his line of action.

He now gave a faint smile and said, "Meher, do you think your Abbu is a weakling? Do you think your Abbu will allow any rascal to come and spoil your life? No my child, No. I have the strength to desist these terrorists. I can prevent them from touching my family, or me. I will keep them at bay from you all at any cost. They won't get a chance to fire a single shot. I won't let anything like that happen," Wali's voice was soft yet determined.

Both the women now were looking at Wali with certain expectations. He got up and walked to the window once again. The two pairs of hopeful eyes followed him across the room. He peeped out through the curtain. It was almost dark outside but Abdul had switched on the veranda light. He could see all four fearsome men in the compound. They definitely appeared restless for they all were walking back and forth aimlessly. No sound seemed to have leaked out from the room for the men appeared unruffled. Satisfied, Wali came back.

Meher couldn't restrain herself anymore. "What have you decided Abbu Ji?"

"I have made certain plans. I was given one day to make arrangements for the *nikah*. And I utilized the whole time to plan our escape," Wali informed them in murmurs.

"Escape?" Both the women spoke in unison. But they were careful to be extra soft this time.

"There is no other choice. I have tickets for the night bus to Jammu. We must reach the main road by eleven from where we will be picked up by Wasim Bhai. Once we reach Jammu, we will be safe. From there we will board the first available train to Delhi. We are going to Salim," Wali spoke with authority, feeling blissful to perceive an element of pleasant surprise on the faces of the women.

Meher instinctively rushed to hug her father. Wali too embraced her lovingly. They both laughed and cried at the same time. Meher then kept her head on her father's lap and continued to reprieve her emotions through tears. Sakina remained glued to her seat. Tears were rolling down her cheeks once again but a faint pale smile too had appeared on her face. She nodded in appreciation, her expression clearly defining that her faith in her husband's capabilities had soared prodigiously.

Wali proceeded to caution them of the perils of the venture they were about to undertake. He was a practical man who believed in straightforwardness. Giving the women false assurance when they were about to tread on a bed of smouldering coals, wouldn't be fair. Moreover, if the ladies were acquainted with the dangers they were likely to encounter, they would be more vigilant. "I want to warn you that it is not going to be easy. Our attempt is fraught with dangers. Firstly, if we come face to face with any one of these men, our expressions should not reveal our inner thoughts. We will continue to conduct ourselves normally till dinner is over. Once the men are sent to their sleeping quarters, we will slip out, say around ten thirty. It will be before time, but the men probably will not suspect us to slip away that early. That time should be to our advantage; when they might be less watchful. Abdul will take care of the rest. He has already been instructed his course of action. In case, we get into any trouble, then do not panic. We will face the consequences together, and bravely." He didn't need to say more. The women knew what to expect of the men involved in subversive activities. From the prevalent circumstances in the valley and the experience of the unfortunate, they knew well that to expect mercy from them would be like patting a man eater and expecting that hungry tiger to lick in return.

Meher and Sakina vigorously nodded their heads, which indicated their whole hearted cooperation. Their faces too had begun to acquire grimness of resolve now.

Wali patted Meher's back and said, "Now go and pack your luggage quietly. Take as little as possible, only bare essentials. There should not be any noticeable hectic activity in our rooms. Work calmly. Sakina, I will manage my packing. You too make sure you carry only as much as you can easily carry yourself. Escape won't be possible if we are overloaded. Things can be bought in Delhi if need be. Carry your jewellery for that is valuable. If you think there is anything really important, then pack it. But each one is allowed only one bag. Wasim Bhai is coming to take Ammi-Jaan first at exact eight thirty. Sakina, I will be with the villains at that time eating dinner so you will have to handle it carefully. She thinks that she is going to see ailing Ayesha. That is the reason to be given to her by you. Feed her well in time and send her off from the back kitchen door with the least noise. Abdul knows it all and he will be with you. We do not have much time so hurry up. Dinner must be served on time." Both the women kept nodding with eagerness throughout the directions. Wali fell silent after the instructions were over. He felt exhausted. The events of the previous few hours had been gruelling. But he also felt quite at ease now, as compared to the rest of the day, for one major task had been taken care of.

The room was almost dark now. No one had any will to switch on the lights. They were afraid of getting exposed to more man made vicious plans. They wished that the four walls of their house could hide them. They were obviously reluctant to leave their home. It had meant every thing to them; it had meant happiness, security and glow of love. The same house was becoming an unsafe place today from where they were to run like fugitives. Wali sighed deeply and got up to switch on the lights. A dark room could raise the curiosity of those who should be kept unperturbed tonight. Moreover, time was running out.

With the click of a switch, everyone woke up to the reality. Meher jumped up to go to her room. "Ammi ji, I am going to pack my things quickly. After that I will come to help you," she whispered and left in a haste.

"Sakina, get the meals ready first. It is seven thirty now. By eight twenty-five our abominable guests should be at dinner, for Wasim Bhai will be here at exact eight-thirty. I will do my packing meanwhile. You can pack after making sure the dinner is served on time and after sending Ammi Jaan away. Show yourself or let your voice be heard clearly once or twice while we are at meals. That will satisfy the scoundrels of your presence. I will try to shake off the villains by nine. That will give us some time to rest. But first get two bags for both of us. And hide this somewhere, perhaps at the back of the closet." Wali picked up the packet that Wasim had handed him and gave it to Sakina. Sakina took the packet from her husband and peeped inside it.

"It is a lady's dress. Why have you brought it?" She asked.

"It was Wasim Bhai's idea. No, it was in fact Nusrat's idea." And Wali quickly explained the reason behind bringing that dress home, and also how useful it had been to fool the self appointed guards outside their house.

Sakina smiled faintly and carried the packet to the store room from where she then fetched two bags. One of them was Salim's old backpack. Wali immediately laid claim on it, for that would keep his both hands free to assist the women down the steep incline tonight.

She then informed Wali, "I was in the kitchen for most of the evening and dinner is more or less ready. I will go now to give the final touches. If you remember anything else you want me to do, you can tell me after dinner." Sakina began walking towards the door. Wali watched with anguish her heavy slow steps; a stark contrast to the briskness that had always characterized her movements. It was as if in a jiffy, her agility and friskiness had been snatched away by some brutal hands. He also noted how pale and terrified she had become. He called out to her softly, "Sakina, I am so sorry. I couldn't think of anything else. We are going to be homeless, and for how long; I have no idea."

"Don't be disheartened. The house is not more important than our daughter. We can't let that mean Shakeel spoil our Meher's life. And as far as being homeless is concerned, who said we are going to be homeless? Doesn't our Salim's house belong to us as well? I know my Salim. He will be too happy to accommodate us. Do not worry anymore. We are together in it now." Sakina's statement was the most comforting aid Wali had received that day. It was as if he had received some reinforcement to continue to fight his battle against evil forces.

He smiled at her affectionately.

Sakina turned to go and then stopped at the door as something had occurred to her and she retraced her steps. She then came to stand in front of her husband and voiced with certain hesitation, "Only you must treat Subina well. She is a sweet person. Do not be angry at her unnecessarily."

Wali gave a sheepish smile and nodded. "When did I say she is not a wonderful girl?" He remarked.

Sakina's face lit up with satisfaction. When she walked towards the door again, Wali couldn't help noting some ease in her gait.

Wali immediately jumped up to pack. His photographs and the camera along with the directory were the first to go inside the bag, before the other bare necessities. It took him barely ten minutes to finish the packing. Sakina's cooperation had left him somewhat light hearted. He had dreaded hers as well as Meher's reaction. But the women had exhibited incredible sagacity.

He next took out the packet of money from the pocket of his *pheran*. After giving some to Abdul, he was approximately left with a little more than Eighty thousand rupees. "Enough money to go for a long vacation to my son," thought Wali sardonically, "But this is no vacation. And for how long will this amount last me?" He wondered. Even if he spent sparingly, it wouldn't last him for more than a couple of months. What after that? Though there was some amount left in the bank, deliberately kept for the day when he would perhaps return. That would be the reserve to renew life once again on the territory that was his real home. If he was never able to return, then at least he would have left some bequest for his children. With the interest earned over the period, it should be a decent amount.

There were whole lot of payments to be collected too, especially from the middlemen of his orchard produce and his handicrafts. The amount should be close to about a few lakhs. How would that money be procured now? He had had no time to discuss this matter with Wasim. Perhaps he might be able to steal some time at the bus stop. But he still had to compute the accounts. He would have to calculate the amount to be secured from various business associates in detail and inform Wasim of the same through correspondence.

"How many of my affairs will Wasim be able to handle?" Wali thought uneasily.

Under the present circumstances, unless Wasim managed that, as well as earned profit from the orchard and sent him the emoluments, he would be a pauper soon, totally dependant on his son for survival. An ironic smile played on his lips and he sighed heavily. It occurred to him that with the hopeless situation like that, he was no more afraid to face the bullets. And if such a situation did arrive, he would die with dignity. But, he was undeniably afraid for Meher, and for Ammi-Jaan and Sakina. For them, he would have to fight till the end.

He divided his money into three portions and put one bundle in his wallet, one in his bag and the last one back into his *pheran* pocket. This was all that was perhaps left in hand from his entire life's labour.

Presently, his riches were reduced to three small bundles of paper notes.

Chapter 20

At five minutes past eight, Wali walked out of his room and down the staircase. He went straight to Ammi-Jaan's room. She had changed into a fresh *salwar kameez*. Her small bag bulging with her belongings lay on the floor next to her bed. On the bed was placed her freshly ironed beige *pheran* with embroidery in shades of sapphire around the neck and front. Wali had always admired his mother for her impeccable dressing sense. Even at home, she could never be caught shabbily dressed. She put the last bite of food in her mouth as Wali entered her room.

Sakina had served her dinner in her room and that was a wise move.

Seeing her in slippers, Wali suggested, "Ammi-Jaan, you must pack your slippers too? You may need them."

"I have decided to wear my slippers to walk downhill in the dark. Due to the corns in my toes, shoes give me trouble. I will be more comfortable in slippers. I have packed a pair of sandals though. But if I am going to be inside Wasim's house most of the time, I don't think I'll need them."

"Yes Ammi-Jaan, if you will be at ease walking down in slippers, then it is fine. Do you want me to do anything?"

"No Wali, I am ready to go. Let me just wash my hands. Has Wasim come?" She seemed quite energized and all set to go to perform her important job. "By the way, why don't you send Meher with me? She will be able to help the patient more. Ayesha too will be pleased if a doctor is at her disposal."

"Ammi-Jaan, I had suggested that to Meher, but she has a headache. She has promised to see her aunt later. I will bring her along, the instant I can break free from my visitors." Then with urgency in his tone he said, "Wasim Bhai should be coming any minute now. I am going to be with my guests, so I won't' be able to see you off. But I will try to I see you as soon as possible."

"Never mind Wali, you just look after your guests. Sakina said she will see me off. She has fed me with real delicious food. And I think I have overeaten." Ammi-Jaan gave a short chortle and disappeared into the bathroom.

Wali's heart had begun to quiver with sudden qualm and he fervidly prayed for the safety of his mother. The first leg of their escape plan was about to commence and his trepidation was immense. He had done what was within his power. Now Blessings from above were absolutely essential. He urged the Almighty to individually watch over each member through their dangerous mission tonight.

Ammi-Jaan was still in the bathroom. If he stayed in the room longer, his expressions might give away his consternation and that would certainly give Ammi-Jaan a reason to be concerned. So, Wali opened the door and silently walked out. There was a lump in his throat, for he wasn't sure if he would see his mother again and he hadn't even hugged her. He wondered which way the wind would begin to blow henceforth. If it turned unfavourable it would bring along a storm…a tornado and suck them all into its vortex. He wished the elements to show them mercy tonight by remaining mild and favourable.

He halted in the parlour to regain his composure. The stillness in the house was nerve wracking. There had always been vibrant atmosphere in the house, even after children had grown wings to fly away. The women's chatting…his discussions with Abdul regarding the days dealings…Abdul's funny narrations followed by his light hearted guffaw…sounds of hectic dinner preparations…it would all add up to keep the house in vivacious spirits. Today, there was deathly silence around and it began to give Wali cold creeps.

He quickly moved towards the kitchen to seek company. The feast was ready. Sakina and Abdul were precociously occupied, though their actions lacked motivation. The usual warmth was missing. Their silence was an indication of the disquiet in their hearts. The kitchen was saturated with the spicy aromas of freshly cooked food. Saffron drenched steam from the pot of rice rose in whiffs and reminded Wali of the vast saffron fields, so exclusive of his land.

Saffron sold almost as expensive as gold. Though it was a labour intensive crop, Wali had been lately contemplating on buying a field in Pampore area, not far from their town to grow his own saffron. But his plans were now melting away before his eyes one by one and quickly dissipating like the steam from the rice pot.

He stood aimlessly looking around. Abdul was readying the steel plates and bowls to be laid with food and taken to the dining area. Wali nodded with approval at the preparations. It was quarter past eight.

"If every thing is ready, Abdul, you may call the guests for dinner now. You can instruct them to wash outside before coming in, like yesterday. That will save you the effort."

Abdul left wordlessly to invite the guests to come inside the house for the first time that day. Abdul's unusual muteness further depressed Wali. He took a deep breath in preparation to face the dreaded men. "Sakina, I am going to be with the guests from now on till after dessert is served. I won't be able to show any urgency to dismiss them. I leave it on you to take care of the things behind the scene. Wasim Bhai will be here soon. These men shouldn't even have an inkling of his presence in the house. But you can speak loudly with Abdul so that you may get heard. And... make sure you and Meher eat well." Sakina nodded and noting her eyes haunted with fear he added, "Have prayers in your heart continuously. Prayers give strength during the weak moments of life." He then gave her a feeble smile and lovingly put his comforting arm around her shoulders.

The reality stirred his mind that this was to be their last meals at home and he looked at Sakina sadly. The vibrant kitchen... fitted with modern gadgets... full of hectic activity each day of their lives...more so when feasts would be readied for guests, would now wait listlessly for their return not knowing when it would be. Sakina returned Wali's gaze, understanding each word his eyes wanted to convey and tried to say something, but her words got stuck in her throat. Her lips quivered, and Wali felt a constriction in his chest. He left for the sitting room in a hurry, before he got besieged by some weakness.

He sat straight and dignified on an armchair and waited for his guests. But after five minutes of wait, he began to be worried. He looked at the wall clock. He then rechecked the time by his wristwatch. Eight Twenty-two. Why were the men not coming? What was taking them so long? Wali picked up a magazine to glance through it. He didn't read a word. He didn't see any picture. His heart had begun to pound with anxiety. Eight Twenty-Five. Wasim would be here in five minutes. Why was Abdul not hurrying them up? Perhaps it was his fault. He should have come down five minutes early. Were the men somewhere down in his orchard again? What if Wasim came face to face with them? He became alarmed. In his agitation, he got up to check the reason for the delay himself and walked up to the main door which had been left open by Abdul. He peeped out into the veranda lit by a sixty watts bulb inside a decorative copper shade.

"Come on. Hurry up Shakeel or eat cold food. I am not going to warm it up for you again. Don't expect that of me eh…" Abdul's welcome voice fell on Wali's ears. "They are coming, *Huzoor*. I don't know why they are so grumpy. Wouldn't get up…till I declared it was no problem with me if they wanted to go hungry to bed. I could enjoy their share of the delicious feast too, that our mistress has prepared. That made the young boy jump to his feet and urge the others to do the same as he was starving," Abdul hurriedly informed Wali before hastening off to the kitchen.

A minute later the four repulsive characters came marching from the direction of the servant quarters. Shakeel was leading the pack, followed by the scowling and moping members of the repulsive assembly. Hashim gave the impression of being the most disgruntled of the lot but then even a mild frown would have been enough to add mortified grief to his revolting countenance. Wali instantly judged that their recent discussions were centred on his conduct and that it was the root cause of their malaise. If the state of affairs had been different, this could have been rather a matter of gratification. But, today they were to be kept amused, so that duping them may possibly turn out to be trouble free.

He noted that Hashim was still hauling his gun along. His sullen looks added to that and Wali's heart experienced a sinking feeling. He was the one to be vigilant of…he was the one to be kept well entertained and perhaps given maximum importance, decided Wali.

"Come in…come in…the dinner is ready. The mistress and Abdul together have prepared some sumptuous feast for us," Wali lured his guests in.

He stood at the door to allow his guests to walk in first. As the last member of the single file, Ahmed, walked past him to enter the house, Wali got a glimpse of a shadow emerging out of the total darkness into the dimly lighted area of the compound. It then quickly retraced its steps to merge with the darkness once again. "Wasim Bhai is already here," Wali realized and felt fortunate that he was the lone witness to the event. As a reaction, he abruptly shut the door.

Uneasy at the awareness that it had been a very narrow escape, he quickly followed his guests and led them to the sitting room.

"Thank you for inviting us inside Wali Sahib, after closing the doors on us for the whole day," Hashim opened the dialogue in ill humour, keeping his rifle rested next to the wall, once again on display.

"Well Hashim, I was out the whole day and I believe so were you. I am sure you do not expect to be allowed inside when only ladies are in the house," Wali reacted with slight impatience.

"You have been inside for the past two hours but this man who lives under your heels still kept us out. This is not the way to treat important guests," Hashim declared.

"Important …my foot! You are the most unwelcome guests ever to step inside my house," thought Wali. He also wanted to say, "Who invited you to be my guests anyway? I never extended any invitation to any one of you. Isn't it funny; to barge inside somebody's house and acquire importance at gunpoint?" Instead he said politely, "Abdul had been busy preparing meals you know. And I had gone to rest meanwhile. I am not as young and energetic as you people. I get tired by the evening. Especially, today was a tiring day for me, so I needed to stretch my back."

"Sakina, I need some help," Ammi-Jaan voice reached them clear and crisp. Wali abruptly looked up at the door, startled by the sound reaching them so distinctly, irked that nobody had thought of closing the doors. It was more worrisome as they all were standing close to the sitting room door. Hashim looked at Wali and said, "Why Wali Sahib, what is the matter? You look very disturbed."

"Oh nothing, really! Ammi-Jaan is not well. I am wondering why she requires help." Wali quickly covered up his reaction. Loudly he called out to Abdul who instantly responded. "Abdul, why is Ammi-Jaan calling out? Just check if she is all right or needs something. If your mistress is upstairs, ask her to attend to Ammi-Jaan," Wali gave him the instructions in louder than his normal tone. He knew that Wasim was probably in the house and Ammi-Jaan was getting ready to go. He wanted to provide a cover up to the activities going on in the background at the same time caution Wasim Bhai to remain alert.

"The mistress was in the kitchen till recently but has now gone to attend to your mother *Huzoor*. If you want, I will go and check too," Abdul answered.

"If the mistress is there, it is fine. You may serve us dinner now," Wali said.

Abdul left to follow up the instructions. Very casually, he shut the door of the sitting room before leaving. Wali somewhat relaxed.

He led his guests directly to the dining area. Once they all were seated, Wali looked straight at all of them. He wanted to be sure they were not distrustful of him. Though, it was quite hard for him to conduct himself normally in his agitated state, but restraint he must. His guests would be grossly suspicious and it was essential to keep them under a blanket of bogus assurance.

There was once again silence in the room. Wali wanted the conversation to keep going so that the men would remain distracted, but like the previous evening, he did not know what to talk about. He searched desperately for a topic. Then he said, "Hashim, is this your first visit to Srinagar? Or have you been here earlier?"

"Hashim Bhai has come to our Valley for the first time," quipped in enthusiastic Shaukat.

Before Wali could absorb this information, Ahmed tried an instant cover up, "Hashim Bhai lives on the high mountains you know. He has come down to the valley the first time"

"Which high mountains?" Wali's attention being divided, the question popped out automatically before he realized his mistake. This topic needed to be discontinued. He had noticed Hashim's vexed stare at Shaukat that made the boy wince in an obvious fright.

He was now absolutely sure that Hashim had come from across the border; fully trained for subversive activities, to mislead the simple minded people with false propaganda and perhaps pick up vulnerable youth of the valley for recruitment. No wonder he looked so dangerous. This realization made the matters worse. Hashim would not hesitate even for a second to pull the trigger. He would not listen to any pleas, even if they came from his team members. Perhaps, Shakeel himself wasn't aware of the blunder he had committed.

"Do I have to give the detailed topography of my place Wali Sahib?" Hashim asked in a sarcastic tone, as if taking revenge for the utterance made by Wali a few hours ago.

"Not really if you don't want to." Wali simplified things for him.

"Wali Sahib, I want to know about this *Maulvi* you have arranged for the *nikah*. I hope he is cooperative. He might endanger many lives if he tries to be clever," Hashim now said.

Wali could grasp pretty well that he was simply flinging another warning at him.

"Does this man know any language other than offensive? He has been thoroughly brainwashed to become a human cannon. The feelings of compassion and mercy are alien to him. Pity has been squeezed out of his system. Instead, he has been converted into a ruthless machine," Wali reflected with revulsion.

"Do not worry on that account. As I said earlier, I took a long trip to Chashme Shahi just for this reason. *Maulvi* Sahib has been very understanding. He will reach here around eleven in the morning. We all need to be ready by then," Wali said, keeping his tone as casual as possible.

Hashim and Ahmed nodded. Shakeel smiled and Shaukat grinned. Wali looked at the clock. Eight thirty-five. "Ammi-Jaan and Wasim Bhai should be on their way, commencing the on foot journey downhill. Another twenty minutes at Ammi-Jaan's pace and they will be heading towards safety," the thought made Wali cheerful.

Hashim must have noted the soft smile playing on Wali's lips and the questions which might have been at the back of his mind till lately, now emerged forth. "Wali Sahib, one thing has been irking me since the morning," he said.

Wali's smile disappeared. He looked at Hashim with certain alarm.

"How is it that you have agreed to Shakeel's proposal so easily? I mean your daughter is a doctor and…here is Shakeel who barely knows how to read and write. Well…in short… he's almost an illiterate man. He might have earned some money but if I were in your position, I wouldn't have agreed to such a marriage. Then…why haven't you expressed your disapproval even a bit?"

Wali was silent for a while. The question had taken him utterly by surprise, for this was the last query he had expected from a person like Hashim. He glanced at Shakeel, and noted with satisfaction that he had turned crimson with embarrassment. He was rightly uncomfortable with this awkward enquiry by a fellow comrade.

Wali decided that it would be in his best interest to be honest now. Perhaps he could make them withdraw their proposal and that would make things simple. Quite obviously Hashim understood the absurdity of the match between the two people totally misfit for each other, therefore, he might relent. Consequently he said, "I thought I didn't have any choice. Or do I Hashim?"

Hashim gave a broad grin for the first time. His crooked, decayed and badly discoloured and teeth got fully exposed for the first time, making Wali recoil. Instead of softening his features, his smile made him look even more dreadful. "You are a smart man, Wali Sahib. No, you don't have any choice. We have… I have given my word to Shakeel and it will have to be honoured. The *nikah* will take place tomorrow morning as decided."

"There is no point pleading with these obstinate, decadent specimens," Wali decided silently.

Abdul entered with two plates laden with food. Wali noted him to be somewhat relaxed and immediately concluded that the first operation had been executed smoothly.

And then sound of footsteps was heard by all. The flip-flop sound was clearly coming from the front side of the compound. "It is Ammi-Jaan walking in her slippers carelessly, oblivious of the danger that the sound may now put us all in," Wali thought with alarm.

Hashim and Ahmed exchanged glances. Wali could feel many pairs of eyes piercing him and he struggled to remain composed. To disguise his panic he threw a quizzing look at Abdul, clearly requesting him to come to his rescue. Abdul remained totally unfazed.

"*Huzoor, do you* remember the craftsmen were to come to report the progress of their work? It could be one of them."

"I will go and check," Ahmed declared and began to rise from his seat. Hashim was noted eyeing his rifle. Wali clenched his fists in terror. If the men decided to verify Abdul's statement, it would be disastrous. They must be prevented from moving out. He gestured at Ahmed to remain seated. "NO…no, you don't bother yourself. Abdul will check, for he knows all the workers who visit to report at this time." He glanced at the men who appeared quite tensed and he hoped they had not read fear in his eyes. He lowered his eyes.

Abdul quickly kept the food plates in front of Hashim and Ahmed, thus blocking their way. "You start your feast. I will check who has come. And why are you bothering yourself when you don't even know our workers? It is anyhow, none of your business so keep your noses out of our affairs." Abdul sounded so genuine that instead of being irked, the men seemed to have pacified a bit and remained seated.

Soon Abdul was heard talking to someone outside who appeared very soft spoken and faintly audible. The person asked for Wali Sahib and after a minute of indistinct conversation Abdul returned. The flip flop sound too began to recede and then slowly faded.

"*Huzoor*, Sillaludin had come to inform that he has completed the filigree work he had been assigned and wanted to know if there were more orders to be completed. I have asked him to come in the morning."

Wali was thankful to Abdul for having saved the tricky situation by instantaneously creating a wonderful cover up. Wali knew that no worker visited at night. It was probably Abdul carrying out conversation with Wasim, who had well understood the tight spot the sound had put them in. Wali nodded gratefully.

He was relieved that the man like Hashim hadn't insisted upon checking the identity of the person who had visited the house at this odd hour. At the same time, he wondered why he hadn't seriously suspected that it could be security personnel summoned for help. Then he grasped that Hashim was quite trained in this aspect and knew that security or any other help wouldn't announce their arrival thus. They would make sure to approach inaudibly and astutely, moreover, never in slippers.

"Abdul Bhai, what are you wearing for the special occasion tomorrow morning?" Shakeel asked Abdul now.

Abdul feigned a puzzled look and asked, "Occasion? What occasion are you talking about? Are we celebrating something?" And without bothering for an answer he left. All four men once again gazed at Wali with expressions spilling over in amazement.

Why had Abdul done that? Wali was mystified and totally taken aback. Perhaps, he wanted them to perceive that his master had not discussed any of his troubles with him so that the men may grasp Wali to be their lone opponent, without any backup. That would keep them reassured.

But why had these rogues taken it for granted that Abdul would be acquainted with the situation? They might have gathered through Shakeel that Abdul was part and parcel of the household and Wali's special confidant. Therefore, they expected him to have shared the circumstances with him. Immersed in these interpretations, Wali also tried hard to pretend that he was the least affected by Abdul's response and as a matter of fact, it didn't mean anything to him. To appear casual, he drummed his fingers on the table and kept his vision focussed on the door, completely evading the chilling stares. Before he could think of an appropriate explanation, Abdul returned with more food-laden plates. He laid a plate in front of his master and then he served the other two. He then quietly went back to the kitchen avoiding to even as much as glance at the guests.

Noticing the grim faces of the men, Wali realized that Abdul had put him in some serious quandary now. Hashim had not touched his food; instead he was still directly looking at him enquiringly. Wali directed his attention on the food laden plate.

"It appears that your servant has no clue about the wedding to be celebrated tomorrow? Is there some specific reason for it?" Ahmed ultimately broke the uncomfortable silence.

Wali answered with complete composure, "Yes, Abdul has not been informed of the proceedings. He is anyway going to be occupied tomorrow in business affairs. A consignment is to be sent and he will be busy and away from the house from early morning. Moreover, you must have noted that he is a big mouth. He can't keep secrets, so I have decided to keep him in dark."

After the explanation, Wali felt satisfied. He was rather pleased that he had very quickly learnt to tell impressive lies. This was what they deserved…only lies, he thought to himself.

"That is all right. We do not want a crowd here tomorrow morning anyway. Especially the big mouths are to be kept away at all cost. It will be safer for them that way," Ahmed responded.

Hashim intervened the conversation at this point, "Wali Sahib, What about your daughter? Did she agree readily to the proposal? She should not create any problems tomorrow during the *nikah*. You must make sure of that. For, you yourself will be responsible for any mishap."

"No, she is not at all happy at what is happening. I have tried to make her understand but she has been crying her eyes out ever since I have informed her of her engagement," Wali said. He knew that all his statements were being weighed for authenticity, especially by Hashim and Ahmed. They couldn't be easily fooled; therefore, he shouldn't make unbelievable statements. He also noted that his declaration had had some effect on Shakeel who now sat with his head bowed. Could he expect it of Shakeel to withdraw the proposal and put an end to all their troubles? Wali gazed at Shakeel expectedly but the foolish man remained unyielding. It was again Hashim responding to his statement.

"Hmmm... She will have to bear it all. Women are supposed to do that. They cannot be given the independence of taking their own decisions. That is why there is no need to educate them highly. That is a drastic mistake you have committed, Wali Sahib," Hashim said with the firmness of a high authority.

Wali chose to remain silent. He knew there was no point arguing with the men who had no respect for the educated. How could they be expected to...when all were unlettered fools themselves? Hashim too didn't seem to have had even formal schooling. It was easy for them to kill and blast people than to toil day and night with books. They may remain up all night wandering around in search of their victims but burning midnight oil to pass examinations was too much for them. The strenuous brain work was simply beyond their means. Shakeel had proved that by kicking away the opportunity given to him.

"Let's eat or the food will get cold," Wali announced.

Everyone's attention was now drawn towards the plates laden with Kahsmiri cuisine. There were *Yakhini* and *Gushtaba* filled in the bowls. A few pieces of *Tabak-maaz*, the pan-fried lamb ribs flavoured with saffron, were tastefully served in the main plate. The aroma was mouth watering.

"Soooo... many dishes? Abdul Bhai has been feeding us well since the morning but I am still hungry. In one day, I have satiated my cravings of months. Shakeel, will you bring me along on your next visit here?" It was young Shaukat commenting.

Wali felt pity on him. He was still a boy. How he had got entangled into the vicious net of the terrorists, Wali wondered. Perhaps there was still time and he should get out of the mess. Wali wished to help him but knew he couldn't, at least not today. Right now, he was desperate to get out of the mess himself.

The men waited and Wali understood that they wanted him to start the feast. It was strange to observe politeness in the ruffians. But before he could take a bite, Hashim said, "Why Wali Sahib, Abdul has served you much less than the others. This is not right. Here exchange plates with me," Wali was astounded. No one ever behaved in that manner. Moreover, the food appeared almost of the same quantity. Then why was he exchanging plates? Before he could protest, Hashim, who was sitting right opposite to Wali, picked up his plate and it reached Wali after passing through the hands of the other men. Wali felt a sudden wave of revulsion, as if the food in that plate was defiled. But, he was left with no option other than to offer his plate to him.

"That was not required but if you insist it is fine with me," Wali simply said, though the reason behind the gesture had become clear to him. Hashim was being extra careful. He was trained to be. Did he think that his food was laced with sleeping pills or perhaps poison? And Wali was thankful they hadn't planned any such course of action.

"Enjoy your food," was all Wali said, and he proceeded to eat form the exchanged plate. He noted that Hashim did not begin to eat immediately. He waited till Wali had eaten from each bowl. Wali had been hungry, but now his appetite was gone. His mind was once again distraught with worry. This man was being excessively cautious. Giving him a slip was beginning to appear a formidable task.

"The food is delicious! Your servant is a good cook," Ahmed remarked.

"But Abdul Bhai never could cook that well when I was here," Shakeel protested.

"The main cooking is done by the mistress. Abdul only helps with the odd jobs," Wali clarified.

He did not want to talk unnecessarily with these men any more, now that Ammi-Jaan was safely out of the house. They were not worth making any conversation with, Wali decided. He continued to eat quietly. The men ate with gusto. Abdul went in and out of the room occasionally to fetch more food and serve everyone. He had been instructed to over feed them, to make them drowsy. Therefore, even after their refusal to eat more, he insisted upon refilling their plates, as a gesture of a good host. Though a sharp brain would have wondered at this change of his behaviour, the greedy guests complied by unrestrained gluttony.

Abdul now brought bowls of sweet dish, *Phirni*. More fragrance of saffron exuded from the rice pudding decorated with chopped pistachio nuts. The men eyed the bowls greedily.

When they were towards the end of the feast, Sakina came to stand behind the door. "Are the guests satisfied with the food? Was there enough to eat?" She asked softly, addressing Wali.

"Yes, Sakina I think we all enjoyed the food. It was pretty good." And Wali looked around at every one. He found them all nodding. "Why don't you eat now? And see to it that Meher eats well too. She should not go to bed hungry," Wali added.

Wali noted that this time even Hashim had nodded with extra vigour, perhaps satisfied that the women of the house were quite submissive and cooperative. Wali discerned that Wasim was absolutely right and this act was essential to fool the imprudent men. Then he noted that Hashim hadn't taken his eyes off Sakina and had continued to stare at her. Wali was livid with anger at his lewd stare and immediately voiced, "Sakina, you go and rest now. Abdul will manage the rest." Sakina well understood and withdrew instantly.

When the feast was over and dishes removed, Abdul walked in and sat cross legged on the floor near Wali. He then addressed Wali, "*Huzoor*, I wanted to discuss a matter with you. I thought now will be the right time for I know that you like to rest soon after the meals."

"What do you want to talk about, Abdul?" Wali asked.

"*Huzoor*, you never got time to visit the orchard today. But when I was there, I noted that some fruit had been eaten…in fact a whole lot…more than to my liking."

"We didn't touch any fruit today," Shakeel immediately protested.

"When did I say that you have eaten any fruit? Have I blamed you? Why would you hold yourself culpable, unless…you were genuinely guilty?" Abdul gave Shakeel an interrogative stare and continued, "The fruit is quite unripe to be consumed by humans but…as far as you are concerned, it is a different matter all together. By the way, some half eaten fruits are still hanging from the branches of the trees and I know only animals can eat that way." As an after thought Abdul added, "You probably cannot devour the fruit in that manner… though I am not quite sure. You have been doing lots of unexpected things anyway." Abdul chuckled with childlike delight at his drollery and this ridicule straight away granted Shakeel, a sullen face.

"You mean some animals have been raiding the orchard?" Wali asked with concern, purposely drawing Abdul's concentration away from bantering Shakeel.

"Yes *Huzoor*. It could be some bears who come down from the mountains sometimes and raid the orchards. Remember two years ago, they had caused us a big loss in their overnight feasting? It is again the same area, bordering the woods. Something needs to be done before they cause further damage tonight. What are your orders *Huzoor*?" Abdul asked.

Wali was about to add that their land facing the woods had been fenced off after the last experience with the bears then how could they enter the orchard, but something in Abdul's expression advised him not to divulge that fact. He realized that it was perhaps again a ploy for reasons known to Abdul alone.

"Abdul what can I say? You have brought the news quite late; however, we can't lose more fruit. Just take a few rounds of the orchard at night but be careful. Bears can be very erratic in their behaviour. Tomorrow we will see what can be done about it," he suggested.

Shaukat quipped in now, "How can Abdul Bhai alone deal with the bears? They will make a feast out of him."

"I know how to deal with all kinds of animals. For this particular animal species, creating a din is the simplest way of keeping them away. Besides, what are you here for? This is your opportunity to pay me back for the extra labour I have endured due to your unannounced visit. You will help me to keep the bears at bay tonight," Abdul declared.

Shaukat's disgruntled expression unmistakably indicated his displeasure. It was also obvious that Abdul's statement hadn't gone well with the others too. Wali wanted the men kept mollified, more so, as the time to dodge them was fast approaching. He desperately needed to put it across to Abdul but found him engrossed in glowering at the visitors with his challenging stare. He was singularly focussed at conveying to the guests what he thought of them. Hence, Wali completely failed to attract his attention.

Hashim then stood up abruptly to go out, quite clearly to avoid further conversation which was turning unsavoury for them, and the others followed suit. Well registering their displeasure, Wali began to feel uneasy.

Least affected by the demeanour of the guests, Abdul too got to his feet and declared, "I am famished and going to eat now."

'Don't forget to prepare *kahwa*, Abdul Bhai?" Shakeel's request sounded almost an order.

"Didn't you hear I am famished and haven't eaten dinner? And do you think I am your personal servant? Or, do you consider yourself to be some VIP guest? Forget it. I am not serving any *kahwa-wahwa* tonight."

Hashim stared at Abdul with eyes blazing with anger. Wali was scared stiff that he might react to Abdul's statement rashly. He could well construe Abdul's indignation towards the men and agreed that he was absolutely justified in feeling so, but he also felt that his bluntness was crossing the limits. He should know that this was the moment to appease the men, not annoy them. Wali immediately grasped the opportunity to calm down his vile guests, despite the fact that he was impatient to send them to their sleeping quarters. "Abdul if there is hot water ready in the kettle, there is no harm serving some *kahwa*," he requested.

In reply, Abdul looked at the wall clock. The time was five minutes to nine. In about an hour and a half the family should try to depart. There was time for *kahwa*. He nodded.

Then Hashim spoke to Abdul quite rudely, "Don't prepare *kahwa* for me. I have no time for it." Turning towards Wali he said, "Wali Sahib, I will take leave now. I will see you tomorrow morning. Make sure everything is arranged on time." Next he looked at Ahmed and Shaukat and said, "Let Shakeel rest tonight. He should not be disturbed as he has a busy day and night tomorrow." The men sniggered and Wali fought with his anger to remain normal. "Cheap rascals," he wanted to say loudly.

"Go out to wash but come back immediately if you want *kahwa*, or I will lock the door after five minutes of wait. I am starving and can't wait for eternity," Abdul notified the group and slipped out hurriedly to get them *kahwa*.

This time their trip had remained restricted to the outdoor tap and back, Wali was certain, as the men had returned in no time. Abdul's warning had surely borne fruit. Ahmed and Shaukat made themselves comfortable of the plush sofa and Shakeel once again chose to sit on the throne he had chosen for himself the previous evening. Hashim was not with them. Wali wanted to enquire about his whereabouts but decided against it. He was not to exhibit any curiosity. Perhaps he had gone to sleep, he presumed.

Abdul didn't delay bringing in *kahwa*. He served the men in small cups, in fact the smallest cups available at home. Wali would have been amused at Abdul, had it been another time, but right now he had begun to feel cramps in his stomach once again. The time to flee was approaching and his anxiety too was mounting.

The *kahwa* consumption, as desired, was over in next to no time as the men had been served barely three sips each. With this task over, normally the guests would be expected to politely thank the hosts and depart, but this particular type didn't seem to be in mood to exit. Abdul collected the cups to take them to the kitchen but instead of leaving the room, he stood waiting. Perhaps he would be required to shoo away these parasites and relieve his master of the blood-sucking leeches, he judged. Finally Wali got up saying, "Well, I am quite tired. It is also my bedtime. Sleep well every one. We will meet in the morning." With this proclamation the three men were given a clear indication that they needed to buzz off. They reluctantly got to their feet but remained standing indecisively. Shakeel opened and closed his mouth a few times and Wali knew he wanted to say something but he was in no mood to entertain him. To ignore him completely, Wali turned his back towards him and gave pointless directions to Abdul, "Abdul, after winding up work inside take a round of the orchard. But be careful. Don't venture far. Bears are unpredictable and can attack without provocation, so keep a comfortable distance if you spot any. We will cover the trees with nets tomorrow to save the unripe fruit from any further damage."

"Do not worry, *Huzoor*. Shakeel can be an additional guard with me tonight. He has also acquired a gun from somewhere and that can be used to scare away the bears. Shaukat is, as such, accompanying me on my rounds. I would have certainly been afraid to go out in the dark all alone…knowing some dangerous animals were lurking around. But the three of us…and a few guns…will be enough for me to feel safe, as well as to keep the animals away," Abdul suggested with earnestness.

"No…no, I am tired and want to sleep immediately," Shakeel instantly reacted.

Abdul was attempting to entangle Shakeel and Shaukat in his net and now Ahmed cunningly tried to extract them, "I don't think my friends should put their lives in danger. Moreover, since they are afraid of these large animals, they won't be of much help."

Abdul instantly responded to Ahmed's statement. "Oh, I see! Now I get it! You all must belong to a group of people highly scared of animals. No wonder you need to carry your guns along wherever you go. So the mystery gets solved… the guns are for self protection against larger animals! But I wonder…why animals are particularly after you four. They seem to have become choosy these days."

Wali noted three speechless and expressionless faces staring at Abdul. He couldn't help smiling at his sense of humour; at the same time to conceal the smile from the dangerous men, he turned his face away. He wondered how Abdul could remain so witty at the time when the dagger of danger was hanging over their heads. Though, now he could well grasp his strategy of removing a few guards away from the vicinity of the house to craft the escape easier. He had been worried of the fact that if the absence of the family was discovered before Abdul managed to break away from the house, he would be in a critical spot. But due to the tactics he was now trying to apply, these men would become convinced of his involvement and such risks must be avoided.

"Abdul let it be. Don't overdo tonight. Just a round or two should be enough, that too if you seriously want to, though, it will be unwise on your part to jeopardise your life. Moreover, you have a very hectic day tomorrow. And please see to it that the articles are properly counted and packed before dispatching them. Send the consignment through the registered post." Wali gave these instructions on purpose and Abdul kept nodding though he didn't know what was to be dispatched. He pretended to comprehend it all.

Apparently irked by Abdul's remarks, Ahmed now marched towards the door without any further comment or even wishing Wali goodnight and Shaukat followed him. However, Shakeel was not the one to concede easily and he now intruded in, "Wali Sahib, I would like to meet Meher, even if for two minutes before she becomes my bride tomorrow."

Wali's response was spontaneously abrupt; "I don't think she is in mood to meet anyone tonight. She needs to be given time to reconcile with the circumstances."

But the stubborn man would not relent so easily. Distrust was apparently lurking in his mind and he wanted some surety that his scheme was functioning according to his design. Turning towards Abdul he said, "Abdul Bhai, since your master is tired I don't want to bother him anymore. You take me to Bari Ammi so that I may take her blessings tonight."

Wali was alarmed. Shakeel should not march into Ammi-Jaan's room for that would be catastrophic. He knew the way to her room and he had to be prevented at all cost. Wali strode towards the door with the intention of blocking it but before the situation could turn serious, Abdul took immediate command to control it with firm hand.

"Are you mad? You want to trouble our old mistress when she has already gone to sleep? You want me to wake her up in the middle of the night that too when she is unwell? The blessing-wlessing can be taken in the morning before you leave for good, though I am sure our senior mistress wouldn't want to waste her blessings on a scoundrel like you."

On one hand Wali was troubled at Abdul's candour, on the other, he realized that it was perhaps his natural behaviour that would keep the men from being suspicious.

And he was right. Shakeel frowned with annoyance but then decided to swallow Abdul's comments. He was evidently reserving his ire for the day when he would become Abdul's master, and then would take full advantage of his position to harass Abdul to his heart's content. It was, therefore, imperative to make certain that his devious plans should remain remotely distant.

"Ok, we will then go and rest for tomorrow is a hectic day." Seemingly infuriated Shakeel then strode towards the exit door in a huff.

Shaukat was at the moment standing at the door waiting for his buddy though Ahmed had already walked out. On reaching close to the door Shakeel turned once again to face Wali. "Wali Sahib, do you realize that the servant quarter no more suits my status as your family member. You should have invited me to sleep in the house tonight."

"The obdurate fool will not relent so easily. Making him sleep inside will mean our doom," reckoned Wali. "He requires some assurance before being pacified. Since the shrewd most of the three is out of sight, perhaps a soft stance will work," he further mused. For the first time he smiled directly at Shakeel and said, "Do not lose your patience my boy. The ceremonies are planned for tomorrow morning and the groom to be should not enter the house before that. Go and have a good night rest. Tomorrow morning will be another day."

The smile, without doubt, worked. Returning Wali's smile, Shakeel bent slightly to wish *adaab* and walked out in seemingly lighter spirits

The men had finally left the house. Wali waited in the parlour to make sure the main door was locked securely.

When Abdul came back after closing the door, he informed Wali in undertones, "So far so good. *Huzoor,* everything seems under control. The men do not appear suspicious, yet we can't take it easy till we have thrown dust into the eyes of these scoundrels and have left them licking their wounds. *Inshallah,* we will do it." Wali sadly smiled at Abdul and nodded in agreement. He wished he too could be as flamed as Abdul at the moment but apprehension had begun to surpass his other responses. Abdul well read the fear in his master's eyes and continued, "You needn't be troubled. I will take care of the things on the front side. The bear raid was an excuse to be out around the time you will leave. I would have taken the two of them away from the house into the woods and then would have tricked them into getting lost there in the dark. You should have allowed my plan to be implemented."

"I had judged your intentions Abdul, but didn't want you to risk your safety. Moreover, these men were not ready to go with you and had you insisted further, they might have become suspicious. We will still manage well with these fools skulking around. And your bear incursion theory may still work by keeping the men inside the quarters," Wali gave Abdul a weak smile of reassurance.

Abdul nodded, recognising the validity of Wali's point and then added gravely, "I will quickly wash the dishes and go out to keep eye on these mean men; no less ferocious than bears though."

Wali's heart was filled with admiration for his humble old servant. Tonight, he had saved him from so many tight spots and was still trying his best to render his unconditional help, caring the least for his own safety. It would have been much easier for him to have left his master in a lurch and vanish from the unsafe locale. But such a possibility wouldn't have crossed the mind of the unassuming man who was the foremost example of those rare humans who are sincere to the core of their hearts. Wali made a silent resolution that after today, Abdul would be his equal partner in whatever business he would be able to carry out. The man who had remained loyal in the face of such threat surely deserved that honour.

Breaking the silence Abdul said, "Remember Wasim Sahib will be waiting for you two curves down the main road after the footpath meets it. You know that deep curve; we chose the spot after a good inspection of the area. A vehicle parked on the side, next to the mountain wall will almost be invisible in the dark."

"Yes, I know the place and that is for sure an ideal spot," Wali said approvingly and then immediately added, "Abdul, I am extremely worried for you. Once we leave, you will be left all alone to deal with these scoundrels. You must try to slip out at the first opportunity."

"You don't worry about me, *Huzoor*. I know how to trick the rogues. I will try to reach Delhi day after tomorrow. If I am late by a day or two, don't be anxious. I will manage somehow. You only worry about taking Meher *Beti* as far away from these rascals as possible. She is in grave danger and her safety is our priority." Abdul whispered his instructions and Wali gazed at him in gratitude. He knew that Abdul was as indispensable as Wasim in today's plot and they couldn't have managed without Abdul's support at all.

"I am glad I have you on my side today Abdul, and want it to remain so forever. Once we are out, you must begin to concentrate on your departure. And thank you Abdul, thank you for everything. May *Allah* be with you and protect you."

Abdul nodded and added in a quivering voice, "*Huzoor*, each time I see Shakeel, I feel like strangulating him. If he didn't have those fearful armed men with him, he would have been posted at the gates of hell by now, waiting to be admitted there."

Wali smiled feebly and whispered, "If the fearful armed men were not on his side, he wouldn't have dared to face us. Abdul, it is all the power of guns. These men would run like chickens without their weapons. Unfortunately, they have found easy victims in us. But tomorrow morning, they will know who the real weakling is."

Both the men stood there wanting to say so many things yet became wordless. When has bidding farewell not been painful? And this farewell was, as such, laced with so much uncertainty.

"*Khudah hafiz*, Abdul," Wali said and slowly walked away

"*Khudah Hafiz*," whispered Abdul and watched the slumped back of his master moving away. He had never seen his master walk with that kind of a hunch and knew that he was drooping with the heavy burden of the circumstances. "May *Allah* be with you too," he spoke softly even when Wali was outside the hearing range.

Wali's feet instinctively moved towards Ammi-Jaan's room. Her room was empty. Thank God! one member was safely out of the house, Wali felt satisfied. He opened Ammi-Jaan's closet and shuffled through her things. He wanted to see if there was anything that she might need. They wouldn't be coming back for a very long time. He picked up Ammi-Jaan's thickest woollen shawl. She might need it during the winters. Next, he picked up her book on religious doctrines from the table. It was the one she had been reading. Satisfied, he quietly came out of the room and bolted it from outside. Giving one last glance around, Wali quickly climbed up the staircase to his room.

Chapter 21

When Wali reached his bedroom, he found both Sakina and Meher all geared up for the journey. They even had their footwear on, as if, set to move out immediately. They had been discussing something seriously and Wali's arrival caused interruption. Wali noted that the tearful expression they had formerly acquired now seemed to have somewhat dissipated. Their creased brows were smoother and both appeared slightly eased though still despondent. Three packed bags were kept ready near the door.

Wali's entrance into the room caused them to look at him for reassurance. Speaking in undertones he informed them, "All is well so far. The villains are well stuffed with food and have been sent to their living quarters. Their drowsiness should make them comatose and hopefully, they should be dead to the world as soon as they hit the bed. Abdul is winding up the kitchen work quickly and then will move outdoors so that he may be able to keep the man on guard duty distracted. Was Ammi-Jaan's sent off trouble free?"

Keeping her voice low to match his, Sakina informed him, "Yes, there was no problem at all. Wasim Bhai hardly stayed for a few minutes, during which he quickly escorted Ammi-Jaan out. That didn't give her time to speak much. All Wasim Bhai said while leaving was that he would be at the decided spot at eleven."

Wali looked at the sorry figure of his daughter, who looked so fragile, so much shattered by the events. The proposal of running away from the home that had been hers ever since she was born must have been very tormenting. She was also too young to be stoical. The thought that a bleeding wound had been inflicted in the young heart of his darling daughter added to Wali's misery.

"And what have you been discussing with your Ammi, Meher?" He asked her, lovingly running his fingers through her silky smooth hair.

"Abbu ji, I was formulating my future plans. I was telling Ammi ji not to worry about my job any more. I was doing it simply for gaining experience. In a few months, I would have resigned anyway to pursue my post graduation. Now, I will send my resignation from Delhi." She paused to watch her father nodding his approval. She noted his sunken eyes filled with pain. She then added, "Abbu ji, I am so sorry to have been the cause of your sufferings."

"I am only doing the duty of a father, *Beti*. It is all *Allah*'s wish. He has decided to test us and we have to accept His will." Wali found that his own statement had an effect of ice on a burn. He felt calmer.

"And what are your future plans?" He then asked her with an indulgent smile, sitting down on the side of his bed to face her directly.

"Abbu ji, the head of the neurology department, Dr. Khera, was keen that I should do specialization in that subject. He had wanted me to try admission immediately, after I had finished my internship but I wanted to be near you for a while. Now since we all are going to be together, things are more or less decided. I will join the post graduation course and support myself to begin with. Once that is over, you and Ammi ji will be equally my responsibility as Salim Bhai's. You need not worry at all regarding the loss of your business," Meher laid clear her plans.

"Yes, Meher, you are far informed about things than I am now. You can select your future course as you wish. Your Ammi and Abbu are getting old now. We are going to let you children take up the rudder and lead us down the stream of life. We are going to relax in the boat now. But more recently, we should be able to successfully slip out of the clutches of the dangerous men who have surrounded us," Wali said.

Both Meher and Sakina nodded their heads in agreement.

"We have a little more than an hour with us now. It is nine twenty. At about ten thirty, we must try to leave. Though it takes only ten minutes to reach the main road, yet we should have extra time in hand in case of emergency. Meanwhile, let us all rest. I don't need to change. You two seem dressed too. Why Meher, you are even wearing your sports shoes. Is that for a marathon?" Wali tried to joke to ease out the atmosphere.

Both the women faintly smiled. Then Wali noticed Sakina's footwear. It was a pair of sandals with small heels. He frowned at her sandals. "No Sakina that will not do. Wear something practical like Meher. The incline is steep and we will not be able to use the torch. It is quite dark outside. The moonlight too is very faint."

Sakina Protested, "I have always been walking down in this kind of footwear and managing well."

"We are not using the regular path. Well, I forgot to tell you that we will be slipping away from the back side, from the kitchen door. Meher, do you remember the shortcut you and Salim used to take to school?" Meher nodded vigorously, almost pleased to be reminded of it. "We will be going down that way, for there is a security guard in front." Wali then moved towards the window and opened it. He stood at the window as if enjoying the cool breeze and the crescent moon. As expected, Shaukat was sitting on the low boundary wall. His gun was kept next to him. Wali could see it all from the corner of his eyes, though he pretended not to be looking in that direction. He also knew that Shaukat was looking at him. "I think I will close the window. The breeze is cold tonight," he said aloud before shutting the window. He then drew the curtains once again.

He came back and sat on the bedside once more. "The guard duty for the first quarter of the night has begun," he informed the women. He then slipped his feet out of the slippers. That reminded him once again of Sakina's footwear and he looked down at her feet. She had not made any effort to change her sandals.

"Sakina, please wear something comfortable," he requested her again.

"This is the most comfortable footwear I have," she said, "I used to wear sports shoes as a young girl. Now for years I have worn nothing but sandals. For, I have never been required to run up or down the slopes till today. This pair has the lowest heels. Other than this, then I have only a pair of rubber bathroom slippers," she added.

"No…no, bathroom slippers will be loose and slippery, not suitable if we need to run. They won't do at all. I am slightly apprehensive about how you will walk down with these heels," Wali said.

"I will be fine. I am used to wearing heels, even higher than these," Sakina answered.

"Hmmm…." Wali nodded, though he was still uneasy with Sakina's sandals.

"We can't sit like this till we leave. Lie down until it is time to go. Meher go and rest and come here at ten twenty five. Switch off the lights now and pretend to retire for the night. Do not switch on the lights after that," Wali instructed.

Meher immediately left for her room. Sakina removed her sandals and sat on her bed. Wali switched off the light and stretched himself on the bed. Now they didn't have much to do except wait. Remembering something Wali got up again.

"Now what is it?" Sakina asked.

"We cannot switch on the light anymore. I will therefore fetch the torch. We may need it though we will avoid using it. We are familiar with every step, so it shouldn't be difficult to walk in the dark. I will also keep the pencil torch in my pocket."

Wali brought the torches from the cupboard and kept one under his pillow. He kept the pencil torch in the pocket of his *pheran*, which he had kept ready on the chair close by.

They both now lay on the bed silently for a while, each engrossed in one's own thoughts. Wali held Sakina's hand and found it absolutely cold. He patted it to comfort her. It was a silent reassurance of his presence. He was there to see to their safety.

Then Sakina whispered, "When do you think will we be able to come back?"

Wali thought for a while making up his mind and then said, "Sakina, I am not sure myself. I have no idea when will it be safe to return. These rascals may keep a tab on us and could return anytime to take revenge. At least, Salim and Meher should not return to this place for a long time to come. We will watch the circumstances. Wasim Bhai will keep us informed. Then, you only said that we were going to our son and that his house is our second home. So, don't bother yourself so much."

After a long pause Wali continued, "Sakina, I don't even want to give you false hope. We are about to undertake something very dangerous. I don't know what is going to happen in the next few hours. I am not even sure if we will see another dawn. But whatever is in store for us, we are together in it. *Inshallah*, victory will be ours."

Thus, they both lay listening to the ticking clock, silently praying to God to help them successfully escape from the cruel assassins. After staring at the ceiling lit dimly by the light falling from the veranda for some time, Wali closed his eyes.

He must have dozed off due to the tiredness of the hectic day, but some noise outside his door woke him up with a start. He looked at the glowing needles of the clock. The time was ten past ten. The door was softy pushed opened. Meher stood at the door.

"Abbu ji, is It time to go?" She whispered.

She then moved towards their bed. In her anxiety she walked right into the side table, stumbled over it and lost her balance. She grabbed at the table to escape falling on the floor. In the process she knocked the brass vase kept on the table. It came down crashing to the floor.

The three hearts together skipped their beats. Wali jumped out of the bed and rushed towards the window. He set the curtain aside slightly and peeped out. Shaukat was standing and looking at the window of their room. He then picked up his rifle. From his earlier experience, Wali instantly evoked the easy means to escape from the predicament. He walked towards the bathroom in big strides and switched on the light. After counting a few seconds, he flushed the toilet. He then found the bathroom window ajar and realized the blunder. He immediately shut it, the sound not bothering him. He then switched off the lights and came back to his room. He again peeped out. Shaukat had now been joined by Abdul. He was stating something to Shaukat who then nodded in understanding. They then went to sit on the wall together. Wali breathed slowly in relief and blessed Abdul in his heart. He was trying his best to keep the unwanted guard distracted. Seeing Abdul keeping Shaukat engrossed in some talk, Wali decided that it was the time to slip out.

"Pick up your bags. Let us leave now," Wali commanded and put on his *pheran*. He then sat down to quickly put on his shoes. Sakina wrapped her shawl around her shoulders and slipped into her sandals. They softy moved towards the door. Each one picked up one bag. Wali put on his backpack. He then went back and picked up the torch from under the pillow.

The three of them halted at the main door for a while. Wali gestured them to move down. "Go slowly and steadily. Do not hurry and make no sound. Wait for me at the kitchen door," he whispered.

He waited till he was sure the women had reached the base of the staircase. He then went back to the window once again. Setting aside hardy an inch of the curtain, he peeped out once again. Abdul and Shaukat were still sitting on the wall. Shaukat was smoking and Abdul was successfully keeping him diverted by his colloquy. "Abdul is firmly guarding him." Satisfied, Wali backed off. He paused at the door once again. A pain of being torn away from his roots engulfed his whole body. "No point getting attached to things. I have to take care of lives tonight," he thought and quickly walked out of the door.

Chapter 22

Softly on his tiptoes, Wali climbed down the staircase. The women must have reached the kitchen door by now, he guessed. No noise had reached him while they were descending. They were being cautious and that made Wali satisfied. The parlour was dark. No light from outside seeped in the heavily curtained room. Abdul had switched off the veranda light but that wasn't a problem. Wali knew the way well. He had exact judgment of where each piece of furniture was kept. Circumventing and avoiding any collision, he too reached the kitchen. A faint moonlight drifted in softly through the uncovered panes of the window. His eyes too had become accustomed to the dark. He could clearly see the silhouettes of the women standing next to the door. He reached the door from whence would be launched their perilous mission.

The kitchen door was not bolted. Abdul had gone out through that door. He would be using that door till he could lock it from outside before his departure. The rest of the house was locked and secure. Sakina and Meher moved aside to let Wali lead them.

Wali softly pushed open the door. He peered through it. Intense silence welcomed him. He walked out and stood in the compound. The servant quarter, where the dangerous men were housed, was to his right. There was a straight brick wall facing him. Wali was thankful for the design. There was no window facing the house. Only a part of the veranda of the servant quarters was visible. It was empty. A faint sound of music being played on a radio was now picked up by Wali's alert ears and he nodded with approval.

Abdul had provided a good distraction to the men residing in his rooms. Making sure of no presence, Wali beckoned the women to follow him.

The three huddled figures rushed towards the edge of the compound. "Meher, you lead us down," Wali whispered. Meher promptly obliged. Wali held Sakina from her elbow and they followed Meher. Cautiously and slowly, they began to descend in near darkness. Wali kept turning back to watch out for any figure making sudden appearance and ruining their plans. In case anything like that happened; they were prepared to duck before being spotted. They had covered half of the steep incline when an untoward thing happened. It coincided with the timing when Wali had turned to look back. The heel of Sakina's sandal landed on a small stone and she slipped. Wali tried to control her with both his hands, in the process the torch he was holding in one hand fell and rolled down making a distinct sound. Sakina fell with a thud…another distinct sound. A subdued squeal of pain escaped her lips, like the cry of a wounded rabbit…the worst sound of all. Wali instantly bent down and his hand shot out involuntarily to cover Sakina's mouth to muffle her sound. It all happened within a few seconds followed by complete silence. All three froze in their positions. "Meher sit down low," Wali softly commanded. He too reposed flat on the incline, making Sakina to follow suit. They waited with bated breaths to know if somebody had heard the sound. Should they dash down, Wali considered. No, running down would be even more perilous at the moment…too risky…the sound sure to draw the attention of the alert men who would then come chasing them with their guns. Three people loaded with bags would be no match to their agility. Their best bet would be to wait and watch till they got the all-clear signal.

"We may now be caught trying to escape from our own house," Wali thought shaking his head in disgust at the paradoxical situation.

For a few seconds, there was no activity. The stillness was overwhelming, broken intermittently by the whispers of the fruit trees shaking to and fro in the mild breeze. The shadows of the trees too coordinated with their movements playfully, relentlessly changing the stroked patterns in silver streaks, a colour obviously lent by the moon. Only if these shadows could swallow them completely, making them oblivious to the eyes of the possible hunters, wished Wali. Before long, a cicada suddenly broke out into a screeching song shattering the intensity of the silence to which no one paid heed, except its mating partner which responded immediately. There appeared no unnatural sound which the three people hiding awaited and dreaded at the same time.

Few more seconds passed without any occurrence. Wali began to relax and slowly raised himself on his haunches but instantly froze in that position. They heard the soft approaching footfalls, distinct footsteps. He once again ducked as low as he could. The sound became louder. It was now coming from the far end of the compound. And then Abdul's voice fell into their ears, "I tell you it must be those animals. I will now make them run for their lives." He was extra loud, so was the sound of the footsteps which hadn't stopped. Abdul then continued his insistence, "Come Shaukat, help me locate them. I want to teach them a lesson of their lifetime. They think we work day and night to grow dinner for them? Let's give them a clear message so that they will never again venture into our orchard."

No response.

"Where do you think you are going? The sound came from here," Abdul spoke again, the passageway the family was to embark on, being in his full knowledge.

"No, I think the sound came from ahead, from the hillside down there," Shaukat spoke now. And his footsteps continue to come closer.

"Look, there is something here! I can see one big shadow. My God, it appears a huge animal! Shaukat come and see," Abdul was urging him. There was clear desperation in his voice now. The footsteps stopped. From the place where Wali was positioned, he could see a pair of shoes. The rest of the frame was hidden behind a large fruit tree. A few more steps and Shaukat would undoubtedly see them hiding.

There was a sound of something falling and rolling down from the distant corner now. The legs retraced. "Where?" It was Shaukat speaking now. He seemed to have got interested. Wali began to breathe again.

"There, behind that cluster of trees. I saw an animal move down there," Abdul claimed.

"I can't see anything. There is no animal. Abdul Bhai, you have lost your mind. The sound came from further up. I am going to check that side," Shaukat said. His footsteps once again began to near.

Wali shut his eyes as if that would somehow aid in going undetected. His heart beat intensified. Thump…, thump   he could hear it so clearly. Perhaps Shaukat could hear it too. He instinctively put his arm around Sakina. She was shivering. He instantly made up his mind that he would face the terrorist alone, after commanding the women to run for their lives. It would give them a chance to escape. But he wasn't sure if Wasim Bhai had reached the main road with the vehicle. They were a little early. That could pose a problem now.

The footsteps were fast nearing and Wali was engrossed in a desperate planning, when there was a loud thud of something heavy falling followed by a moan. "Oh! Shaukat help me. I have fallen down. Please come quick. The bears are dangerous animals. I don't want to be eaten alive," Abdul's pleadings sounded absolutely genuine.

"What a troublesome man you are? Where have you disappeared? I can't see you." Shaukat was heard now, noticeably annoyed. The footsteps retreated.

"Here…I am here…I have slipped down. Help me please. Pull me up… be quick, before a bear reaches here," Abdul was heard begging.

"How did you manage to fall down? And if you are so afraid of the bears, why were you ready to hunt them down? In front of your master, you were bragging as if you are a valiant hero. He should see you now; a gutless chicken. I have every intention of inviting your master for a reality show."

"You dare not trouble my master by waking him up from his sleep. And who is not afraid of bears? I bet even you would be…without your gun? I am bold today precisely because you are with me…and you have a weapon. That is the biggest support," Abdul was heard explaining.

"Here hold my hand. Why are you hanging on to my arm? Make some effort yourself too. Oh! Don't pull me down…try to pull yourself up. Yes, that's right. Apply more force."

The instruction continued for a while after which Shaukat's piqued comment was heard, "Abdul Bhai, you are a real buffoon."

"What, what did you call me? A buffoon? Have you seen your age? A chit of a boy calling a man fit to be his grandfather a buffoon?"

"Bhai, a buffoon will be called a buffoon. Age does not matter here. A young clown becomes an old clown with age." And Shaukat gave a short boyish chortle, his mood obviously lifted at his ingenuity.

"How dare you call me that?" And Abdul tried to sound annoyed.

"Don't eat my head," Shaukat snapped at him. "You look after your orchard and the bears and I let me do my duty."

"What is this duty you talk about? Are you on some kind of a job? Aren't you out here with me to keep out the trespassing bears?" Abdul asked him feigning complete surprise.

"Who is bothered about your bears? I am guarding the house right now. Ahmed Bhai has asked me to be extra vigilant tonight. He and Hashim Bhai don't trust your master, Wali. They were saying that he agreed to the proposal a little too easily. And he was out for unnecessarily long time today. He was practically out the entire day. Shakeel and Hashim Bhai went to the town but couldn't locate him. They were worried that he might have gone to report our presence to the police. Even though Shakeel is my good friend, I am sure Wali is definitely miserable giving away his doctor daughter to him in marriage. I have heard that she is very beautiful. I wanted to see her today but you kept the doors closed on us the whole day. You must be conniving with your master against us."

"What nonsense are you talking? Who is getting married? And why are you bringing in the police? What are you all up to?" Abdul was heard asking all these questions, pretending complete ignorance once again.

"We are the freedom fighters and want to avoid police at any cost, especially now when there is a wedding tomorrow," Shaukat said.

"Did you say Shakeel is forcing my master's daughter to marry him? Has he gone completely crazy? Hasn't he ever seen himself in a mirror? He is an exact replica of a monkey…no a black faced langur. He can't even read two letters of a word and aspires to marry a doctor? He must be completely out of his mind. No…no, this cannot happen. You people definitely need to be reported to the police. The best place suited for the langur will be behind the prison bars," Abdul was quite vehement and convincing.

"Why is Abdul taking things that far? He is only supposed to keep these men distracted. He should not risk his life. These are the most unpredictable men he is dealing with and he doesn't realize that," Wali began to get worried for Abdul.

"We know how to save ourselves from the police. We will easily escape. But before that we will make sure no one in this house survives. That includes you. It has already been planned. Except of course the beautiful daughter, on

Chapter 22

whom Shakeel has a crush. Hashim Bhai had suggested kidnapping her, but that smitten Shakeel wanted *nikah*." Why was Shaukat revealing so much to Abdul? What were the intentions of the group? Wali was rightly worried.

"I think you are all traitors," Abdul said. He was then heard stomping away in anger towards the front side.

"I am not a traitor. People like you are the traitors," Shaukat's angry voice resonated. He now seemed to be following Abdul. Wali began to relax.

"How can simple hard working men be traitors; the men who do not know how to fire a shot from a rifle?" Abdul's sound was quite distant now.

They must have been sitting there for close to five minutes but it seemed an eternity. Now the sounds were far but were more heated. They were no more comprehensible but disturbingly loud. Wali was full of anxiety, for Abdul was taking chances. He was going beyond keeping Shaukat diverted. These men shouldn't be infuriated. At the same time, he was relieved that Abdul had managed to remove Shaukat from the area quite successfully. Wali slowly stood up. If they managed the first two curves without being detected, rest would be comparatively easy. The path would no longer be visible from the vicinity of the house. The women followed his example. "Hurry up! Let's go," Wali said in undertones.

They had barely taken two steps when they heard the cracking sound of a shot being fired from a rifle. The sound resonated through the quiet of the night, shattering its peace like a rock blasted with explosives. The three heartbeats stopped momentarily before quickening their pace. "Abdul!" Wali whispered to himself and he felt his legs going weak.

He had to think of something quick. What was he to do now? Was Abdul hurt? Was the shot fired at him? Wali was in a terrible fix. "Meher, take your Ammi along. Both of you move on. Keep going. Don't wait for me. I will join you as soon as possible. If I am delayed, you must reach the vehicle. You know where it will be parked. Catch the train to Delhi if I don't come, if I am stuck here to take care of certain things. Here take my wallet. It has the tickets and money. Take my bag too. There is more money in it. Now, quick! Go on. Don't dilly-dally. I must go and check on Abdul," Wali's whispered command demonstrated his desperation. "And Sakina, look after Ammi-Jaan," Wali added as he turned to go.

"Wait Abbuji," Meher spoke in an undertone. "I can better tend to Abdul if he has received any injuries. Why don't you and Ammiji walk down! I will catch up with you after attending to him," Meher suggested quite fervidly.

"NO...not at all! You are not going in front of any of those ruffians. If Abdul needs help, it will perhaps be immediate shifting to a hospital, and I will manage that. Now don't waste time. Start walking down, both of you," Wali ordered rather assertively.

The women obeyed him meekly this time, though they appeared highly frightened. Wali heard a sob escape Sakina's lips. There was no time to console her. He rushed up the hill. Reaching the edge of the slope, he pried the area. The sound of the outhouse door being opened came clear. Then two pairs of steps rushed out and ran towards the direction from where the shot was fired. Wali waited till the sound of the steps receded. Then in one leap he hauled himself up onto the compound, dashed through the compound in few dives, reached the door and quickly entered the house once again. He sprinted through the kitchen and the parlour. He rushed up the staircase three steps at a time and finally entered his room. He then switched on the table lamp rushed to the window and opened it. It was all done in almost a minute. The exercise had made him totally breathless but controlling his tone, he now said loudly, "What is happening? Why are shots being fired?" He was almost choking and it was a real effort to keep his voice normal.

Ahmed and Shakeel were standing with Shaukat who was holding his rifle in his hand. Abdul's absence was conspicuous. Wali's eyes sought him on the ground in an earnest but couldn't spot him. The worry along with the breathlessness and palpitation made him suddenly sick. He felt his head spinning. "What has this juvenile killer done to Abdul?" He became panicky.

"Nothing Wali Sahib, we were trying to scare away the bears," Shaukat said.

Abdul now appeared on the scene. It seemed he was sheltering behind the boundary wall and on hearing Wali's assuring voice, he came out of his hiding place. "*Huzoor*, he is lying. He fired the shot to frighten me. It could have hit me," he complained.

Wali was washed with relief. Abdul was safe.

"No, I fired in the air," Shaukat tried to explain.

"Not exactly. Your gun was pointed at me. Fortunately your shot missed me," Abdul contradicted him.

"I pointed the gun up in the air before firing," Shaukat tried elucidating.

"Shaukat please constraint yourself. There is no need to take risks with precious lives like Abdul's. Besides, my mother is not to be disturbed at any cost. We too are trying to sleep. This is no time to play games like this. Moreover, firing shots will mean inviting other people to see what is happening here," Wali tried to sound as annoyed as he could, and spoke it all in one breath. He hoped his heavy breathing wouldn't be noticed by the men.

Wali now saw Ahmed nodding at the statements. He spoke in undertones to Shaukat followed by hitting him lightly on his head. Shakeel followed his example and gave Shaukat another light smack. Looking up at Wali, Ahmed said, "Sorry Wali Sahib, he won't do it again. You may sleep now."

"Thank you," Wali said loudly and coldly before closing the window with a deliberate force. He then stood in the dark leaning against the wall, trying to regain his composure. His comfort at seeing Abdul unhurt and alive was beyond expression. With deep gratitude, he thanked God. His breathing was returning to normal now. The nausea that he had felt recently too began to recede. Then without further delay, he once again began his journey to the compound. He peered out from the kitchen window and saw Ahmed and Shakeel walking up the veranda of the outhouse. He noted the music this time which could be heard quite loud through the open door. He waited till he heard the sound of the door being shut; the fading sound of the music was an added proof...an added indication of the storm blown over.

"The coast is clear. This is the time now," Wali said to himself and rushed out again. Scrambling through the compound he rushed down the declivity. This time he didn't bother to turn to look behind him, for he was sure of each person's location and intended to create maximum distance from them in minimum possible time. A Fleeting thought crossed his mind as to why Hashim had not made his appearance in the compound hearing the shot fired from a gun. It could have meant serious trouble for these villains and Hashim was the one planning strategies for the group. Perhaps he was sound asleep...having drained himself in his daylong bootless errand, judged Wali. He smiled thinking that he had managed to leave the crafty men pouring water into a sieve the entire day.

Chapter 23

Running down in short but sure steps in no time he completed the slope and reached the main footpath. Thereafter he dashed down, making sure not to produce any sound and caught up with the ladies quickly. They had barely covered three curves distance. They were walking quite slowly. Meher was carrying three bags; one at the back, one hung across her shoulders and one in her left hand. With her free hand, she was holding her mother's arm and helping her to walk. Sakina was limping badly.

"What has happened?" asked Wali with concern.

"Ammi ji has sprained her foot in the fall. She can barely walk," Meher answered. "Has Abdul been harmed? Was he shot at by that reckless stupid boy?" She asked in the same breath.

"Abdul is fine. That daft boy Shaukat had fired in the air," Wali answered.

"Thank God," said Meher softly.

"*Allah* be praised," added Sakina in a whisper.

Wali now spoke softly to himself, but irritation was apparent in his musings, "This injury had to occur at this time when danger is looming over our heads." Then he instructed the women in the same soft tone, "We can't continue at this pace. In fact, any delay will be foolishness on our part. We must distance ourselves from the house as quickly as possible."

"But Ammi ji is in terrible pain. She can barely walk," Meher stressed.

"Meher, you carry my backpack but give me your Ammi's bag. The backpack will be easier to carry. I will help your Ammi." Wali took Sakina's bag and hung it on his left shoulder. Instructing Sakina's to put her arms around his neck, he wrapped his arms around her waist, almost lifting her. She wasn't light and Wali managed to lift her only a bit. They quickened their pace. Sakina was almost being dragged but she did not complain and fully cooperated.

Wali resumed his vigil by continuous survey of the area, more behind him to spot any undesirable company so that they may react well in time to avoid being caught red handed. Although, he couldn't imagine how they were going to do that now, with Sakina incapacitated. Dashing down was out of question. He prayed that their absence shouldn't be detected till they were safely out of the reach of the rogues, and not till the morning when Abdul too would be safely out of the town.

The footpath was completely deserted and to much of his relief they didn't encounter anyone on the way. In fifteen minutes, they were on the main road.

The road too was completely bereft of traffic. There was not a single vehicle on the road at the moment. This was not unusual. There was always very less traffic at this time of the night. Only inter-city buses or trucks with goods plied with regularity at night. Ever since the terrorism problem had started in the valley, very few private vehicles could be seen on roads after dark. People preferred the safety of the indoors.

There was an electric pole at fifteen metres distance and some light from it was reaching the road here. It wasn't well lighted though.

"Let's cross over to the other side. Walking next to the mountain will be easier and undetected. The car too will be parked on that side," Wali suggested.

They continued their slow amble next to the mountain wall. Wali's arms were aching by now. He loosened his hold on Sakina. They could relax a bit now, he decided. The moment Sakina received more pressure on her foot, she moaned. Wali immediately tried lifting her but she disallowed it. She knew that he had already overexerted his muscles. Although she was finding it difficult to walk, she carried on by gripping on to the mountain wall to ease the pressure on her foot. Negotiating two curves they reached a deeper arc. There was no light here and thus it was quite dark. That suited them well as it would be easy to be concealed in the coverlet of darkness.

There was no vehicle there yet, though Wali was sure that this was the place where Wasim would be coming. Wali took out the pencil torch from his pocket and switched it on. He strained to check the time without his spectacles and managed. It was ten forty. Wasim would take another fifteen-twenty minutes to come. Should they wait standing on the roadside till then, Wali pondered.

"No," he decided. The night was too full of risks. They couldn't take any chances. If the men missed them sooner than expected, they would come rushing down. Wali inspected the surroundings. The hillside here was not straight but rather inclined. At about four metres above their position, there was a flat patch lined with trees. That would be the ideal waiting spot, Wali decided. Then he whispered to the women, "I feel we are not safe standing on the road like this. We will be waiting for Wasim Bhai up there, hidden behind the trees."

Considering Sakina's condition, he hesitated for a while. "I am being unnecessarily finicky," he thought. When he had left home, his oppressors appeared unperturbed and Abdul too was keeping them well distracted. He doubted that their absence would be detected immediately. Yet, there was a feeling of edginess within him. Finally, he decided to let his instincts prevail. He made up his mind to climb up to the patch and wait there. He instructed Meher softly, speaking almost in her ears, "I am going up first. You pass me the bags and then help your Ammi from below. I will pull her up."

It was not an easy exercise to reach Sakina up but Wali and Meher together managed it after a short struggle. They then selected the darkest corner and sat huddled together, waiting for Wasim to rescue them from the harrowing wait.

"Ammi ji, is your foot hurting badly?" Meher asked once they were settled. Although she had not spoken loudly, her sound was crisp clear in the silence of the night.

"Shhh...do not talk. Remain absolutely still and silent. We aren't yet out of danger," Wali instructed.

They were safely away from the house, then why did he have some kind of foreboding fear, Wali wondered again. Perhaps the gun shot had unnerved him. Or, perhaps he wouldn't be easy till they all reached Delhi safely.

Furthermore, he couldn't afford to be careless.

They must have been sitting up for about ten minutes when shadows of two men emerged from the direction of the main town. Their features were not clearly visible in the dark. The men were engaged in some absorbing discussion. They were incomprehensible to the listeners due to the distance. The three people concealed behind the clump of deodar trees watched them with total lack of interest.

A truck now approached from the opposite direction. It made the men on the road to step aside and wait for it to pass. The headlights of the truck fell on them. The two figures got clearly revealed. Wali stiffened and drew in a quick breath, the sound of which was luckily covered up by the roaring engine of the truck. In an automatic reaction, he extended his arm to cover the women and shoved them back. He threw a fleeting glance at Meher and Sakina. They were concealed in the darkness. Fortunately, the light from the truck wasn't reaching their hiding place.

He now looked at the men once again. The tall figure belonged to the most vicious of his terrorist guests; Hashim. The other man with him too was known to him. They both were walking up towards the house.

The women well understood his reaction; that the men were dangerous. Sakina recognized the tall man too. She hadn't liked a bit the way he had stared at her that evening when she had gone to perform her duty as a hostess. She had also seen him from the kitchen window in the morning, walking around her house. He had been surveying the house keenly. Once when she had walked out of the kitchen door to throw some waste in the bin kept outside, she had almost come face to face with him. He had run his eyes over her, giving her creeps, before greeting her frostily. His cold and savage expression had made her recoil in fright. She had simply nodded in reply and had quickly withdrawn into the safety of her kitchen. The door had got shut rather abruptly but she couldn't care less, for he was one of the eerie undesirable visitors. Seeing him now so close, she flinched.

Wali was almost shocked at this unexpected appearance of Hashim. It immediately occurred to him that God was with them tonight. For, had they been delayed, or had they decided to leave later by fifteen minutes as planned, they would have met this rifle toting terrorist on the way, on the footpath leading to their house. Not only would their plan have collapsed then, but he was quite sure, he would have killed them there and then; shot them all dead!

Wali was exceedingly thankful to the power that was guiding them tonight;

someone who had given him the sense to hide in this patch and not wait on the roadside, someone, who had given Wasim, the astute not to hire a taxi. For the man now walking with Hashim was an employee at Hassan's transport office. Wali was quite sure. He had had business dealings with him a number of times and till today he couldn't even have dreamt of his involvement with the terrorists. Surely he was Gulam, the same medium built man who sat at the reception of the private transport office belonging to Hassan. Did Hassan too suspect of the involvement of Gulam and some taxi drivers with the terrorists? Was that why he had offered his own vehicle?

The revelation had come as a shock to Wali. What if they had hired a taxi? By now, their plan would have lain revealed to the dreadful group and they wouldn't have been sitting here. Instead, the experience they might have undergone was something he wouldn't want to befall on anyone, not even on these obnoxious men.

But why was Gulam going to his house with Hashim? What were the plans of the group? Why was Gulam ready to reveal openly his involvement with men like Hashim? Did Hashim have his own secret strategy, unknown to his group?

Wali's heart was pounding, his stomach churning and his mind furiously at work.

The truck disappeared around the curve. Once again it was dark. The eyes dazzled by the strong headlights took time to adjust. Meanwhile, the two figures got lost in the obscurity of the night's dark blanket.

When the eyes became used to the darkness once again, the two repulsive figures had reached directly opposite to where the three of them sat hidden. And fatefully, they halted there. Their conversation too became discernible now.

Gulam was saying, "Yes, yes, you do not worry. I will get you the details. But it will cost money."

"Money is not a problem. You will get what you want, but the information should be valid and in details," Hashim was heard instructing.

"Once tomorrow's schedule gets through, I will proceed with the next job," Gulam said.

"Tomorrow's schedule is a miniscule crack. I expected some trouble initially but this man, Wali, has turned out to be a chicken, posed no problem at all.

Though, I would have loved to point my gun at him to see him shaking with fear…begging for mercy, but not even once did he forthrightly refuse marrying his daughter to an illiterate man indulged in the line of work unpalatable to him. In fact, he had been out the whole day organizing tomorrow's ceremonies; arranging a *Maulvi* to read the *nikah* and buying a wedding dress for his daughter. He has also bought some gold and that will for sure come handy in exchanging for money." His snigger sounded a roaring laughter and Wali wished he could pounce on him and send him tumbling down the hill. Hashim continued, "He is cooperating well, though I know that from inside he is a highly distressed man. He is in torment but pretending to be normal. He thinks that I do not know it. I am a guy who can see through people."

"Naturally, Wali couldn't have agreed so easily to marry off his daughter, who is a doctor, to an illiterate man who was once a meagre domestic servant in the household," Gulam was saying.

"I know that well. But he is scared stiff of the guns we had exhibited immediately on arrival. He might not have seen so many guns displayed thus ever in his life. And I am making sure he doesn't forget their presence. " A short chortle followed the statement and then there was aloud proclamation, "But even his dead ancestors can't rebuff me when I am resolute. He knows either he has to be in agreement with us or it will be the end for him. We will take away his daughter anyway. So, he is being sensible in being cooperative."

"His daughter shouldn't pose any problem tomorrow."

"She better not, or she will have to witness the most unsightly and haunting spectacle of her life; of the blasted head of her father. I have no patience for the trouble makers." Hashim's voice sounded easy, as if taking life was an effortless job, not worth any botheration or second thought. Wali had never in life met such a diabolic being whose every utterance was drenched in barbarity.

"What about the rest of the family?" Gulam inquired next.

"They are not much of a trouble. Only there is that blabbermouth servant of theirs. I would have sent my bullet shooting across his crafty head long ago but he is required to serve us and is doing a good job. That has kept the big mouth alive till now. Apparently, he will be away on a job tomorrow morning. Then the old grandmother is as such enfeebled by age and is lying ailing on her bed…that leaves only her mother; hmmm….an attractive woman for her age…quite tempting…"

Wali simultaneously reached out for his wife's and daughter's hands and found them trembling. He pressed them lightly for assurance.

"I have heard that his daughter too is quite beautiful. She is a treat to see," Gulam now commented.

"From tomorrow, she will be a treat for my eyes too."

A loud, boisterous laugh followed the crass comments. It made Wali furious. He wanted to hit Hashim right across his face to shut him up. He was terribly embarrassed for Meher as well as Sakina. To have his young daughter be exposed to such drivel was the last thing a father could endure. But this nauseating conversation had brought some relief too, for he was now sure that the men held no clue to their escape plan. Moreover, his suspicion that the men were merciless was now an established reality and it was also ascertained that he had made the right decision by choosing to leave the town relinquishing all his assets.

The sound of a lighter vehicle approaching from the opposite direction reached them and the crude talk of the two men got covered up by the louder welcome sound. Negotiating the curve, the vehicle slowed down. It was a Maruti van. The light from the vehicle once again exposed the dreaded men to their full view. The three pairs of eyes watched them, paralyzed with fear. Gulam now gestured at the vehicle to stop.

"Is it a taxi? Can you give us a lift?" He loudly asked the driver.

The vehicle slowed down further and then stopped slowly a few metres ahead. It was clear that the driver was quite hesitant to halt. "No, it is not a taxi. And I am going home now." The man driving the vehicle replied dryly.

"We are also going in the same direction. It won't be any special effort to give us a lift," Gulam insisted.

"I am getting late. Where do you want to go?" The driver now asked, raising his voice a little. There was clear annoyance in his speech. And in the silence of the night the voice was loud and clear.

All the three people concealed in the darkness recognized that voice. It belonged to Wasim. Wali began to get worked up again. "What if Gulam recognises Wasim? Does the man know about me and Wasim being closely related?"

Wali saw Gulam turn towards Hashim, clearly to make him give the directions. Hashim first looked around and then up towards the house.

"I don't have the whole night to wait. I am in a hurry," Wasim was heard speaking in irritation.

"They can't read the registration number of the vehicle in the dark. Otherwise Gulam would have definitely recognized the vehicle that belongs to his employer. But if they get inside the vehicle, there are chances that something there will make Gulam identify it." Wali's assumption caused added worry.

"Why are you getting cross? We have only asked for a lift. We haven't asked you to surrender your vehicle," Gulam spoke quite rudely.

Things were turning unpleasant. Wali's shivering body experienced another bout of weakness. The men should not get into the vehicle; he prayed and waited with a bated breath.

"I don't think we need to take a lift, Gulam. I know the house we need to go to. It is up on this hill. I think the footpath begins from after the next curve. Go on man, you get lost. We do not want a lift from a reluctant man. If we hadn't reached our destination, we would have thrown you out of your vehicle." It was Hashim talking brusquely to Wasim.

There was no reply from Wasim. He simply changed the gear and pressed on the accelerator. The vehicle continued to move uphill, unhurried. Probably Wasim hadn't recognised the dangerous men, thought Wali.

The men on foot too treaded on. Wali watched the vehicle disappear around the corner.

"Did you see the cheek of the man? He dared to be rude to us? If we didn't have things to finish tomorrow, I would have shot a bullet right through his head," Hashim's infuriated tone gave Wali jitters. The snigger of the other man too was crisp clear in that stillness. Their conversation after that became subdued as the distance between them increased. The footsteps began to fade. The two men melted after turning around the curve.

Once again there was intense silence. Only three hearts kept on hammering fast.

The only concern in everybody's mind was; what a narrow escape it had been! Ten Minutes! Ten minutes of delay…and all would have been over and done with...under the sound of gunfire. They were even more convinced now that Hashim was the type who wouldn't have hesitated slaughtering them like animals in an abattoir.

But where had Wasim gone?

They kept sitting glued to their places for the next five minutes. Nobody tried speaking. They knew that it would be the most sensible thing to do; to continue to remain mute and under cover till Wasim came back. The escape was becoming wrought with problems. They hadn't expected it to be smooth but now it was getting packed with complications.

Wali cursed himself for being so careless. He should have checked the reason for Hashim's early departure after dinner. He had just presumed that he had gone off to sleep early, whereas he had gone to the town, to meet this man, Gulam. So Gulam was their contact here. Was he the man who had been spying on them and supplying the terrorists with the information regarding Meher's whereabouts?

Wali was sure, he was the man.

Was Hashim taking Gulam along for extra surveillance around the house tonight? Gulam probably knew Abdul. On some visits to the transport company, Abdul had accompanied him. Was that a plus or a minus point for his safety? Wali was not sure at all. He was now seriously worried for Abdul. Abdul had been taking unnecessary chances with the men. His straightforwardness had surely piqued the mean minded. He was being foolhardy, taking unnecessary risks. But he was gem of a man and had taken those serious risks to help them escape. Wali hoped that he was clever enough to evade five dangerous men and sneak out before the men discovered the absence of the inmates of the house. He should not become the target of their wrath. They were going to be fuming hot once they discovered that they had been hoodwinked. Abdul had shown his presence of mind during their close shave with Shaukat. Abdul couldn't have been sure but he had certainly presumed that the family was on the run and had for some reason made the undesirable sound. He had already prepared an excellent cover up. In his desperation, he had deliberately fallen down, no, perhaps jumped down and pretended to have fallen. He should similarly be able to fool the men and slip away in time.

Wali thus silently and fervently prayed for Abdul's safety. Without him, leaving the vicinity of the house would have been impossible tonight. He had stood by him at the hour of need. That was the true revelation of the character of the man. Wali wanted him by his side always. He wanted to honour him as the family's best friend.

From where he was seated, he could see a part of the footpath leading to his house. He now stared at the two repulsive silhouettes walking up slowly, unhurriedly; up on the same path from where they had rushed down a while ago. Their confidence lay in the fact that they were the intimidators and not the intimidated. An ironic smile played on Wali's lips as he thought of the incongruous situation, "We had trodden that footpath for years without any hitch, it rightly belonged to us, today we are being forced to forsake it in fright. This is an unknown road for them, yet, they are walking up the same assertively."

The helplessness combined with anger made Wali silently invoke, "It is not fair. I beseech *Allah* to make them pay for what they are doing to an innocent family."

The two vile figures had reached the corner of a curve traversing which they disappeared from his sight once again. He never wanted to see these men again. None of them. Never again.

After another five minutes of agonising wait in the dark hush, Wali began to be concerned why Wasim had not reappeared. Had there been some kind of misunderstanding regarding the waiting spot? Should he walk in the direction where Wasim had vanished? He was wavering in uncertainty when he heard a faint sound of a vehicle approaching from the direction where Wasim had driven a short while ago. The slow moving Maruti van now became visible once more. It stopped right below where Wali and his family were hiding. Wasim's figure emerged from the driver's seat. He jumped out of the vehicle and on to the road. He now looked up in the direction of the house and murmured to himself, "What do I do now? Wali, what do I do? How to save you? My mind is not working. Oh my God! What will happen now? What will happen to the innocent family? *Allah*, Please help them, save them," Wasim's whispers sounded almost hysterical.

Wali instantly realized the reason for his trauma. He was wrong that Wasim had not recognized Hashim. He surely had. He had seen him with Shakeel that morning. That was why he had driven on, deliberately unhurriedly, so as not to raise the men's suspicion. He had seen him going up towards the house and knew that his time coincided with the decided time of the escape. He had taken it for granted that the family was on their way down and was now sure to meet the dangerous man en route to their house.

"Wasim Bhai, we are safe up here," Wali said in a tone loud enough only to reach Wasim's ears.

Wasim looked around anxiously. "Wali, is that you? Where are you? I can't locate you," he said.

'Here, up on the hill. We are coming down," Wali said. Wasim watched with much relief as the three figures emerged from some dark corner and began to scamper downhill.

"What were you doing up there? I was worried sick for your safety. Did you see those two men who wanted a lift in my vehicle? Did you recognize them?" Wasim bombarded Wali with questions the moment he touched the hard surface of the road.

"I saw them Bhai and I thought we were now done for. You did a very clever thing by not stopping here but moving on. Did you realize who they were?" Wali said.

"Wasn't the tall one the same man who was with Shakeel today? Wasn't he that dangerous Hashim?" Wasim asked.

"Yes Bhai, he was the same man. And perhaps you recognized the other one too," Wali added.

"No, I don't think I know the other man," Wasim said, shaking his head.

"Why Wasim Bhai, you didn't recognise Gulam who works at Hassan's transport company?"

That brought immediate concern on Wasim's face. He almost shouted, "What? That fellow works in Hassan's office?"

"Bhai, speak softly. We are still in the danger zone," Wali warned him.

Wasim lowered his voice but continued in horror, "Oh my God! What a narrow escape! Thank God, we didn't hire a taxi. And thank God, I didn't go to Hassan's office today. In fact, I have hardly been to his work place. I meet him once a while at his house only."

"Didn't you go to his office to arrange for the taxi?" Wali asked, rightly surprised.

"No, I had called Hassan on his cell from Nusrat's place. He was at home, down with viral fever. So I had gone straight to his house. He was in bed and didn't require his car. That is why he offered it to me," Wasim explained.

A faint smile played on Wali's lips, "We are definitely under Mr. Virus's debt." His statement brought smiles on the faces of otherwise petrified women. Without wasting more time, they got into the vehicle.

"I think, *Allah* has decided to protect us in our venture today. Lots of coincidences have been happening and thinking of them now, I have begun to realize that it has all been turning in our favour," Wali said once they were all inside the safety of the vehicle and moving farther and farther way from the house at 50 km. per hour.

"What other coincidences?" Wasim was genuinely interested now.

"To begin with, if Meher hadn't dropped the vase with a loud bang, we wouldn't have decided to leave early. We left about fifteen minutes in advance than the decided time and that has turned out to be the major advantage today," Wali explained. He then kept Wasim Bhai alarmed with the details of the escape story till they reached the main streets of the town. Although this area was more or less flat, Wasim slowed down the vehicle. The police and army patrolling was evident. They could spot border security force personnel in their combat gear patrolling the streets. A fast moving vehicle could raise doubts.

But the presence of the police helped everybody to feel more relaxed. Only Wali was still disturbed.

"Wasim Bhai, I have an immense feeling of guilt to have left Abdul alone to cope up with the dangerous men," Wali expressed his apprehension. "He is surrounded by not four but five dangerous men now. What if they decide some trick to judge if we are at home; like firing a shot again. Shaukat had no qualms about letting off his gun when we were supposed to be resting. It could be done again. Wasim Bhai, I will never forgive myself if something untoward happens to Abdul."

"Hmmm... the situation is no doubt serious. But I don't think they will start shooting just like that. Shaukat's gesture was of an immature boy. Hashim will not allow it, for it will lay them exposed. That is the last thing they would want," Wasim tried to calm down Wali.

Wali saw logic in Wasim's explanation. But he still felt perturbed. "Wasim Bhai, Abdul has to spend few more hours in the company of those terrorists. It is really making me uneasy."

Wasim responded with a smile, "Wali there has been a change of plans. I also realized that there was no need for Abdul to stay in the house till late night. Once your bus leaves, it becomes safe for him to leave the house. So I have already fixed with Abdul to meet him at the same spot at twelve thirty."

"You will be going back to fetch Abdul?" Wali asked with surprise.

"That's right, Wali. I thought it was rather risky for Abdul to walk all alone to the bus stop in the middle of the night. It would have meant a walk of about at least an hour, even if he ran all the way. And that walk could be packed with dangers. Moreover, he would have to wait alone at the bus stop till the morning. So I decided that I will pick him up and bring him to my house. He will at least have some safe place to take refuge in, till the time of his departure. I will see to it that he boards the first morning bus to Jammu, before Ayesha and I leave. It leaves at 7:30 am. I have already bought his ticket," Wasim informed Wali.

"Bhai, you have really unburdened me of my guilt. I was worried stiff for Abdul. Thank you. But when did you make that arrangement? Abdul never told me about it." Wali was pleased with the latest tidings.

"It had occurred to me much later that Abdul too should be evacuated from the house as soon as possible. When I had gone to fetch Bua-Jaan, I had met Abdul in the kitchen and had fixed up the meeting with him then," Wasim informed him.

Wali almost choked with emotion in gratitude for Wasim Bhai's unconditional support and indispensable help. He was sure that it was due to the men like him that the world had not yet been shattered by the savagery of the satanic elements.

He had always been a religious man, but today's strange events had managed to augment his faith manifolds and he could feel some kind of guidance, as if there was a steering hand in today's happenings which was negating the evil forces. His heart if was filled with praises for *Allah*'s mercy and benefaction.

Chapter 24

There was not much traffic on the roads of the town and it took them another ten minutes to reach the station. The moment they got off the vehicle, Wali put on his spectacles to check the time once more. Never before in life had he checked time as frequently as today. It was eleven thirty. There was still half an hour for the bus to depart.

What were they going to do meanwhile? If the men discovered them missing, they were sure to come to the bus station looking for them, Wali thought. He began to calculate how much time it would take for the men to appear at the station. Hashim would have reached the house by eleven fifteen, for he was walking up quite slowly, almost leisurely. Even if their absence was discovered immediately, though it was not likely, and the men left straight away, they would not be able to catch up with them. The bus station was about six kilometres from the house. Even if the men were to run fast, they couldn't possibly reach by twelve. By the time they would be on their way and out of their reach. Wali smiled with certain glee after completing his calculations. But he immediately frowned. Abdul was still there and till he was safely out, there was nothing to feel pleased about.

They hurried through the main entrance of the station which had a big signboard of "Srinagar Bus Terminus" written in bold letters on its arch. The group's first task was to go and meet Ammi-Jaan and Ayesha, who were waiting for them somewhere there. Wasim had dropped them both at the station entrance before coming to pick them up. They would have to be located.

The station was almost empty. A few coolies were sitting in a group, chatting and sharing a *hookah*. The gurgling sound of the *hookah* was the most prominent in the missing bustle at a station. Most of the eating stalls had closed down except a small teashop, ordaining lethargy to the atmosphere. The huddled and familiar figures were soon spotted by the escaped quartet after a brief search. They were sitting on a bench in a dark corner.

When Wali's eyes fell on Ammi-Jaan sitting in a bowed submission, looking quite shaken, he realized that Ayesha had revealed the truth to her which had made her so despondent. She had her face covered with her scarf and had probably been crying. Ayesha was sitting with her consoling arm wrapped around her.

"Ammi-Jaan, I am sorry. I had to lie to you today. But the circumstances were such that there was no alternative," Wali voiced his regret softly the moment he reached her.

Ayesha stood up immediately to allow Wali to sit with his mother. Wali put his arms around Ammi-Jaan and hugged her. Ammi-Jaan lost whatever cool she might have been exercising till now began to cry uncontrollably. Sakina and Meher sobbed too; expressing their pent up grief openly. Ayesha wiped her eyes with her *chunni*. Wasim subtly turned his back to avoid being seen with tearful eyes.

Wali let the tears flow down his cheeks unhindered once again. But these tears were different. These were more the tears of relief than grief. They were at last away from immediate danger. All the constrained feelings of the past many hours were now getting emoted through the flowing tears.

Wasim then said, "Let us not sit out in the open and expose ourselves. There is still some time for the bus to leave. Let us sit inside the tea shop. We will sit next to the window and keep an eye on the outside. I think we have enough time for tea."

The group immediately complied and moved inside. Ammi-Jaan was still clinging on to her son, her staggering feet indicative of her being still in shock. Though outwardly she had now calmed down, what Ayesha had revealed to her had stunned her beyond reckoning and it would take days for her to come in terms with the changed circumstances. The grief she presently felt for her son's family was immense, almost incurable.

When they all were seated, she spoke for the first time. "Wali, what is this rubbish that I am getting to hear? Is it right that Shakeel had visited us with indecent ideas in his mind?"

"Yes Ammi-Jaan, he had come to threaten us into submission. Tagging along were three other armed terrorists, who not only appeared quite dangerous but are confirmed so, especially the one who has come from across the border. And I couldn't think of any other way out. We have to leave to save Meher from their clutches. But do not worry. We will be fine with Salim in Delhi," He explained to her. In the same breath, Wali then asked his mother with eagerness, "Do you approve of the decision I have taken?"

"I think there is no option. You did the right thing son, for only fools take risks and then pay for being foolhardy," Ammi-Jaan now said. 'And do not think that I was crying for we have temporarily become homeless. Mine were the tears of happiness to see you all safe with me. Till all of you hadn't arrived, I was half dead with worry."

Ammi-Jaan's statement was followed by a reprieved silence. Each member of the group appeared drained out. They sat quietly waiting for the next part of the journey to commence. What was there to discuss anyway! Uncertainty had thrown its shroud over their lives and suddenly overturned their fortunes. Some had lost a lifetime of labour. The question in every mind was whether it was a temporary loss or a permanent one…whether the road they were about to tread had any return. The only thing they were somewhat certain now was that they might be able to witness another sunrise.

Thus they sat there; numb, without any expected reaction; like jubilations and celebrations for having defeated the enemy. To win this battle, they had lost a lot. And then it was only partly won. Their hearts felt empty; yet they were filled with emotions, their brains confused; yet crammed with thoughts. Only their eyes were alive with expressions. And each one understood what the other wanted to convey, for it is not always the language of words that are needed to express sentiments.

Increase in the activity outside brought them back to the immediate present. People could be seen embarking the bus. Their total belongings, which had been reduced to a small bag each, were picked up and the nomadic travellers were ready to move on and begin life all over again.

At the door of the bus, Wali was handed an additional bag by Wasim, his black bag with all the papers he had compiled in the morning. "Wali, you are required to take care of your assets yourself. That is surely *Allah*'s desire and His ways are great."

In return, Wali bowed his head in a quick prayer to thank the Almighty for shielding them from harm so far. He then quickly hugged his brother one last time, performed *adaab* to Ayesha and then helped his family board the bus.

Every eye was wet, every heart aggrieved. When they bid the final farewell, it was only through their gaze; their words, having been strongly seized by pain, continued to be voiceless.

Once the bus crossed the city limits, Wali's overworked nerves began to settle down. At last his plan had worked. The might of the brain was yet again proven to be stronger than the might of the weapons. Even if their absence was discovered now it would not be possible for their stalkers to catch up with them. This was the last bus to leave the town and the next one would leave at 7:30 in the morning. That gave them solid seven and a half hours lead. Wali smiled with contentment. There was some mitigation in the consternation he had felt the whole day. They had left behind the lined deathly steel, at the moment lying ineffectual against a wall. Wali's dwindling confidence in his capabilities was at last restored. But then his smile congealed on his lips.

The deathly steel could still be aimed at an innocent. Yet another absolutely unmitigated innocent!

How could he be so callous? Abdul was still a captive of the trigger-happy brutes. He was possibly trying to break away from their clutches at this very moment. There was no one to help him escape, no one to distract the treacherous men to facilitate him to get away. Would he be successful in the attempt? The thought increased Wali's heart beat and agitation and he knew it wouldn't be possible to feel tranquil till Abdul successfully managed to flee. Though, he knew that Abdul was smarter than all the four fiends put together. Wali had strong conviction in his ability to pull the wool over the eyes of the idiots yet again.

For them too, the danger was yet not over. If their absence was uncovered even now, the terrorists could hire a taxi to follow them. Gulam could easily and quickly arrange that. The images of the bus being stopped and the family asked to alight and line up against a wall made Wali break into a cold sweat. Many Pandits of the valley had faced similar fate and it was awful. He could foresee Hashim's piercing cold eyes ready to press the trigger. He shuddered. The disagreeable thoughts made him hot and suffocated. Leaning across Sakina sitting next to the window, he pushed opened the window. The draught of cool breeze pried in. In an automatic reaction, he peeped out to look as far behind as possible. Sakina made no protest at being crushed under his weight. She understood each of his actions.

Total stillness in the landscape pacified him. He couldn't spot trailing headlights of any vehicle. He breathed deeply with relief. Pure air filled his lungs. "Abbu Ji, the moment you enter Delhi you feel as if you have entered a gas chamber," He now recalled what Meher had told him when she had come home on her first vacation after joining the medical college there. "The air of our Valley is so clean that here I can feel my lungs getting rid of the pollutants collected in the metropolis" Involuntarily, Wali filled his lungs in a succession of deep breaths. He would have to tolerate the smoke and smog of the big city. He hoped that it wouldn't play havoc with Ammi-Jaan's health. They would perhaps get used to it but she was too old for such natural adjustments.

Seeing Sakina shiver mildly, Wali closed the window, letting only an open slit for fresh air. Each needed to carry lungful of it till it would last, he thought.

He now surveyed the occupancy of the bus. It was one third full. Most of the passengers were either fast asleep; apparent from their deep breathing, or making efforts to sleep; moving restlessly in an endeavour to find comfortable positions to doze off. They all seemed locals, but today how many of them could be trusted. Perhaps no one. At least, he would not be able to trust his fellow men for a long time to come. This was the donation given to the peaceful Valley by the terrorism. The blight of distrust had been sown in the productive orchard.

Meanwhile, he had to go on with his existence; for the precious gift of life was perhaps given to him the second time. He would have to make the best of what was left. To begin with, he should rest so that he could take care of the others. He closed his eyes.

A baby cried. The young mother, sitting across the aisle opposite to Wali, tried to pacify her child. A few restless heads turned to stare, to lodge silent protest as if the baby would understand and obey. The mother began to hum softly to soothe her baby. The cries subsided. The sweet hum began to affect Wali and he began to drift into the welcome arms of sleep, though the lullaby was for the baby.

Both Meher and Ammi-Jaan settled on the seats in front appeared to be dozing. With his half closed eyes, he glanced at Sakina and was content to see her snoozing too.

He drifted into a fitful slumber, haunted by a dream of drowning in the lake. He was desperately moving his arms and legs but he couldn't swim. Something kept pulling him down and wouldn't let him progress even an inch. He could see Wasim's houseboat he wanted to reach but his arms were getting tired and he was finding it difficult to move them anymore.

He had barely slept for half an hour when some activity in the vicinity woke him up with a start. He tried moving his arms but they had become numb as they had got pressed under the weight of his body. Then blood rushed back into them causing uncomfortable prickly sensation and pain. He stretched them and looked around to see if all was well. Meher was helping Ammi-Jaan who was half out of the window. Wali remembered with concern that Ammi-Jaan was extremely prone to motion sickness and they had completely overlooked it. To top the hassle, they were without any water. Meher could medicate her but it wouldn't be possible without water. Wali immediately offered to change seats with Meher.

To Wali's alarm, his mother kept throwing up through the window of the moving bus every ten minutes. He didn't know how to make her comfortable except wrap his arms around her and rub her forehead.

When the bus stopped for a fifteen minutes break after five hours of journey at a small habitation, Wali rushed to procure a bottle of water. He handed over the bottle to Meher through the window and she right away made Ammi-Jaan swallow a tablet. They had some time for tea as well. Requesting the boy at the teashop to take three cups to the bus, Wali took his steaming cup of tea and sat on a rock looking at the eastern horizon. By the time he had finished his tea, there was a dramatic change in the intensity of the darkness. The black of the night was fading away slowly revealing the serene pure white mist flowing like a woman's veil down in the valley. The stars were gradually losing their brightness and the sky was turning lemony.

As soon as the bus began to move, Ammi-Jaan vomited out the tablet. Wali was worried stiff lest his mother suffered from dehydration, though Meher was trying her best from the limited store of medicines in her first aid box. She exchanged seats with Wali once again, for she wanted to administer oral hydration to her patient and was also worried for her distraught father. He was the one for whom rest was obligatory.

Wali chose the window seat this time. His eyes would no more close to rest. In fact, they were glued to the horizon in anticipation to the appearance of the Sun that, he had felt, had bid him a final goodbye the previous evening. Like a child keenly awaiting the arrival of his father with arms full of presents, Wali now awaited the appearance of the sun. For him, the sight of the sun would be confirmation of his triumph.

Soon, the brightening horizon in hues of violets and pinks declared the much awaited approach. Wali watched in esteem as a part of the dazzling phosphorescent orange disc made its slow appearance. He watched it breathless, although its brilliance almost blinded him. He was unmindful. He had witnessed yet another sunrise and it was more beautiful than the sunset he had seen the previous evening. He was ever so grateful for being given more opportunities to watch this glorious phenomenon of nature. Till yesterday, he wasn't sure if he ever would. "In routine so many things cease to be meaningful despite their indispensability. You begin to value things only when they have either been completely lost or almost lost," Wali mused.

When they reached Jammu, the Sun was high up in the zenith. It was a relief for the whole family to have covered the first part of the journey safely, but For Ammi-Jaan it was another matter all together. The moment she alighted from the bus, she felt magically cured.

They headed straight to the railway station on a hired three wheeler. For the four of them he needed to hire a taxi, but Wali's affluence had been wrecked overnight. He would have to be extremely careful with his money now. He had therefore haggled with the auto driver and made him agree to charge ten rupees less as well as carry all four of them crammed together in his small vehicle.

Wali managed to procure tickets in the second-class sleeper compartment for the evening train that would leave for New Delhi at 6:30 pm. It was a slow train and would reach them at their destination only sometime by noon the next day. Though he wanted to leave as soon as possible, as well as reach the place of safety as fast as possible, but all the other trains were fully booked. They were left with no choice but to wait the six more gruelling and straining hours at the station.

Wali was still apprehensive that the livid men might have decided to follow them. By now their flight had surely been uncovered and the first thought that was likely to strike the bruised men would be of revenge. This set him to worry all over again for Abdul. He realized that it would be another twenty-four hours before he would feel absolutely secure, only when they all were together under the safe roof of his son's house.

Wali had no acquaintances in Jammu with whom these few hours could be spent in security. Where could they go in this city of strangers? Theirs was a physically drained group with broken spirits, which neither had the will nor interest to find a better resting place. Wali managed to find a bench in the shadowy corner of a retiring room and made his family as comfortable there as was possible. For himself, he chose a seat next to the window for constant surveillance. They should not be caught napping.

Every character either resembling in built to any of the terrorist they had left behind, or a person hidden behind the anonymity of head to toe clothing sent his heart fluttering. Wali kept awake, in a confused and tired state of mind while advising his family to close their eyes and sleep. If they could.

Wali left his seat only to procure food and water. Lack of exercise was rendering his body stiff but he was unmindful to it. He was focussed on his mission's survival.

The hours passed without any untoward event and Wali was thankful for that.

As the train chugged slowly out of the station, Wali threw a last glance at the entrance gate. Abdul should be entering through it shortly and Wali expected that if the second operation had been executed successfully, he should be about to reach Jammu.

Chapter 24

Chapter 25

As the train raced cutting through the dark night, Wali Mohammad Khan's stress began to ebb further. The success of his venture and the increasing distance from his tormentors was a matter of fulfillment. He stretched his aching body on the upper berth and closed his weary eyes. But the unnerving events had made him so insecure that his fear would not subside so easily. The vulnerability he had recently encountered made him instinctively open his eyes a moment later. In the faint light of the compartment, he glanced at Meher to check if she was comfortable. She lay curled on the opposite berth with her back towards him. He gazed lovingly at her frail profile. A doctor by profession, bound by oath and dedication to save lives and alleviate pain of the suffering humanity, yet reduced to such helplessness herself! His Meher had undergone intense trauma. Not that his sufferings were any less, but he was a mature and strong man and his Meher was young and susceptible. He felt a surge of emotions for his treasured daughter; a mixture of relief, sympathy and love. He was glad that he had managed to save her from some decadent elements. He felt contented that he had the courage to take strong decisions and not crumble under threat. He felt a sense of pride that he hadn't weakly accepted the vile demands of some depraved humans. He felt satisfied that he had executed his responsibility as a father as well as was possible in the given circumstances.

The worst was perhaps over. They all could afford to relax now. They needed to rest their overworked nerves. "My daughter, who has suffered intense humiliation, needs to rest the most," judged the loving heart of a father. The whole day he had been immensely aggrieved...lacerated at the sight of her strained pale face...suffering throes of pain watching her sitting helplessly for hours on stretch on a hard bench of the dingy retiring room at the Jammu railway station. Apart from tending to her mother and grandmother, she hadn't spoken much since their departure from home. She appeared fazed and withdrawn. It was only after boarding the train that a smile of relief had appeared on her face. She was obviously apprehensive all the while, perhaps like him scared of the stiff reprisal. Also, Hashim's cutting remarks must have had an effect of hot chillies on her wounds. He hoped that she was getting over the harrowing experience and was sound asleep.

Ammi-Jaan and Sakina had been made comfortable on the lower berths. Meher had given first aid and administered painkillers to her mother, who was finding it difficult to walk, her injured foot having swollen to double its original size. She had also given antidepressant drugs to her grandmother, insisting that she needed that for a comfortable journey. Were they sleeping or else were they lost in their own thoughts, inferring the past events in their own light? Or had the tiredness overtaken them and sent them into restful slumber? Wali couldn't really make out but he felt deeply satisfied that all his women; his mother, his wife and his daughter were strong and had proved thus at the time of the present crisis. He was grateful to Sakina who hadn't even once expressed remorse at leaving behind all her opulence or at the family being instantly reduced to destitution. It was a mother's heart; which was much richer than all the riches in the world. And Ammi-Jaan was beyond all material attachments at her age. Safety of her family was her greatest consolation.

As far as he was concerned, strangely, he too had begun to feel a kind of numb detachment with the property he had left behind. To be able to save them all, had perhaps overshadowed all other aspects. Yet, there was a strange ache in his heart, an ache he oddly now recalled having felt on his first day at the primary school when the teacher had pulled him away from Abba-Jaan who had come to drop him at school. He wanted to scream but no sound would emerge from his throat. He had simpered watching the receding back of his father. Those forlorn feeling were intense, as if he had been rejected by the father he loved and he would never see him again. Then, Abba-Jaan had returned to pick him up after school and life had once again begun to move smoothly. Those forlorn feelings had erupted yet again and he knew there would be nothing to pacify them now. Perhaps, this time there would be no return. A long phase of his life had got left behind. All he would now be remained with were the countless memories, which were no different from the withered and scattered leaves of the *chinars* towards the conclusion of the autumn, when the winds would blow them around uncontrollably before they would be lost forever, their existence completely obliterated and their place on the trees taken over by the others. That was the law of continuity in nature. It had to be accepted.

Life in Delhi wouldn't be easy. It would be claustrophobic living in small congested spaces. They would be burdening the young couple with aided responsibilities. And how was he going to pass time without much to do? Perhaps, he would find some part-time job and try to keep busy. But would he be given a job at this age without any experience in any particular field, except tending an orchard? Wali sniggered lightly at the fickle fate that had lovingly led him till a junction and then had abruptly abandoned him. Blindfolded.

In the milieu of teeming millions, he was going to be on his own. Wasim and Nusrat would be a thousand miles away. Who would provide him with unconditional help in need? He would have to develop close rapport with his children. His Salim too was a man now. They would have to learn to stand for each other.

Keeping in mind the current state of affairs, it would be in their best interest to be lost in obscurity and live where no one knew them; where there wouldn't be a single individual interested to give directions to the vicious men regarding their whereabouts. As such, it was a frightening prospect that from hence forth there would be some depraved humans waiting to avenge humiliation at his hands. An anonymous life was the only indemnity towards safety.

The events of the past few hours had also shaken Wali's conscience out of its slumber.

His eyes were heavy with sleep. He had hardly slept a few winks in almost two days. For how many hours exactly had he been awake, his tired mind couldn't even calculate any more. But sleep still eluded him. A long chapter of his life had prematurely reached its conclusion. All that he had laboured for in his life was gone. He would have to undo the blindfold and begin afresh. He would have to open another chapter; he would have to learn to tread a new road.

Thankfully, they had been spared the sight of four guns directly pointed at them.

On one hand, Wali's mind had attained peace, for his Meher was safe. All the sacrifices were worth making; to see that pink hue back on her face and the innocent smile making her eyes sparkle yet again. On the other hand, the turmoil inside him was unremitting.

And one illiterate person was responsible for all this; an illiterate mind, incapable of rationality.

"'Wali, the difference between an educated and an illiterate mind is not the bookish knowledge but the capability of appropriate interpretation, of accurate analysis of situations and not getting swayed by hysterics." Abba-Jaan's voice was so clear and close. It was in his heart. "An educated mind seeks logic. It clearly distinguishes between the right and the wrong. It has the intelligence to probe, infer and find answers. It is the mind that cannot be easily moved by irrational frenzy, but seeks the truth through inquest."

"An illiterate mind is like a sightless person. It can easily be controlled and misguided, for it lacks its own direction. The unscrupulous and the power hungry wolves are always in the lookout for such minds; for they can easily be manipulated and corrupted. These fools are provoked into violence, whereas those cunning minds watch the destruction from a safe distance and wait to reap the profit."'

"How true are Abba-Jaan's words! It was as if he had studied Shakeel's mind and had reached its deep recesses. Only people like Shakeel can indulge in depraved acts of killing the unarmed harmless innocents. Only such minds can harness such wicked ideas as he has been fancying. And religion, which is meant purely for keeping the human race within certain moral and ethical principles, is being misused to incite such men to perform evil deeds. Fools like Shakeel do not even realize that they have been turned into sinners."

Through half closed, sleep heavy lids and the blurred darkness, Wali's mind kept on pondering over many speculative issues.

The most perplexing one that now occurred to him was that the men involved in many terror attacks including the one on the World Trade Centre were not unlettered like the group that had visited him, but some of them even held professional degrees. Then, why were their minds not revolted by the very idea of senseless violence? Why had they allowed to be brainwashed and get involved in subversive activities? Why some of them had slighted the blessing of life and carried out the suicidal attacks?"

For the first time Wali gave thought to this baffling problem, slowly afflicting the contemporary civilized world.

Chapter 25

"Perhaps their understanding of *Allah* and His wishes had become obscured in their minds. Perhaps these lettered men had allowed their learning to be auctioned in the haberdashery of misconception, pettiness and hatred. Somewhere in life, they had lost their path, willingly or unwillingly, and got disoriented under negative influence. To achieve their ill-contrived conviction, they didn't mind turning innocent men, women and children into sacrificial lambs. Such are some easily influenced violent minds, incapable of compassion and mercy. May be, they were never taught that each heart carries an essence of *Allah*, therefore is equally important to Him. These men possibly are not the true followers of any religion, for; every religion shuns violence, especially against the innocents," Wali concluded.

"There is another breed of men, men like Gulam, who are never hesitant to auction their morality…their integrity on the platform of greed. They are the chameleons keen to change colours to match the profitable locales…forever ready to sacrifice others to realize their own interests. Gulam doesn't seem to harbour any guilt in helping to nip an innocent and promising life in its bud. What does he think? Does he expect to be made a governor or an equivalent in case men like Hashim assume power? He doesn't realize that he will be thoroughly squeezed and the moment he ceases to be of any use, be discarded like a mango pip. He has no future beyond that. He will forever remain a clerk in some small company. And if he thinks these contenders of violence will be able to mitigate his struggles of life, he couldn't have been more mistaken. He will then have to do the same work but with a gun pointed at him, in case he refuses to undertake vile jobs. The fool is totally unaware that he is helping to bring about the rule of the unruly."

"I am a criminal too." The next thought caused a stabbing pain in Wali's heart. "There are two categories of criminals; the ones who commit the crime, and the others who watch the deplorable acts without protesting. I have committed the crime of being a mute witness to the atrocities being committed against humanity. I felt secure thinking the new terrible breed of terrorism had risen against another race…against people belonging to different religion. I watched mutely their houses being erased to ground. I was wrong. When the bloodthirsty taste blood; it doesn't matter whose blood they shed."

"Today when my house was raided by those who are drenched in innocents' blood, I have realized the pain of the wounds inflicted on so many innocent Hindus of the Valley. I watched the Pandits leave their homes…their belongings…their entire life's labour and running away to save their lives. I watched them becoming homeless paupers from affluence overnight. The Valley was their home too. They had lived there for generations. We all had lived harmoniously together as kinfolk. Their presence was a proof of the unbiased and tolerant character of the inhabitants of the valley. Where did that *Kashmiriat* get lost subsequently… in the hands of these deplorable beings?"

"And when the mischief was played, we blamed the elements from across the border. Didn't some among us harbour those elements? Didn't people like me remain silent?"

"The land and property abandoned by the displaced was grabbed at the first opportunity and many revelled in the riches they had thus acquired. Were these raiders so blind that they were not able to perceive having become poorer by the loss of thousands of their brothers and sisters?"

"But, what do the ravenous for materialistic gains know about the richness of love and benevolence? Why would they bother to realize that they are building their citadels on the soil destabilized by the tears of anguish and sufferings? But such ill acquired wealth certainly cannot last long."

"If you do not help to douse the fire in your neighbour's house, do not be complacent, for it may turn into an uncontrollable inferno, threatening to engulf whatever comes its way; including your house. The fire reached my home yesterday and almost burnt it."

Wali's thoughts made him restless. He turned his side to face the partition wall of the compartment. But there was not enough room for a woeful person to breathe and he felt suffocated. He turned to face Meher once again. She was facing him now and seeing her soft regular breathing, he felt satisfied that she was in protective custody of restful sleep. He too wished he could sleep soundly like her but a gnawing worm of unrest kept wriggling inside him. The chain of his thoughts had bound him like a prisoner and he was being released link by link. Till all his guilt feelings were out and he had paid through self reproach, perhaps he wouldn't be able to sleep. And he continued to reflect.

"We let the terrible ideas to grow unchecked and looked the other way. We never considered it as our problem. It is because no one thinks that one day you could be the one hunted. It could be your house burning. It could be your tears flowing."

"We should not be instrumental in bringing tears to the innocent eyes; We should be the ones readily available to wipe them."

"We are taught values and morals at home, and how easily we forgo them? We forget that our actions carve our destiny. Over and above, all deeds must be paid for in one's lifetime."

"If I am a true *Mussalman*, I should have condemned the prevailing prejudice. I should have at least tried to prevent the misled men from digging graves of their innocent victims. I could have expounded that the seeds of opulence never sprout on such graves. Someone might have heeded my words. A few lives saved and a few recuperated souls would have been a great achievement, enough for an individual like me to accomplish. But I was afraid. I knew what was happening was extremely wrong, but I had also known the fate of those who had openly condemned the violent activities. So, I chose to be a silent spectator."

And these troubled reflections wouldn't allow Wali to sleep a wink.

The faint light of the dawn reminded him that yet another day was being ushered in. He anticipated that the new dawn would bring new hope for him; hope of good times with his family. And it would bring new hopes for the next generation. He wished that the world should not come to an end before many generations had seen the beauty of the sunrise, ripples in the undulating blue waters, the green vastness of the Valleys, the colours and fragrances of nature, the stark beauty of the mountains and the serene sound of a flute being played by an unknown Shepherd.

These hopes finally lulled Wali gently into the tides of sleep.

When he woke up with a start, there was bright sunshine outside. He looked around in a daze. He had been dreaming of some faint distant music flowing in soft whiffs. Was it a dream of the sweet music emanating from a shepherd's flute that had caused a strange yearning in his heart and woken him up? Fully awake, he realized that it was not an imaginary flute being played by some shepherd on a distant mountain. It was real music. It was sweet sound of a song being sung from the adjacent cubicle that reached his ears now.

"Awal *Allah* noor upaya...."

He lifted himself on his elbows and peeped out of the window. There was a lot of activity outside. The train had halted at a station.

"Where have we reached Bhai?" He asked a middle aged passenger sitting right across, on the corner of Ammi-Jaan's berth.

"We are at the Ambala junction," The man replied.

Meher was still sound asleep. It was good for her…she needed the rest. Wali peeped down to see if the ladies were awake. Both Ammi-Jaan and Sakina were sitting up to accommodate the day passengers who must have recently boarded the train. Having occupied the window seats, they both were viewing the chaotic bustle on the platform and failed to respond to Wali's surveying peek.

His vision traversed through the rest of the compartment. A whole lot of people had got on the train while he had dozed off. Wali's eyes checked the new comers one by one. All were strangers and appeared harmless. He had already scrutinized the ones sitting below his berth next to Sakina, at a glance. The totally unfamiliar faces granted immense respite. Finally, he had managed to distance his family from the danger zone.

His attention once again got drawn to the melodic singing.

"Who is this person singing in his golden voice? Is he a Sufi saint?" Wali asked the same man.

"No, he is a *ragi.*" The man replied. Then noticing the frown of blankness on Wali's face, he continued, "He is employed at a Gurudwara and is a trained musician. Like me, he lives in Ambala city and daily boards this morning train to get off at Shahabad Markanda station. He is a *Bhai* at the Gurudwara there. Though, he travels barely for half an hour, he begins our day in the right spirit by singing devotional songs in his angelic voice."

"But he is singing in praise of *Allah!*" Wali openly showed his surprise.

The man slowly nodded and smiled openly at Wali. "Where are you from?" He asked. The unrelated question slightly surprised Wali but he immediately responded to the query, "We have travelled from Srinagar."

"Hmm…I thought so. Your diction is unmistakably Kashmiri and you look like one too. Well, he is singing Gurubani from the Guru Granth Sahib." The man informed him.

"Praises of *Allah* in the holy Granth of the Sikhs?" Wali was even more astonished.

"Why brother, don't we have different names in different languages for the vast blueness above us? It doesn't cease to be anything but the sky. Aren't *Allah,*

Waheguru, God, Ishwar, the names of the same Holy Father in the Heaven above? Don't we, the members of the human fraternity, have the liberty to use any language when we want to remember Him?"

Wali slowly nodded his head in agreement. The man was speaking his language…the language he had learnt from Abba-Jaan…the language he had been pondering over for the past many hours…the language he had given his children; and would give to his grandchildren.

He sat cross legged leaning comfortably against the partition wall of the compartment. Closing his eyes he channelled his concentration on the rhythmic language, trying to comprehend the wordings of the hymn. As he listened to each word with deliberation, its powerful spirit began to manifest itself, revealing its lucid solemnity, effusing forth like bright sunshine over quiescent environs after a spell of violent storm. The song made him spellbound.

Awal Allah noor upaya kudrat ke Sab bande

Ek noor te sab jag upjaya kaun bhale kau mande

Supreme is the Light of the Almighty, the Creator
and the entire world is the creation of this Supreme Power.
When the complete life form was born of the Same Divine Soul,
where is the question of some being high and some being low?

The whirling mists of the notes flowed around him engulfing him in their embrace. They condensed and fell on him like cool drops of rain on a heat tortured body. He allowed the notes of the music seep deep into his spirit unconstrained. For the first time in many hours, Wali felt peace spreading through his mind and soul; peace as serene as the cool light of the dawn. The music continued to flow elating his spirit; ordaining it to rise above the petty human conflicts; awakening his consciousness to realize the true essence of life. And he decided to let the tides of life take him along at their free will; like the strains of the unrestrained music.

He was now ready to face his uncertain future. He was now ready to confront his destiny stoically. He was ready to accept what the fate had in store and accept it happily. It was heavenly to realize that the possessions that mattered to him were intact, and the ones which were lost, were only the superfluities.

And Wali wished that the songs of wisdom could possibly reach the depths of all the defiled hearts in need of solace. "For, more than at any other time, today the world is in dire need of wisdom; also of compassion, mercy and cooperation. The acrimonious forces like greed, jealousy, hatred; violence against the innocents; the scramble for power; the nuclear-arms race will only take the world towards its downfall; into a dark abyss. The world needs more people with pure hearts for its survival and love in every heart is the only assurance towards the continuity of human species on the planet."

He raised his hands towards heaven to pray for the preservation of the beautiful life on Earth, for he could clearly envision that humanity was precariously balanced on a verge: On one side was the assurance of safety by the likes of Abdul, on the other, deep chasms created by Shakeels to push the world into a murky void.

The man sitting across looked at Wali in surprise wondering what he meant; when with eyes still closed he uttered aloud, "And, the choice is ours!"

Impressions

When the next moment remains uncertain, tomorrow is yet far off.

Nurturing hope of a smooth journey through the unknown trail of life is optimism, but anticipating unavoidable roughs on the way; wisdom. Under the inconsistent circumstances, it is the courageous who brave the obstacles, traverse over the barbs and cross the violent waves in an endeavour to unearth the terrain of absolute tranquillity.

But what if during the search for solace, fate takes dramatic twist and things no more remain under control? What if life gets thrust towards more violent seas? What if the attribution to the adversity lies beyond ones power and life becomes an affair not controlling the circumstances anymore but being controlled by them?

At this juncture, temptation to halt the efforts to find the lost track may be overwhelming.

But, if one fears the tough trials of life, the golden opportunities to test hidden strength will be lost forever.

Hence for the brave, it is the time to begin all over again. It is the moment to achieve unwavering faith in self. It is the instant to realize that it is feasible to defeat the detrimental forces and control the rudder to find the lost direction once again.

For how can the valiant abandon the path which directs towards the elevated self and ultimately to true spiritual happiness?